# Mighty Quill

# Mighty Quill

## Emmaline Strange

*For **Gary**, who taught me to believe in happily ever after.*

# 1



The posting was probably a prank.

It had to be a prank.

I flicked back to the pic I'd taken of the student center bulletin board.

*"Roommate wanted. Furnished room. Utilities included."*

Below that, a price and a phone number.

And a name.

It *had* to be a prank.

*"Inquiring parties please text Thor Ambrose."*

What the fuck kind of name was Thor? Were people actually named that? But the price was right and I was desperate enough to text the number and risk humiliation. Risk being butchered by some kind of Craigslist Killer wannabe.

I stood in front of the building, trying to convince myself to go inside. The building seemed nice, more like a converted old multi-family house, far homier than a sterile high-rise. I double-checked the address, and when I couldn't stall any longer without being late, I buzzed the bell for number three, which did, at least, have a tiny nameplate beside it reading, "T. Ambrose."

I waited to be buzzed in and tried to conjure up the image of a person to accompany the name Thor. He was probably some big alpha male type, who'd turn everything into a damn pissing contest. His apartment was probably a disgusting bachelor man-boy hole with the aroma of sweaty socks clinging to every surface. He probably had the IQ of a potato, and hosted parties every weekend that would make sleep and studying impossible. I sighed.

The wooden stairs creaked as I ascended to the third floor.

I faced the door, still debating if I should even bother, but I didn't have much of a choice. Classes started in less than a week, and it was either this or live under a bridge, so I knocked.

The guy who answered the door stood a good head shorter than me, his frame was skinny, bordering on scrawny, and he drowned in an enormous green Grandpa sweater. He blinked up at me through shaggy dark bangs and thick, horn-rimmed glasses. I stared.

"Yes?"

"Uh—sorry. I'm Cassian. Rhodes. I'm looking for..." I choked on the name. It *had* to be a prank. "Thor?"

He slid his glasses up his nose, a small, tired sound escaping between his lips. "That's me."

"No shit?" I said, and immediately clapped a hand over my mouth.

He flushed and looked at his feet. "You'd like to see the place, I assume?"

I nodded, feeling like the world's biggest asshole, and followed tiny Thor inside. The building was old, but the living room was huge and bright, with hardwood floors, lots of windows, and what looked like an actual fireplace.

"This is the living room," Thor told his shoes.

"It's nice."

Silence.

"Big."

He blinked up at me, the eyes behind his glasses big and brown, rimmed with long, thick lashes. The phrase "doe eyes" popped into my head, which, was weird. Thor turned and gestured vaguely behind him. "Kitchen," he said.

I almost drooled. The kitchen was small, but had a big, hooded Viking stove—a six top—and an island in the center to eat at. Everything shone sparkling clean and meticulously maintained, and I itched to get cooking straight away. After a year in dorm housing with nothing but a microwave, the little kitchen with the oversized range seemed like heaven.

Thor cleared his throat and took off down the hall, so I followed him. "My room," he said, pointing at a closed door down the very end of the hallway. "Bathroom. And your room."

I stuck my head into the bathroom, which, like the kitchen, appeared small but outfitted with beautiful new fixtures. The room Thor referred to as mine was spacious, had plenty of windows, and an inviting queen-sized bed.

"If you have furniture, we can put this in storage." He chewed the inside of his cheek. "Or bedding."

It was my turn to blush. I had budgeted for this school year down to the penny, which did not include new bedding. My stupid dorm sheets from last year would definitely not fit. Thor didn't seem to need an answer to that, however, as he turned on his heel and returned to the living room.

I followed, awkward silence thick on the ground.

"So," said Thor Ambrose, crossing his arms over his chest.

"So?"

He waved his hand toward the manilla envelope crushed between my bicep and rib cage. "Oh. Right. Here." He'd asked for a lot of materials: bank statement, personal reference, resume, and transcripts. Thank God he hadn't asked for records of my conduct at school.

I handed him the envelope, and he stuck out his other hand. "I'll be in touch?" It came out like a question.

"Sure, yeah. Thanks. It's great—I mean. The place." I had no idea why this guy made me feel so damn awkward. I shook his hand, and he gasped, a sharp intake of breath like I'd squeezed his delicate fingers too hard.

When I released his hand, Thor slid his glasses up his nose again. "Anyway." He clutched my paperwork and gestured at the door like he couldn't wait for me to leave. His big eyes darted away, then back to me, then to his shoes, so I took the hint. If I wanted to live here, I'd better not piss off my new roommate before moving in.

"Oh, well, uh. See you."

Back on the sidewalk, the knot of anxiety in my chest did not let up. I walked down the street, wrenched open the door of my ancient Impala, and drove back toward the shitty motel I'd been staying in while I looked for a place. I felt nauseated because my entire academic future now rested on the shoulders of a scrawny nerd in a cardigan.

———

## THOR

It had started about two weeks ago, at lunch with my sister. Circe was my oldest sibling, and she'd gotten married last year to her mated partner from a totally respectable shifter family. Needless to say, as the oldest of the Ambrose brood, she was killing it.

"Dad's worried about you," she told me, sipping from her cappuccino.

"Yeah, right." I was the middle child, like Jan Brady. Most

of the time, I did my best to escape the notice of my parents. Dad had no reason to be concerned.

"He is," she insisted. "I heard him talking to Mom about it."

"Oh?" Anything that stood out to my father was bad news. My entire goal in life was to fly under his radar. It was the least I could do as the resident family disappointment.

Circe eyed me over the top of her menu. "He thinks you're failing," she said bluntly.

My stomach tied itself in knots. "Failing?"

"Socially," she said. "For the most part. You live alone. You never go out. You haven't even tried to meet someone."

My parents had been trying to set me up for years, and I had yet to find anyone to whom I could form a mating bond. Being twenty and unmated put me well on my way to becoming an old maid, in their eyes. My siblings had both made great matches just out of high school, tying our lineage to other powerful shifter families, and our parents couldn't be prouder.

It was galling that they came down so hard on me, considering my parents hadn't begun their courtship until college. Perhaps my single life wouldn't be such a scratch on the family crest if it weren't for the other thing.

"I don't want to meet anyone," I said. "I love being alone."

"Do you really?" Circe scrutinized me as she spoke, like she could peer right past my eyes into my head. She had always been astute. I wouldn't go so far as to say we got along, but of everyone in my family, Circe had always been the only one who really saw me.

The truthful answer, of course, was no. I liked my space, but I didn't love being alone. I'd always hoped to find a mate, like just about everyone else in our world. But it hadn't happened, and I didn't mind my lonely life. It was quiet; it was tolerable. And it was infinitely better than whatever alternative I was certain my father was going to propose.

"Anyway," said Circe. "He thinks you're too immature—don't look at me like that, his words—to be on your own."

My mouth ran dry, the bite of crusty Italian bread in my mouth transforming to wet sawdust. *No, no, no.* The backs of my knees started to sweat.

"He's considering breaking your lease at the end of the year so you have to move back home. He thinks you need more social grooming."

And there it was. Gods help me. It took a moment of high, white panic before I could form my next words. "What do I do?"

"Well, you can start by calling Rafe Nardini."

I groaned. This fall, Rafe had enrolled in my school, Fremont University. He'd also just come out as gay, the only reason my parents had not fostered an introduction before this point. He was a year younger than myself, so my father had encouraged (nagged) me to "show him around campus," which was, of course, code for "lock him down and put a ring on it." Or rather, a mating bite. I hadn't called. In my defense, Rafe had not called me either. It was not hard to figure out why. I'd seen him around campus––tall, handsome, and popular. Running back on the football team. His *fauna* was an elegant Aesculapian snake, so he had that going for him too.

And me? I was nothing. Once I hit puberty, the time when our kind traditionally experienced their first shift into our animal forms, I had remained despairingly, resolutely, human. The emergence of one's *fauna* was a celebrated, sacred time for our kind—and, nothing about me was celebrated. Or sacred. When my sister had experienced her first shift into an elegant panther, a sleek and deadly predator, my father had gone misty-eyed and said she inherited his mother's speed and strength.

Then he'd look at me and say I inherited her near-sightedness.

My teen years were not happy ones. I'd learned since coming to college that the way shifters reared their young wasn't strictly...typical. Or ethical. But I shut that away in a teeny little box and moved on with my life. Because I was free. I had my own apartment, my own space. The thought of losing that and being brought back under my father's scrutiny was unacceptable.

When I hadn't undergone a shift, my father had tried all manner of things to "inspire" one, everything from spells to foul-tasting potions; anything he thought would unleash any latent animal instinct. Doctors in the know, holy folk of our order, and even witches were summoned and then dismissed as failures. As I grew older, my father's shame grew, and his methods grew more desperate.

He took any and all suggestions from the people we knew. For a while, he put me on a diet of raw meat. When I'd nearly died of a stomach parasite, he switched over to acorns and roots. He tried shoving me out the window, tossing me into the lake. Had my brother jump out at me in the form of his *fauna*, a massive grizzly. My father even stalked my footsteps himself as a wolf, trying to ignite the wild that might have merely been hiding inside me.

He'd even gone so far as to force me to camp naked in the woods behind our estate. That was the second time I'd almost died, of exposure in that case, and the last of his more drastic attempts. It had been obvious at the time he'd given up on me. I knew a year or two of relative peace, and when I was accepted to my parents' alma mater, where I'd have my own place, my own sanctuary, I had lit candles and incense and uttered tearful prayers of gratitude to our wild gods. I didn't consider myself religious, at least not compared to the rest of my family, but occasionally, when emotions ran high, I leaned on the crutch of our multi-theistic faith.

Now, my safe haven would be ripped away if I couldn't get my act together. The lunch with Circe had been a wake-up call. I needed a plan, and I needed my own money. If I could prove to my father I was not—to use his words—failing, all to the good. I'd call Rafe Nardini and I'd make an attempt to be more social. But I needed my own security net, as well. That way, if my father cut me off, I would be able to keep paying rent.

Or...perhaps I could move away from here. I could transfer schools and leave Douglas Crest behind. Be *normal.*

Be free. The thought terrified me almost as much as it thrilled me.

If I had a roommate, I could sock away their rent money, and if I could pass them off as a friend—even better. Cassian Rhodes was the fifth I'd interviewed. He seemed okay, all told, and really, *really* cute. My hand still tingled where he'd shaken it; his fingers were callused and warm, his hand dwarfing mine. The big hand suited his tall, broad frame. Between that and his thick, sandy hair, his dimpled smile, and freckles, I'd practically been swooning. And he smelled *incredible.*

My father had always said response to smell and touch were the most reliable indicators of mating compatibility. I tried to stuff that thought away. Cassian was looking for a roommate, not a suitor, and besides, I'd all but decided to leave this whole world behind me. I'd go through the motions and contact Rafe for a date, but after that, I hoped it would be a non-issue.

I shuffled through the paperwork Cassian Rhodes had brought with him. I saw he played for the hockey team, which made sense, given his body. He got surprisingly good grades. Based on his course load, he didn't seem the type to spend a lot of time partying, so perhaps he was the lesser of many possible evils. I typed a text telling him he could move in as soon as his deposit check cleared, but I hesitated with my thumb hovering over the send button. I didn't want to seem too eager; I'd already gone weak at the knees when he'd shaken my hand. I certainly didn't need to let him know I was thirsting over him, on top of everything else.

So, I decided to wait until tomorrow at least. I considered what my father would say about Cassian Rhodes.

*Look at me now, Dad,* I thought. *I made a new friend, and he's a popular jock. Isn't that something?*

# 2



I woke up to a text message from Thor, inviting me back to the apartment to sign paperwork and get a set of keys. I threw back the musty comforter and sprang from the mattress like I'd been shot from a cannon. If I could get out of here before nine a.m., I could avoid paying for another day.

I'd never stayed in a motel before, and it was a very sad experience. I felt like a cheating husband. The pit of guilt in my stomach did *not* help.

But I almost laughed, giddy with relief that I'd have a decent place to live, near campus. Despite my blunder of epic proportions last year, I could continue my education, graduate, and start helping earn money for my family. It was just my dad and me to take care of my younger siblings since my stepmom had passed away. I couldn't tell him I'd lost my scholarship. So, I'd gone home last summer, pretended everything was fine and spent as close to zero dollars as possible while working my ass off. I'd budgeted the school year down to the nickel and prayed to find a halfway decent apartment.

The text message from Thor felt like a miracle. I flung myself around the motel room, shoving stuff in my bag and checking out as fast as possible.

When I arrived at the apartment building, I saw the nameplate for number three had already been changed. It now read "*T. Ambrose & C. Rhodes.*" I was oddly touched. Inside, Thor was as clipped and awkward as he'd been the day before, tense silence blanketing us as I signed the lease he'd drawn up.

"Do you need help bringing in the rest of your stuff?" He asked.

It was, by far, the longest sentence he'd spoken, and I took that as a sign we were trending in the right direction. "Nah," I said. "This is all my stuff." I didn't have much.

I brought my few bags into the second bedroom, and saw Thor had set a small vase of cut flowers on the nightstand. I dragged my fingertip over the lip of the vase, and looked up to see him watching me. When I caught him looking, he spun on his heel and departed without a word. I heard the front door slam. He seemed like a weird dude, but I could work with that.

I only had a short while to whip my ass back into shape before hockey started up again. The season may not start until winter, but there was plenty of pre-season training. I changed into my gym stuff and left the apartment, a definite spring in my step. My guts had been too churny to do much working out, but now that I had a place to live, I could focus on moving forward. That meant making sure the team and the coaches knew what my priorities were: hockey, school, requalifying for my scholarship, and keeping my nose clean.

As I ran on the treadmill, I decided I should cook dinner for my new roommate, as a thank you. Grabbing a quick shower in the locker room, I turned over possible favorite recipes in my head. Thor had told me to help myself to anything in the kitchen, but to let him know if I used the last of something so he could replace it. Obviously, I planned to do my own shopping, but for tonight I'd work with what he had.

Unfortunately, I'd left without getting a copy of the key like a fucking moron, so when I returned to our building, I had to ring the buzzer again. Thor must have returned home because he buzzed me in immediately.

Opening the door to the apartment, a spicy, smokey scent struck me, like cigars and cloves. It wasn't a bad smell, just an unexpected one. It seemed to be coming from a tall, funny-looking candle on Thor's mantlepiece. Beside it sat a wooden statue of a man with horns. Thor himself sat curled in a chair by the fire, limbs tangled up like a pretzel, deeply engrossed in a thick leather book that looked like a prop from a B movie about wizards. He didn't look up as I entered. He had a glass of some kind of amber liquid resting on the arm of his chair. Scotch maybe? His nostrils flared several times as I watched before he looked up.

"Hey," I said.

He went immediately back to his book, but said, "Got you a key."

I wandered over to the kitchen island, finding a keyring with two keys: one smaller one, presumably for the mailbox, and a larger one, stamped with a bright cartoony print. "Hockey sticks?"

Thor flushed, finally looking me in the eye, and he pushed his glasses up his nose. "You play, don't you?" He asked, his voice a bit defensive.

"Yeah," I said. "I play."

He nodded, went back to his book, and turned a yellowing page, his eyes roving over the text, brow furrowed in concentration. I had the overwhelming feeling like Thor was an emotionally distant father figure I was trying to impress.

"Reading?" I said, like an idiot.

"Yes," said Thor. He sounded tired. "It's a book my father wanted me to look into."

"Looks cool."

"Yeah, it's not," said Thor, and then he looked surprised, like he hadn't meant to say that at all. "It sucks, actually."

I laughed, a startled little bark. Thor grinned too, laughing in a high-pitched, breathy way, like he'd forgotten how. It made me feel a bit better about everything, like maybe we'd get along and this wouldn't be eight months of painful silence. "I was thinking of cooking dinner," I told him. "For you." I flushed. "For us, I mean. As a thank you, for letting me move in."

"You cook?"

The eager lilt of his question made me smile. "A bit."

Not one for chit-chat, he didn't reply. With my back to the living room, I searched through the cabinets, getting the lay of the land. I turned to ask Thor if he was in the mood for anything in particular, and found that he'd already perched himself eagerly on a stool at the kitchen island, hands clasped on the counter, watching me. "Jesus," I said. How did he move so quietly?

"Sorry," he said, but his face shone with anticipation.

Thor let me move around his kitchen, observing me. He didn't ask questions, which I liked. One of the worst things about cooking in a new kitchen was when people hovered, asking if you needed help, jumping to ask what you're looking for, and generally kibitzing. Thor didn't kibitz. He watched, engrossed, like someone might watch a football game. Maybe watch wasn't the right word—more like, he analyzed.

I opened the refrigerator, thinking to get inspiration for the meal, but the interior was shockingly sparse. Meticulously clean of course, but empty except for a dozen free-range eggs, Irish butter, and some bacon that looked like it came from an honest-to-goodness butcher, wrapped in that crisp white paper and everything. The freezer wasn't much better: ice trays, a bottle of vodka, and a package of English muffins.

I searched every cabinet twice before I finally gave up. "Well, I was going to cook but..."

"But what?"

"But you don't have anything!" Not even garlic or onions or rice or pasta. I had never seen a kitchen this empty before. At least he had a bowl of fruit, so I assumed he didn't starve, but I was at a loss.

"Just tell me what you need and I can have it delivered," said Thor, pulling out his phone.

"I don't mind going to the store for a few—"

"Or we could just go out, instead."

I really, *really* did not have it in my budget to go to a restaurant. "Tell you what," I said. "How about I make breakfast for dinner tonight, and I can make us something more exciting this weekend."

"Sounds great," he said. "Just tell me what to get."

"I really don't mind going—"

"I have a service," said Thor brusquely.

I hadn't meant to cause him more stress and give him an errand to do, but he seemed adamant. Perhaps he had some kind of food allergy and had to be careful about what he bought. "Okay man. I'll send you a list. How does eggs Benny sound for tonight?"

Thor looked at me like I was some kind of witch. "Sounds perfect."

I set about gathering my supplies, thankful there was at least a lemon in the fruit bowl, but miffed that Thor didn't even have a spice rack. I'd have to make my Hollandaise without cayenne pepper, but I was still pretty sure it was going to blow the glasses right of Thor's face. Thor watched me in awe like he'd never seen his stove turned on before, and I couldn't help the cocky little smile on my face as I whisked my egg yolks and melted butter together. The Viking cooked like a dream and I couldn't wait to make a more complex meal. Ideas for our weekend dinner already coursed through my head.

When I finished, I turned toward Thor with a flourish, and the look on his face was so funny I couldn't help but say, "Ta-Da!" as I set his plate in front of him.

He shot me a shy little smile and dug in. I took my seat, which was a little weird, both of us sitting on the same side. Thor was silent for a good several minutes before saying, "This is like, *really* good."

"Thanks." I couldn't help feeling a warm glow of pride.

We ate in silence for most of the meal, until I gave in to my burning curiosity. "Is Thor your real name?"

He set down his cutlery with an aggrieved sigh and dug a slim hand into his pocket. He fished in his wallet for something and slid it over to me. It was, in fact, a driver's license. It read *Thor Giles Ambrose*. Yikes, this dude's parents really didn't give him a chance at all, did they?

"And this is real?" I asked. How could I not?

He glowered at me. "Why would I get a fake ID that says I'm only twenty?"

"Fair point."

"You done?" He didn't wait for my answer but snatched the plate right out from under me, bringing both of our dishes to the sink and scrubbing them like they'd done him some kind of personal grievance. I kicked myself, because the mood had been verging on pleasant before I'd opened my dumbass mouth. I hadn't intended for him to have to clean up, either.

"I can do those," I said, but he ignored me, shoulders tense as he scrubbed. Well, fine.

———

THOR

I felt immediate guilt for being short with Cassian. The eggs Benedict had been divine, better than any I'd ever had in a restaurant, and really, who wouldn't be curious about my stupid name? I opened my mouth to apologize, but instead blurted, "Cassian is a weird name, too."

My face flamed. *Some apology.* But Cassian only laughed, for the second time tonight, and my immediate thought was that I'd do anything to hear that laugh again. Glad I was facing the sink because I was blushing like a cartoon, I added a feeble, "Sorry."

"Nah," said Cas, waving me off. "It's a fair point. That's why I usually go by Cas."

"Cas," I said, testing the sound of it. I liked it. "Okay."

"My parents had me when they were young." He hesitated, and I could feel his uncertainty through the air between us. "I guess my mom had been studying Roman history when she got pregnant with me so...here we are."

I turned, looking at him with my head cocked. "It's a beautiful name," I said before I could stop myself.

He laughed again. "You just said it was weird!"

"It can be two things," I said, embarrassed, and turned back to the sink. I could tell he was waiting for me to explain my own, similarly weird, name. "My father likes history, too. That's where Thor came from."

Cas joined me at the sink; I'd taken his plate while he still had his fork in hand. Our elbows brushed as he dropped the utensil in among the rest. "Thanks for doing the dishes," he said, as I coughed to cover my shiver.

"Thanks for cooking."

After I finished clearing up, I knew I had to get back to my research. With only a few days remaining before classes started back up, I had to make the most of my time. This book was merely the latest in a long list of titles my father had asked me to look into. When I'd been accepted to Fremont University, as he had, he'd been over the moon about their famous collection of really old books no one in their right mind would care about. My mother and father had first met while attending the school.

This particular book contained a long-winded personal history of a Celtic druid. I'd already decided most of the text would amount to little more than a story, but if I didn't provide copious notes, Dad would chase me down and demand a full report on the book anyway.

The wild magic that had flowed through the veins of every single person in my family dating back untold generations, had, apparently, skipped over me. And my father was obsessed with finding the reason why.

I was nothing. All of those things my father had tried, none of them worked. I was simply human. I had accepted it, for the most part, but my parents never had. So, here I was, reading the last diary entries of a man rumored to know something about our origins, taking notes, and delivering them back to my father. I'd been doing it since last year when I'd enrolled at Fremont U.

The problem––well, one of many––was that my failures as a progeny essentially influenced my entire life. My major? Evolutionary biology, selected by my father. My second major? Folklore, also chosen by him. The folklore major gave me access to the rarest sections of the campus library, and its oldest books, like the one in my lap.

At least the folklore was interesting. The evolutionary biology was decidedly not, and it was a demanding major. Between the two of them, the extra work for my father, and the internship position he insisted I take with the daughter of one of his oldest friends, it really shouldn't have been a shock that I had trouble maintaining a social life. I barely had time to sleep, let alone go out to parties.

"Are you alright?"

I startled, so engrossed in my notes that I had entirely forgotten Cassian—Cas—was here. "What?"

"You're scowling up a storm over there."

I realized my self-flagellating train of thought had clouded my expression. "Oh, sorry."

"You don't have to be sorry," said Cas. "I was just wondering if you were okay."

"Oh." I had to admit I already found having someone in my space to be taxing. Exciting, in a way, but taxing. I gritted my teeth, turned a page in my book, and reminded myself it only had to be for a year. I could stick it out for a year. I'd lived in discomfort and anxiety for six before that, after all. Cas fidgeted where he sat on the couch, and I got the distinct impression he expected something of me, but I had no idea what. Even if I had, I was sure to fall as woefully short of his expectations as I did of everyone else's. I was about to get up and go read in my room in blessed solitude when Cas spoke again.

"I like your candle."

I blinked up at him, surprised, sliding my glasses up my nose. "Yeah?" I'd debated moving the candle and my statue of Cernunnos out of the living room and into my room out of respect for Cas.

"It's comforting," he said, smiling at me.

"Thanks. It's tobacco and—"

"Cloves?" We said it at the same time.

"Yeah," I said. Then, with no idea what possessed me to do so, I kept talking. "It's a traditional thing. My family is sort of...religious."

"Oh yeah? Are you?"

"No," I said, returning my face to the book. But Cas was

still looking at me, and I squirmed under his attention. "Not really. I just like the traditions."

"And what's the tradition of the candle?"

Cas had fixed his eyes on me, smiling like he was genuinely interested. "It's just—we—" I stammered. "We always light a new candle at the start of something new. Like a new season, a new year—"

"A new living situation?"

"Yes." I went tingly from scalp to toes.

When I went to bed that night, I marshaled my courage. Thirsting over my human roommate was a recipe for disaster, and I needed a distraction. I pulled out my text thread with Rafe, and before I could change my mind, shot him a message about making hard plans for a date.

# 3

CAS

Figuring out a routine with my squirrelly new roommate was like a puzzle. I'd moved in on a Monday, and classes were going to start the following Monday, so we had a week to adjust to each other's company. Thor seemed nice enough, but prone to strange turns. For example, the day following our eggs Benedict experience, I woke up at my usual six a.m. and found him still awake, hunched over his laptop at the kitchen island, typing frantically. When I greeted him, he seemed to come out of a trance, spooking and retreating back to his bedroom without another word.

The next day, I'd come home from the gym to find him on the sofa, brooding in silence. As soon as I crossed the threshold, he left to hide in his room for the rest of the night.

I entertained the thought that perhaps he didn't like me. That was fine, really. I didn't have to be friends with everyone. But it bothered me, perhaps because something told me it was more complicated. Thor was eccentric and interesting. I wanted to figure him out. He was quiet and solitary, sure, but thoughtful. I saw it in little gestures: the hockey stick key, my name on the plate by the buzzer. He'd even pinned a little schedule to the refrigerator, filling in my regular comings and goings alongside his own, so we'd know when to expect each other. I hadn't told him my schedule—he'd just observed me, and made note. When I'd sent him the shopping list for the dinner I planned to cook that weekend, I found Thor also purchased an entire spice rack, as well as a host of pantry staples. Based on what I'd seen of his cabinets before, it was clear they were for my benefit.

He'd waved me off, looking uncomfortable, when I offered to pay him back for half the ingredients. That was one of the first things I learned about Thor. He preferred things to pass without comment. So, whenever I noticed new ingredients in the kitchen, I simply started using them, for both our benefit. I always woke up early, and loved breakfast, so I cooked for us every morning. The first day, Thor emerged from his room, bleary-eyed and grouchy, but when I put a plate in front of him, he dug in and seemed much happier. After coffee, he became downright cheerful.

Soon enough, it was Friday. I planned to make my big dinner for myself and Thor Saturday evening. I'd come up with the perfect, hearty menu for a fall evening: wild mushroom and butternut squash risotto, served with roast duck. Risotto was one of my signature dishes, and I was eager to impress Thor with the meal.

I had to survive today, first.

It was my first practice since I'd completely blown everything.

Last year, I'd had a full ride to school: part academic scholarship, part athletic. It was the only way I could afford to attend a school as nice as Fremont U, where the accounting program was top-notch. I was determined to major in something with high earning potential, so I could start sending money home to help the family.

The whole year had gone great, until finals, when I absolutely tanked a huge paper and freaked out. Certain I'd blown it, I'd gone out to a party with some of my teammates, and—let's just say we got caught doing something stupid. Really stupid. My athletic scholarship had a strict code of conduct by which I had to abide, and in exchange for my performance on the ice, offered me room and board. My performance on the ice had been beyond reproach, but getting caught red-handed trashing a professor's office did *not* fall into that code of conduct.

And of course, the capper to all that, on the last day of the semester, my professor had announced he was dropping everyone's lowest grade, meaning my academic scholarship was intact after all. Long story short, I'd fucked myself. Big time.

When my teammate, Jack Benson, had suggested going to trash Professor Kendrick's office, I should have backed out. Better yet, I should have put a stop to it. The fact that I went along with it had me feeling spineless and weak, but I'd been drunk. I'd been scared.

The paper I'd bombed for Kendrick's class had been my best attempt, but Kendrick's class was hard, and he was a ruthless grader. I should have been instantly suspicious when Benson leaped onto my drunken, wound-licking pity party. That guy never did anything when there wasn't something in it for him. As we downed beer after beer, he let me in on his plan. Knock Kendrick down a peg and blow off some steam. I never, ever would have agreed to it sober, or if I didn't already think my college career was shot to hell. It was like some reckless stranger had possessed me that night.

We'd left the party around eleven: me, Benson, and two other guys from the team. Essentially, the entire offensive line, plus our Goalie. I should have questioned their desire to help me get revenge on Kendrick, but I didn't. The idea was to trash his office—nothing permanent, nothing too destructive. His office was on the first floor of the science building, so climbing in through the window had been easy enough. Kendrick taught mostly post-grad classes, but I'd had him for one of my core courses, introduction to biology. I could still remember the way my hair stood on end in his office—nerves at what we were doing, coupled with the creepy vibe the place gave off. Skulls and jarred specimens lined the walls, and the lights from our phones threw eerie shadows on the wall as they refracted through the glass. While my drunk brain needed all its RAM to focus on adorning the interior of the office with toilet paper, my teammates were busy on Kendrick's computer. By the time I realized what they were doing— loading his computer hard drive with nude pics of Benson's ex-girlfriend—I could hear the security officers approaching from the end of the hall.

Benson and his ex had a rather public, ugly break-up, and there were rumors of her fooling around with a professor. I didn't know if that was even true, let alone if the professor in question was Kendrick—and I didn't think it mattered to Benson. He just wanted to humiliate her and didn't care which teacher got caught in the crossfire.

Panicked, I stayed behind to delete the pics and ended up taking the fall for the entire prank.

I might have been an absolute moron, but I was no snitch.

The other guys had been more than happy with that arrangement, and they'd avoided me like the plague since. Today was the first day we'd all come face to face, and I was dreading it.

When I arrived at the athletic center that housed the rink, I heard a shriek.

"*Cas!*"

In spite of everything, I cracked a grin to see Lucy Myers

jogging toward me. Lucy was five ten, gorgeous, and played for the Fremont volleyball team. She was easily my best friend on campus, and also happened to be queer as a three-dollar bill. I'd tried asking her out last year, at the first party of the fall semester, and she'd spent about twenty solid minutes laughing her ass off. Weirdly, that was how we became friends.

"Dude," she said, folding me into a hug. "I thought you *died*. You dropped off the place of the planet!"

I sighed, returning the hug gratefully. I'd been so ashamed of myself that I'd absolutely stuffed my head in the sand and avoided everyone all summer. "Sorry, Luce," I said. "Just busy."

She slugged my shoulder, giving me another smile, but I thought there was something knowing in her eyes—like maybe she'd heard something. When she asked, "So, where are you living this year?" I was certain of it.

"Got a place off-campus," I said evasively.

"Oh yeah? Nice?"

"Very."

"Cool, cool. Listen," she said. "I gotta get to practice, but are you free this weekend? We have to catch up."

"Can't," I said. "I have plans with my new roommate. Next week?"

"Definitely. I'll text you." She paused. "Oh, hey. Who's your new roommate? Does he go here?"

For some unknown reason, my face burned. "Thor. Thor Ambrose."

Lucy raised her brows. "Really?"

"Yeah, why?"

"He's kind of...weird, isn't he?"

I shrugged. I'd thought as much myself, but her question made me defensive. "I guess? He's just kind of quiet."

"If you say so, dude. Anyway...I'll text you later!" And with a wave, she was gone. I carried on toward the locker room, wondering if I could fill a social gathering with enough "catching up" to avoid talking about last year. Lucy was a ride-or-die type of friend, and she never would have let me get away with taking all the blame. That's why I couldn't tell her what happened.

After practice, Coach Merle called me back after everyone else had packed up their gear and showered off. He wanted to see me in his office, so I went, shoulders up around my ears because I had a suspicion what this was about. I'd hoped that Merle and the assistant coaches would assume that since I showed up, played well at practice, and didn't mention anything, I wasn't about to rat the other guys out.

I was wrong.

Coach Merle sat me down, stared at me, and then gave a bunch of veiled threats that basically amounted to how much they valued the team's entire offensive line more than they valued me, personally. He also all but confirmed what I'd already suspected: the only reason they hadn't booted my ass from the team entirely was that I'd protected the other guys.

Being devalued to my face left me feeling wrung out, empty, and sad. When they finally dismissed me, apparently certain I wasn't going to rat Benson and the others out to the Dean, it was after nine. I hoped to find Lucy leaving the girls' locker room because all I could think about was getting another hug. I needed one real bad. But the building was a ghost town. Everyone had gone home for the night, and my only company was the sound of my own squeaky shoes in the hallway.

Outside, the night air was warm, but a breeze ruffled my sweat-damp hair. All I wanted was to get home and hide under some blankets.

A shrill yell cut through the silence of the night and I was off running, charging toward the noise before my brain even had a chance to register what it might be.

One of the security lights next to a bench on the walking path fell on Thor, who was backing away from something twitching on the ground. Something crawled out from under the bench. It was a hand, followed by a pale arm, and the hand had latched itself onto Thor's ankle. Approaching behind him, I circled my arms around his middle and yanked, pulling him out of the thing's grip and practically into my lap as we fell onto the damp grass.

"What the f—"

But the words died in my throat as the rest of the thing crawled out from under the bench and into the light. Saying "thing" might sound a little cruel, because, I think it was a man? Once, maybe? At least, it was man-shaped, but his skin was pale and greying, and the hand that had grabbed Thor's ankle appeared blackened and burned where it clawed the grass. As my eyes adjusted, I saw that he looked like he was wearing some kind of scaly glove, except that the scales traveled up his wrist to blend seamlessly with his skin. As he hauled himself further into the light, it looked like someone had put him together wrong. There was no other way to describe it— he appeared as if someone had a bunch of action figure parts and tried to stick them together onto the same doll. Some of his ribs were outside his skin, and though I could not see any blood, his lung dragged along beside him, pink and veiny and glistening. It expanded feebly like a wet whoopie cushion.

I glanced at Thor, whose face had run bloodless, his mouth gaping in horror as we watched the man continue moving into the light. We scrabbled backward, away from him, and when he turned his face toward us, my guts lurched. As if the rest of this rich tapestry wasn't enough, the guy's face was oddly flat, primitive, and expressionless, like pictures of early man in a textbook. His head was as bald as the rest of him, no eyebrows or lashes, and his expression vacant. There was no light behind his eyes.

When he drew breath, it rattled, so labored I could feel it in my own chest, and I tried not to look at his exposed lung. I found my voice. "Are you alright?" I asked him.

"Cas!" Thor clutched my arm so tight I could feel his fingernails digging into my skin.

"Can you hear me?" I called louder, ignoring Thor.

The guy kept crawling, revealing that he was naked, and patches of the scales spread down his back, up over his skull, and in other random patches on his body. He opened his mouth, revealing a thick, purple tongue split like a snake's before drawing one last breath. Then he went still.

Silence.

Then, the night seemed to remember itself, crickets and animals and distant traffic resuming in the periphery of my perception. "I'm—I'm calling the cops," said Thor, but his voice felt far away, despite the fact that his fingers still pressed into my arm.

I shook him off, pins and needles shooting up from my fingers to my elbow. I knew I'd have little bruises on my bicep. Crouching carefully beside the man's head, I pressed my fingers to the side of his neck. His skin was already icy cold and clammy and I felt no beat of life beneath my fingertips. The police arrived, and detectives tried to ask a bunch of questions but could tell Thor and I were useless.

"We'll have to bring them to the station," a voice penetrated the dull fog.

"Sir, I—"

"Now, Detective Davis."

In the back of the cruiser, Thor sat rigid and pale, staring at nothing. He had one slim leg drawn up close to his chest, his hands wrapped tightly around his own ankle, the one the dying man had grabbed.

"Hey," I whispered.

Thor didn't seem to hear me, so I rested my hand on his leg. He jumped about a mile.

I had no idea what to say to him, but his eyes shone giant and terrified behind his glasses, which were fogged up and smudged, probably from his brief grapple with the man before I'd yanked him to safety. I had to do *something,* so I reached out and slid the glasses from his face, polished them gently on my shirt, and replaced them on the bridge of his nose. He didn't react.

"Thor," I said gently.

He turned to me, his lips pressed into a thin, grim line.

"It's going to be okay," I said, though in all honesty I had no idea. I didn't know why I was whispering, either.

Certainly, the detective—Davis, I guess his name was—could hear us from the driver's seat no matter how quietly we talked. He caught my eye in the rearview mirror, giving a reassuring smile. "He's right," Davis said kindly. "You guys aren't under arrest. We just need to get some statements for the investigation."

Thor nodded absently, and I was certain he wasn't worried about being in trouble. Without really knowing why, I reached over and pried Thor's hands from his ankle, gave them a squeeze, and set them on his lap. He glanced at me again, shell-shocked.

For my part, I was glad the police had come. The whole thing seemed unbelievable, like a dream with a lot of gaps in it. Or a nightmare, I suppose, but there was a nagging part of me that was glad I hadn't seen it alone, glad that I had other people there to confirm what I'd seen was real.

When we arrived at the precinct, Davis led us through the bullpen of desks into an honest to goodness interrogation room. There had been part of me that thought they really only existed on TV shows. He sat me and Thor down, and promptly left the room. Thor behaved like a sad little mannequin, allowing Davis to move him toward a chair, push him to sit, but not moving on his own. I began to fidget, squinting at the mirror in the room, trying to see a shadow of someone moving behind it.

Eventually, Davis returned and I had enough wits about me to get a good look at him. He was stocky, disheveled, and tired-looking, but he had a kind and honest face. He set a manila folder down on the table in front of us.

"I need you two to start from the beginning," he said, "and tell me everything you saw."

Considering it had all happened in the whirlwind of about a minute or so, it took a long time for Thor and I to—haltingly—tell the tale.

"I was on my way home from a date," said Thor.

"You were?" I turned to him, surprised.

"Um, yes," said Thor, his cheeks getting some color back.

"Why didn't you—"

"You two know each other?" Interrupted Davis. "Before tonight?"

"Yeah," I said, annoyed at something I couldn't put my finger on. "We're roommates."

"But you hadn't planned to meet up at that spot?" Davis asked.

Thor and I looked at each other, frowning. "No," he said. "Total coincidence."

"I wouldn't have even walked that way if I hadn't heard him screaming."

"I didn't scream," said Thor, coming back to himself a bit. He seemed insulted.

"You absolutely did."

"I did not!"

"Okay, then, what did you do?"

"I don't know, he grabbed my ankle and I must have..." he cast around for a different word. "Shouted."

"Fine," I said. "I would never have gone that way if I hadn't heard him *shout*."

Davis noted a few things, and then said, "Alright, boys. I need to show you a few photographs. It's probably going to be disturbing—do you think you're up for it?"

"Yes," I said, and Thor nodded.

Davis flipped open the folder and laid three glossy photos of the dead guy on the table before us. There were two close-up shots of his face, and one of his whole form, with some sticky notes covering the more grotesque aspects of his body, which to be honest was sickly amusing considering we had literally just seen his entire body.

"Do either of you recognize this man?"

"No," I said.

"No," echoed Thor. His voice broke, and he shifted in his seat, moving closer to scrutinize the photos.

"Are you certain? You've never seen him anywhere on campus?"

I could feel Thor trembling beside me. He stared transfixed at the pictures, like he was willing them to tell him something about what happened to this guy. He seemed to be on the verge of some kind of panic attack. I snapped. "Listen," I said. "Is this some kind of joke?"

"I don't—"

"You think we really wouldn't have noticed some bald, scaly, inside-out zombie motherfucker shambling around campus?" The voice coming from my mouth was high-pitched, bordering on hysterical. I barely recognized it. When had I stood up?

"Cas." Thor's quiet voice came from somewhere to my left. A small, warm hand fell on the crook of my arm and tugged me back down to sit.

"Sorry," I mumbled, already embarrassed. I'd been trying to stick up for Thor, but really, I was just as freaked out.

"*I'm* sorry," said Detective Davis gently. "I know this is disturbing, especially after what you've already been through tonight, but I have to ask these questions."

Thor and I stared back at him, and Thor didn't move his hand from my arm. I was glad to have it there as a reminder I wasn't by myself in this surreal nightmare. There came a soft rap on the mirrored glass, and Thor jumped. He pulled back his hand and I immediately missed its weight on my arm.

"Excuse me, for a moment, boys. We're almost through here."

Davis got up, but he left his folder on the table.

Without knowing what possessed me to do so, I whipped out my phone as soon as the door clicked shut behind him. "What are you doing?" Thor hissed, but I ignored him.

There was something about this man that unnerved me down to my bones—and not just the visuals of his horrific death. I had this weird feeling that when we left this room, we'd never hear about it again, like once we left the police station tonight the victim would not exist. So, I used my phone camera to snap a few pictures of the photographs on the table. I was just stuffing my phone back into my pocket when Davis returned. He carried two steaming mugs and set them in front of us. Hot chocolate. Thor wrapped his fingers around the mug, clutching it like a lifeline. I merely leaned down and inhaled the scent of chocolate, infinitely comforting.

After a few more questions, Davis confirmed we were free to go, and offered us a ride home. The drive was silent, and I had this weird impression, like a shift in the air. Taking the photos had used the last drop of courage I had in me, and it had made room for a lot of fear. Thor, on the other hand, seemed significantly calmer. My heart pounded and sweat poured over my forehead. Meanwhile, Thor's breathing had steadied, and his eyes no longer threatened to bug out of his head.

I didn't even know if I thanked Davis as we got out of the car. With a hand on the small of my back, Thor guided us both upstairs, unlocked the front door and steered me over to the couch. He sat me down and set about immediately lighting his candle and setting a fire. The scent of tobacco, cloves, and woodsmoke filled the apartment. Meanwhile, on the couch, I shivered violently.

"Why am I so cold?" I asked, annoyed.

Thor startled, like he hadn't expected me to speak. "Huh?"

"Cold," I said louder, and my voice still sounded young and panicky. "Why am I so cold? It wasn't even cold out tonight."

"Probably shock," he said. Thor reached for a knitted blanket that draped over the back of the sofa and wrapped it around my shoulders. He sat down beside me and pulled my hands into his own, rubbing warmth into them.

I was so out of sorts it didn't even strike me as odd until much later. "What do I have to be shocked about?"

"Well, what we saw—"

"Yeah, great, but nothing *happened*. Not to me, anyway. Why am I being like this? Why—" I jumped up, rambling, to pace back and forth. I shook the blanket from my shoulders, and a shiver wracked my spine again. "What about you, are you alright? He grabbed you. Are you hurt?"

"Cas, come sit down."

But I ignored him. "Why did I *do* that?"

"Do what?"

"Take pictures!"

"I don't—"

"There's got to be something seriously wrong with me. Am I a fucking sociopath?"

"Cas, please. Come sit."

I allowed Thor to pull me back toward the couch and wrap the blanket back around my shoulders. "What kind of person takes a picture like that?"

Thor sensed the question was a rhetorical one, and said nothing. I couldn't sit still, my knees bouncing, my teeth chattering. Thor's hand rubbed circles on my back, somehow finding the tense knot right below my left shoulder blade. He kneaded it with his thumb, soothing me. He didn't speak, just kept massaging little swirls through my flannel as I slowly calmed down. I took a few deep, heaving breaths, focused on the feel of his palm and the crackle of the fire. The scent of cloves.

Eventually, I relaxed. I clutched the blanket around my shoulders like a cloak and leaned my head back against the couch. Thor moved his hand out of the way, and his fingers found their way up into my hair, scratching against my scalp. It felt wonderful and beautifully familiar, though we barely knew each other. I let myself take comfort in his fingers, and it seemed to soothe him too, having something to do with his hands, someone to care for.

All the frantic energy whooshed out of me, like Thor's dexterous fingers had drawn the tension out from my scalp. I sighed, and closed my eyes.

———

## THOR

I woke up with a stiff back, but warm, with the most enticing aroma curled around me like a hug. A hot weight rested in my lap, and something cornsilk soft tangled around my fingers. On a happy exhale, the memory of the night before came screaming back to me. My eyes popped open and my entire body went rigid with panic.

Cas.

My roommate, who I'd literally known for less than a week.

His head was on my lap, and my hand cupped tenderly around his skull, moving through his soft, shaggy mop of sandy waves. With every brush of my fingertips, somehow more of his scent dislodged, filling my belly and chest with heat, all while I quietly panicked. Cas's natural aroma, heightened by the adrenaline that had wrung him out so thoroughly last night, had some...*effects.*

As I tried to wrangle my thoughts and my instincts to avoid poking him in the temple with an errant erection, Cas stirred.

He sat up with a start, taking my arm with him as he pulled out of our impromptu cuddle fest.

"What the—*ow!*" As he jerked back, my fingers tangled in his thick hair, pulling at a snarl at the back of his head.

I yanked my arm back, grimacing at Cas's wince. "Sorry," I whispered.

"It's fine, it's—what time is it?"

"No idea. I just woke up."

"Oh. I guess I should...get to bed."

"Yeah, me too."

We stared awkwardly at each other for a beat before Cas fled to his room and slammed the door. In truth, I was just as drained, my head spinning from what had happened earlier.

I'd just left my date with Rafe, which naturally had been a disaster. He was perfectly lovely, polite, good looking—but there was no spark there, no ease of spending time in each other's company, and certainly no strong mating pull. Nothing like what I felt toward...I shook my head. No. Rafe and I had parted ways with a stiff, formal handshake, and I'd walked the long way home to clear my head.

I cringed, even now, thinking about it. Remembering my terrible date was far superior to dwelling on what I'd seen immediately afterward. Twisting in my sheets, I grabbed my ankle again, because I could feel the phantom touch of the dying man even now.

My stomach roiled. He had been horrible to look upon, especially his blank expressionless eyes. A dead guy with animal traits? A pretty safe bet my kind were involved. Unfortunately—or, fortunately, depending on where you stood—I didn't recognize the man. That in itself was unusual. Of course, there were shifters the world over, but my family was at least acquainted with everyone in this area.

He had to have come from somewhere else, the poor man. His face had been profoundly wrong, his features almost... primitive. Like he hadn't developed the facial features of an adult human. To say it was disturbing was the understatement of the century.

Eventually, I did fall asleep, because I woke in the morning to my usual Saturday alarm. I rolled over, groaning, trying to decide if facing Cas after our awkward encounter last night was worth it to get some coffee. The dull pounding behind my eyes said yes.

When I reached the kitchen, I smelled something heavenly. Something besides coffee. Cas was already up and elbow deep in a huge breakfast extravaganza.

I approached the side of him to get coffee from the pot brewing at his elbow, and when I reached over, he finally noticed me and jumped. "Jesus, Thor," he said.

I flinched. "Sorry."

"It's fine," he said, clearing his throat. He waved his spatula dismissively. "You move so quietly."

"I wasn't trying to sneak up on you."

"I know."

The silence was loaded, everything we'd seen, plus our little moment last night, weighing heavy in the air. Finally, Cas said, "I really wanted to make pancakes."

A classic comfort food, sweet and hearty. "Pancakes sound great."

We ate in silence, and I was already making plans to avoid Cas for the rest of the day to forestall any further awkwardness. At the first bite of pancakes, however, I was totally lost. In heaven. Cas could never move out and I potentially had to contrive some way to chain him to the stove. He had already taken to making breakfast every day since he moved in, but never had he made something like this before. I moaned out loud.

"Good, huh?" He asked, and I glanced over to see his cheeks go a bit pink.

"Perfect."

After breakfast, Cas told me he was planning on deleting the photos he took last night.

"*What?*"

"I don't know what made me take them. I feel gross about it. Probably illegal too, now that I think about it."

No doubt, it was illegal. But I needed to get my hands on those pics. "You can't delete them!" I blurted, grabbing his wrist.

We looked down at where we touched and I dropped his arm immediately. "Why not?" he asked.

"Don't you want to find out what happened?"

Cas laughed. "What, and you and me are going to figure it out?"

"Maybe."

"I really don't feel right keeping them," said Cas doubtfully.

"Can you send them to me? I know someone who might

be able to make sense of..." I left the rest unspoken. Whatever the hell had been wrong with that poor guy.

"Who?"

Who indeed? Last year, my father had arranged for me to get a research position for a PhD candidate in the postgraduate evolutionary biology department at Fremont.

Leda Templeton was tall, blonde, and beautiful. There was also a time when I thought she'd be my future wife.

Leda's father was my dad's oldest friend, a guy he seemed to like far better than most of his blood relations. The two of them had been putting Leda and me together since we were kids, hoping we'd form a mating bond. Now, of course, on some level I'd always known I was gay, but when you're a kid, you don't really have the full concept of adult notions like marriage, or in our case, mating bonds. Leda was a few years older than me, and had approximately zero interest in being my mate, thank the gods. I thought, too, that she was a bit relieved it hadn't worked out between us. Her *fauna* had emerged right on time—an elegant Tundra Swan—and I was, well, me. Her father was as relieved, if not more—being shackled to a genetic failure like me would have tarnished their family's reputation.

I wouldn't go so far as to say we were friends, but now that I wasn't the dumb little kid trailing after her, she seemed to tolerate me okay. Outwardly, her PhD was in a niche area of evolutionary biology. Something to do with yeast, I think. However, her real work was with shifters. While she studied our biology, I dug into our history.

She studied under her mentor, Dr. Sean Kendrick, who was well known in our circles for his work on developing shifter pharmaceuticals. He taught advanced courses here at Fremont, but I knew he had his own private lab facility where he developed drugs and medical treatments specifically geared toward shifters. Our kind tended to metabolize medications differently than humans did, and he'd spent a lot of time and money researching those differences. I knew my father wrote off hefty monetary contributions toward his work, as did many of the shifter elite.

I signed in with security in the science building where Leda had a small office and lab space with equipment to work on her dissertation, and by extension, her shifter studies. When I walked in, the sight of her in her pristine lab coat, hair pulled back in a French twist, filled me with relief. With all of the chaos of last night, and the awkwardness of this morning, Leda could be counted upon as a constant.

"Thor," she said, by way of greeting. She didn't look up from her microscope. "Come look at this."

I shrugged into my own lab coat and hurried to her side. Most of my assistant position involved double-checking figures, confirming results, and preparing slides. It was far from fascinating but it was soothing, methodical work and I was good at it. Leda loved it, of course, spending more time in the lab than out of it. As I confirmed what she was looking at on the slide, I heard her take a sharp inhale.

"What?"

Her nostrils dilated furiously. "You met someone."

It wasn't a question. "Uh, What?"

Leda scoffed. "Oh, please," she said with a wry smile. "You have horny boy shifter stink all over you."

"Oh my *God*."

"It's not a bad smell." She returned to her tablet for a moment before saying absently, "I'm glad for you."

"Yeah?"

"Of course," she said, sounding surprised. "You've always wanted to find a mate."

I wasn't sure what to say to that, so instead I said, "What about you?"

She sniffed delicately. "I don't think I'm cut out to be

anyone's mate," she said. "I have neither time nor inclination for such nonsense."

"Well, consider yourself lucky. It's complicated."

"Oh?"

"He's human," I told her. "And, uh. I think he's straight."

"Ah. Well. If you're giving off pheromones this strong, I would be very surprised to learn that he's straight."

"Pardon?"

"Your inner *fauna* can tell. It wouldn't lead you astray."

"You forget," I said sourly. "I don't have a *fauna*."

"You don't have a *presenting fauna*," she amended. "I still don't believe there's *nothing* going on in there." She poked my chest.

"Regardless," I snapped, uncomfortable all of a sudden. "I actually had something far more important than my dating life to discuss with you."

"Color me intrigued."

I pulled out my phone, eager to move the subject away from my stirring feelings for Cassian. After a lot of wheedling, I had convinced him to send me the pics from last night by telling him Leda was doing work with infectious diseases. That had possibly done more harm than good, because Cas was now even more freaked out at the idea of a pandemic than he had been at the idea of one dead body. Handing my phone to Leda, I said, "My roommate and I found a dead body last night."

Leda slid her stylish black glasses up her nose, staring at the picture. "Fascinating."

"Excuse me?"

"And horrible," she added. "Fascinating, but horrible. Where is the specimen being held?"

"He's not a *specimen,*" I said. "Anyway, I think he's down at the police station, in the morgue. You don't...you don't recognize him, do you?"

"No," said Leda. "I've never seen his like before."

Odd turn of phrase. "What do you mean, his like?"

"Well, he doesn't have the craniofacial structure most shifters have—in their human forms, I mean."

She zoomed in on the photo, and I knew she was referencing the man's strange, flat features. "That was odd to me too—but don't you think it could be because he died mid-shift?"

"I'm not certain," she said. "This is the photo of a photo. I need to see the actual corpse, perhaps take some samples."

"I don't know how you think we're going to manage that."

"Well," said Leda, as though explaining the obvious. "We're going to have to break into the morgue."

I laughed, before I realized she wasn't kidding. "Come on," I said. "You can't be serious."

"Of course I'm serious," she said. "Kendrick would flip if he lost the chance to examine something like this."

"Well, I understand that but I really don't want to be arrested for tampering with a criminal investigation."

Leda pursed her lips. "Help me out, and I'll make sure it gets back to Kendrick...and your father."

She had me there. My dad had been dying for me to get an internship working with Kendrick. This would definitely help me convince Dad I was doing my part to tow the family line.

"Okay, fine," I said. "What are we going to do?"

I had Leda's insane plan chasing itself around in my head the whole walk across campus, not to mention the fact that I was giving off mating pheromones. How humiliating. This stupid crush of mine had to be squashed before it took on a life of its own, and ruined mine. The date with Rafe had gone nowhere, so my next bet was to actually ask my parents to set me up with someone else. *Shudder*. No doubt they'd be over the moon at the request, and it would help my cover of at least trying to find someone in our world to mate with. Still, I hesitated. The idea was even more unappealing now, for some reason.

When I got home, I distracted myself—or tried to—by picking up one of the books I had been studying for my father.

I realized I'd been reading the same passage over and over without comprehending a single word of it, when the door burst open and Cas came thundering over the threshold. He didn't notice me sitting there as he charged directly toward the refrigerator. His hair stuck to his neck and forehead with sweat from the gym, and the scent was unlike anything I had yet experienced. It hit me like a baseball bat, filling my mouth with saliva. All my senses turned way up, every single one of them focused on Cas. He bent at the waist to rummage in the fridge for something, and I gripped the arms of my chair, white-knuckled, because all I wanted to do was press up against his ass, to rub myself all over his body possessively, to blend my scent with his. I watched a bead of sweat slide down his neck, heard his heartbeat, his pulse. The scent was so thick and strong in the air it was like I could taste him, and before I could get a grip, I realized I was legitimately panting, drawing more of Cas into my lungs.

Cas finally heard me, or noticed me, or something, because he straightened up and turned around in surprise. His smile faltered and he said, "Are you okay?"

A strangled noise came from my mouth, and I stood from my chair, concealing my groin with my book, my own back breaking out in sweat. Cas took a step toward me, and I took a step back. If he got any closer, I didn't know what I would do—lick his neck, probably. Good grief.

"Aren't you going to shower before you cook?" I blurted.

Cas looked like he'd been slapped. "*Excuse* me?"

I opened and closed my mouth a few times before turning and fleeing the room before I said anything else moronic.

Back in my room, I sat on the edge of the bed, scrubbing my hands over my face. I felt like the worst sort of asshole. There was no polite way to tell someone to kindly, please, wash the stink off themselves, and yet in a sea of bad options I somehow picked the worst one. At least I hadn't tried to spin it as a positive—that would obviously have been even worse.

I needed to get a handle on this crush, because there was no way it was going to end well. The best-case scenario was I'd get rejected and humiliated; the worst-case scenario was that I'd freak Cas out so badly he'd feel like he couldn't live here anymore.

His scent punched me in the chest, like Cas had reached through it, grabbed my heart, and squeezed. And pulled. Toward him. Ugh. I tried my best to squash it down but my body hummed, alive with desire and aching want. I heard the shower, and while I was relieved that the heady scent of Cas's sweat was being washed down the drain, my brain suffused with images of what he'd look like under the spray, water rippling over him, clinging in droplets to his golden eyelashes, suds trailing down over his chest...

I grabbed my pillow, pressed it into my face, and screamed. After that, I felt a bit better.

After skinning down my jeans and masturbating furiously, I felt a lot better. I cleaned myself up, changed clothes, and ventured cautiously out of my room. Cas remained in the bathroom for a while, and part of me wondered if he'd decided not to cook dinner for us both. Of course, I felt badly that I'd insulted him so egregiously, but also, I was starving. I'd been looking forward to this meal all week.

I picked up *The Wilde Histories* again and started thumbing through, but my eyes were trained down the corridor, waiting for the bathroom door to swing open. Cas stepped out in a billowing cloud of steam, the towel barely hanging on for dear life around his hips, water dripping sinfully over his abs. The scent was manageable now, but the visuals seemed just as likely to do me in. Thank the gods I'd taken myself in hand already, or there would be no preventing myself from falling to my knees and worshipping every inch of Cas's body, scrubbed and pink and clean. I ached to dirty him all over again.

With a second towel, he scrubbed the excess water from his hair, leaving it adorably tousled. When he lowered the terrycloth, he caught my eye and glowered before stomping into his room.

# 4

Wat the actual fuck. As I scrubbed myself clean, I thought about what Thor said, scouring my body in hopes of calming down. What a rude thing to say to someone! I was sure I hardly smelled like perfume and rose petals after my workout, but goddamn. Like he smelled so perfect after he...I frowned. I had no idea if Thor worked out. Probably not. He was so skinny the tiniest free weight would probably knock him on his ass. Picturing that broke my anger like a fever, making me snicker to myself.

I did, however, take my sweet ass time in the shower, because if Thor was going to be a dick, his fucking majesty could wait until midnight to eat for all I cared. Still though, this tension between us could probably be chalked up to everything that had happened last night. As if to remind myself of that, I glanced down at my bicep, and the four tiny bruises left by Thor's fingers when he'd grabbed hold of me. I brushed my wet fingertips over the marks, and shivered.

After pulling on some loose sweats and a comfy tee, I

emerged from my room to get dinner started. I'd been looking forward to cooking this meal all week, so I decided to let Thor's rudeness go.

Thor sat on the edge of the couch, perched like he often did when uncomfortable. He leapt to his feet when I came in. "Cas! I am *so* sorry—"

"Don't worry about it, dude." I waved him off. "I probably wouldn't want someone sweating all over my dinner, either."

But Thor crossed the room to me and said, "It was so rude. I—I'm just used to living alone, so I guess maybe I lost my filter a bit. I'm so sorry."

It felt nice that he acknowledged his mistake. Usually, I would have shrugged it off, but his earnest apology was oddly validating. I had started pulling some tools from the kitchen cupboards, before finally saying, "Yeah, you know what? It was rude."

Thor froze, looking taken aback by my bluntness, and he let out a breathy, nervous laugh.

"But," I said. "Thank you, for apologizing."

The tension broke after that, and I went about my cooking, blissful with the Viking stove and all of Thor's top-of-the-line kitchen tools at my disposal. I noticed some new things—a huge new cutting board, and a set of chef's knives set in a wooden block. They definitely hadn't been there before. I pulled one out, brushing my thumb over the blade to check the edge. "Did you just get these?"

Thor sat in his spot at the island to watch me cook. He looked away, pushing his glasses up his nose. He shrugged. "I thought you'd like something decent to cook with."

I knew a thing or two about knives, and these were some extremely nice ones. "You didn't have to do that," I said, feeling squirmy and embarrassed. This was a really nice gift. Why would he spend so much money on me?

Thor shrugged, looking equally uncomfortable. "Don't worry about it."

"Well," I said. "I suppose it's kind of for your benefit too, since I'll be feeding you."

With a small smile, Thor nodded and went back to studiously examining his fingernails. Like the groceries and the spices, I knew Thor would have preferred it if I never mentioned the knives, but I couldn't help it. No one had ever gotten me something so thoughtful and expensive before.

So, I vowed to make the absolute best risotto Thor Ambrose had ever tasted.

The smell of shallots, butter, and roasting meat filled the apartment, and I realized I was starving. By the time dinner was ready, it was pretty late, but Thor raised no word of complaint. In fact, he raised no word at all, seeming happy to sit in total silence and watch me cook. My family was usually far too chaotic to calmly watch me make dinner, and I didn't think I'd ever cooked under such scrutiny before.

As I neared the end of preparation, Thor rose and gathered plates and wine glasses. He lit his candle on the mantlepiece and got some red wine from the counter. He poured us each a glass as I dished up the risotto, topping each steaming portion with a crispy-skinned, perfectly roasted, juicy duck breast.

"This is a Borolo," Thor said. "I picked it out to go with the duck."

"I'm sure it's perfect." I knew fuck all about wine unless it was literally an ingredient in a recipe.

We sat at the kitchen island, side by side as usual, and dug into the meal. I was about to open my mouth, try to make some casual conversation, when Thor released a quiet, strangled moan. I jerked my head to the side, watching him as he closed his eyes and savored the first bite. With a grin, I decided not to talk and let him enjoy it. I couldn't lie; I loved how much he loved my food.

However, several tense minutes later, I was uncomfortable and rather hot under the collar. At first, I thought Thor was pulling my leg, moaning and groaning his way through about half his plate without saying a word. My own fork hung between my plate and my mouth, frozen as I watched.

When Thor sealed his lips around the fork, sucking the risotto off the end with pornographic gusto, almost like he was moving in slow motion, I cracked.

I cleared my throat, still at a loss for words, and Thor opened his eyes to find me staring. "What?"

"You're, uh," and my voice came out weird and strangled. "You're making some real weird noises, dude."

Thor dropped his fork. "I'm not. Am I?"

I decided to go easy on him and said, "So, you like the food?"

Cheeks pink, Thor nodded. "It's amazing."

"Cool."

A weird humming silence settled over the table, and Thor seemed to be hyper-aware of any further noises—though occasionally a muffled squeak would emerge. He broke the silence and said, "So, where did you learn how to cook?"

It was my turn to feel weird. "My stepmom taught me," I said.

"Oh yeah?"

"Yeah," I said, swallowing nervously. "She uh—she passed away several years ago."

Thor grabbed my hand. "Oh, Cassian, I'm so sorry. I shouldn't have brought it up."

"No, no, it's okay." This is where I'd usually clam up. I was very private and protective about my family, but for some reason I didn't mind talking about it with Thor. "There's five of us. Siblings, I mean. It's hard for my dad, so I started doing a lot of the cooking for the younger kids."

"That's a lot of responsibility," said Thor carefully.

"Yeah." My dad had given me—us—absolutely everything he possibly could. He worked endless shifts, always sacrificing his own time to make sure we were taken care of. I felt guilty complaining. Almost like, he could hear me, and he'd be ashamed he hadn't been able to do even more. "It's hard, being away from them."

Thor scrutinized me, a shrewd look on his narrow face. "You feel guilty, being here at school, don't you?"

I frowned. "Yes." I turned back to my plate, pushing rice around in circles with my fork. "I do. That's why I have to be careful this year, requalify for my scholarship. Then I can send home any money I would normally spend on rent."

Thor nodded thoughtfully, digesting this. "What happened to your scholarship?"

Again, I would normally have shrugged off the questions and changed the subject. But Thor's earnest curiosity did not grate on me the same way questions from others did. I told him, briefly, about my egregious mistake of the spring.

"Jack Benson is a jackass," said Thor with a derisive snort.

"We're still friends," I said. Then I paused. Were we? "Sort of."

Thor clearly had some thoughts about that but he kept them to himself, taking a sip from his wine glass.

"What about you?" I asked, definitely ready for a subject change.

"What about me?"

"You know, what are your plans? For next year."

Thor shrugged one shoulder. "I might transfer schools," he said.

That took me aback. "Oh?"

"Yeah, my family has a lot of plans for me that I don't

really...anyway. I'm actually saving your rent money into a little stash to help me move. Maybe California, I don't know. A fresh start."

"Huh," I said, unsure why that idea made me so unhappy. "Well, here's hoping both of our goals for the year come to fruition."

We clinked glasses, and Thor looked uncertain, like he hadn't meant to share that much with me.

I cast around for another topic change. "We should make this like, a weekly thing."

"Huh?"

"Fancy dinners like this."

"Really? You want to?" Thor looked genuinely surprised.

"Yeah, this was really fun. Your kitchen is amazing and I have a ton of cool recipes I've been wanting to try."

Thor beamed. "That sounds great," he said.

I found myself mirroring his smile.

———

## THOR

Leda was determined to carry out her insane tissue heist as soon as possible, citing the fact that we didn't know what would happen to the body the longer we delayed.

This was how I found myself crouching behind the police station, a scraggly bush my only cover. I had positioned myself below a window. Leda's plan, though reckless and criminal, was fairly simple. Since the police had already seen me, Leda would enter through the front, claiming to be a girl with a missing brother. That way, the coroner would let her in the morgue to identify the body, where she'd fake a meltdown and ask for some privacy with the deceased. After a quick check for cameras, she'd hoist me in through the window and I'd help her collect the necessary samples.

Easy peasy. So why was I sitting here with my breakfast churning around in my guts? Well, aside from the fear that I'd get thrown in jail for tampering with evidence in a criminal investigation, I felt guilty concealing this from Cas. I knew the body had disturbed him, though he hadn't brought it up again. Solving the mystery might set his mind at ease, but it would have the teeny, tiny side effect of outing my family and the entire shifter community. It was a risk I couldn't take.

With any luck at all, this poor man's fate was a fluke, or a tragic accident, and I could go on forgetting about it as well.

The knock on the window startled me, and I leapt to my feet, narrowly avoiding banging my head on the windowsill. Leda slid the window open and grasped my forearm to pull me inside.

Not one for small talk, Leda said, "You take the photos and keep a lookout, I'll harvest the samples. I don't know how long we have."

I whipped out my phone and Leda pulled back the sheet covering John Doe's body. I took a few snaps of his placid, underdeveloped face, and the chart with the case information hanging from the end of the gurney. Squinting, I realized the cause of death had not been filled in. Well, it had kind of been filled in—someone had written "suffocation" and about six question marks. As Leda bustled around the table, visually examining every inch of the corpse, I took a ton of photographs. My stomach roiled, but Leda was the picture of composure.

Finally, she opened her purse and pulled out a leather case that contained her tools: forceps, scalpels, and scissors. She also had a dozen or so jars, some pipettes and slides, zip-lock bags and sealed containers. Her pocketbook was like that of a serial killer version of Mary Poppins.

Though I'd assisted Leda in the lab for almost a year now, this sort of treatment of flesh was foreign to me. Usually, her specimens were relegated to vials and petri dishes by the time I saw them. I turned around to survey the room. It was clean, and surprisingly bright—I'd pictured a morgue to be a dreary, depressing place. Despite the faint odor of bleach and formaldehyde, it was pretty unoffensive. So, what raised the skin on the back of my neck?

Something prickled in the periphery of my awareness, a feeling like judgmental eyes on my body. I turned, almost expecting the other two corpses to sit up under their respective sheets and point at me. They didn't, of course, but still—I felt a pull, some niggling sense of dread. I approached the closest gurney, labeled for a Jane Doe. The case number matched the one for our body. I shuddered, turning back to Jane. The feeling of dread increased its pressure on my shoulders, but I couldn't stop myself from pulling back the sheet.

It took everything I had not to cry out in fear, in revulsion, in sheer disbelief at what I was seeing. I practically teleported to the third and final body to expose his face as well. Some sort of strangled sound must have escaped because I, at last, caught Leda's attention.

"Thor, you've got to—oh what the *fuck.*"

I'd never heard Leda curse like that before, but most of my awareness centered on the horrors in front of me. While the scaled man had been plenty unsettling, seeing two more bodies made it worse, a million times worse.

Jane Doe's face was obscured by bouquets of thick, sleek black feathers which exploded from her mouth, nostrils, and eye sockets. Leda reached a gloved hand toward one and gave it a gentle tug. "They're growing from her," she whispered, her voice breaking. "The feathers are coming out of her."

She looked like some sort of strange effigy, and we didn't dare uncover the rest of her body to see what else may have befallen her. Leda used her forceps to excise a few feathers, and we covered her back up before we looked at the third and final body, a second male victim, and his face, neck and shoulders were covered entirely with thick grey fur. On closer examination, rough, hairy skin grew over his eyes, nostrils, and the place where his mouth would have been—unbroken skin stretched across his airways.

"What the hell is going on here?" Asked Leda, and I hoped the question was rhetorical because my tongue had seized in my mouth. She took a few final photos of the other bodies and covered everyone up while I stood there like a plank of petrified wood.

Without another word passing between us, we worked together to cover our tracks, and Leda boosted me up and out of the window. I landed on my feet, but overbalanced a bit and hit the ground, gravel and dirt digging into my hands. I stood up, blinking stupidly at my palms. I didn't even bother to crouch behind the bush again—a lucky thing no one came around the building until Leda found me standing there. She grabbed my wrist and tugged me along back to where she'd parked several blocks away.

"I think we're in the clear," she said, and her voice had a strange high pitch to it.

I didn't answer, merely staring down at the grit still embedded in my palms.

"Are you alright?" She asked me.

I nodded.

"I'm going to drop you at home and head straight to the lab. I want to get these samples preserved as fast as possible."

I nodded again, glad she didn't expect me to help her out yet. The one body had been bad enough, but three?

# 5



Thor had been acting weird all week. Weirder than usual, I might add. Distant, cold, and jumpy. He also had definitely not been sleeping. By the time our second fancy dinner rolled around—for which I was making bouillabaisse—I was worried something was very, very wrong. I realized while Thor was in class on Friday that I had forgotten to get fresh fennel for the stew, so I headed to the market. He'd gotten the groceries delivered as usual, but I'd forgotten to mention the fennel, an inexcusable lapse. I added a few other things to my cart, like soap and deodorant, and I passed by a little table full of candles. A sage green one called "brisk spring" caught my eye, I picked it up, closed my eyes and inhaled. It smelled clean and fresh. Remembering Thor's candle and the meaning behind it, I thought maybe it would cheer him up a bit.

Back at home, Thor came in, dropping his bag and making immediately for his liquor cart. He poured himself a glass of whisky and swirled it around. I watched from the kitchen as his nostrils flared rapidly. His eyes flitted to the mantle, where I'd set the new candle beside his original one, and lit them both.

"Did you buy a candle?"

Suddenly, I felt very stupid, and possibly like I'd done something hugely insulting. "Yeah," I said defensively.

"Why?"

"I don't know." It was just a stupid candle. "It's a new tradition, right? Us doing our weekly dinner thing?"

Thor *beamed,* showing me his lopsided grin for the first time in a week. "Okay," he said, positively glowing. "Yeah, you're right. Thank you."

The bouillabaisse was a challenge. Unlike the risotto, which I considered a signature of mine, I'd never made it before, so I was pleased when it came out great. Though Thor seemed determined to keep his appreciation, let's say, PG, it definitely put him in a much better mood than he'd been in for days. I counted it as a win.

Thor washed the dishes when we'd finished eating. I was debating trying to get in some studying when my phone rang. It was a number I didn't recognize, but the area code was local.

"Hello?"

"Mr. Rhodes? This is Detective Davis from the Douglas Crest police department."

"Oh, hi, Detective," I said.

Thor spun from the sink, ignoring the thick suds dripping from the plate in his hand to the floor. His face went pale.

"Listen, Mr. Rhodes," said Davis. "We're going to need you and Mr. Ambrose to come back down to the station. We uh, have a few more questions to ask you both about the case."

"Alright, when—"

"Tonight, would be ideal. As soon as possible."

"All right," I said, and we hung up.

"What was that about?" Thor's voice had gone high and squeaky.

"Detective Davis needs us to go back and answer a few more questions," I relayed. "I can drive us."

"Oh. Uh, okay. Um."

Thor made his way around the kitchen island as I grabbed my keys and jacket. "You might want to lose the gloves. And the sponge."

He looked down at his hands like he'd forgotten what he was holding, and dashed back to the sink.

The car was silent as I drove, and I could feel the tension coming off Thor in waves. I wasn't sure why he was so nervous; certainly nothing *more* crazy could have happened since we'd found that body, right?

Detective Davis, looking haggard, herded us into the same interrogation room we'd been in the week before. A second officer joined us and sat beside Davis on the other side of the table. He was older, his face deeply lined, but his eyes were piercing and harsh.

The four of us stared at each other for quite some time.

"So," I said, breaking the quiet. "What is this about?"

While the other man merely continued to stare at us with mistrust on his face, Detective Davis gave me a long, searching look. "Well, Mr. Rhodes, we wanted to make absolutely certain the two of you had nothing else you wanted to tell us about the incident you witnessed."

*No way,* I thought. There was no way this was the only reason they called us in. I sensed a trap. "We told you everything," I said flatly. "Right, Thor?"

He nodded, and I could feel him trembling beside me. Under the pretext of getting more comfortable, I shifted my chair closer to Thor's and pressed my leg alongside his shaking one. I wasn't entirely sure why; I just knew I wanted to offer him some kind of secret comfort, something to keep him steady. The move had been instinct, and it surprised me—what surprised me even more was that it seemed to work. Thor stilled at the touch.

"Well," interrupted the other cop. "We had the body of the victim in our local morgue, right here at the precinct. Did you know that?"

"No," said Thor, too quickly.

"No," I echoed, shooting him a look. "Well, I mean, I assumed it was in a morgue somewhere."

"Aside from yourselves, there were no witnesses. We didn't release any details about this case to the public. And yet, somehow, a woman who claimed to be the sister of the deceased reached out to us. She came in, saw the body, and left without providing any contact information."

He stared at us expectantly, and I met his eyes.

"Would either of you have any idea why that might be?" Asked Davis. "Or how she may have heard of the victim's presence here?"

We shook our heads.

Davis opened a folder and pulled out a glossy, but blurry, black and white photograph of a blonde woman wearing a cap and dark glasses. "Do either of you recognize her?"

I really and truly did not. I shook my head while Thor said, "No," again, but his voice broke.

Both cops stared at him, and I gave him a subtle nudge under the table. I knew he was nervous but he was acting suspicious, and I didn't want either of us to get in trouble.

"The strangest thing," said Cop number two, "was that after she left, the body of the victim seemed to have been tampered with."

"It was missing hair and teeth, and showed signs of injection sites in the arms that had not been present during the initial autopsy."

"Well," I said, slowly, "She's obviously the one who did it, right? We weren't anywhere near this place."

"Yeah," said Thor. "What would we want with dead bodies?"

Davis's shrewd eyes snapped to Thor's face, narrowing in suspicion. "Bodies? Plural?"

Thor blanched, and something like a warning bell went off in my head. "I meant body," he said hastily. "I misspoke."

I hadn't known him long, but something told me Thor knew a hell of a lot more than he was telling them. It struck me that he was the first on the scene the night we'd found the poor guy. What if something more had happened before I'd arrived? What if Thor's yelps of distress had been a cover?

I hated to think of him as capable of something sinister, but there was something going on. However, some instinct convinced me to give Thor the benefit of the doubt, at least, for now. "Listen," I said, with more confidence than I felt. I pulled from the depths of my cop show knowledge. "We've told you everything we know. So, either charge us with something and let us call a lawyer, or let us go."

When they did release us, Thor couldn't flee the station fast enough, but Detective Davis grabbed my arm before I could follow. He lowered his voice. "If you think of anything else," he said, "Please. Call me."

I trailed after Thor, following him to the door of my car. I waited until he had climbed into the passenger seat and fastened his seatbelt before saying, "Okay, man. What the fuck is going on?"

"I have no—"

"Come on, dude. We both know I covered for your ass in there. So, start talking or I'll drive right back there and tell them."

"It's kind of hard to explain," said Thor. "You wouldn't believe me if I told you."

"Try me."

"Okay, I think—I think I'm going to need some help explaining."

I squinted at him suspiciously. Thor looked truly distressed, and he didn't seem the kind to have a good poker face. "It better be one hell of an explanation, because where I'm sitting, this looks like some real serial killer shit."

"Okay, just, please—give me a second." Thor pulled out his phone, tapped the screen a few times and held it up to his ear. I could hear it ringing in the weighty quiet of the car. No one picked up. Thor hit dial again, and a third time. "She's not answering," he muttered, almost to himself.

"Who's not?"

"My boss, Leda. She's the girl in the picture they showed us."

I almost crashed the damn car. "What the hell?"

"I know, Cas. I know it's a lot, but she's not answering. It's late. Can we maybe, go meet with her tomorrow?"

"First thing tomorrow," I said emphatically.

Thor nodded. Out of the corner of my eye, I watched him as I drove. He had his phone out the entire remainder of the drive, thumb brushing over the screen. My head spun. What the hell was Thor involved with?

I slept with one eye open, so to speak, though I was confident if it came to a fight I could easily best Thor. He weighed about as much as my gym bag, so even if he did turn out to be a serial killer, I think I still had the upper hand.

Nonetheless, I almost jumped out of my skin when he knocked softly on my bedroom door in the morning. "I finally heard back from Leda," he said, sounding troubled. "Let's go."

We walked across campus, and it was broad daylight on a Saturday, so I didn't suspect any sort of trickery. I had no idea what he was going to reveal, if anything, that would change my mind. I couldn't explain to myself why I hadn't outed

Thor to the cops yet. I supposed I still could, if his explanation was too flimsy.

Thor and I swiped into security at the lab, and didn't speak as we waited for the elevator to take us up to one of the top floors.

For some reason, my fight or flight response hadn't woken up yet to warn me to stay the hell out of their creepy scientist lair. I think I was just too damn curious.

Leda had her back to us when we entered, and started speaking immediately, like she recognized Thor by the sound of his footsteps. "Thor," she said, her voice sounding raspy like she hadn't slept. "I don't know what any of this means, but I've begun the process of—"

She turned and saw me standing by Thor's elbow, and clammed up. She was definitely recognizable as the girl from the photo, despite her hair being pulled back and the absence of sunglasses.

"Are you alright?" Thor asked her, real concern in his voice. I could understand why; this girl looked like hell. Bags under her eyes, greyish pale skin, and her hair was greasy and lank.

"I'm fine," she waved him off, and spread her arms in attempt to block whatever she had on her worktable. She stared at Thor, he stared back, and I watched as the two of them appeared to communicate solely through blinks and pupil dilation.

Finally, I cleared my throat. Thor glanced at me before saying, "Leda, this is Cassian. He's my—"

"Roommate?" she finished. "I recognize his scent from the other day."

Thor blushed, a shade of dark, pinky peach that I recently had found myself watching for every time he got embarrassed or flustered, which was often. I, however, was flummoxed. Maybe I did absolutely reek after all. First Thor had commented on my scent, and now this girl was claiming she could detect hints of it on Thor. "Uh," I said.

"The police know about the samples," Thor told Leda, still looking mortified by her scent comment.

"What samples?" She asked, her voice far too innocent, as she moved her body to further obscure her worktable.

"I need to…" Thor looked at me. "The police have a picture of you in the lobby of the precinct. Help me explain it to Cas. He thinks we had something to do with it."

"Well, we didn't kill them!" Leda blurted.

"Them?" I echoed, feeling faint as I remembered Thor 'misspeaking' the night before. "*Them?*"

Thor sighed, pulling out his phone. He handed it to me, saying, "We went to the morgue to collect some samples of the body you and I found, and there were two more in there."

Staring at the pictures, I almost ralphed. I shoved the phone back at Thor. "What the fuck," I said. "What. The. Fuck?"

Leda winced as I practically shouted the last word, pressing a finger to her temple.

"Cas, just let—"

"No," I said. "No. This is so fucked up. There is nothing you can say that'll prove you didn't have something to do with this!"

"Oh, for fuck's sake," snapped Leda, and then all hell broke loose.

I legitimately thought I'd lost my marbles. Where Leda had been standing seconds before, an enormous swan now wrestled its way out of a blouse and a lab coat before my very eyes. I clutched the doorknob, seeking anything to help me stay on my feet, as my knees threatened to give out. The bird flapped and wiggled its way out of Leda's clothes, her stylish glasses clattering to the floor as she preened her feathers and honked.

I turned toward Thor, open-mouthed, and saw he looked only mildly taken aback—not nearly shocked enough for this to be a new revelation to him. "Leda," he hissed, lunging forward. "What were you thinking?"

The swan merely honked again, flapping her enormous wings to display flawless white plumage. Thor gathered Leda's clothes and set them on the table. Then, he held out the lab coat like a matador's cape, and Leda shot back up behind it. Thor bundled the naked girl into the lab coat as if it were a bathrobe, and she groped on the table for her glasses. Sliding them on her face, she said, "There," matter-of-factly, as if her turning into a giant ass *bird* explained fucking anything.

I staggered over to a stool and collapsed on it.

"The victims..." Thor said. "They are like Leda." He gestured between Leda and himself with a resigned sigh. "Like us."

There it was. Those two quiet syllables finally, *finally* triggered my fight or flight response. I launched myself off the stool, and without the backward glance fled the lab, fled the building, and practically sprinted all the way across campus, not stopping until I got to my car.

"Drive," I told myself. Commanded really. "Just drive."

———

## THOR

Leda sighed, carrying her folded clothes into the little stall that held the chemical decontamination shower. "Well, that went horribly," she said as he dressed.

"What were you *thinking*?" I asked her, horrified.

When she emerged clothed from the shower stall, I squinted at her. She really looked like she'd been to hell and back since I saw her last. "What is up with you? You don't do anything that impulsive."

Leda shrugged and went back to her worktable.

"I'm serious—what if he goes to the police now?"

"He won't."

"You don't even know him!"

"But I know people," she said calmly. "Do you honestly think the police will believe him, if he tries to tell them what he saw just now?"

"No?"

"No," she confirmed. "And Cas isn't an idiot, I don't think. He knows that as well as I do."

I mulled over her words, but something still didn't sit right. The Leda I knew would never take such a gamble. "Why didn't you answer me last night?"

A scared, lost expression passed over her face. "Yesterday is...fuzzy."

"Fuzzy?"

"Missing," she clarified, chewing her lip. "Thursday night, I went out for drinks with a friend, and I guess we got a little crazy because I don't even remember how I got home."

I stared. This was highly unlike Leda, always so composed focused on her work in the lab. She never partied. I could tell by the look on her face that she wasn't satisfied with her own explanation for her missing day. "Are you alright?"

"I think so," she said. "Just really, *really* hungover."

"Well," I said. "You should be home recuperating."

"I had to check on some of the results," she explained. "I can tell you about it later. You should go find Cassian."

Oh, hell. My head spun. This was too much to process in one day.

I walked back across campus, and I wasn't shocked to find Cas wasn't home. I waited for him, though. He could very well be back at the police station, despite Leda's assurances.

While her transformation proved the situation was more complicated than he'd thought, it didn't necessarily prove our innocence. Was Cas going to divulge our secret, a secret kept for centuries? Was he ever going to come back here, or was he fleeing as far and as fast as he could?

I sat, stewing. The sound of the door swinging open scared the hell out of me. Cas came in, stared at me for a second, and then headed to his room. Every instinct in me screamed to follow him, but I knew he needed some space. If and when he needed more information, I would have to let him come to me.

A surprisingly short amount of time later, Cas busted out of his room. "What the fuck?" He asked, for the third time.

In his defense, I hadn't really answered either time he'd asked before. I exhaled a long, slow breath, trying to keep my voice even. "Um, what, specifically, the fuck, are you asking about?"

Cas paced back and forth in front of the mantel. "I don't know," he spat. "All of it?"

"Will you please come sit?"

"No—no. I can't. I gotta..." He trailed away and stomped into the kitchen. I watched in silence as Cas seized the cutting board, an onion, and a knife. He peeled the onion and began chopping. I took this to mean he was waiting for me to begin my explanation.

"Okay," I said. "So, Leda, I guess."

Cas didn't answer, but the rhythm of his chops faltered.

I took a breath, looking down at my interlocked hands. "So, Leda is a shifter."

The knife stopped and I looked up to see a question unasked in the pitch of Cassian's brows.

"Sorry, that's kind of, slang. Short for shape-shifter."

The chopping resumed.

"And...I mean. I guess, so am I."

"*Ow,* fuck!"

I jerked my head up to see Cas clutching his finger. He'd dropped the knife, and he turned toward the sink. I just about flew to his side, but when I laid a hand on his shoulder he flinched away. "Please," I said. "Let me."

Reluctantly, Cas held out his hand, where he'd given himself quite the slice on the side of his pointer finger. I dabbed it with a clean cloth, then instructed Cas to apply pressure while I stooped to get my first-aid kit from below the sink. I tugged Cas over to the couch, forcing him to sit. I wrapped his finger in some sterile gauze pads and bandaged it up.

We stared at the bandaged finger, and I did not want to let go of his hand, afraid if I did he would run, screaming, from the apartment.

He gingerly pulled his hand out of my grasp, and I felt like any possibility of us having a friendship was slipping through my fingers as his hand did. I sighed.

"So," said Cas, inspecting the edge of the bandage with laser focused intensity. "You can...you're..."

I flushed with shame, because not only was Cas *so* horrified by the idea of shifters, but the fact that I wasn't even one, not truly, hit me hard. It was like I was the worst of both worlds. "Technically yes," I said. "I don't have a power like Leda does. But the rest of my family can shift, yes."

"Into swans?" he blurted. "You're a bunch of wereswans?"

I couldn't help a small, hysterical laugh. "No, not exactly. My immediate family are all mammals when they shift. My father's *fauna*—that's what we call our animal sides—is a wolf. My brother's a bear. Like that."

"And you're...?" The question was there, and my face heated, boiling shame and the feeling of failure rising in my throat.

"Nothing," I said. "I don't have a *fauna*. But yes, technically I am one of them. Us."

Cas digested that, fear and confusion and curiosity warring on his face. "So, the bodies..."

"We don't know," I said truthfully. "We don't recognize any of them, which is odd. It's not a vast community. They look unlike anything either of us has ever seen before."

"That's why you needed the samples?"

"Yes."

Cas chewed on that a minute, and I could see the cogs turning in his head as he tried to figure out what to ask next. "Are you in trouble?"

I started. That was just about the last thing I expected him to concern himself with. "I'm not certain," I said. "I haven't noticed anything else out of the ordinary."

He nodded, sitting in silence for a while, fidgeting with the edge of the bandage I'd wrapped around his finger.

"Listen—Cassian," I started, but he leapt to his feet, putting distance between us.

"Yeah, um. Tho..." He choked on my name, like he couldn't even bring himself to say it. He couldn't even look at me. "I gotta go."

And as suddenly as he'd arrived, Cas had gone again. I sighed, rising slowly from the sofa to put away the partially chopped onion and clean the cutting board of Cas's blood. I'd thought once I had a chance to explain he would understand, or at least accept that I meant him no harm. In fact, I barely even counted as anything paranormal. But the truth was, we hadn't known each other long enough to establish that base-line of trust.

Worried, I scrubbed the counter and the sink, and then swept the floors, cleaning to distract myself from everything. Cas hadn't flat out *said* he wasn't going to report Leda and me to the cops. He still might. And now, he knew our secret. My knuckles went white where I gripped the broom at the thought of what my father would say if he found out I'd let Cas leave this apartment, knowing what he knew.

Oh, gods. What if Cas reported us to the FBI? What if some kind of paranormal investigation unit came in, wearing black suits and dark glasses and hauled me and Leda off to be dissected in some Area 51 lab?

I couldn't stay put, worrying all night. Considering I was wired, I figured I'd capitalize on it. What I really wanted to do was write––take some time to work on my own novel, my secret passion project––but I knew I wouldn't be able to focus. So, I packed a few things and headed over to the Greely Building, which housed the oldest library in the country, and boasted a massive collection of rare manuscripts.

I'd been sifting through dusty old volumes for a year now, and most of what I found was fearful human nonsense, but I'd uncovered a fair amount about our history. For example, our earliest written creation myth centered around the founding of Rome, and the tale of Romulus and Remus. Twin brothers, raised by a wolf.

I checked in with Stacy Chandler, the librarian and curator of the ancient texts. I moved toward a different topic than usual, searching for old medical texts. The more outlandish the claims, the better. It was hard to quantify, but after reading what felt like hundreds of these books, I had developed a sense of what had a kernel of truth, and what was merely superstition explained as magic. In fact, often times, the things *not* claimed to be magic turned out to be evidence of just that. This work I enjoyed. I think, perhaps, I would have found the process more enjoyable had it not always brought to mind the reason my father had me digging through these texts every spare minute.

Today I was on the hunt for anything that would shed light on what had befallen the shifters found by the police.

While the police could hardly put down the grotesque corpses as having died of natural causes, I was not convinced of foul play. Not yet anyway. It could be some sort of genetic disorder. Diseases cleaved human lives daily. It stood to reason, that different illnesses would develop in congruence with our species, too.

I soon had a stack of books surrounding me like a fortress, and I sank my teeth into the work, focusing all my energy on the words, on deciphering hidden meanings behind the text. A lot of times, my hours spent in the library were spent using books to find more books. By the time I tossed down my pen, rubbing my eyes beneath my glasses, I had a solid list of titles for which I could go hunting. Any the library didn't have I would find online and order. My father would cover the cost, and be happy to do so if any of the research bore fruit, leading to the cause of my...failings.

Unfortunately, that thought brought me right back to the topic I'd been hoping to avoid, and my mind filled with Cas's face, his hazel eyes wide with fear and revulsion as he learned what Leda and I were.

I stayed at the library until closing time, prolonging the moment of returning home to find Cas still gone.

# 6



I didn't have a destination in mind when I left the apartment, knowing only that I had to get out. I had to get away, I had to...I had to grasp onto something normal. I guess that's how I found myself at Lucy's. I put on my best laid-back demeanor, and while I occasionally caught her looking at me sidelong, we had a fun night shooting the shit and watching dumb movies. I cooked dinner for us both, and got a chance to play my favorite game—scrolling through Lucy's online dating app and matching or rejecting potential girls for her.

I crashed on her couch, and in the morning, I woke up and pretended, just for a moment, that everything was fine. That I hadn't seen a dead body a week ago. That I wasn't under suspicion by the police. That I hadn't watched a girl turn into a swan, and found out my roommate was not human. I looked at my phone, half expecting to see a text from Thor, but there was nothing.

I couldn't work out if I was disappointed or relieved. Some mixture of both, maybe.

"What are your plans today?" Lucy asked me, handing over a mug of coffee.

"Not much," I said. "You?"

"Fuck all. It's the last Sunday I'll have free for a while, though. And we're off class tomorrow."

"Oh, true." I'd forgotten. "We could go to my place," I heard myself say. *What the fuck was I thinking?* "Tho...my roommate has just about every video game system known to man. We could day drink and play Mario Kart."

"Sounds dope!"

Part of me didn't want to involve Lucy in our mess, but the much larger part of me was terrified of going back to the apartment alone. I drove us there, and when I opened the door, I realized Thor had cleared out. I breathed a sigh of relief, and went over to the bar cart to fix us a couple drinks. Lucy followed me inside. She'd barely made it over the threshold when she said, "Holy crap. Your roommate is rich."

I paused at the drink cart. "Huh?"

"He is filthy stinking rich. No wonder he's so weird."

*You have no idea.* "What are you talking about?"

She waved me off, inspecting the kitchen stuff and then moving into the living room. She scrutinized the sofa, its cushions, and the drapes. The entertainment system. "Rich people are always weird."

"How do you know he's rich?" I wracked my brains, momentarily distracted from the paranormal of it all, trying to remember if Thor and I had ever discussed his family's background. Now that Lucy mentioned it, I was sure we hadn't. A few things clicked into place—his ability to buy expensive things for the apartment without a second thought, his penchant for eating all his meals out before I moved in, and his grocery delivery service. He hadn't let me buy groceries once yet. Suddenly, I felt a little crestfallen, like Thor's thoughtful gestures held less meaning because money wasn't as much of an issue for him. I also called to mind his talk of family obligations, and the wheels started spinning out in my brain. Was he a part of some kind of supernatural mafia?

"Just look at all this *stuff*," she said. "You're a cook—can't you tell this stove is like, super fancy?"

"Now that you mention it..." I wasn't sure why this made me so uncomfortable, especially in comparison to the other stuff I'd learned about Thor's family of late. For some reason, finding out about his wealth was almost as strange as finding out his dad was a wolfman.

Almost.

Lucy eventually let it drop, I handed her a drink, and we got down to being super competitive about Mario Kart.

"So," Lucy said. "What's he like?"

"Who—*fuck!*" A blue shell came out of nowhere, slamming directly into my character and costing me my significant lead.

"Thor! Is he like, weird, or really weird?"

"He's...shy," I said, an uncomfortable heat rising in my face.

"Aw," said Lucy playfully. "He's *shy?*"

That rankled, for some reason. I turned toward Lucy, momentarily losing focus. "I just meant—Oh, goddamnit!"

Lucy's character sped past me at the last second, and the cartoony slide-whistle sounded her victory. "Ha! You are way too easy, man."

Keys jingled on the other side of the door, and my guts filled with ice. I turned to look at Thor, who came in with a look on his face like a deer in headlights, despite the fact that it was his place. "Hey," I said.

"Hi." Thor paused, gripping the strap to his bookbag with fitful intensity. "I um, I didn't realize you had company."

"Why don't you join us?" Lucy said, and I jerked my head toward her, eyes wide.

"Oh, no," said Thor. He gripped the strap of his bag even tighter. "I don't want to...*intrude.*" The way he said intrude and shot me a significant look shook something loose in my brain.

I couldn't help the laugh that busted out of my mouth. "Just come join us," I said. The idea that Thor thought Lucy and I were on some kind of date—and he was trying to do me a solid, was such a bizarre attempt at roommate normalcy. It made the entire situation even more surreal.

"Oh my God," Lucy hissed at me, as soon as Thor had escaped down the hall to his bedroom.

"What?" I asked, panicked that she had somehow figured things out.

"He's into you!"

"He's..." I laughed again. "He's *what?*"

"He is totally into you."

This made me squirmy, thinking about how I'd fallen asleep with my head in his lap, how he'd made those noises at dinner. How my touch had soothed him, and vice versa. "I don't even know if he's gay," I said.

Lucy laughed. "You're cute."

When Thor emerged from his room, I pressed a drink into one of his hands and a controller into the other, and the evening bumped along about as smooth as it could have, given the circumstances. Thor was terrible at Mario Kart, which earned him a lot of ribbing because they were his game systems after all.

Somewhere, somehow, over the course of the evening, we stopped playing video games, and switched from mixed drinks to shots of Wild Turkey.

Someone, and I think it may have been me, suggested we

play I Never. The idea of spilling secrets weighed heavily on my subconscious.

My heart quickened. *Never have I ever turned into a bird*, I thought. *Never have I ever ripped the tooth out of a dead body.* "Never have I ever..." I faltered. "Skipped school." Lame.

Both Thor and Lucy drank, which surprised me because Thor had seemed like too much of a goody-goody to skip. I was learning all kinds of things about my roommate recently.

Lucy had been giving me significant looks over the course of the evening—getting less subtle and more maniacal with every drink she had—and seemed like she had something to prove.

"Never have I ever...slept with a guy," she said, waiting eagerly.

Neither Thor nor I drank.

When it was her turn again, she said, "Never have I ever had a boyfriend."

Still, nothing.

And finally, "Never have I ever...kissed a guy."

Thor rolled his eyes, his body and demeanor getting looser with each drink. He shot us a look that was hard, challenging, and kind of cocky. I'd never seen that look on his face before. Thor lifted his glass in mock salute, and knocked back his shot. He pondered as he refilled his glass, sloshing some whisky over his knuckles. He turned to us with a mischievous smile, another new expression, and said, "Never have I ever kissed a girl."

Lucy and I laughed, cheersed, and drank. Then, Lucy surprised us all by seizing Thor's cheeks in her hands and pulling him in for a quick, hard kiss.

Something confused and hot flared inside me at the sight, and to compensate I said, "Ha. You both have to kiss next time. Drink. You both have to drink both next time." Good *Lord* was I drunk.

Lucy pointed at me and Thor and said, "Now you two kiss, and all three of us can drink next time!"

Instant back sweat.

I set my glass on the ground and settled on my knees, looking at Thor, whose eyes were huge and round—and, a little unfocused—behind his glasses. I watched his lashes, fascinated as he blinked rapidly. Girls wore all kinds of makeup to get lashes like that, I thought. We leaned in closer, closing the gap between us, inch by agonizing inch, while Lucy looked on with the air of one who had a lot of money riding on the outcome of a prizefight. Thor's eyes floated closed, and then, he clapped a hand over his mouth.

He scrambled to his feet and took off at a run down the hallway. I heard the sound of spectacular vomiting from what I sincerely hoped was the bathroom.

*Oh.*

I woke up on the rug.

The wooden floor creaked, and I opened one eye to see Thor emerge from his room and shamble down the hallway like a zombie. He looked quite a bit worse for the wear, his hair sticking up in all sorts of directions, and as far as I could tell he was only wearing boxers and one sock.

He approached the fridge, squinting into its light when he opened the door. After grabbing a carton of OJ and swigging directly from it, something I'd never seen him do, he wiped his mouth on his hand and shot me a look of pure venom before replacing the juice and shuffling back toward his lair.

"Nuhhhh," I said to the room at large.

"Stop screaming," said a voice, and I realized Lucy must have passed out on the couch.

I felt a stab of annoyance that she hadn't woken me up and shooed me to my room, or to the other end of the giant sectional, on which we could both easily have fit. My back felt like a bundle of broken twigs as I sat up and stretched. "My head."

Lucy grunted. Then she said, "Breakfast?"

The thought of lifting a skillet made my head spin, so eventually we rallied and made our way to the little breakfast place on campus. Lucy returned to herself with annoying haste, slurping happily on a frozen coffee drink. I nursed a plain black coffee and scowled at her, the lights in the café pounding behind my eyes.

"What are you so fucked off about?" Lucy asked finally.

I wasn't even sure. "What was all that stuff last night?"

"What?"

"All the kissing guys stuff."

"I was just trying to make a point," she said.

"A vague and confusing point."

"Thor wanted to kiss you! I could tell!"

"Clearly," I said, annoyed. "As evidenced by the way he immediately fled and then puked his guts out."

"Yeah, I'm sure that reaction was only about you, and not the quart of Wild Turkey in his stomach."

"Ugh, please don't say the word 'stomach' to me right now."

"Why does it bother you so much?"

"The word stomach?" I asked, deflecting, because I totally knew what she meant.

Lucy raised a brow, but let the subject drop.

Of course, the teasing was only part of it. This whole debacle was problematic on several serious levels. First of all, I wasn't into dudes. Second of all, I barely had time to breathe, let alone have a relationship. Third of all, Thor was my roommate. It would be hella awkward if he came on to me, or asked me out. We were becoming friends. I didn't want to hurt his feelings, and I definitely didn't want to end up homeless partway through the semester. After everything I went through trying to find a place, all the stress—I couldn't go through that again.

This all would have been true if we had this little drunken adventure last weekend.

Now, there was the added fun of the enormous were-swan in the room.

After finding out about Thor's friend Leda, I'd considered hopping in my car and driving straight home, but something had stopped me. The knowledge that I'd rather be twisted up in some weird paranormal shit than give up on school and face my family as a failure, was strangely heartening. I'd make this work. I had to.

"Cas?"

I looked up, realizing Lucy was staring expectantly. "Look, can you just drop the whole thing with Thor? I'm serious."

Her face broke into a shit eating grin, and she said, "I was just asking if you wanted to get together for dinner some night this week."

"Oh." I could feel my cheeks heat, and I refused to meet her eyes. "Yeah. That sounds great—sorry. I have a lot on my mind."

"Hmm," said Lucy drily. "I wonder what that could be."

———

## THOR

Getting a few meager sips of orange juice to remain in my stomach without making another appearance was a labor on par with slaying the Nemean Lion. I stared at a spot on the ceiling from the center of my mattress, willing the pounding in my head to subside. I had never, ever gotten that drunk before. In fact, I had never been drunk at all with anyone outside my family.

I reached across the near-insurmountable distance to grab my phone from the nightstand, the room swooping and spinning around me as I tried to bring the screen into focus. I let it fall to my chest without processing any notifications, cursing Cas and his friend Lucy.

To be fair, I certainly wasn't cursing her as much as I had the night before, when I'd thought she was Cas's girlfriend. In fact, I had to calm myself multiple times throughout the evening, to remind myself that just because Cas wasn't involved with Lucy didn't mean he would ever be willing to become involved with me, especially after everything he had learned. In fact, the look of pure horror on his face when Lucy suggested he kiss me had been like a bucket of cold water thrown on me.

I'd had fun with them, though. They'd only included me to be polite, but I was grateful. I parceled my time down to the minute, carving out time to maintain top grades, assist Leda in the lab, to research shifter history for my family, and, if the stars aligned, work on my own fiction and practice some yoga so I didn't totally lose my mind. Usually, I was happy to trade a few hours' sleep to get all of that into my rigid schedule, and I'd planned on shutting myself away in my room last night to give Cassian some space and get ahead on a few things.

However, apparently, a few hours hanging out with Cas were *not* to be gladly traded. I hadn't even considered it. When Cas had first appeared on my doorstep, the axis of my world had tilted, my priorities and goals shifting around to accommodate him like tectonic plates.

I realized part of it was this ridiculous mating pull. I had to imagine, if not consummated, the irritating tug in my chest would fade eventually, right? Or maybe it was simply the universal pain of an unrequited crush.

Like heartburn.

Speaking of, I massaged my chest and grimaced. I couldn't remember a Monday morning with a less auspicious—oh *shit.*

Monday.

My father had arranged a breakfast for me with Dr. Kendrick, Leda's mentor and the man who guided her studies in shifter evolutions and biology. Dad was doing his best to ensure I ingratiated myself to him in order to secure an internship this summer, leading to a job after graduation. If I wanted to keep up appearances, I could not miss this meeting. I gritted my teeth, flung the covers off myself. I had two hours to rally.

I stretched, and stood. A shower and coffee would be the first orders of business to get me feeling like a person again. My feet felt weird. I looked down, realizing that sometime in the night I must have toed off one of my socks.

Oh *gods.*

I had walked out to the kitchen earlier, hadn't I? Dressed —or rather, *undressed*—like this? I had waltzed right out into the kitchen in front of Cas *and* his friend half naked. More than half.

Please, *please,* let the earth open up and swallow me whole.

I pulled on a pair of sweats and ambled out to the kitchen, which was, blessedly, empty. After coffee and a couple aspirin, I felt marginally better.

A shower set me mostly right again. I absorbed water like a bullfrog in a pond, and by the time I'd toweled off my head I felt much better.

I met Kendrick at a café on campus, and I was a bit surprised. He looked more like a football player than a scientist––about my father's age, well-muscled and tall. We shook hands, and he gave me a squint, like possibly he could tell I had gotten up to some unsavory shenanigans the night before, but made no mention of it.

"Well, Thor, I'm glad we're finally getting the chance to meet," he said warmly, gesturing for me to sit.

"Yes," I said. "I've been following your work closely, and, of course, Leda has spoken often of what she's learned from you."

"She is a brilliant scientist," he said. "I find I learn plenty from her, as well."

My head gave a throb, and I clenched my jaw, hoping my coffee wasn't about to make a reappearance. Perhaps I had overestimated my ability to be out and about just yet.

"So, Thor," said Kendrick. "Your father has spoken often of you, and your ambitions."

*My ambitions,* I scoffed internally. Out loud I said, "Well, I find the study of our history fascinating, and plan to make a career of marrying the folklore of our kind to scientific inquiry."

I had rehearsed this line, and I think my hangover affected the earnestness of my delivery. Judging by Kendrick's smirk, he could tell. He regarded me thoughtfully across the table. "I went to college with your parents, did you know that?"

"You did?"

He nodded. "The three of us attended this very university."

I wondered why my parents had never mentioned it, and Kendrick seemed to know what I was thinking.

"We didn't run in the same social circles then," he said. Kendrick's tone was mild, but I heard something there, something painful. Something tinged with regret. "I had something of a crush on Freya, but I fear at that time I wasn't much worth her notice. Or your father's. I have a feeling you know what I mean?"

"Yes," I admitted, curious as to what he was getting at.

"Sometimes, it seemed better to...escape their notice." He raised his brows significantly. "I think, perhaps, it is easier to discover what we truly want, when we're free to explore in private."

"Perhaps," I said carefully. I didn't want to admit to anything that would get back to my father. Just because Kendrick was astute at reading people didn't mean he would take my side over my father's—especially given how much my father had helped him fund his research. "We don't always have that luxury, though, do we?"

He sighed. "No, we do not. Regardless, I have looked over your transcripts, and Leda has only wonderful things to say about your work ethic. I think, if you're interested, we would have an internship available for you this summer."

I unclenched in relief. "Oh, yes, thank you Dr. Kendrick. I am definitely interested."

We chatted a bit more about his current work, which involved using DNA samples from shifter children to predict their *fauna's* form before it presented in adolescence, which reminded me of mine and Leda's conversation, and of course, the samples in her lab. "What are your thoughts on the case?" I asked him, when we reached a lull in conversation.

Kendrick frowned. "What case?"

"The Jane and John Does Leda and I took tissue samples from? The shifter corpses?"

Kendrick looked bewildered. "I have no idea what you're talking about," he said. "Leda hasn't mentioned anything like that to me."

"My mistake," I said, floundering. Why would Leda avoid showing her mentor the samples? She might be brilliant but the both of us were far out of our depth here. "Perhaps she was still gathering data before she discussed it with you."

"Yes," he said, looking suspicious. "I'll ask her about it when I see her next." Kendrick dabbed his face with a napkin. "Listen, Thor, it was wonderful to finally get to meet face to face, but I have to run off. Can we arrange a time for you to come tour the lab? I know your father wanted you to see the facility. I think he was interested in coming, as well."

"Yes, of course. You have my email address, right?"

"I do indeed." He stood, and we shook hands.

"Thank you so much for meeting with me, Dr. Kendrick. It would be an honor to work for you next summer."

"The pleasure is all mine, Thor. I'll be in touch."

After Kendrick left, I bought half a dozen donuts to bring home and share with Cas, hoping the offer would help diffuse some of the awkwardness of our near-kiss incident the night before. I wasn't even certain if it counted as a near-kiss, but it was certainly the nearest *I'd* been in quite some time. At any rate, he was home on the couch when I got back, and he had the kindness not to rub my nose in my humiliation. In fact, he suggested inviting Lucy over for dinner this week, something far more low-key than the three of us getting drunk off our asses

"How about Friday?" I asked him.

"Oh..." Cas looked strangely disappointed. Like maybe he was looking forward to our new ritual.

"Or another night?"

"Yeah?"

"I didn't want you to feel like you had to cook some big thing twice."

"I don't mind," he said, a grin pulling over his face. "So, it's a plan?"

"It's a plan."

A few days later found me in the lab with Leda, and my first chance to ask her a burning question. "Why didn't you tell Kendrick about what we've found?"

Leda looked at me sharply. "*You* told him?"

"Only because I assumed you would have!"

Leda looked very distraught. "Well," she said, flustered. "I didn't want to bring him in until we actually *knew* something."

"Why not? He can help."

"This is my career, too, Thor," she said. "My future. I wanted to make sure we were organized, that we had some findings to show him, and make a proper presentation of our theories."

"Is that all it is?" I asked her.

"Yes, of course. What else would it be?"

I didn't know, but something still felt off. I opened my mouth again but Leda cut across me.

"I wanted to show you what I *have* found so far."

She had been working diligently to extract as much information from our stolen tissue samples as she possibly could. She'd performed a karyotype on each of the bodies, though looking at the transparencies, it seemed a few were incomplete.

Together, we studied the shape, size, and number of chromosome pairs present. As any high school biology student could report, human beings had twenty-three pairs of chromosomes. Shifter DNA proved a bit trickier to decipher. We had the base human twenty-three pairs, plus an extra pair that broke down when we shifted into our *fauna* forms. Pair twenty-four broke down as a shifter transformed—working something like a supercharged helicase enzyme, programmed to disassemble itself, bond with the other chromosomes, braid and change them all on a cellular level. Post-transformation, shifter DNA most closely resembled that of our *fauna* counterpart.

This was no small feat, and shifters often experienced a period of confusion and fatigue following a transformation as their genetic code literally rewrote itself.

"What I'm seeing here isn't making a lot of sense," Leda said, shoving her fingers up under her glasses in order to rub her eyes.

"Are you alright?"

"Yes," she asked. "Why?"

"You look...distracted."

"I look like shit, is what you're saying."

"Your words."

She slid her glasses up her head, and said, "I must admit, the day missing from my memory has me quite on edge. I haven't been sleeping very well."

My stomach twisted nervously. "Oh?"

"Yes. But I would rather not discuss it. Can we focus on this, instead?"

"Of course." I hovered by her shoulder, staring at the karyotype backlit on the wall in front of us. "What am I looking at?"

"I extracted as many of the chromosome pairs as I could from the samples, but…"

"Well, this doesn't make any sense," I said flatly. She had about forty pairs of chromosomes.

"I know."

"Is this…is this showing DNA from multiple victims?"

She shook her head. "This is all comprised of tissue from Jane Doe. The cells were of course decayed, but still…"

Yeah, *but still.* "Maybe it's because she was partway through a shift when she died?"

"Perhaps," she said. "But there's something else."

"What is it?"

"Visually at least—Jane Doe was almost all the way through her shift back to human," said Leda. "But…"

I squinted at the transparency. "Where's Pair Twenty-Four?"

"It hasn't begun to break off yet—or, I don't know. I couldn't find any trace of it. Usually, it begins to detach itself at the beginning of a shift. Otherwise, she shouldn't have been able to get this far."

"Do you have workups for the other victims?"

She shook her head. "Not yet. I started with this one because…"

"You're the most familiar with avian shifter genetics."

Leda nodded. She looked deeply, deeply troubled. "Thor," she said, her voice almost a whisper. "What the hell did we stumble on here?"

Her fearful question repeated itself in my mind, over and over, the entire walk from the Lab, across campus toward my apartment.

"Hey," said Cas, when I got inside. "Where have you been?"

"The lab," I said. Leda's scared, exhausted face swam in my mind's eye. "Do you think we could invite Leda for dinner, with Lucy? I think she could use a night out if—if it's alright with you."

Cas paled, but nodded. I knew he was terrified of Leda, another reason I wanted to invite her. I desperately wanted Cas to know there was nothing for him to fear from either of us, and that would never happen if he avoided her entirely. "If you trust her, I guess that's enough for me."

"Really?"

He shrugged. "Yeah," he said, but he didn't sound sure. "Yes. At the lab, did you find out anything...new?"

"Sort of," I said heavily. "Although what we seem to have found is just more questions. The victims' DNA is...screwy. It's kind of hard to explain. I'm starting to wonder if they were sick."

"Sick?" Cas asked sharply.

"Not like, black plague sick, more like...a genetic illness. I don't know." I didn't like the idea that everyone in my family's world could be vulnerable to such a horrific ailment.

"Hey." I looked up and realized Cas had put down his utensils to come around the kitchen island to stand in front of me. His arms twitched at his sides like maybe he was debating between patting me on the shoulder and giving me a hug. "Do you want to cancel tonight? Just hang in, the two of us, instead?"

Tempting, but no. "No, of course not, you've been cooking all afternoon!" I said. "I'm fine."

Cas crossed his arms over his chest, seeming to decide against touching me. I shouldn't have been surprised, of course, but I really could have used that hug. Stuffing my own hands in my pockets, I said, "Anything I could help with?"

"Nah, I'm good here. Just take it easy."

I sat in my usual seat at the kitchen island, resting my elbows on the bar and my head in my hands. Cas went to the fridge and poured me a glass of wine. "Thanks," I said, and settled in to watch him cook.

When Lucy and Leda arrived, the apartment seemed to boil over with warmth and cheer—honestly, something I wasn't used to. Cas was shocked to find that Leda had never been over here before, considering how long we'd known each other.

"So, you knew little baby Thor?" Cas pressed.

Leda grinned. "I did. He was an annoying little shit, to be honest."

"I was not," I said, aghast.

"Oh, please. He kept trying to get me to agree to marry him." She eyed me critically. "Even when we were kids, I knew that would never work out." Leda's eyes, clear and blue, darted over to Cas's friend Lucy, who blushed. I was kind of astonished, actually, because I hadn't thought Lucy to be the blushing type.

Lucy, for her part, teased Cas mercilessly—explaining to Leda that I would rather make out with the toilet bowl than with Cas. Ugh. If only she knew.

The conversation flowed easily like a river, carrying us all along. I didn't always contribute, but I didn't feel weird or awkward or like I didn't belong. I was like a rock in the river.

Sometimes it simply flowed around me, but it wasn't a bad feeling at all.

After dinner I completed my usual ritual of washing up, and Lucy made noises about calling it an early night. "I have a paper and I was hoping to hit a yoga class in the morning," she said.

I perked up. "You do yoga?"

"Yes! Do you practice? You should totally come." Lucy grabbed my arm eagerly, and I startled. She was a very touchy-feeling person, and I was still a little flabbergasted that she had kissed me the last time we had hung out.

"I do," I said. "Where is the class?"

"Hold on," said Cas. "*You* do yoga?"

I scrunched up my nose, uncomfortable now that all eyes were on me. "Every day, if I can."

"I can't even picture that," he said.

"Why not?" And why would he want to picture it?

"You're just so..." he gestured at me. "Uptight."

"Why do you think I do it?" I asked, eyebrows raised.

Cas looked indignant, like I'd been hiding it from him.

I turned back to Lucy. "I'd love to meet you for the class," I told her.

"Oh, *yay!* You'll love it. Give me your phone so I can text you the address."

Once we'd all said our goodbyes and the girls had left, I returned to doing the dishes. The silence settled over Cas and me. It gave me a thrill that I'd thrown him off with something besides my family's ability to transform into a safari.

"How can you do yoga every day?" He blurted. "I have literally never once seen you do it."

I wrung out the sponge, shrugging. "I used to do it in the living room, but I figured when you moved in, I'd start doing it in my bedroom."

Several more minutes of quiet passed before Cas said, "You don't have to do that."

"Oh?"

"Yeah, man, it's your home." He gave me a piercing look, like maybe we were talking about more than yoga. "You shouldn't feel like you have to hide."

And the tectonic plates shifted again.

# 7



It was official—I was losing my marbles. I could not stop watching my roommate. And, I could also not stop thinking about what Lucy had said, about him being into me. September gave way to October, and Thor continued to spend long hours in the lab with Leda, presumably doing more science-y shit. I didn't know what all they could do without fresh samples, but every time he came home, he seemed more troubled. I didn't like it.

I also didn't like how much it bothered me that he was upset.

Something in me wanted to *fix* it, but I knew I couldn't. All of it was sort of tangled up in my head, protective instincts and friend stuff, and for some reason my brain fixated on the amount of time it had been since I'd hooked up with anyone. All of that, with the added spice of Lucy's determined match-making, made for a pretty confusing brain soup.

What did *not* help matters, like, at all, was my dumb ass insisting Thor do his yoga in the living room. So, one day, not long after our dinner with Leda and Lucy, I came home from class to Thor doing just that. His bare chest aglow with candlelight, bent in all kinds of impossible shapes. I froze in the doorway, watching, as he thrust his ass up into the air.

I had never consciously checked out a guy's ass before, but, lo and behold, here was one presented for me like some kind of illuminated trophy. Thor had on light grey joggers that didn't leave a whole lot to the imagination, especially when stretched across a surprisingly firm little ass that was, presently, staring me in the face.

So, I stared right back.

It was a nice ass.

Objectively speaking.

A nice ass was a nice ass, no matter who it was stuck on. I realized I'd been staring for some time, because Thor had a quizzical expression on his upside-down face, peering at me from between his legs. The blood had rushed to his head, giving his cheeks a heady blush, gravity pulling his thick curls down toward the yoga mat. He cocked his head to the side. "Uh," he said. "Hey."

I think my exact words were, "Fwuh?"

Thor dropped into a plank, the cords of his surprisingly defined muscles straining as he bent his elbows, tight against his torso. I watched in what could only be described as a stupor as he flowed like liquid through a series of poses, arching his back before tucking his toes and rolling his body back to sit on his heels. He peeked over his shoulder at me, flushed and coy. "Is it still okay if I practice out here?"

I nodded, because my vocal cords had stopped working, and fled before my suddenly very interested dick could speak for me. Because if it could talk, it would have said, "Hell yeah."

I leaned against the closed door of my room, looking downward at the damning evidence twitching earnestly against the fly of my jeans.

I refused to acknowledge it further, because this was ridiculous. I wasn't about to be bossed around by my dick. But clearly, I had some stuff to figure out.

I'd always loved girls. I think, maybe though, when all the guys around me were figuring things out, figuring out which magazines to steal from their parents, which websites to go to in the private browser, I'd simply stopped inquiring further once I realized I liked girls. On some level, even then, there was part of me that had been relieved. Like, okay, cool, one less thing for me, and by extension my dad, to deal with.

Now though...

Okay. Just because Thor and his dinnertime sex noises and sultry yoga pretzels had sort of knocked this idea loose in my brain, and certainly just because Lucy was meddling in the whole business, didn't mean I had to pursue anything with Thor. Or anyone. While it had indeed been a while since I'd hooked up, I enjoyed being single. One less thing to worry about, one less complication in my already over-stuffed life.

In the interest of objective investigation, however, I decided to try to tease apart the things happening in my brain and apply them to guys who weren't my roommate. The next day, at the gym, I tried to passively check out some dudes. Not in the locker room, of course—I didn't want to be *that* guy— but on the gym floor where everyone was mostly dressed.

Unfortunately, I couldn't help comparing everyone here with Thor. Especially with the images of him doing yoga so fresh in my mind. Him, bent over, thrusting his hips into the air like he was waiting for someone to grab hold of them...I shook my head. This wasn't what I was supposed to be doing. I cleared my throat, ramped up the speed on my treadmill, and casually swept my eyes over the guys working out around me. A lot of big, hard bodies, glistening with sweat. More traditionally buff, gym rat types—compared to a lot of the guys here, even I was on the smaller side.

I didn't...hate it? There were hot girls here too—and I experienced distress, wondering if now looking at *anyone* hot would get me horny. But no matter who it was, I compared their bodies with Thor's, and found that no one compared favorably. Perhaps super athletic just wasn't my type anymore.

That brought me up short. I stumbled, and grabbed for the emergency stop button on the treadmill. Panting, I clutched the handrails and tried to steady my pounding heart. My, my, my. How quickly I had gone from "I think I'm straight," to having guys who were, or were not, my type. I tried to clear my head, rubbing over my face with a towel while my heart slowed down.

Then, a grunt and the clang of a dropped free weight scared the hell out of me. Perhaps the gym wasn't the best place to check people out.

So, not being prone to half measures, I decided to check out some gay porn. Thor stayed up crazy late, so I couldn't have the sound on, but I figured being on mute might make things a bit easier anyway. I didn't need the stilted dialogue. I was here for one thing and one thing only: to gauge my body's reaction to the very real sight of two dudes fucking.

With the lights off and my laptop propped up on the side of the mattress, I stripped down naked and rested one hand on my dick while I browsed Pornhub with the other. I wasn't hard yet, too tense and nervous, but electrified at the same time. The hair on my arms stood on end, and I shivered.

I decided to dip a toe in, at first, just watching my normal kind of stuff to get in the mood, and relax. Since most of the porn I usually watched was guys with girls, it at least had guys *in* it. It seemed like an okay place to start. However, I was so nervous, and none of my old favorites were really doing it for me. So, I decided, fuck it, and switched over to the gay side of Pornhub.

I scrolled through the first few pages with disinterest until one video title caught my eye. "Twink nerd gets bred by football stud." I could not deny the concept piqued my interest, so I clicked play.

The setup was minimal, but the video delivered on the promise in the title with quick efficiency one can expect from porn. The actor playing the "twink nerd" didn't really resemble Thor at all, except that he was slim and had brown hair—it was more of a mousy color than Thor's dark waves. He was cute enough, I supposed, but what really grabbed my attention were his glasses. Big round Harry-Potter-style ones that magnified his eyes.

I wondered if Thor would leave his glasses on during sex.

With a strangled gasp, I realized I was fully hard seconds into the video. I watched hungrily as the two of them got naked and started fucking in a steamy locker room. The "football stud" was a lot bigger than the nerdy guy, and I was fascinated by the way their bodies looked together, the hard lines of them somehow braiding together into something soft—despite the fact that they fucked like animals on the low wooden bench.

Since I had the video on mute, my brain decided to be super helpful and provide its own soundtrack for my enjoyment. The noises Thor made while enjoying the hell out of my risotto played in my mind over and over, and all of a sudden, I was jacking my dick like my life depended on it.

I was looking, really looking, at the parts of them that were unlike girls—their balls swinging, the hair in their pits, the way their hips tapered to narrow vees, and of course, their dicks. At one point in the video, the nerd guy twisted around, a wild, desperate look on his face as he grabbed for the other guy's head—like he'd *die* if he didn't get a taste of his partner's lips. When they met in a kiss that was almost violent in its intensity, I came so hard a strand of cum splattered onto my cheek.

Holy shit.

I could never, ever, make risotto again.

———

## THOR

Cassian was avoiding me. I was certain of it. But he was avoiding me in a very weird way, because when he wasn't avoiding me, he was staring. At me. Like he was trying to bore a hole in the side of my head with his eyeballs.

He would come home from class, or hockey practice, cook, and then immediately retreat to his room to study. Sometimes, it seemed like he only existed in the kitchen, a ghost who haunted my stove.

This reluctance to spend time together seemed only to apply when it would be just the two of us. We hung out with Lucy most weekends, and Leda with increasing frequency. In fact, I had begun to suspect some sort of flirtation between the two of them, but Leda and I didn't have the sort of relationship where I felt comfortable asking her. We all went to Cas and Lucy's home games, hockey and volleyball respectively. Overall, I preferred spectating Lucy—but only because the stands at the volleyball court were heated, unlike the rink. However, I did love to see Cas on the ice. Even with all the padding, he looked amazing—and the skates made him even taller. He moved like a predator out there on the ice, focused and fast.

Leda and I, unfortunately, had stalled out big time on our investigation. We'd performed karyotypes on the samples we had from both John Does, and aside from further confirming they had an unusual number of chromosomes, we had nothing. Similar to the genetic pattern of Jane Doe, the two males seemed to have met their end through some kind of spontaneous genetic unraveling mid-shift. Something had gone wrong, the transition from animal to human failing catastrophically.

With no new samples, we were up against a dead end. Despite our investigation losing all of its forward momentum, I still worked my usual hours assisting Leda, and with my studies, as well as all of the books I promised my father I'd investigate, the cracks were starting to show.

I knew it, but I really didn't have much choice, so I soldiered on. Apparently, there was a bigger difference in my freshman and sophomore year course load than I had anticipated.

I was exhausted, doing my best to juggle the dual major, my research, my job, and my own fiction, which had been shoved very far to the wayside of late. All I wanted was to write, but it seemed destined to be sacrificed in favor of my other responsibilities. Not to mention, I still tried to fit in some yoga from time to time so I didn't totally lose it, *and* my fledgling social life. Again, I had to wonder how my parents expected me to cultivate any extracurricular relationships with my schedule this packed. But, of course, that was for me to figure out and handle gracefully.

Partway through October, I could feel myself coming down with something, but I couldn't let it get to me. A cold was the last thing on the planet I needed as I barreled toward mid-term exams. I was oddly touched, because, while Cas was behaving strangely, he seemed to sense something was up with me and began cooking massive amounts of comfort food. I suddenly found myself up to my eyeballs in soup. To be fair, it may have been what he wanted to make and not expressly for me. I appreciated it all the same.

I hung on, by spite, by stubbornness, and by sheer force of will as long as I could. However, my flu or whatever caught up with me and I was forced to spend an entire weekend comatose in bed. Cassian had been MIA since Friday night, which only made my mood worse. I was in a codeine-induced fog until I emerged, sweaty and shaking on Sunday morning, and honestly ready to make a scene because Cas had not cooked breakfast in three days, and I had become quite accustomed to it. I managed to make myself coffee and eat a toast before my phone began to ring, the incessant buzzing almost as bad as the buzzing behind my eyeballs.

It was my dad. I groaned, and answered. "Yes?"

"Do you know what day it is?"

"Sunday?"

"It's the seventeenth."

"And?"

"Did you, or did you not, have something to do on the seventeenth?"

Oh, *hell.* "Oh."

"Yes, oh," my dad snapped. "I met Dr. Kendrick at his lab today, and we stood around waiting for an hour for you."

"Why were you—"

"He told me when you had planned to tour his facility, and I thought it would be good to remind him that he was taking an Ambrose under his wing."

"Fabulous," I muttered, recalling my conversation with Kendrick. "Well, I'm sure you smoothed things over." It's what he did.

"Well, he's a busy man, Thor. I can tell you he didn't take kindly to be blown off."

"I didn't blow him off," I said, voice thick. I grabbed a tissue and blew my nose. "I've been—"

"I don't care," he said, which to me, his son, was obvious. "He took this meeting as a favor, and I had to pull a lot of strings to convince him to offer you an intern position. He is on the cutting edge of shifter research, and honestly the only selling point on your resume was your name, and your reliability." He snorted. "And your wits, I suppose..." and he gave a little scoff to show what he truly thought of *that*—of anyone being duped into thinking I had anything of value to offer them. "He won't have time to reschedule this semester."

"Well, then, that's his business," I said. Then I immediately clapped a hand over my mouth. I think cough syrup made me brave. Or stupid.

The line was silent for a good, long while. "Thor," my father said, and he sounded frustrated and tired. Which was funny, because that's how I felt. "You have certain responsibilities as a member of this family. It would be excellent, if for once, you could try to shoulder them with a little dignity."

He hung up. Super.

So much for towing the family line.

When I hung up, I realized I had a bunch of texts from Cas.

**C**as: *I should be home tonight.*

**I** stared, uncomprehending. Had he gone somewhere? I scrolled backward through our text thread. Above a few memes and an emoji of a smiling bowl of soup was an explanation for Cas's absence this weekend.

**C**as: *Just a reminder I'm away at Bell State this weekend for that tournament. I tried to tell you Friday night but you were very out of it.*

**T**hen, a time gap.

. . .

Cas: *There's chicken noodle in the fridge.*

Then, another gap.

Cas: *Feel better!*

I smiled, for the first time in days, and headed to the refrigerator to heat up some soup. I took a selfie of me and the bowl and sent it to Cas.

Cas: *YOU'RE ALIVE!*

Thor: *Somewhat.*

Cas: *I'll take it. How's the soup?*

Thor: *As if you don't know it's heavenly.*

. . .

He sent a string of gifs of people bowing and curtseying. I felt much better after the soup, and sent Cas a pic of the empty bowl before I strolled into the living room to take a nap on the couch. It was late afternoon when I woke up, and no sign yet of Cas, so I decided to check in with Leda. After that, I made my way home. Enjoying the brisk fall air, I took the long way, enjoying the serene evening. I was about half a block away from the apartment when the serenity was shattered by someone seizing my arm. "What the fuck are you doing?"

I yelped and squirmed, until I realized it was Cas. "What is the *matter* with you?"

"With me?" Cas grabbed both my upper arms and gave me a little shake. I hadn't picked up his scent as he approached because I was so congested. "What are you thinking being out here alone?"

I almost laughed. "What are you talking about?"

Cas looked at me like I was nuts. "Someone has declared it open season on shifters, and you go strolling around the streets in the dark by yourself?"

I froze. "I didn't—"

"Jesus, Thor." He released my arms, suddenly, like he hadn't realized he'd grabbed them. "You have to be more careful. If I was able to sneak up on you, some murderer definitely could."

My brain struggled to catch up. "What makes you think there's a murderer? Leda and I thought—"

"Thor," said Cas. "Wake up. Even if the victims were sick, based on what you've told me, ninety-nine percent of the world has no idea shifters exist. Do you think that would still be the case if your kind went staggering around naked and changing back and forth into their animal forms in public?

Why weren't they at home? Or a hospital, if they were sick? You guys have your own doctors, right?"

I honestly hadn't thought of that. My head pounded again; I needed to share this theory with Leda. Despite it being a logical one, neither Leda nor I had even considered the fact that someone out there might be specifically targeting shifters.

Cas's expression softened. "I didn't mean to scare you," he said.

"It's fine," I said robotically, but it wasn't. I was unnerved. Shaken, by the idea of a killer, and abraded by Cas's protectiveness of me. Especially because—

"Thor, what is it?"

"Shh," I whispered, moving toward the bushes on the side of the road.

"What--?"

"Cas, shut up!" I hissed, more harshly than I intended. There was something moving in the bushes, something rustling and making faint noises of distress. Pushing aside the branches, I squinted in the dark, and found the source of the noise.

I crouched, trying to make sense of what I was seeing. An adolescent swan, by my guess, judging by the color of its plumage. It had clearly just died, which would have been sad enough, without the rather horrifying addition of a human ear growing out of the top of its head, and the human foot that emerged from its wing joint.

"Cas," I said, and my voice seemed to have risen about twelve octaves. "Come—come here."

He joined me on the ground and let out a whispered curse. "We have to call the police."

"No," I said. "We should bring it straight to the lab."

"You're joking."

"Cas, if what you're saying is true—I don't think Detective Davis will consider it a coincidence that we've now called about two dead bodies, do you?"

"No, I suppose not."

I pulled off my hoodie, wrapping the poor dead bird in it before lifting it up. "Get my phone," I told Cas. "Tell Leda we're on the way."

Even in the dark I could see Cas blush as he reached gingerly into my jeans pocket for my phone. He fired off a text as we walked across the campus. The night air had gotten colder, and I shivered as we walked.

"Here," said Cas quietly, and he draped something over my shoulders. I nearly stumbled, the warmth of his jacket surrounding me, the gesture intimate and sweet, despite the fact that Cas hadn't meant it that way.

"Thank you."

When we arrived at the lab, it was around eight o'clock, and Leda had her lab coat over a chic little black dress. Cas and I stared. Her makeup was far more dramatic than usual, her hair curled and tumbling around her shoulders instead of pulled back in her customary French twist.

"I was on a date," she snapped, before we could ask. "This better be good."

I had a suspicion who Leda had been on a date with, but now was not the time. "Here," I said, laying the swan on her examination table.

Leda pulled on a pair of latex gloves, ire at her disrupted evening forgotten as she bent over the swan. "What on earth... Where did you find this?"

"About half a block from our apartment."

"Well," said Leda, examining the body. "We had been waiting on fresh samples..."

Cas snorted. "Careful what you wish for, I guess."

We didn't speak on the walk home. I could tell that

Cassian wanted to, but I kept my eyes on the sidewalk, my thoughts a tumult.

I intended to go straight to bed, but before I could make my way down the hallway, Cas seized my arm again, turned me around, and to my surprise pulled me into a tight, swift hug. I let out a small *oof* of surprise, and he whispered "It's going to be okay," into the top of my head. "You're going to figure out what's going on."

With him this close, it was impossible to keep his scent from fighting past my head cold, and I took a moment, just one tiny moment, to let myself pretend this hug meant to him what it meant to me.

When I finally got to bed, I tossed and turned all night, my dreams full of strange, shambling figures who chased me through the woods. They were slow, but I was slower, and yet whenever one grabbed me, it would burst into an explosion of downy white feathers.

# 8

The feel of Thor in my arms as I'd hugged him lingered for quite some time. I also had, somewhat purposely, neglected to ask him for my jacket back. It was an old one of my dad's, and I'd always found it comforting to wear, the old denim and soft flannel lining felt like having a piece of my dad here with me at school. Somehow, seeing it on Thor seemed just as right. I did not fail to notice that he wore the jacket several times after the night we brought the dead swan to Leda.

Leda and Thor had thus far confirmed the mutilated swan was not anyone they knew personally—but otherwise had not determined a whole heck of a lot.

Meanwhile, I spent an inordinate amount of my free time watching every video on Pornhub starring that bespectacled twink and beating off like a fucking maniac.

When I was in public, and had time, I did a fair amount of reading on gender and sexuality. There was a *lot* out there, but if I was being honest, it was a lot more fun exploring my sexuality with my hand on my dick than it was reading stuffy articles on JSTOR about gender through the years. I had hoped that getting away from campus for the tournament over the weekend would help me shake loose whatever fixation I had on Thor, maybe make it so that he wasn't at the center of this phase of self-discovery. However, as soon as I caught a glimpse of him walking down the street alone, I'd seen red. Some kind of crazy protectiveness had flared up inside me, and I was back at square one all over again.

Regardless, I had now jerked off enough with nary a gal in sight to solidify myself in my brain as "not straight." From there, however, I wasn't really sure where to go. I thought perhaps it was time to face facts, and talk to an expert. Namely, Lucy.

So, we met for coffee one morning. I took a deep breath. "Lucy," I said, all serious. "I think I might be bi."

She stared at me, expectant. The silence stretched on for a long ass time before she finally squinted and said, "Okay, and?"

I sputtered. "Good grief, isn't that enough?"

"Oh, sorry," she said, schooling her face into a look of cartoonish surprise. "Egads! You are a bisexual! We must tell the church."

"Stop," I said, falling forward and letting my forehead rest on the table.

She chuckled and patted my shoulder. "Sorry, but truthfully this was a long time coming."

I straightened up. "What?"

She gave me a long, searching look. "To be honest, Cas, you've always kind of been a question mark to me. When we met, you were pinging my queer-dar, big time."

I didn't quite know what to make of that, so I said nothing and waited for her to continue.

"But then," she said, and here she grinned indulgently.

"You did the like, peak straight guy thing and immediately asked out the biggest gay at the party, so I thought I had it wrong."

"Huh."

She shrugged. "Queer-dar isn't always flawless." She took a sip of her coffee. "So, what about Thor?"

I felt the heat rise in my face, like somehow my coming out also revealed that I'd been jacking off daily to a facsimile of my roommate. "What about him?"

My nonchalance was fooling no one. "Come on, Cas. He has something to do with all this, doesn't he?"

I made a face. "Maybe," I said. "But it doesn't matter. We're roommates. I have no idea what I'm doing, and it would be way too messy. Right?" I asked, like I really needed her to confirm I was making the right call by keeping some distance.

Lucy considered this a moment. "I, personally, am fond of mess," she said, a twinkle in her eye. "Speaking of which, I wanted to let you know."

"Let me know what?"

"I slept with Leda."

"You—I'm sorry, you what? How?"

"What, do you need like, a diagram?"

"Christ, Luce, no. I don't need a diagram. I just need to wrap my head around this for a second."

"We went out the other night," Lucy said. "She said you guys called her, so she had to leave the restaurant. But she came by later, and—well."

"Um. You're welcome?"

Lucy cackled. "Stop. I just wanted to ask you—what's her deal?"

I choked on a sip of coffee. Coughing, I said, "What do you mean?"

"Just curious if you think she's cool."

My heart hammered, and I felt seconds away from blurting, that yeah, Leda was beautiful, smart and witty—and oh, she had a cool little talent for transforming into a bird. "I don't—I guess I don't know her all that well."

"Hmm," said Lucy, stirring her ice coffee with a straw. "I suppose I'll just have to do my own investigating then."

Lucy's expression was playful, and I felt torn. Did I owe it to Thor to protect his secret? Or did I owe it to my friend to tell her something so earth-shattering about her new girl-friend? When had my life gotten so fucking complicated?

"Seriously though, Cas. Thank you, for telling me. About this part of yourself. I don't mean to make light. How are you feeling about everything?"

"Okay, I guess," I said, though really, I felt like this conver-sation had given me more questions than answers. "I don't think I'm ready to really *do* anything about this yet. Or ever. I have no idea, really."

"That's okay, Cas. And it doesn't make it any less true, okay?"

I nodded, still mulling.

"I'm serious," said Lucy, taking my hand. "And you know you can always talk to me about anything, right?"

If only.

I went home, buzzing from our conversation. For at least a week, Thor had been puttering around the apartment, clearly sick and refusing to mention it or ask for help. I was a bit annoyed. He was sick enough to be in a cold medicine coma all weekend, and I would have thought we were good enough friends now that he could have asked me for help—or at least asked me to grab him some Vicks on my way home or some-thing, but he seemed determined to tough it out alone.

Now that I was back from the tournament, he seemed to be still recovering, so I continued making more soup than I'd ever made in my entire life, hoping it would help him feel a bit better. Even if he didn't say so.

Totally unrelated, when I got home from my chat with Lucy, I checked Pornhub for the umpteenth time, wondering if the actor with whom I'd become obsessed had been tagged in any new videos. He hadn't.

Being honest, out loud, with Lucy—at least, about my shit—had filled me with restless energy. Should I tell Thor?

That would maybe be...odd. Thor had never told me point blank that he was gay. Or into guys. Whatever. All I knew was that he had, by self-admission, *kissed* a guy. Weirdly, I wanted Thor to know I was open to the possibility of dating guys (was I?) without actually having an explicit conversation about it.

Okay, so, maybe I wasn't ready to drop that bomb. I was just as likely to trip, clutch the bomb in my arms and allow it to detonate, blowing myself to smithereens.

I was all up in my feelings when I arrived at practice the next afternoon. As I geared up, I reflected that I hadn't spent all that much time with the guys on the team since the year started. I felt as though we didn't have much in common all of a sudden. There was also a heady dose of shame every time I saw them, remembering what had gone down last year––our stupid prank and how much it cost me.

However, going away for the tournament reminded me that I missed hanging with them. They were rowdy and fun and most times made me feel light. So, when Benson came up to me in the locker room after practice and invited me to a party, I accepted. It would be nice to hang with everyone again, cut loose and have some fun. It had been a goddamn weird couple of weeks.

"And hey," Benson added. "Why don't you bring your roommate?"

"Thor? Do you know each other?"

"Not really, just figured the more the merrier. There's going to be a lot of hot girls there."

I must have made some sort of twitchy expression, because Benson eyed me curiously.

"What?"

I shrugged, embarrassed that I didn't have a better poker face—or one at all. "I'm already kinda talking to someone," I said, like a fucking idiot.

"Oh, dip," said Benson. "Bring her!"

Ugh.

Later that night, I couldn't sleep. It was just one of those nights where everything caught up with me. I couldn't get comfortable, couldn't shut my mind down, couldn't drift off. Lying in bed, I flailed around, huffed and puffed, and tried to manhandle my pillow into a comfier position.

With a sigh, I checked my phone. 4:17 a.m. My alarm would ding in forty-three minutes, so there wasn't much point of even trying to fall asleep. I rolled onto the edge of my bed, sat up and stretched. That's when I noticed the light sneaking into my room under the crack in the door. How unusual. Thor compulsively turned off every light in the place, sometimes before I'd even finished up in a room.

I got dressed for the gym, packed my books and some clean clothes, figuring I could get in an extra-long workout. Moving quietly so as not to wake Thor, I walked down the hallway. When I reached the living room, I saw the reason the lights were still on.

Thor had clearly been working on something last night and fallen asleep. He was perched at the kitchen island—how he hadn't fallen sideways onto the floor was beyond me— laptop open on the counter, body slumped over the keyboard. His cheek pressed into the keys, his glasses knocked askew, and he snored softly. I couldn't help but smile.

I certainly couldn't leave him like that, poor guy. His spine was at a right angle, his neck twisted all around like an owl's. I crouched beside him, gingerly slipping one arm under his knees and the other around his shoulders. His snores sputtered to a stop, and he said, "Nuh," but otherwise didn't wake up.

As his cheek lifted from the keyboard, the laptop hummed and the screen blinked to life. I couldn't help it; I glanced at what he was working on. Most of the on-screen portion of the document was taken up by gobbledygook, the result of his face smushing the keys. It was bunch of disjointed letters and a few words autocorrect had valiantly tried to supply, and the whole paragraph ended with a bunch of backslashes and the word, "Buhhhhhhtable."

The document title was, "A Lover's Treasury of Monsters." Didn't seem like a paper for class, but without doing some legit snooping I was unlikely to figure out what it was. I shifted Thor's weight against my chest so I could reach down and close his laptop. He was so light in my grasp. I hoisted him more securely and felt a tug at my collar. Glancing down, I saw Thor's hands had fisted into the fabric of my tee. I smiled to see the little grid pattern imprinted on his cheek from the keys.

Halfway down the hall, I stopped dead in my tracks.

What the fuck was I doing?

This was so fucking weird. Why hadn't I woken him up and shooed him off to bed? If he woke up and I was carrying him—and I flushed, realized I was legit carrying him bridal style—he would think I was such a creep. I'd also never been inside his bedroom before. It felt forbidden, like some mysterious hideout he kept from me and the rest of the world.

Well, I certainly couldn't stand here dithering. It's not like I could put him back where I found him and if I woke him up now, he'd know I was being weird anyway. So, I nudged open the door to his bedroom with my foot and carried him over the threshold.

He was snoring again, happily resting against my chest, still gripping tight to my shirt. The bedroom was dark, and for the most part it was dominated by an enormous king-size bed with a fluffy white comforter and matching pillows. I released one arm to turn the blankets down, and Thor clung to me like a monkey as I lowered him gently to the mattress.

"Unnnhhh," he said, an annoyed little sound, as I tried to jostle him loose without waking him. I overbalanced a bit, dropping Thor and almost falling on top of him. As I extricated my shirt from his grasping hands, the tip of his nose slid across my neck. He inhaled deep, nuzzling against me for the briefest second before releasing his grip. Goosebumps burst across my skin in the wake of his hot breath, and then I was free.

I straightened up, disconcerted, and fled the room before anything else could happen. At the doorway, though, something stopped me. I crossed back over and slid the glasses from Thor's face, folded them closed, and left them on the bedside table.

———

## THOR

My eyes fluttered open. I groaned, disoriented in the dark. I had no idea what time it was. Did I sleepwalk to bed? I had been working late. When I looked around, the room was fuzzy, so I groped around for my glasses. Odd, I was still wearing my jeans and cardigan, but somehow during the night I seemed to have toed off one of my socks.

As I shifted around, a faint smell hit me that set my whole body quivering. *Woah.* I tilted my head, giving my shoulder a deep sniff. The shiver hit me again, so I kept on sniffing. *Cas.* Vague memories surfaced of strong arms lifting me, carrying me down the hall, and tucking me into bed. The smell was barely there, nothing like the day he'd come home all sweaty from practice, but it was softer, far more intimate—and just as intoxicating. I pulled my cardigan off and bunched it up on my pillow so I could bury my face in it. This was something I had read about, how the smell of one's potential mate could drive one crazy. I had never really understood, till Cas had entered my life.

I'd been trying to fight it for weeks, but my reaction to Cas couldn't be denied. After all this time, I'd found someone with whom I wanted to form a mating bond. Too bad he was human. Too bad he was horrified by my entire world. So, I did my best to try to squash the achy pull that had taken root in my chest, but I carried on sniffing my cardigan for Cas's lingering scent.

I must have forgotten to set my alarm, because when I woke up it was well past noon and I'd slept through my morning class. Something woke me up though, and that something was yelling my name from the kitchen. I considered, briefly, if there was somewhere I could hide. There wasn't.

There was no hiding from Lysander Ambrose.

I got up, thankfully still dressed, and ambled down the hall. "Hi, Dad."

My dad scoffed, crossing his arms over his broad chest, each one of them almost as thick as my whole body. Not really, but that's how he always seemed to me.

I didn't want to imagine how I always seemed to him.

"Thor," he said, and the way he said my name had me wincing. He frowned, looking me up and down. "You look like hell."

"Thanks?"

"You know what I mean," he said, waving his hand impatiently.

I didn't, but okay.

"I don't have long," he said. "I just came by to check on you. You've been acting strangely."

"No, I haven't."

He glared. "Well, you're shirking your responsibilities. You blew off Dr. Kendrick."

I shrugged. "I was sick," I said.

"Well, tough. I can't believe you would embarrass me like this."

Lack of sleep, lingering traces of illness, and my temper got the best of me. "You're not even mad that I missed the meeting. You're just mad that I missed a chance for you to throw your weight around in front of Dr. Kendrick."

I think, for once, I had actually shocked my father to silence.

"He's a reasonable guy," I continued. "I'll explain I was sick and he'll reschedule the tour."

"But what if—"

"If one mistake is enough to lose me this internship, which I doubt, then so be it. I'll figure something else out."

"You will *not*," Dad said, pure venom in his voice. "There is far too much riding on you getting this position."

"What?"

"I have been courting Kendrick for two years now, funding his research, because I am hoping against hope that he will be able to *fix* you."

That hung in the air for several long moments. "What are you talking about?"

"This is all very hush-hush," said my father. "Dr. Kendrick was going to talk to you about this at your meeting, but since I can't seem to get you to take it seriously—"

"*Dad*," I said. "What was he going to talk to me about?"

"He is working on a gene therapy for shifters," he explained. "Something that can give a *fauna* to someone born without one."

*Like me.* "Wait, why? I thought I was the only one who—"

"You're the only one of—whatever you are, locally. He

agreed to meet with you as a personal favor to the family. He's considering you for the pilot program for the gene therapy."

I bristled. "There is nothing wrong with me," I said, and hated myself because there was no denying the doubtful tremor in my voice. My dad didn't believe my claim, and neither did I. "What if I don't want to get some insane experimental treatment?"

He balked, looking at me like I was out of my mind. "Well, of course you would. Don't be ridiculous."

I knew there was no arguing, and in all honesty, I wasn't even sure why I was arguing. A *fauna* was all I had wanted my entire life—wasn't it? I frowned, crossing my arms over myself protectively.

"I've got to run," said Dad. "So, get your head on right. Call Dr. Kendrick and apologize. And if you're sick, book a damn physical."

Then he was gone. That was my father, always tearing in like a March storm and disappearing just as quick, leaving me wrong-footed, disoriented, and cold.

I stewed for the rest of the afternoon, contemplating everything he'd said about how I had to be fixed.

Like I was broken.

I mean, it wasn't really that big of a leap, I suppose.

When Cas came home some time later, I glanced at our schedule on the refrigerator. He usually didn't come home at this time of day. "Hey," I said, as he set down his bag. I waited for the immediate lift in mood his presence usually brought, but it didn't come.

"Hey."

He balanced a tray from the coffee shop with his class stuff, and I hastened to take it from him.

"Thought you might need one," he told me, gesturing once his hands were free.

"Thanks." I set the tray on the counter and took one of the coffees. "Did you skip practice?"

Cas grimaced. "No, I'm still going. I didn't sleep much last night, either, so I was hoping to grab a quick nap before I drag my ass to the rink."

"Fair enough." The silence between us grew, thick and heavy, so I had to break it. "Thanks for uh, getting me to bed last night."

For some reason, Cas turned beet red, and I had to steady myself on the counter. The blush came with a direct infusion of his scent. It seemed as though my senses were tuning in more and more, tuning in to him. He looked down at the ground, grinning shyly. "I figured I had to, before you slid off the stool and broke your neck?"

I laughed. "True."

"So, uh, what were you working on so late?"

"Nothing," I stammered. What a stupid lie; I could have said I was working on a paper.

Cas frowned at me, and I could tell he wasn't buying it. "You can tell me, dude, if you want. I already know..." he trailed off.

"It's..." There was no reason why this was so hard for me to say. "A book. A novel."

"No shit," said Cas, looking genuinely impressed. "That's awesome."

"I've never told anyone that before," I confessed. I didn't think I'd ever even said the words out loud.

"Why not?"

I shrugged. "Because," I said. "I know it's never going to happen." My conversation with my dad today made that clearer than ever. If I stayed here to attempt this cure, I'd have to surrender fully to whatever my family asked of me. I wouldn't have any time to spare on something so frivolous.

"That's a weird thing to say."

Which was odd, because I thought *that* was a weird thing to say. "Huh?"

"I mean—you're smart. Why can't you be a writer?"

The question hung in the air, so unencumbered. It was the type of thing a kind, guileless college student *would* ask. The question made me angry, mainly because that's all I wanted to be. Just me, just normal. But also, angry because I didn't have the words to answer it. Cas knew about my family, sure, but there was so much I hadn't explained to him, so much he didn't need to burden himself with. I finally said, "My major is evolutionary bio."

Cas frowned at me. "You can change your major. Like, if you want."

"No, I can't," I snapped.

"Woah," said Cas, looking startled. "Okay."

"I have way too much going on for writing to be anything other than a hobby."

"You have way too much going on, period."

"What's that supposed to mean?"

"Thor, man, you look like shit."

"Thanks!" I said, insulted. That was the second time today!

"I mean it," said Cas, refusing to back down. "You've been sick and you're not sleeping. You study, you work at the lab. You stay up all night working on this so it clearly means a lot to you. Something's got to give or you're going to kill yourself."

"I'm fine."

"No, you're not." Cas stood close to me now, and his smell was overpowering. It left me feeling frayed and raw, like a vulnerable animal. If he stepped any closer, I'd come entirely unglued. "Why don't you cut back on something? Maybe the reading for your dad?"

"I can't do that!"

"Why?"

"Because, I can't," I said. "It's none of your business, Cassian, okay? Just back off."

Cas looked like I'd slapped him. "Wow," he said quietly.

In all honesty, I didn't know what had me so wound up, or why I was taking it out on poor Cas. Realizing this, however, did not improve my temper. "Listen Cas, you don't know me. We're just roommates."

"Jesus," he said, holding his hands up. "Fine."

The silence stretched until I said, "Thanks for the coffee."

"Yeah." Cas shouldered past me into his room and shut the door—not quite a slam, but definitely a bit harder than necessary.

Damnit.

# 9

*Just roommates.* The phrase rattled around in my head. So much for getting a few hours' sleep. I tossed and turned as much as I had last night, angry and confused. I had no idea why Thor had taken my suggestion so badly—the guy was clearly pent up, and there was something on his mind. *Just roommates.*

I knew what he meant; just roommates as opposed to old friends—but it sounded like it had a lot more weight to it than that. To me, anyway. I groaned into my pillow, trying not to be too hurt or angry. It wasn't really working. Part of me wondered if I shouldn't invite Thor to the party this weekend after all, like maybe he really didn't want to be friends, let alone anything else.

On the way to practice, I dithered back and forth quite a bit, and in the end, I decided I'd ask Thor over text. Then I'd invite Lucy too, as a buffer. Come to think of it, Lucy might already be on the invite list, considering the varsity sports teams at Fremont all seemed to run in the same circles. She could invite Leda—maybe if we went as a group, it would be less awkward. *Just roommates.* Thor had no way of knowing how deep his words had cut. I had the feeling his little freak out had less to do with me than it did with how much strain he was plainly under. A party, a chance to cut loose and maybe meet some people, would do him some good. So, before practice I pulled out my phone.

C*as: I forgot, there's a party this weekend. Thinking of asking the girls if u wanna join.*

Then, I stuffed my phone into my locker before I could obsess any more.

After practice, I practically sprinted to the locker room to check my phone, but there was no reply.

However, when I left the building, the evening chill sending shivers down my sweaty back, I saw Thor waiting for me, wearing my jacket and holding a little white box.

When I approached him, unsure of what to say, he pushed off the wall where he'd been leaning. "I got you a cupcake," he blurted, handing me the box.

"Is this an 'I'm Sorry' cupcake?"

He slid his glasses up his nose. "Yes."

"Okay, well, then. I accept." I opened the box and peered inside. "What flavor?"

"Carrot cake."

"I love carrot cake," I admitted.

"I know."

So, naturally, I had a doofy smile on my face as we walked back to the apartment. Part of me knew I should have pressed the issue, maybe talked about some of the stuff that had been left unsaid between us, but for now, I didn't want to ruin the moment. A conversation was coming, though. Or it should be. This thing, this tension between us, I was pretty sure now that Lucy had been right about Thor liking me at least a little. Maybe at the party, after a few drinks, we could sneak off somewhere for a private chat, and slash or some other private stuff.

I was getting way ahead of myself.

Finally, Saturday rolled around, and I was in my room getting ready for the party. I was weirdly worried about what to wear, something I had literally never once in my life worried about. It's not like I had a ton of varied options, so I settled on some dark grey jeans and black V-neck tee shirt. I would normally have worn my denim jacket, but I didn't want to ask for it back from Thor.

As I laid out my clothes, debating if I should try to style my hair, there was a knock at my door. I hastily pulled on my jeans and called, "Come in!"

Thor entered, looking nervous. He swallowed, his eyes widening behind his glasses, lingering on my chest, and I think my abs. I took that as a good sign.

"What's up?"

"You're not ready!" he said. Thor was dressed in his usual skinny jeans, Converse, and cardigan. The cardigan, however, was a thinner grey material, and fitted close to his trim body, very different from the giant baggy ones he usually favored. Under that, he had on a black button-down shirt with the festive addition of a white bowtie. The whole look really worked for him, in my opinion.

"You look nice," I said, before I could stop myself.

He flushed. "Thank you. But we're going to be late."

I pulled on my tee with my back to Thor. "It's not an 'arrive right at the start time' thing," I explained. "What, is this your first party?"

Silence. Oh, Jesus. I had been kidding but, damn. I turned

to face him as I put on deodorant. "Maybe," he said, squinting at a spot on the carpet.

"Well," I said, recovering quickly. "Trust me. We'll be fine if we're not right on time."

"Okay," he said. He turned and left my room without another word.

I chuckled, and turned to the mirror to fuss with my hair. I decided against styling it, largely because I never did, and didn't really know how.

When I finally made my way to the living room, Thor had been perched anxiously on the sofa and sprang up as soon as I entered. "Ready?"

I couldn't help my smile. "Yeah, man. Let's go."

The party was in full swing by the time we arrived. Lucy was on her own, ensconced in a doubles' beer pong tournament with a couple of other girls from the volleyball team. Thor and I threaded through the crowd towards them to watch.

Benson caught my eye and waved before his gaze fell on Thor, and his face broke into a twitch sort of grin.

He ambled over. "Hey, man."

"Hey," I said. I placed my hand on Thor's shoulder and squeezed. "This is Thor, my roommate."

"We've met," said Benson, his voice curt. "Nice to see you again."

I frowned, because it had been Benson's suggestion to invite Thor, who was now openly scowling at Benson. However, he said, "You too. Thanks for the invite."

"Sure." Benson turned his back to Thor. "Where's your date?"

*Fuck.* "Oh..."

"You said you were talking to somebody."

I wished to evaporate on the spot. The noise of the party swelled around us, and Thor tensed beside me. I was scared to even look his way. "Yeah, uh." I swallowed. "Couldn't make it."

"That's a shame," said Benson. "But I guess it means I could introduce you to—"

"Excuse me," said Thor icily. "I'm going to get a drink."

And he stalked off before I could stop him. I tried to keep my eyes on him as he fought the tide of party-goers toward the bar area that had been set up toward the front of the living room.

Feigning interest in Benson as he described whoever he was planning on introducing me to, I settled in to watch Lucy finish her game of pong, which she dominated. Thor didn't come back though, and when I looked around for him—why was it so easy for me to pick him out of the crowd?—I saw him leaning against the wall, sipping from a solo cup. A taller guy stood next to him, leaned into Thor's space.

Immediately, I prickled, clenching my jaw. Thor batted his eyelashes and lowered his cup, a little smile on his face that made me want to hit something. Who the hell was this guy? He was tall, maybe taller than I was, though it was hard to tell with him leaning over into Thor's airspace like that. He had short black hair and deeply tanned skin, and I guess he was kind of good-looking.

Or whatever.

"What's up with you?" Lucy asked, pressing a beer into my hand.

"Nothing," I said, but she followed my eyes.

"Ah," she said. "Well, Leda blew me off tonight, too. So, let's be miserable together."

"Better yet—let's get drunk off our asses together," I said, knocking the neck of my bottle with hers.

"Cheers to that!"

———

## THOR

I had no right to be upset that Cassian had been planning on bringing a date to the party. However, I would have thought he'd at least *tell* me if he had been seeing someone. And despite my brain knowing I had no right to be angry, I still was.

To cap it off, Jack Benson was not only the host of this party, but being reminded that he was Cas's friend further confirmed that Cas and I simply had nothing whatsoever in common. Benson was insufferable. We shared a major and had crossed paths in several classes. I wasn't sure if he was a complete idiot, or a complete slacker. Perhaps both. I had no idea how he managed not to drop out of school. The last time he and I shared a class, we'd been paired on a project and I had done the whole thing myself while he ignored my texts and emails.

After the project, our professor had asked us to rate our partners, and I had been furious so I torpedoed him. I think it must have gotten back to him, because he'd hated my guts ever since.

When I'd seen Rafe Nardini across the room, I'd leapt at the chance to extricate myself. Though our blind date had ended awkwardly, he was cute and polite and I knew him, so I grabbed a drink and tried to engage him in conversation.

I had mixed myself a vodka cranberry, ratio heavily favored toward the vodka. I stared up at Rafe, who had dark blue eyes and neat black hair, trying to focus on what he was saying. He was nice, and good-looking, but mostly I wanted to escape, and I already regretted coming to this party.

So, I downed my drink quickly, and under the pretext of getting a refill I shook Rafe loose. I felt tingly in my sinus and made a mental note to pace myself a bit better on this second round. I wandered around the party, people-watching, wondering if I should just sneak out and head home. A few rooms had been given over entirely to amorous couples, so I avoided those. I found a room with pounding music and saw all the furniture had been pushed against the wall. I was about to flee when an arm looped through mine. "Hey," said Lucy, leaning in to yell in my ear. "Finish your drink and let's dance!"

"I don't really dance," I said, for all the good it did me.

She didn't take no for an answer, so I gulped my drink, set down my cup, and let her pull me onto the dance floor. Two drinks in quick succession and I was a little less terrified of dancing in front of people. Besides, it was dark, and everyone here was already drunker than I was, so I decided to let loose.

Lucy and I ended up doing a few shots with some of the girls from her team, and between the alcohol, the press of bodies, and the dancing, I realized it was *hot*. I loosened my tie, but I was still sweating, so I extricated myself from the ungraceful, dancing pileup to peel off my cardigan and drape it over the back of a chair. With a frown, I realized I couldn't see Cas anywhere. I hadn't seen him in a while. I wandered back to the bar and got a refill, meandering through the crowd. My feet were a little reluctant to follow my instructions, so I thought maybe some fresh air would do me good. I saw Rafe head outside to the porch so I decided to follow him. I didn't really have any reason to hide from an innocent flirtation.

I approached him where he leaned over the railing. "Hi."

"Hey," he said warmly.

He had a pretty smile. I set my drink down on a rickety little card table and sidled up beside him, but found I had absolutely no idea what to say. There were a few people milling around on the porch, talking and laughing. To my annoyance I caught sight of Benson lurking next to some girl over in the corner. It seemed like his eyes were fixated on me over her shoulder, so I turned my back on him to focus on Rafe.

He watched the lawn, where a few people had gathered around a bonfire.

I shivered. Where had my cardigan gone? "I'm cold," I blurted.

I hadn't meant for that to come out as flirty, but Rafe's eyes darkened and he shot me a grin. As he moved closer, he said, "Wanna go sit by the fire?"

But being cold made me think about Cas's jacket, and the hug he'd given me while I wore it.

I swallowed, mouth dry. I grabbed blindly for my drink, and it took me a second to find it. I must have moved it from the table to the railing, where Rafe had set his cup, too. I took a huge gulp to hide my nerves and handed Rafe his drink. I glanced toward the fire, and with a start realized Cas was one of the people standing around it. "Let's dance," I said abruptly. Then it dawned on me that I had left my cardigan in the room with the dance floor, anyhow. Perfect!

Rafe took my hand, which felt kind of weird, but I gulped down the rest of my drink and let him lead me back through the party.

# 10



This party kind of bit.

Well, I guess that wasn't entirely fair. It seemed like an okay party, and I had some fun playing pong with Lucy and drinking with the guys. Several beverages later, I found myself buzzed and standing alone by the firepit on the lawn. I hadn't seen Thor in like, an hour. It twisted my guts to think he was somewhere making out with that guy he'd been talking to, so I supposed I didn't look all that hard for him. Lucy had made some noises about dancing, so I'd made myself scarce. Dancing wasn't really my thing.

What a trainwreck. If this had been last year, or even a few months ago, I would have been in the thick of things, maybe trying to find a date, or at least flirting with someone cute. My definition of someone cute had expanded recently, so with the help of my beer, I passively tried to look at some of the guys I might consider flirting prospects. No one really stood out to me, and it left me with a hollow sort of feeling in my gut. The beer certainly wasn't helping that. It wasn't a happy buzz, more like a grumpy one.

Someone grabbed my arm. "We have a problem."

I turned from the fire, a bit night blind, blinking to get my bearings. It was Lucy. She chewed her lip, scared, her eyes wide. Something was definitely wrong. "What is it?"

"It's Thor," she said. "I think—I think someone may have slipped him something."

"*What?*"

"We were dancing, and he was dancing with that guy Rafe, but *he* started feeling sick so he left. Then Thor, I dunno, Cas —he got all weird and like he couldn't talk or stand up right."

"Maybe he's just drunk," I said.

Lucy shook her head. "No, I don't think so. Unless he did ten shots in the span of like, five minutes. It's real bad."

I went cold all over. "Show me."

Lucy and I shoved our way back through the press. She led me to a bathroom on the second floor of the house. The hallway was mercifully quiet, and Lucy knocked.

A slurred voice came from the other side. "Go away."

We ignored the voice and opened the bathroom door with a soft click. Thor sat on the tiled floor, slumped down against the wall beside the toilet. His eyes were closed tight, and his skin was sweaty and pale.

"Cas," he said, without opening his eyes. His voice sounded faint and weak.

"Hey, buddy," I said, not even questioning how he'd known it was me. I crouched down and touched his forehead, finding it clammy and warm. "What happened?"

But telling us to go away and mumbling my name seemed to be all he could manage. He slid over, colliding with the side of the bathtub. I couldn't stop touching him, so Lucy wet a washcloth and handed it to me so I could dab it on his forehead.

Finally, Thor said, "Dancing. I dunno. Got sleepy."

"Did someone do this to you?"

He frowned, like thinking of it was too much for him right now. He opened his mouth like he was going to answer, but his face went immediately slack and he fell asleep.

"Jesus," I said. "I gotta get him home."

"Should you take him to the hospital?" Lucy asked.

It was on my tongue to say "Good idea," but something stopped me. *Should* I? I had no idea what Thor's internal makeup was like—if I brought him to the doctor, would his entire family be exposed? In my moment of hesitation, Thor opened one eye, peering up at me in a hazy, unfocused way. He shook his head. "Home," he managed.

"Are you sure?"

A tiny nod. I draped the face cloth over the edge of the sink and seized Thor under his arms to haul him to his feet. He swayed, so I wrapped an arm around his waist to steady him. His head lolled to the side, and he opened his eyes. "Hi."

I smiled, but my heart had leapt up into my throat. Not in a good way. "Hi," I said back, trying to keep my voice steady. "I think maybe we should take you to the doctor, bud."

His brows knit together and he shook his head so hard he nearly fell over. I caught him before he went down, but that settled it. If he stopped breathing or something, I'd call 911 in a heartbeat. In the meantime, once we got home, I'd give Leda a call.

Thor clearly wasn't going anywhere under his own steam, so with no other options I scooped him into my arms, like I had the other night. He curled contentedly against my chest and something squeezed around my heart. I took a step, swaying a tiny bit myself—I was definitely not sober enough for this shit.

With Thor held as securely as possible, I pushed out the bathroom door and down the stairs. There was no way not to make a damn spectacle as we left, but there also wasn't much I could do about it. People stared, but I ignored them and marched out into the chilly evening.

Lucy called us an Uber and made me promise to keep her in the loop, and soon enough I was hauling Thor up the stairs at our place, fumbling with my keys to let us into the apartment. I may or may not have banged him up a bit on the way up the stairs, and by the time we reached the door I was sweating and huffing.

"You're strong," he mumbled.

"You're heavy," I shot back.

At last, I dropped him on his bed and went to get him some water. As I filled the glass, I heard a soft, plaintive cry from his room. Panicked, I hurried down the hall to find Thor trying to undress himself. He had his button-down half undone and was trying unsuccessfully to yank it over his head.

"M'stuck," came his muffled voice from behind the shirt. It covered his face and pinned his arms against the side of his head.

"Hang on, before you strangle yourself." I peeled the shirt off him and turned away as he wiggled out of his jeans and collapsed on the bed.

I fetched the glass of water and moistened a washcloth from the bathroom for his head. I placed the back of my hand on his brow again, feeling the heat of a slight fever, so I removed his glasses and laid the damp cloth on his forehead.

Then, I was kind of at a loss. I had texted Leda, and was waiting to hear back. I didn't know if it was okay to leave him on his own, he was so out of it...but the idea of staying here made me nervous, too. In the end, I figured I'd set up camp on the reading chair on the other side of Thor's bedroom.

"Cas?" Thor's whisper was so quiet I almost didn't hear it.

"Yeah?"

"Stay."

"Of course. I'll be right over—" I gestured toward the chair.

He shook his head. "No, please. Stay with me."

I had a lot of self-control, or so I thought, but the small, weak plea undid me entirely. I slid out of my own sweaty tee and jeans and moved to sit stiffly beside him on the giant mattress, propped up against the headboard. Thor rested his head on my thigh, and the wash cloth fell into my lap with a wet plop. I replaced it as best I could, and left my hand to cup the back of his head, stroking his soft, thick hair. With my other hand, I pulled out my phone. Leda had messaged me back, giving me a list of things to check for; a list of warning signs that meant I should ignore his request and get him to the hospital. It was a relief to know I had that option available without exposing the entire secret shifter society in the process.

Satisfied that we could manage for now, I set my phone aside and rested my palm between his shoulder blades to feel the steady, reassuring huff of his breath, counting each inhale and checking the clock to make sure there wasn't any immediate danger. My eyelids drooped, the nerves and adrenaline fading in the quiet of the room, but I forced myself to stay awake, to listen to Thor breathe for an hour. Then I pushed his shoulder gently, to see if he would wake. He did, briefly, squirming back from the disturbance and rolling over, but it was enough to ensure he wasn't passed out unconscious, just sleeping.

My shoulders came down from around my ears, and I hunkered down a bit lower against the veritable mountain of pillows on Thor's bed. All of a sudden, Thor rolled over, curled into my side, and snuggled against my chest. I laid there, rigid as a corpse, all too aware of his body and mine, wondering why I hadn't taken the time to go into my room to get some actual pajamas.

Or possibly a hazmat suit.

It was going to be a long night.

In the morning, I woke up to three things.

First: A hangover.

Second: The most. Fucking. Comfortable. Bed. It was like being hugged into a cloud.

Third: I was rock hard. My dick nestled perfectly against a soft, warm thing. My proper brain wasn't awake yet, but my lower brain sure as hell was. Before I was even fully conscious, I was rolling my hips, mushing my pelvis against the soft, warm, heavenly thing that seemed custom-made to cradle my shaft.

Mush. Mush.

A wiggle and a sleepy mewl greeted me. I tightened my arm, and the person under that arm yawned, stretched, and ground their ass back toward my very receptive dick.

Fuck.

My actual brain woke up all at once, thank God. Sleepy, drunk "consent" might get a pass for snuggles, but I knew better than to fucking dry hump someone before I knew for sure they wanted me to. I rolled away as fast as I could disentangle my limbs. I needed caffeine and long shower.

I *nyoomed* to the bathroom, ripped off my boxers and jumped into the tub. I turned the dial to maximum heat and before the spray even hit my chest, I was cranking my dick like jacking off was about to become an Olympic sport. It was fast, sloppy, and rough—just what I needed to clear my head. I was hungover and horny as hell and really not ready to process the events of the night before.

Plainly, Lucy's queer-dar had been right on the money and I was about as straight as a paperclip. I had told her I might be bisexual, but I hadn't really considered any other guys besides Thor, and I was *definitely* considering him. Hard. So, was I gay? Pan? Whatever the fuck? I'd learned a lot of words over the course of my research, and finding a name for how I felt seemed less important all of a sudden.

All I knew for absolute fucking sure was that I wanted Thor. Bad.

I wanted my friend, my roommate.

I wanted to snuggle him, protect him. Kiss him. Touch him. My dick was clearly happy with that idea. Vivid fantasies burst into my mind's eye with a battering ram. I imagined Thor with me here in the shower, on his knees to suck me off. Through the beauty of fantasy, I switched our places mentally, and it was the idea of me on my knees for him that had me spurting all over the fancy shower tiles.

A moan slipped out, and I rested my aching forehead on the cool wall of the shower, letting the water run down my back. I sighed deeply. Maybe I should cook us a nice breakfast. We plainly had a lot to discuss—which I knew would take some serious coaxing.

Plus, holy fuck. Forget about me. Thor had been drugged. Maybe us cuddling last night had been purely platonic, because he'd been afraid and vulnerable and I made him feel safe. Something fierce swelled in my chest. Of course, I made him feel safe. If someone fucks with my friend, they fuck with me. Someone slipped shit into his drink, and regardless of my desire to christen every surface in this apartment with Thor's tight little body—they were going to pay for that.

I got out of the shower and dodged toward my room so I could pull on some comfy flannel pants and towel dry my hair. Pancakes sounded good. I went to the kitchen and started grabbing what I needed to make a big breakfast feast. Bacon, fluffy buttermilk cakes, and fried eggs on top. Lots of coffee. Just what Thor needed to rouse, feel comfortable and full, and tell me whose ass I needed to kick.

My mind became a tangle of violence and romance, so

distracted that I failed to hear a key turn in the lock. The door banged open.

"Who the hell are you?"

I nearly jumped out of my skin. Framed in the doorway was a fucking giant. "Uh," I said.

The guy crossed his arms over his chest, glaring at me like I had broken into his home to make pancakes in my pajamas. He was in his early fifties maybe, and I didn't know much about clothes but the suit he was wearing probably cost more than my dad's car. He was huge, towering over me, straight back and broad-shouldered. His eyes glinted steely and unforgiving, and his dark greying hair gave him a distinguished supervillain vibe.

"Well?" he demanded.

"Uh," I said again, forgetting the fact that, you know, I lived here. I even had a lease.

"Dad?" Thor emerged bleary eyed and tousle-haired from his bedroom, in boxers and a big t-shirt. Holy shit, my t-shirt.

"Who the hell is this?" The giant jerked his thumb in my direction.

"That's Cas, my uh," his eyes found mine, and he hesitated. "Roommate."

The word sounded different this time—less like a slam, and more like a secret. Clearly Thor's dad thought so, too, because something knowing flickered in his eyes, and he looked me over with an appraising sort of stare that left me feeling naked.

He stuck out his hand. "Lysander Ambrose," he said.

I shook his hand and found my voice at last. "Cassian Rhodes," I said. "Sir."

"Good handshake," he said, his tone warming so fast it was alarming. "You look like you work out, Cas."

What a weird thing to say. "I play hockey."

"You any good?"

Thor watched this interaction with his arms crossed and a scowl on his face. To see him in the daylight, he still looked ill. "Dad," he interrupted. "What are you doing here?"

"I can't come to visit my son?"

"It would be nice if you knocked once in a while," Thor muttered. It seemed that standing and having this conversation took a tremendous effort. I resisted every instinct that told me to go to his side and pull him against me, to shield him. How could his own father not see that something was wrong?

"I have a key," Lysander said.

Thor sighed, a look on his face that told me was considering getting his locks changed. I stood there like a walnut watching their conversation. It was so early and already way too much had happened today.

"So, anyway, Cas," Lysander said, shifting focus back to me. "You play varsity?"

"I do, sir."

"Grades?"

"I do okay." Suddenly a lot of weird things about Thor were making sense to me.

"Better than okay," Thor put in. "Cas has an academic scholarship. He's on the Dean's List."

I startled, flush with a weird, squirmy sort of pride to think Thor had looked at my transcripts with such care when we first met.

"Brains and brawn, huh?" Lysander turned toward his son. "I approve."

Thor looked like he wished to evaporate on the spot, and his pale pallor suggested he might do just that. He rolled his eyes heavenward. "*Dad.*"

Truthfully, I had no fucking idea what was going on.

"Well, Cas, I didn't think my son had it in him."

I frowned. Had what in him, exactly? Thor looked small

and miserable, slouching, pale and sickly with his eyes on the floor. After the night he'd had, the last thing he needed was his dad barging in and shitting all over him. This guy was a jackass. I opened my mouth, about to tell him so. "Listen—"

"Now, now," he said. He clapped me on the shoulder like we were old buddies, giving me what he must have thought was a winning smile. "Cas! Do you have plans for the Thanksgiving break?"

I was startled by the change of subject. "Huh?"

He squeezed my shoulder. "You should come home with Thor for the long weekend. We really do it up right. Plus, then you can meet the whole family."

"Dad—"

"Oh, don't be uptight. It'll be fun. Don't you think, Cas?"

"Uh, I guess?" My dad usually worked on Thanksgiving, trying to pick up some overtime to dilute the cost of the rest of the holiday season. My siblings dispersed to the homes of various friends, or their grandparents on my stepmother's side of the family. Last year, I hadn't even gone home.

"Well," said Lysander brightly. "That's settled. I'll leave you boys to it then, shall I? Son, I'll talk to you soon. Lovely to meet you, Cassian."

And like that he was gone, slamming the door behind him. Was it my imagination or did he literally leave a ringing silence in his wake? All of a sudden, it came to me that the man in my kitchen just seconds ago could transform into a wolf. He could have transformed right there and torn my throat out. Did Thor's family know that I knew their secret? I turned back toward Thor, opening my mouth to ask if he wanted to sit down and talk over some pancakes, but he cut me off.

"I'm going back to bed."

"Oh," I said, disappointed. "Okay."

He stomped off down the hall and I stood in the kitchen

feeling like an idiot. I put away the ingredients I'd pulled out, and when I closed the fridge and straightened up it was to Thor standing there with his hands on his hips and an expectant look on his face. *"Jesus,"* I said, startled. How did he move so quiet?

"Well?" He asked.

"What?"

"Aren't you coming?" He didn't wait for an answer, but turned around and marched off again.

Sure I'd misheard, I trailed after him down the hall, hesitating at the door to his room. Thor pulled back the covers and climbed onto the mattress, looking so small in the giant bed. Timidly, I approached the side of the California king, waiting for something to happen, like Thor jumping up and yelling, "Gotcha!" or something. When he didn't, I sat on the edge of the bed.

"Do you want to talk?" I asked finally.

"No." He rolled over and curled up, dwarfed in the puffy white comforter. "Will you just get in here?" He sounded exasperated, like we did this every day and he couldn't fathom why I was so confused.

Smiling slightly, I swung my legs up into the bed and sank down into the luxurious pillowtop. This really had to be the world's most comfortable bed, and napping the morning away sounded like a perfect hangover remedy. On some level, still afraid I had grossly misread this situation, I carefully inched my way closer to Thor. As I scooted toward him, I remembered something. "You're wearing my shirt," I said, snaking an arm around his waist.

Thor immediately snuggled closer, pushing his back to my chest with a contented sigh. "Uh-huh."

I smiled against his shoulder blade.

———

## THOR

I woke up a few hours later--the feeling like a railroad spike plunged into my temple lessening a bit--to warm, warm, *warm* and soft snores tickling my ear, completely surrounded by sleeping Cas. Beneath the heavy, debilitating fog lingering from the events of the previous evening, I had enough mental capacity to be amazed at myself for commanding Cas into my bed. He wanted to be here, that was plain, but after the party debacle last night and my father this morning, Cas probably thought I was close to a breakdown.

Taking stock of my body, feeling safe with the pressure of Cas's strength surrounding me, I tried to call up last night, to piece together what had happened. My last memory was Rafe staggering off the dance floor, his face suddenly gone slack and wan where he'd been alert just moments ago. By the time I'd put the pieces together, the warning going off inside my head had been far, far too late.

Rafe, I recalled, did not drink alcohol. The only logical conclusion, then, was that something foreign had found its way into his cup. And mine. I cursed myself for my lack of restraint; I'd been buzzed at the time, so even my trustworthy memories, from before I'd come-to briefly on a stranger's bathroom floor, weren't super clear.

I'd gone out to talk to Rafe on the porch and then...it was like a smash cut to us on the dance floor, him retreating with fear and confusion on his face, then another jump in time, to the cool tile of the bathroom, and being called back into consciousness by Cas's scent. I inhaled that scent now, letting it fill me with courage to probe the missing areas of my memory, the jagged edges I could hopefully seam together.

I recalled seeing Benson, lurking in the shadows, certain my fear at the missing, hazy memories amplified the sinister look on his face. Cowering from it, I let the warmth in this little cocoon of comforters and Cassian pull me back under.

I woke again, my brain whirring to life like an internet dial-up connection from the nineties, my mouth dry and foul. I fidgeted for a moment, wondering if I could disentangle my limbs without waking the snoozing guy glued to my back.

"Nnnnf. What?"

No such luck. I cleared my throat and whispered, "Nothing. Go back to sleep."

"No—I'm up. I'm up. What do you need? Water?" Cas was already moving, sandy hair all mussed from the pillow.

I rolled over, watching him stretch as he stood. In that moment I wanted nothing more than to kiss the little dimples at the base of his spine, or push my face between his shoulder blades and breath him in. But my burning throat would not be denied. "Water. Thank you."

He took off down the hall, and I heard the water running. Cas always forgot I had a filtered pitcher of water in the fridge, and routinely drank from the tap. He came back and sat on the edge of the bed, handing me the glass. I scooted up against the pillows, gulping water gratefully. When I set the glass down on the bedside table, I saw Cas staring at me with a worried look on his face.

"What?"

"How are you feeling?" he asked, and I knew he didn't mean the hangover.

I hated the pitying look on his face, hated anyone making a fuss. "Fine."

"You have to tell me what happened."

Part of me wanted to confess my suspicions, but I didn't have any proof, not really. How much could I really tell from one glare? Besides, Cas's friendship with Benson made things much more complicated. To be frank, I'd rather forget about the entire thing. "Why?"

Cas narrowed his eyes. "So I make sure I kill the right person," he said, voice rough and angry. "Was it that slimy guy you were talking to?"

It took me a second to put a name to Cas's description. "Rafe?"

"Whatever. Was it him?"

"No," I said, certain.

"How do you know?"

"I just do, Cas. I know him."

Cas blinked at me in surprise. "You do? How?"

What did that matter? I felt myself flush, and the pain in my head returned with a vengeance. I wanted to go back to sleep and avoid this talk entirely. "We went on a date."

If anything, Cas's expression turned even darker. "What does that prove?"

Was he...was he jealous? This was making my head pound again. "Nothing—it was a setup. Our families go way back."

"Wait—is he...?"

I sighed. "A shifter, yes. And..." I hesitated. "I think...I think someone got him too."

"*What?*"

"Before I..." I trailed away. "Anyway, he was sick, too. Shit —I need to check on him. I need to—"

Frantically, I scrabbled against the surface of my bedside table for my glasses and my phone, and knocked the glass to the carpet where it landed with a thud. I lunged for the glass and almost fell out of bed, a swooping, sickening dizziness seizing me.

"Easy," said Cas, alarmed. He grabbed my shoulders, the warmth and steadiness of his palms like an immediate balm. "*Easy.* If you're sure, I can reach out to him and make sure he's alright. Does he know Leda?"

I nodded. We all knew each other. Something cold and hard found its way to my palm; Cas had found my glasses ahead of my clumsily questing fingers. I slid them on. "His number's in my phone," I said meekly. I knew I didn't have the strength to stay awake much longer.

"Alright," said Cas, his tone soothing. He opened his mouth again, presumably to press the issue but I cut him off.

"I *really* don't want to talk about this anymore."

He gave me a suspicious little squint. "Okay. You hungry?"

I shook my head. In truth, my stomach was a sea of quease and the mere suggestion of food had it lurching unpleasantly, even Cas food. "I might just fall back asleep," I said, squirming down into the covers again.

Cas struggled with himself for a moment before reaching to brush the shaggy hair back from my forehead. It took a lot of self-control not to push my cheek against his hand like an affectionate cat. His eyes bore into mine. "Do you need to go to the doctor?"

"No," I said emphatically. "I need some rest, but I'll be fine."

"Alright, if you're sure." Cas stood and I hated how much I wanted to beg him to stay. He turned and left the room, so I pulled the blanket up over my face. I hid there until I felt the mattress dip, a weight returning to the bed. I peered out.

"Is this okay?" Cas held up a battered, used copy of *1984*. "Will the light bug you? I need to do this reading by tomorrow."

With the covers pulled up so high, Cas couldn't see that I was grinning.

# 11



Thor slept most of the day, waking up for a slice of toast around eight p.m. and falling right back to sleep again. Per his request, I did message Rafe, using all my willpower not to snoop in their messages.

I also let Leda know Thor's suspicions, and she promised to check in on Rafe as well. I refrained from asking her why she had blown Lucy off and skipped the party. One romantic shifter crisis at a time. Thor getting drugged still occupied most of my brain. I had no idea who had done the deed, but I was determined to find out. I contacted everyone I knew who'd been at the party, trying to piece together the timeline without making Thor more upset I hadn't let it drop. I wasn't sure if Rafe or Thor had been the target. From what I understood, they'd been together on the porch—talking, just *talking*, I repeated to myself—and perhaps the person hadn't known whose solo cup had been whose. I hit a lot of dead ends. Benson suggested Rafe was to blame, but Thor was confident it wasn't him—and anyway, he wouldn't have drugged himself. No one knew anything, and most people thought it had been some kind of ill-advised prank. I extricated myself from those conversations before I totally lost my cool, and over the next several days returned my focus to the extremely confusing matter at hand.

After Sunday, Thor and I slept in his bed every night for a week. Just...slept. I would never have assumed he wanted me to keep coming back, but if you could have seen the ocular lashing Thor gave me Monday evening when I slinked uncertainly toward the door to my room—well, let's just say, I knew where I was expected to be.

We didn't talk about it and by the following weekend I was ready to crawl out of my skin. It had taken a bit of soul searching to re-route my brain—the brain that had thought it was straight—and to be frank, now that I had figured things out, I was pretty eager to dive into the hands-on experimenting phase of my newly discovered sexuality. Namely, I wanted to get my hands on the bullet body pressed head to toe against mine under the covers every night.

Thor stayed up quite a bit later than I did, and every night I tried my best to stay awake, to wait for him to come to bed in the hopes that something would happen, but my training schedule had my eyelids drooping by nine thirty. Without fail, when my alarm went off at five in the morning, a warm ball of Thor would be squashed tight against my side, happily snoozing away. In my entire life, I'd never slept better. I dunno what dumbass nineties comedian started the smear campaign against snuggling, but I'm here to tell you, it fucking rules. No matter what position I started in when I fell asleep, I'd wake up wrapped around Thor like he belonged in my arms. I didn't know if he wormed his way in on purpose, or we found our way toward each other in our sleep. Either way, it was so sweet, so addicting. I'd always been a morning person, but suddenly I found getting out of bed to be a huge challenge.

Sure, the bed was criminally comfortable, but I think it had more to do with the company. There was no way to describe a sleeping Thor besides "cute," except possibly "adorable." Perhaps even "irresistible." Leaving him in bed made me ache in a way I wasn't super comfortable examining yet.

Not much had changed besides us sleeping together. Again, just sleeping. In fact, I would have thought Thor had no interest in moving our friendship, relationship, whatever, beyond its current stage. He showed no interest in changing the status quo between us, except when I caught his eyes on me in the rare moments he thought I wasn't looking. The things I read in his eyes had me burning up. His gaze was on me when I cooked for us, when we ate. As we watched a movie, bowl of popcorn nestled on the couch between us.

There was intention in those big brown eyes, perhaps something you might not notice if you hadn't spent as much time watching them as I had. The looks said, plainly, that Thor wasn't waiting because he was nervous, or inexperienced, but waiting because he wanted to. Waiting because he liked where we were, and perhaps wanted to savor it. And waiting, maybe, because he liked to watch me squirm.

Friday night, after I'd cooked beef Wellington for dinner, I was trying to finish an outline for a paper because I had an away game in the morning. I looked up from my computer, and my eyes met Thor's across the room. He grinned, sliding his glasses up his nose, and then he took a long, slow sip from his wine glass, never moving his gaze from mine.

Oh yeah. He definitely enjoyed watching me squirm.

When I finally gave in and decided to go to bed, I was pent up as hell. I considered jerking off, but I didn't know how soon Thor would be coming in. What if he caught me? And why was that notion insanely hot? Fucking hell. I collapsed on the bed, pressing my pelvis against the mattress like I was trying to suffocate my dick. I couldn't deny the idea of being caught by Thor was an enticing one—but I still didn't *know*...ugh. I groaned, flopping onto my back and laying an arm across my eyes. Part of me thought this might be some weird battle of wills, and for some twisted reason, I loved it. And, if it was a battle of wills, I was determined to win.

When my alarm dinged at six, I expected to wake up to Thor passed out on the mattress beside me, sleeping like the dead, as usual. However, I opened my eyes and immediately startled. Thor was wide awake, propped up on one elbow to rest his head in his hand. Staring at me. His face had that open sort of look people with glasses got when they weren't wearing their glasses.

"Morning," I said, voice scratchy and hoarse from sleep.

Instead of answering, Thor nudged my shoulder till I laid on my back. He swung his leg over, straddling my thighs, looking at me like he was a cat and I was a canary he'd batted out of the air.

He chewed his bottom lip, considering me for a minute, and I didn't even dare breathe, or blink. His pretty eyes fluttered shut and he leaned down, pressing his lips to mine.

My body lit up like a Christmas tree. I was so ready. I tangled my fingers in his thick, dark hair and opened my mouth, hungry for his tongue. The taste of our morning breath aside, this was a kiss to end all kisses. Epic, murderous. Under the humming arousal unfurling through my sleepy limbs was the dim awareness of how different Thor felt in my arms, against my lips. Different from other bodies I had held, different from other mouths I had tasted. But all that math added up to the following: different clearly equaled superior. His lips were soft, and despite his clean-shaven face, the slight burn of stubble against my cheeks lit a fuse inside me, and I found myself ravenous to taste him everywhere.

Growing bolder, Thor nipped my bottom lip, tugging it between his teeth and pulling back till I moaned. He seemed to like that quite a bit, because he rolled his hips, grinding his rock-hard dick against my own. With both of us in boxers, there wasn't much left to the imagination. I grabbed his butt, squeezing it with both hands to pull him closer, to chase the friction he offered with each roll of his pelvis against mine. Our lips locked, tongues thrashing, and I didn't want this moment to end.

All at once though, Thor pulled back and rolled off me, panting. I made to pounce on him, but he kept me at bay with a firm palm on my chest. He shot me a lopsided grin. "You have to go," he said.

Go? No, obviously what I had to do was quit hockey and drop out of school so I could spend the rest of my life in this bed. "Huh?"

Thor pushed against me. "You told me your team bus leaves at seven."

"Finding it difficult to care," I told him, dodging his hand and lowering my lips to his neck.

Thor stretched and sighed, writhing against me as I covered his body with mine. He was playing with me, and maybe I was losing our game—but I had never been happier to lose. He arched his back, pushing up toward me all while saying. "Seriously, Cas? You have to go."

I groaned, pushing my forehead against his collarbone. "Fine."

Head spinning, I summoned what dignity I could—a challenge given the serious heat I was packing in my boxers—and rolled off the mattress.

Thor watched me go. I could feel his eyes on my back as I walked to the door and couldn't resist peeking back at him stretched out on the bed. Huge mistake. His eyes were hooded, a bit dazed, his hair an absolute disaster, and the generous bulge in his boxer briefs drew my eyes like a magnet.

"Go," he said, but he pushed his hips up a bit. Fucker. He scooted back, propping himself on his elbows. "I'll see you tonight?"

"Fuck," I breathed. "Yes."

———

## THOR

When I heard the front door slam behind Cas, I broke out all over in shaky giggles. What just happened? Never, never had I done that before, been like that, felt like that. Teasing Cas was so easy, and fun, and for some reason he seemed to really, *really* like it.

And I loved it. Gods, he was so cute all week, flustered and pent up. Something about seeing the want in Cas's eyes, so clear to me now, allowed me to locate some internal well of confidence I hadn't known I possessed. For the first few days, I waited for his restraint to crack, for him to kiss me—but eventually it became clear that he wasn't going to, and then I really just wanted to see how riled up I could get him. Sometime yesterday, I decided it was time for me to make the first move. When I'd looked at him before he went to bed last night, he'd made a soft little noise, somewhere between a sigh and a whine —and the best part was, I didn't think he even realized he'd made it.

While I gathered Cas had far more sexual experience than I did, something about this relationship between us seemed fragile and delicate, something that required perhaps a more precise, careful hand. A hand like mine. And, to be honest, being in charge thrilled me.

More than I thought it would.

It was like Cas had danced joyfully into the little trap I had set for him, beyond happy to be caught. I was happy too, happier than I could ever remember being. Sleeping in the same bed with him was everything. I'd never shared a bed before—not like *that* anyway. Waking up being held, surrounded by the smell of him and the warmth of his skin was absolute heaven. Cas was so sweet, gentle, and solid at the same time, but I could tell he was ten seconds away from exploding and jumping my bones like an animal.

Part of me felt a little guilty sending him off with such a bad case of blue balls, but the much, much larger part of me couldn't wait for him to get home after his game, dripping with sweat and adrenaline.

I wondered what he'd do when he came home. I wondered in bed, lounging and daydreaming. I wondered in the shower, till the hot water ran out. Then I snapped a pic of myself wearing just a towel and sent it to Cas.

After that though, I had to take a break from wondering. Cas would be home tonight, and I had other stuff I had to deal with in the meantime.

Once I'd recovered from my own hangover, I'd been relieved to hear that Rafe was alright. Unfortunately, he seemed to have suffered worse—perhaps because he hadn't had anyone to watch out for him. I seethed with guilt that I hadn't realized something was wrong until it was too late. Rafe was missing a whole day in his memory, just like Leda.

Cassian had been correct. Someone was targeting shifters. But why? And why were both Rafe and Leda released unharmed, unlike the victims that had been found by the police?

Leda's examination of the tissue samples she'd harvested from the corpses in the morgue, and the necropsy she'd performed on the dead swan, had not yielded a lot of answers. Or any, really. So, without Cas to occupy my time, I returned to the rare manuscript library on campus. Science wasn't getting us there, so maybe history would.

Part of the problem was knowing what to look for. Some of the old stories were obvious allusions to shifters, like those of werewolves and selkies. Others, however, you had to dig a bit deeper, comb the lore for the story that truly hid beneath the words. Some of the books in here were so fragile, it was impossible to check them out—the oldest volumes carefully monitored by the curator of the collection. In order to view them, I had to book time in the climate-controlled archival study room, reserving the texts in advance by appointment. It was a real headache. I spent a few hours in the stacks of the larger sections of the library, coming up with a list of titles I could check out, and ones that I could make an appointment to peruse later.

By the time noon rolled around, I had a stack of books almost as tall as I was and a crick in my neck that I couldn't shake. However, when I left the library, fishing in my pocket for my phone, I grinned when I realized I had a new message, a reply to the pic I'd sent to Cas. I shifted the books in my arms so I could read it.

C*as: Are you trying to kill me??*

A nd it was followed by several sweaty face emojis. When I got home and set the books on the coffee table, I tried to leaf through them, but all I could think about was Cas. By the time he got home, he would have had quite a long day, so I thought it might be nice for him to come home to a meal he didn't have to assemble for once.

Obviously, he was the superior cook, but I wanted to do

something for him. Plus, these days, the fridge was always stocked with ingredients. I was certain I could figure something out. I set about preparing what I thought was a simple meal: roast chicken and vegetables. By the time I loaded the pan into the oven, the kitchen looked like a bomb had gone off. After getting it scrubbed down, I still had some time to kill, so I spread my new books out around me on the sofa and got to work. The first phase was always a preliminary perusal; before I wasted too much time on each volume, I had to figure out if they were the kind of books that would have worth in my search.

Which was especially challenging when I didn't even know what I was looking for yet. I must have lost track of time, because all of a sudden, the door banged open and scared the daylights out of me.

"Thor? You home?" Cas said, before turning to find me sitting flabbergasted on the sofa, frozen with my pen between my teeth.

I frowned around my pen. He sounded upset. Taking the writing implement from my mouth I said, "Hey. Did you guys lose?"

"Yes," he snapped. "Wait. No. I don't know. Whatever. What's burning?"

My dinner! I raced around the kitchen island and pulled open the oven door, now billowing smoke. The detectors blared, and I grabbed a stool, hauling it to the center of the room so I could climb up and bonk the smoke detector with my broom handle.

"What on earth are you doing?"

"Cooking," I said, exasperated. Smoke filled the apartment and I stood grumpily on the stool, clutching my broom.

Cas opened the windows to let the smoke dissipate before coming back to stand in front of my perch. "Come down from there," said Cas, offering up a hand. "We need to talk."

I hopped down from the stool and set the broom on its hook.

Cas steered me into the living room. "Sit," he said.

I sat. This seemed serious. Cas immediately began pacing in front of me. "Well?" I asked, anxious. Had I screwed this up already, somehow?

"I know you don't like to talk about stuff," he said. "But we have to."

"Okay. Why are you so upset?"

Cas froze, turned toward me for a moment, and then exploded. "I just fucking came out to the entire varsity hockey team!"

He stared at me, expectant, but I wasn't sure what to say. "Uh...congrats?"

"Congrats!?" He looked furious, and I truly had no idea what had him so riled up. "Thor, I just came out to a bunch of dudes, my coaches, and the bus driver and I don't even know..." he trailed away, distraught.

"Know what?"

"Know what we are! Or what the hell we're doing. What are we?"

"Oh."

"Yes, 'oh.'" He crossed his arms over his chest, waiting.

My stomach did an anxious sort of flip flop, and I wished we could go back to our flirty little game instead of discussing this. "Um..."

"Well?" He prompted.

I stood up and walked closer. "What would you like us to be?"

Cas let out a little snort, but his gaze softened a bit. "I am...crazy about you," he said.

I felt like someone had filled me with boiling water. "Yeah?"

"*Yes*," he said. "You fucking idiot. I thought I was straight until I first laid eyes on you."

I certainly grinned at him like an idiot, but I could tell he was still agitated.

"I've been twisted up in knots for weeks, and then we start sleeping together, you never say anything—then, you *kiss* me!"

"I thought it was a pretty good kiss," I said, looking at the floor.

Cas put two fingers under my chin, pushing my head up to face him. "It was an amazing kiss," he corrected. "Amazing."

More smiles, while I allowed myself to preen a little bit under the intensity of his stare and the earnestness of his praise.

"So," he said. "What are we?"

"Boyfriends?" I said it like a question.

"Yes."

"Exclusive boyfriends?"

"What—Jesus. Fucking *yes.*"

"Okay."

"Okay."

We stared at each other for a while. His eyes flicked from mine down to my lips and I had about half a breath before Cas dove for me, grabbed me by the waist and full-on smashed our lips together. I may or may not have let out an embarrassing little yip, but that didn't seem to bother Cas any. He forced his tongue between my lips, licking into my mouth and kissing hard enough to bruise. As I'd imagined, he was hot and sweaty from the game, and the smell of him had my legs trembling below me. He kissed down my neck. Biting and teasing, his big hands on my hips pushing me toward the sofa. "Wait—wait," I gasped. "What about dinner?"

Panting, Cas glanced over my shoulder toward the open oven, still spewing smoke, and the charred lump within. "Let's order takeout."

# 12



"You okay, man? You look distracted."

I had arrived at the bus leaving for the game that morning with two minutes to spare, flustered and disoriented from my morning with Thor.

We'd kissed. *Kissed.* I had woken up in bed with a dude and we'd kissed. And I had fucking loved it. I couldn't wait to get home and...I went tingly all over. What was going to happen when I got home?

So—that kind of stuff rattled around in my brain all morning as we drove hours to the game. The bus ride seemed endless, especially with the fidgety restless energy coursing through me. Every time I thought too hard about how I'd woken up...well, suffice to say, I was glad to finally arrive at Carfield University and burn some of it off.

The game had been—fine? I wasn't lying when I told Thor I barely remembered it, especially because when I settled back onto the bus and dug my phone out of my bag there was pic waiting for me, a pic that told the captain of my brain ship to take the night off and let my dick be in charge of running things.

It was a selfie of Thor, damp hair clinging to his forehead, a towel wrapped around his tiny waist. His hand rested on the knot of the towel like he was about to rip it off. He wore a shit-eating grin, and water from the shower still beaded on his chest.

*Fuck, fuck, fuck.* A grin pulled over my face and I tapped out a quick reply.

"I know that look!" Benson crowed. "Rhodes just got nudes!"

Before I could even protest, he'd snatched the phone out of my hand.

"Bro," he said, staring at the picture. "What the fuck is this?"

A weird sort of calm washed over me and I held out my hand for the phone. "I told you I was talking to someone."

"Yeah but—" he looked scandalized and dropped the phone back into my lap, like the pic was going to give him cooties. "Dude!"

"What's going on?" Some of the other guys turned toward us.

"Perfect, let's get more people involved," I muttered.

"Rhodes is looking at gay porn!"

That got everyone's attention.

"I am *not*," I said. My cheeks grew hot and I was sure I looked guilty as sin. Everyone stared. I had to say *something;* it wasn't the "gay" that bothered me so much as the "porn." Who looked at porn on a bus full of people? "My..." my what, exactly? I cleared my throat, face burning. "It's not porn. The guy I'm talking to just sent me a pic."

"A dick pic?"

"No!" I squeaked, as good as a confession.

The rest of the tortuous bus ride passed much the same,

everyone grilling me, with no regard for my privacy, or Thor's —even some guys on the team that I knew were out. By the time the bus pulled in at school, I was jumpy, confused, and angry. Everyone on the team knew I was getting spicy pics from dudes, and they had all decided for themselves what that meant about me. Which, to be honest, would have been fine— but I didn't even know what it meant, not really. And for some reason, that made me furious.

Smash cut to me bursting into the apartment, scaring the crap out of Thor, who was well into doing his very best to burn down the building.

And where were we now? Furiously dry humping and making out on the couch. It had been quite a day.

I sucked on Thor's neck, holding him in place while I ground against him, relishing the little noises coming from his mouth.

"The pic was really hot," I mumbled against his throat, feeling him swallow.

"Yeah?"

I locked my lips around his Adam's apple, sucking it, Thor's resulting moan vibrating against my tongue. "Yeah."

Pulling back, loving the disheveled, startled look on Thor's face, I whipped off my sweaty jersey, tossing it to the side. Thor feasted his eyes hungrily, and I tugged impatiently at the bottom hem of his shirt. He slipped out of his cardigan, and I gently removed his glasses and set them on the table. With quite a lot of ungainly grappling, we got out of our jeans, leaving us in just our underwear, finally, *finally* getting back to what Thor had started this morning.

I wanted him under me, I wanted to push my dick up against his and rub off on him. The idea of hard hot flesh and the slight burn of soft cotton between us had taken root in my brain this morning and driven me to distraction all day. So, I pushed Thor onto his back, grabbing his thighs, tracing my pinky down the inside of his leg to the bottom hem of his boxers, lingering there, feeling his skin and marveling how silky it was, dusted with dark hair. Peeking up at Thor, I watched the crown of his head fall back to the sofa cushions, briefly before he shot up like he'd been electrocuted.

"Wait, wait—" said Thor. "We can't—the books, some of them are first editio—*ohh.*"

I grinned against his pec, as I'd just flicked my tongue over his nipple, feeling it pebble as I latched my lips around it, sucking hard. Thor tangled his fingers in my hair and gasped, falling back onto his precious books, his legs splaying weakly open for me to slot between them, to make room for me to rut desperately against his hot cock.

I peppered kisses all over his torso, his skin hot enough to feel fevered beneath my lips, but I needed his mouth again. The faster I moved my hips, thrusting and grinding, the harsher Thor's breathing became—sharp, tortured little pants that I drank down one by one. His hands fell away from my hair and a few heartbeats later I heard a rip, and a clatter, as books went flying to the floor. Thor didn't seem concerned anymore, and his kiss was greedy when our mouths connected again. I rolled myself up, pulling him into my lap, sweaty and sticky and not even caring because Thor pushed his nose against my neck and inhaled, deep and long, then licked the salt from the skin of my collar bone. He breathed in the scent of my body like he was huffing some kind of drug, humping and grinding furiously against me like what he smelled on me really did it for him. I was *not* about to complain.

Something about his eagerness made me bold, and I plunged my hands down the waistband of his boxers to paw at his ass, small but tight and firm, each cheek round and warm and the perfect shape for me to grab, to knead, to spread, to—

A little whimper from where our mouths joined turned into a desperate plea as Thor jerked away. "Wait—wait."

I hadn't realized I'd shut my eyes, and a pulsing warmth, a wet heat pooled between us and before I could process what happened, Thor wrenched his body away, scrambling off the couch, trying to turn from me. *Oh.*

The blush on his body went from his navel to the roots of his hair. "Uh—I—" he took a step away, jerky and uncomfortable.

I hated that he was upset. I hated that he was pulling away from me, so I shot my hand out and seized his wrist. "Wait."

He tried to tug his hand free, so I grabbed his hip instead.

"Where do you think you're going?"

Thor looked everywhere but at my face. "Shower," he mumbled. "Then, probably, I don't know. Changing my name and emigrating."

I laid both hands on his waist, positioning him to stand between my spread thighs. "Stop," I said. "Look at me."

He glanced down at me, then away again.

"Don't be embarrassed. It's kinda...sexy."

"Stop," he said, rolling his eyes at me. He covered his face with his hands.

"I mean it." When Thor peeked out between his fingers, I locked my eyes on his, dipping my thumb under his waistband, swiping it through the sticky moisture I found there. Hell. I sucked my lip between my teeth before whispering. "I've never made a guy come before."

A teeny, tiny smile tugged at the corners of Thor's kiss-bruised mouth, and I could feel my own blush rising. He leaned down, brushing his lips over mine. He dropped gracefully to his knees on the floor between my legs.

"Me neither," he said, and yanked down my boxers.

Oh *fuck.* Before I had time to react, Thor wrapped his beautiful lips around the head of my cock, swirling his tongue around it, tasting it, tasting *me.* I groaned, head falling back to the couch cushions as Thor sucked my entire brain out through my dick. He worked me like a pro. I had always suspected that people with dicks, who liked dick, were probably the best at giving head and I was having that theory confirmed tenfold.

My hips lifted off the couch cushions, trying to fuck deeper into his sweet, hot mouth. I wrapped my fingers in his hair, tugging against his scalp, and the slutty little moan he gave almost sent me over the edge.

It was a needy sound, a private sound, a sound just for me and him and what we were doing here. Thor was always so controlled, so quiet and buckled down, straight-laced. But the uptight façade hid a wild, electric energy that coursed through his veins, a thunderous power like that of his namesake. Thor might be the one on his knees, but he was the god, and me the supplicant, utterly undone by his power. My little Thunder God, I thought—cupping his cheek as he looked at me from below his thick lashes, eyes dark, possessive, and stormy. He would be furious if I called him that, which somehow turned me on even more. I turned my head to the side, Thor's eyes too arresting to be stared at for long—like an eclipse.

Then, I almost launched up onto the ceiling because Thor had drawn me deep into the back of his throat, gagging himself eagerly and swallowing around the head of my cock. His hands fell to my hips, pulling and squeezing, encouraging me deep, deep, *deeper,* until I exploded in his mouth and he sucked me dry.

"*Baby,*" I croaked, my voice hoarse and small as I wilted back into the sofa cushions, shaking from head to scrunched-up toes. I'd never called anyone "baby" before, but then, I'd never been transported to another plane of existence by a blow job before, so I supposed it was a day of firsts. Thor slithered up to join me on the sofa, curling into my side, burying his face in my neck. I wrapped my arms around him, squeezing tight.

When our heartbeats had returned to normal, I said, "So, about that shower?"

———

## THOR

Part of me wanted to flee to the shower as fast as I could, but the other part of me wanted to stay in Cas's lap with my nose buried in the little spot beside his ear. But, the sticky, quickly congealing problem in the front of my shorts would not be denied, so I kissed the side of his neck and said, "Me first."

Cas took my face in one hand as I drew away, searching my eyes for some reason I wanted to shower alone, but ultimately deciding not to question it. While I had clearly hidden it expertly, I was still pretty embarrassed and needed some time to process my thoughts and steam the shame from my pores.

As I stood, legs still a bit shaky, and turned toward the hallway, Cas let out an embarrassed little chuckle. "Wait—you've got something—" he grabbed for my hip.

I tried to look over my own shoulder down my own back, where I realized a torn page from one of my library books had adhered. "Oh my God," I said, face flaming as I spun in a circle like a dog chasing his tail.

Cas took pity on me and unstuck the old, yellowing page, handing it to me with a smile. "Here."

"Chandler is going to *eviscerate* me," I said, turning the page over in my hands.

"Who?"

But I wasn't listening. My eyes had landed on a picture at the top of the page, one of those horrendous medieval illustrations that could depict anything from a cat to a demon to a baby. In this case, it was a cluster of some vaguely lupine creatures, heads at unnatural angles, mouths open, and instead of paws, they had human hands.

Beneath it was a simple title. "The Ferals of Brackenwood."

"Thor?"

I jumped. Cassian stood, moving to my side to see what had me so transfixed. "I think I found something," I said. "What book did this come from? Did you see—"

Cas tugged the page out of my hand. I grabbed for it, but he held me at bay. "Shower first, then dinner. *Then* research."

"But—"

"*Go.*" He nudged me in the direction of the hallway.

"Don't lose that page," I called over my shoulder.

After showering in record time, I dressed and rushed back to the living room. Cas had already moved into the bathroom to take his own shower, so I started organizing the stacks of books, blushing as I lifted them gingerly from where they'd been dumped on the floor earlier. I spread them out, trying to figure out which one the page with the drawing had come from.

The archivist at the library would surely have my hide if I couldn't get these books fixed up before I returned them, adding another edge to the desperation of my search.

By the time Cas came out of the shower, I had found the torn place in the binding and matched it to the page. I was engrossed in the tale.

"Did you order food?"

"Hmm?" I answered, only half hearing him.

"Did you order dinner?"

"Sure," I said absently, not moving my eyes from the page.

A few moments passed in silence, before two fingers pressed below my chin, tilting my head up. "Thor."

I blinked in surprise.

"Focus."

"Okay," I said, momentarily arrested by Cas's eyes, his freckles, and the slight smirk on his face.

"You didn't order food, did you?"

I frowned. "No, not yet—why?"

Cas sighed and pulled out his phone, tapping away to pick something for delivery. "When this pizza gets here, you're putting those books away," he said.

"Oh, am I?"

Cas set his phone on the counter, bracketing me with his arms and leaning in so close I could count his eyelashes.

I could feel the heat radiating off his body from the shower, and I closed my eyes, expecting a kiss but instead feeling his teeth graze my jaw. "Go ahead," he whispered in my ear. "You have about half an hour."

Despite the fact that the temperature of the room seemed to have risen ten degrees with his body so close, I spun in his hold to face the counter, where I'd spread out a few of the texts. "I actually do think I have something here," I said, dragging my finger along one of the pages.

"From the page that was stuck to your ass?"

"Yes," I said. "Now, hush."

Cas pressed his smile into my shoulder before resting his chin on it, peering over it to get a glimpse at the book, waiting for me to go on.

"So, this is an old story—about twelfth century," I said. "There was a small village of people who had to carve out a life in a dangerous area of a forest. Very unforgiving terrain."

Cas remained quiet, his breath ghosting along the side of my neck.

"There was a family of warriors," I went on. "They protected the village. It says here they had magic animal pelts and when they wore the skins they transformed. They were able to fight harder, hunt better—basically, they became animals."

"Sounds fishy," said Cas.

"Yes, it sounds like the kind of thing that, reading between the lines, meant a shifter family could have lived in the village. There're stories like this scattered throughout history. Of course, so many of them are fake, but here—" I pointed to a spot on the next page, and Cas read over my shoulder. The passage went on to explain that as the village grew more secure, and more prosperous, the people began to fear their warriors and their magic pelts. So, when the village had been safe long enough for the people to build their own sturdy walls, they cast the family of warriors out into the untamed forests. Left them only their magic pelts and burned their huts to ash.

"The legend," I finished excitedly, "was that since the warriors had only their magic pelts and no other clothes, weapons, or belongings, they were forced to wear the animal furs for so long they eventually lost the ability to remove them."

"Okay," said Cas slowly. "But what does that have to do with..."

"Well, I'm not sure yet, but with a little more reasearmmmph!"

Cas had cut me off with a deep kiss. When he broke away, he said, "Tomorrow."

"Or after dinner?"

"Tomorrow."

I sulked until the food arrived and over pizza, I brought up something that had been weighing on me. "Do you still want to come to my family's place for Thanksgiving?"

Cas chewed thoughtfully. "Why wouldn't I?"

"Now that we're together, isn't it a bit serious?"

"It wasn't serious before?"

"We were just friends before."

"Were we though?" he nudged me with his elbow.

To buy myself a minute, I took another bite. "No, I

suppose we weren't." I didn't know how to disinvite him from Thanksgiving without making it a big thing. To be honest, I couldn't even explain fully to myself why I was reluctant for him to come. For some reason, Cas had decided he liked me, but if he saw me through my parents' eyes...

"Is everything okay?"

"Y-yes," I stammered.

"Do you not want me to come?"

Well, shit. "Of course, I want you to come."

"Good," said Cas, but he frowned. "Then what's the problem?"

"Well, I mean. You met my dad. He's kind of—"

"A jackass?"

"I was going to say, 'a lot,' but yeah, we can go with yours."

"Okay, he's a lot. So what?"

"So, the rest of the family is like him too. And they're a little...old fashioned." I fiddled with my pizza crust. "They might say something weird, or use like, old, dated language. Some of our traditions are a little out there."

"You don't say," said Cas mildly, and I knew he was thinking that anything would seem normal compared to the ability to turn spontaneously into an animal.

"I just don't want you to get upset if they say something...wrong."

Cas set down his plate and grabbed my hand. "Dealing with each other's weird families is what boyfriends do, though, right?"

I laughed. "How would you know? You've never had a boyfriend before."

"True," he replied, grinning. He squinted at me. "You're sure that's it?"

"Yeah," I said, eyes back on my own plate. "Just don't want you to get freaked out by them, or..."

"Or?"

"This."

He shrugged. "We already live together," he reminded me. "Things already feel pretty serious to me."

I didn't know how he could just say that kind of stuff, so offhand, but nevertheless his words had me warm all over. Truth was, weird traditions aside, I was eager to show Cas off. Maybe Thanksgiving wouldn't be so bad.

I cleaned up after dinner, including the charred mess in the oven. I felt Cas's eyes on me as I scraped the pan into the garbage. "What?" I asked, without turning around.

"You tried to cook for me."

"So?"

"I dunno." He paused. "It's nice."

After dinner, Cas allowed me to return to my books, for which I was grateful, because there was a weird energy between us that I didn't know what to do with. We had sort of done all of this backward, and I didn't think either of us knew what to expect when we went to bed.

For once, I decided to turn in early and give Cas some space. I brushed my teeth, peed, went through my usual evening routine, before pulling out my phone to shoot Leda a text.

T*hor: I think I have something*

L*eda: I'm listening*

. . .

**T**hor: *Can you determine anything about the parents of any of the victims? Including the bird.*

**L**eda: *Why?*

**T**hor: *Call it a hunch. I'll explain tomorrow.*

**L**eda: *K*

**A**nyone else and I'd think the 'k' was a huge screw you, but Leda's brain was probably already whirring, wondering what made me ask that question.

As I pulled back the covers to get into bed, I had a last-minute thought and yanked off my t-shirt and boxers, climbing in between the sheets totally naked. I usually slept nude, and had only been wearing any kind of pajamas the past week because I had company. Well, said company certainly had no objections to my body, and I got a little thrill thinking about how Cas would react. After embarrassing myself earlier, my confidence had taken a serious hit, and part of me wanted to regain the power I'd seemed to wield over Cas this past week.

I noodled around on my phone, waiting for him. After what seemed like forever, Cas shuffled in through the door. Seeing him had my heart beat a little faster, and the shy look on his face had me feeling rather ballsy.

"What are you doing?" I asked him innocently.

He startled. "I was coming to bed," he stammered. "Did you not want—"

"Oh, no. I do. But you're a little overdressed, yeah?"

Cas had on plaid flannel pants and a tight Henley. He raised his eyebrows. "Oh?"

I lifted the edge of the blanket like I was peeking down at myself, then let it fall. "Yeah, I think so."

"Shit," he muttered under his breath, nearly tripping over himself to get naked. Cas paused with his thumbs tucked into the waistband of his boxers. "Hold on," he blurted. "Are we—do you wanna have sex?"

I shivered. So much had happened already today and I certainly wasn't ready for *that*. By the look on Cas's face, he wasn't either. However, I did love to tease him, so I frowned, pretending to consider. "Nah," I said, after a minute. I set my glasses on the bedside table and clicked off the lamp, plunging us into darkness before he could fully disrobe. "Not yet."

He sighed, sounding equal parts relieved and disappointed —exactly what I was going for. When Cas got in between the sheets I rolled back toward him. I could feel his warm breath on my cheek seconds before he brushed his lips against mine. The room was dark, and knowing Cas was naked, inches away, and I could touch him, was thrilling. I trailed my fingers down his side, feeling him shiver, and let my hand rest on the firm muscles of his waist. "Call me baby again," I whispered against his mouth.

"Goodnight," he breathed, after another soft kiss. "Baby."

# 13

That first night, Thor and I traded kisses until we fell asleep. In fact, I think I drifted off mid-smooch. It shocked me how easy it was with him—like, had we always been doing this? Every time I remembered it had only been a matter of hours since we decided to be "together" officially, it surprised me. Him snuggled up against me, every inch of his warm, soft skin pressed to mine, was the most natural thing in the world.

I had Sunday off, and it had been wonderful going to bed knowing I didn't have to set an alarm. So, when my eyes drifted open at ten thirty a.m., I had no designs on getting out of bed. Thor remained dead to the world, so I rolled onto my side to watch him sleep. Part of me was tempted to put his glasses back on his face, because they suited him so well and I thought they were so cute. His thin, toned body was on display for me to feast my eyes on, so I propped myself up on one elbow to enjoy. Thor often drowned in fabric, his big baggy cardigans concealing the actual shape of his body, and with his slim frame, I'd originally thought him no more than a twig.

I have since adjusted my thinking. Beneath my exploring fingertips was a surprising topography of toned muscle and soft flesh, and I planned to chart it all. Aside from the pure hedonistic enjoyment I felt as I touched him, I was also curious, and a little intimidated. This was my very first real-life naked male specimen.

Would it be weird if I snuck a peek at his dick?

I argued silently with myself for a bit. Sure, I didn't have express permission to ogle him in his sleep. On the other hand, though, Thor had insisted we sleep au naturale, so maybe permission was implied?

Besides, I absolutely had to do some dick recon. After yesterday, when Thor and his mouth had fully undone me, I was at a disadvantage. He'd seen quite a bit more of me than I had of him. Throughout my years spent in locker rooms, I'd glimpsed a fair number of dicks, but I hadn't *look* looked. The knee-jerk reaction to immediately avert one's eyes at the slightest glimpse ran deep.

I had to assume Thor would show me his dick eventually, but I was nervous about reacting wrong or making him feel weird. I kind of wanted the space to react to my first IRL dick experience in private.

The thin white fabric of the sheet rucked up around Thor's waist as he lay sprawled on his back. All I had to do was lift it. I let a long, slow breath hiss out between my teeth and grabbed the edge of the sheet with shaking fingers.

To keep from legitimately gasping, I slapped my free hand over my mouth. Thor's cock was fucking enormous. Even soft. Christ. Obviously, I'd felt it pushing up against me on more than one occasion now, so I knew it was no small organ, but feeling and seeing were two very different things. I had not expected him to be this hung.

And he was uncut. That was interesting. A pleasant sort of nerves skittered across my skin, and I wanted to touch. Bad. I wanted to wrap my hand around his shaft and stroke it to full mast, feel it swell under my fingers, see the head poke out from its little sheath of skin, dripping precum, begging for affection. I wanted to see that monster dick hard and proud, framed by the deep vee of Thor's narrow hips.

He had to wake up. Now. I let the sheet fall and shook him by the shoulder. "Hey."

"*Unnf.*"

"Hey," I said again. I shook him harder, and when that didn't work, covered his face with kisses, letting my lips linger at the corners of his eyes, the tip of his nose.

Thor opened one eye. "What?"

"Your dick is huge," I blurted.

"Huh?" He was so confused, clearly still half asleep, hair mussed and adorable. He scooted up against the pillows, rubbing sleep from his eyes.

I could feel the blush coming to my cheeks, my skin searing.

"What? My dick—what?" He looked down at himself, then back up at me, a slow grin breaking over his sleepy mouth. "Did you look?"

"Maybe."

Thor laughed loud and bright. Then he seized the blanket and ripped it off the bed like a magician doing a trick, revealing us both to the morning sunlight streaming in through the windows.

It was the perfect Sunday. Thor and I lazed in bed, touching and kissing, exploring the novelty of each other's skin, and didn't get dressed until three when we went out for an afternoon coffee and I suppose, our first actual date.

We sat in the café, sipping coffee and making googly eyes at each other. I had a lot of studying to do, which I suspected might be next to impossible with such a distraction, so I stayed at the café to do some work while Thor went to meet Leda at the lab. He had some theories based on what he'd found in his ancient books of fairy tales, and was eager to compare notes with Leda.

I had three mid-terms and one last hockey practice before Thanksgiving break, when I'd be going home with Thor to meet his family. I felt a twinge of unease. It hadn't seemed like a huge deal until Thor had pointed it out. He was obviously nervous too, or he wouldn't have brought it up.

After meeting his dad, however briefly, I got the sense that Thor didn't have the easiest relationship with his family. Lysander seemed like a judgmental jerk, all told, and Thor had said his family was old-fashioned, so maybe he was nervous about bringing home a boyfriend?

That didn't exactly track, though. When he'd caught me cooking that morning, Lysander had clearly made some assumptions about my relationship with his son, and seemed most shocked that Thor could...what, find an attractive partner? I scowled at the thought.

Thor was obviously kind of loner by nature, and shy—but the side of him I was seeing lately was confident and sexy. I felt kind of warm thinking maybe I brought that out in him.

With a massive effort, I returned my focus to my books. I had to ace my exams, or I'd be even more of a nervous wreck, and I really, really wanted to make a good impression on Thor's family.

I supposed I was lucky Thor had his own studies, the case, and his writing to occupy him, because he respected my need to study and offered minimal distraction over the next few days. Minimal, however, did not mean nonexistent. Thor was still him, still my Thunder God, with his arresting eyes and shy smile that spoke of dirty intentions. He was still cute and gorgeous and plastered against my body in bed at night. Both of us had exams to worry about, which led to no time for fooling around since our action-packed Saturday and after-glow-y Sunday morning. I had to really, *really* talk myself into getting out of bed, disentangling myself from the press of gangly limbs to get the gym before my first exam on Monday. And Tuesday. And Wednesday.

Finally, though, exams were over. I knew I'd done well, so I finally let myself relax. I got to the locker room in time for the final practice before our break. I had my earbuds in, so I missed the sound of some of my teammates coming in. Under all of the noise I heard my name, and shoved a hand in my pocket to pause my music.

"...he's gonna hear you," one of the guys was saying.

"So what?" That was Benson. I gave no indication of stopping the music, my heart beating a little faster. "I'm just saying I'm still shook that Rhodes is queer."

Okay, fuck this. I straightened up and pulled out my earbuds. "I'm pretty shook over it too, dude."

The startled look on all their faces was pretty satisfying, but Benson wasted no time before hitching a sneer in its place. "I'm more shook that if you were picking dicks to suck, you'd pick that one."

Boiling, I took an aggressive step forward. "You got something to say?"

He threw up his hands. "Just that Thor Ambrose is fucking weird. And he's a pretentious shit."

"He absolutely is not."

My voice had taken on a low, deadly quality, but Benson laughed. "Sure, man, whatever. I've had classes with the guy. He's so stuck on himself. That's why I slipped shit in his drink at the party—take him down a peg. I was hoping he'd embar-rass the shit out of himself, but you carried him out of the party before he could."

His words took a second to penetrate my brain. "Hold

on," I said, certain I had to have misunderstood. "You did *what*?"

"Oh, come on, chill."

"*Chill*?" I echoed, choking on the word. My hands balled into fists at my sides.

Benson was already turning away, like fucking drugging someone was no big deal. "You should thank me. Did you fuck him that night? Probably made it easie—"

*Slam.* Someone sank their fist into the side of Benson's smug face and he staggered into the lockers. One bewildered second later, the pain rocketing up my knuckles told me it had been me.

Benson hopped up swinging. "What the fuck, man?"

I grabbed him by the collar of his shirt and pushed him back into the lockers as hard as I could. We grappled for a minute, and the other guys looked on uncertainly. Benson twisted away and hit me with mean right hook—and I saw red.

It was like time skipped and suddenly I knelt on his chest, drilling him with my fists. "You—ever—*ever* pull shit like that again, on anyone, and I'll personally make sure you end up in jail."

"Bro—" he tried to shield his face with his hands, his voice thick with blood spurting from his nose and a split lip.

"Don't," I said, seizing the collar of his shirt again. "I'm not your bro, asshole. The only reason you're not fucking road rash already is because Thor didn't want anyone to get in trouble. He didn't tell me what happened. So, fuck whatever it is you think you know about him. And if you come near him again, I'll fucking kill you."

I stood, straightening my shirt. Blood pounded in my ears, and the silence in the locker room crashed down, sudden, deafening. I turned and left. I was so shaken up I didn't even bring my stuff. I'd never skipped a practice, but I sure as hell wasn't going out on the ice after that.

By the time I got home I was still seething, but the adrenaline had worn off, and I could still feel the impact reverberating from my knuckles through the bones of my wrists, up my forearms. I glanced down at my hands, surprised to see them raw and bleeding. My eye had swollen too, and I felt a bit embarrassed. I'd gotten into scraps on the ice before, naturally, but nothing like this. I'd never gotten into a fight where I'd really wanted to *hurt* someone.

I opened the door to the apartment to see Thor curled up on his customary chair, reading. The fist clenched around my heart relaxed a bit, but his face read bald shock when he looked up at me. He set his book aside and stood. "What the hell happened to you? Did you skip practice?"

Mutely, I crossed the room and pulled him into a tight hug. I folded around Thor's smaller body and kissed the top of his head.

"What happened?" He asked, voice muffled in the front of my shirt.

"I found out who drugged you," I said.

"Oh."

I squeezed him so tight I was kind of afraid of hurting him. "Why didn't you tell me?"

"It's *humiliating*," he said. "And I didn't want it to be a big thing."

"But it is a big thing. A huge thing. Benson should be expelled. He should be in jail."

He shook his head against my chest and I sighed. Thor pulled back to look at me, pushing his glasses up his nose after I'd knocked them askew. He lifted his hand to touch the bruise I could now feel forming around my eye. "It's a big thing now," he said. "You'll have a black eye when you meet my family."

"Shit." I hadn't thought of that. Not that it would have stopped me. All I had to do was picture Benson's smug face as he admitted to committing a felony like it was just a harmless prank. "I'm sorry."

"It's okay," Thor said, but I could tell it wasn't. "I just don't want you to be hurt. And I can fight my own battles."

I seized his hand and kissed his palm. "I'm fine," I said. "And I know you can. But if someone hurts you, I'm going to want to kick their ass."

He gave me a little smile. "I guess that black eye is kind of hot."

———

## THOR

Leda and I met in the lab. She had been studying the grotesque dead bird that Cas and I had found, looking for answers that would help us figure out who these people were.

She had been able to perform a full necropsy on the dead swan, and taken a proverbial buttload of samples.

"Cause of death?" I asked her, leaning over her shoulder to look at the computer screen.

"Look at these markers," she said, indicating a few places on the chart.

"Starvation?"

Leda nodded, looking troubled. "The digestive tract was… irregular. One thing I'm happy to confirm," she said, though her tone was grim. "This bird was never human. It wasn't a shifter."

There was something she wasn't saying, though. We'd already confirmed the bird had no human parents—or so I'd thought. But that didn't explain its human ear, or foot. I looked at Leda, who chewed her lip, uncharacteristically nervous. "...but?"

"I took your suggestion, and pulled the DNA of the swan. I don't have access to any law enforcement databases, but there are certain things I can tell by comparing the workup to other samples I have already here."

"And?"

"And I have identified one of the swan's parents." She looked at me, miserable. "It's me."

My stomach lurched as Leda pulled up two sets of results. She pointed to the left-hand side. "This is a workup of the swan's DNA, compared to a sample from myself drawn from my *fauna*. This side I tested from the foot, and compared to my human DNA."

Leda looked ill. "Who's the father?" I asked, dreading the answer. She replaced her figures with another workup. There weren't as many markers highlighted to compare, but the number and sequencing were similar. "The father, it appears, was fully avian."

I sat heavily on a stool. "Jesus Christ."

"With electrophoresis I was able to work up the reptilian John Doe's DNA, but we have nothing to compare it to."

"Yes, we do," I said anxiously. "Call Rafe. We can compare it with Rafe's blood."

Leda narrowed her eyes. "You suspect something."

"It's a hunch," I said. "But...your missing day. Rafe's missing memories."

"Where did you get this idea?"

"An old tale I read. I believe a small colony of shifters were forced out of their human village and lived exclusively in their *fauna* forms, for a few generations."

"What does that prove?"

"Nothing, really, yet. Just that, they lost their link to

humanity over time. If a human and a shifter can produce shifter offspring, it follows that—"

"A *fauna* and an animal can produce...whatever these are."

"These primitives, yes," I said. I chewed the inside of my cheek. "But obviously this isn't the case of feral shifters assimilating with nature."

Leda bristled. "It certainly is *not*."

"I know—I just mean. Why would someone want to recreate this?"

"Pull as much research on those old stories as you can, Thor. There might be some older knowledge that can help us. Our people have been doing grotesque things for centuries, without the help of modern science."

"Will do—but I won't be back at the archives for several days."

"Oh?"

I grimaced. "I'm bringing Cas home for Thanksgiving."

"That's brave," she said, scoffing. "Largely because it's not really 'Thanksgiving.' At least, not like he's expecting, anyway."

"No, it is not," I agreed. "What about you?"

"I will be staying here," said Leda. "Having dinner out on Thursday."

"With Lucy?"

She turned to me, pursing her lips. "You know?"

"I have a nose, too, Leda." I grinned.

"Hmm, well," she said. "It's all very unexpected."

I shrugged. "It always is, isn't it?"

"Yes. So, are you trying to scare Cassian off?"

"No," I said, "Though I wouldn't be shocked if my family did it for me."

When I returned home, with feral animals on my mind, I found another in my apartment. Cas paced, agitated, waiting for me to arrive so we could drive to my parents' house.

He was nervous. I could tell by the white-knuckled way he gripped his steering wheel as we drove.

The bruise around his eye had darkened spectacularly, and I didn't know how my family was going to react. It was one of those things that could go either way. Cas's ability to scrap would impress my father, but he was also very into appearances. I also did *not* want them to find out what had caused the fight that had caused the bruise. The last thing I needed was my father to find out that I needed a human to defend my honor. It had been on the tip of my tongue to suggest we stop at a drug store and get some concealer, but Cas was already so worked up, and I didn't want to make things worse.

Cas was always so gentle, I was shocked he'd kicked the stuffing out of someone. Embarrassed though I was, it definitely had me some type of way.

"What?" Cas asked, glancing at me.

"What, what?"

"You're smiling."

I supposed I was. "You like me."

Cas huffed out a laugh. "No shit."

To distract Cas, I told him what Leda and I had discovered, and it appeared to put him in even more of a foul mood than he'd been in before. "That could have happened to you," he said.

"What could have?"

"Whatever this person did to Leda and Rafe. Someone drugged them, kidnapped them, and then did fucked up medical procedures on them."

"I know," I said heavily. "They would have been disappointed by my genes, though, I think."

"It doesn't matter," said Cas. "We have to figure out what the hell is going on before anyone else gets hurt."

Cas's eyes got big and round as we pulled into the driveway of my family's house. I grimaced. The house was big, and, if I was being honest, kind of ostentatious. I didn't want him to feel uncomfortable or intimidated, but there was nothing for it. I tried to fake confidence as I opened the front door. "We're here!" I called into the foyer.

"Hey, boys!" My dad came to greet us himself, which was surprising. "Good to see you again, Cassian—woah!"

Cas stuck out his hand to shake, and averted his eyes. But there was no disguising his magnificent shiner.

"I bet the other guy looks worse, huh?" My dad gave Cas a jocular clap on the shoulder. "Come on in."

I exhaled, shared a relieved glance with Cas, and walked into the proverbial lion's den in which I'd been raised. My entire immediate family was there: my sister Circe, my brother Abraxas, and our parents. Circe's husband, Samuel, was there too—and I knew Abraxas's fiancée would arrive tomorrow with her parents.

Cas looked around the living room, a shell-shocked expression on his face.

"You must be Cas! I've heard a lot about you. I'm Abraxas." My brother crushed Cas's fingers in a handshake, but I don't think anyone but me caught his wince. Abraxas was bigger and broader even than our father, and his grizzly bear *fauna* suited him.

My mother and sister fussed over me, saying I looked thin.

"I always look thin," I muttered, sitting on the edge of a vacant loveseat. A fire roared in the hearth, and I focused on that. My siblings' arrival had preceded mine by only a short while, so luckily, I was able to let the flow of conversation rush past me as my parents fawned over them.

Cas sat beside me, leaning in to whisper in my ear. "What's the deal with PDA in front of your family?"

I grinned. "It's fine," I whispered back.

He immediately snaked an arm around my waist and pulled me closer on the little couch, so we touched hip to shoulder and I felt immensely comforted by his presence. They might be my family, but I still felt like Cas was my only ally in this house.

"Long drive?" Abraxas asked.

"Not too bad," Cas answered.

"Well," said Dad, wordlessly offering Cas a glass of scotch. "I'm thrilled you could join us. Thor has never brought anyone home before."

I tensed. It was starting already. I had really been hoping we could make it through Cas's first meeting of everyone without a discussion of mating rituals, but something told me I'd been a fool to think that. I should definitely have prepared Cas better, but the words wouldn't come out of my mouth, and now, we were here. I took a nightcap from my mother, a glass of red wine. It was late, and I wanted to escape to my room as quickly as possible. So, I may have put a little extra oomf into my yawns, and Cas was quick to my hint. He cleared his throat and said, "Should we bring our bags up?"

"Yes," I said, shooting him a grateful smile. "I'll show you to my old room."

Cas carried our bags like the gentleman that he was, and followed me back through the foyer and up the ridiculous sweeping staircase that led to the second floor. He elbowed me in the side. "Did you ever slide down that banister as a kid?"

I grinned. "I'm really glad you're here with me."

Once we made it down the carpeted hallway, past the ostentatious family portrait of my parents and siblings in their *fauna* forms (I was significantly absent), and into my room, I closed the door behind us and breathed a sigh of relief. One of my favorite things about my room was the old-fashioned lock, with an antique skeleton key that gave a satisfying *thunk* when I turned it. It made me feel more secure, hearing that noise.

"So, that's your family," said Cas, eyebrows raised.

"Yes."

"They're...a lot."

"I told you."

Cas set our bags down in the corner, taking in the four-poster bed, the giant wardrobe, and the door to my private bathroom. "This house is..."

"Also a lot?"

He laughed. "Yeah. But it's beautiful," he added. "It's really big."

"Lonely, sometimes, though."

Cas took a step closer, wrapping his hands around my upper arms. "Not now, though."

I raised on tiptoe to kiss him. "No, not now."

Kissing Cas felt like floating, and when I came down, I drew away, tracing the outline of his black eye with my pinky. The bruise was hot to the touch. "Does it hurt?"

Cas nuzzled into my palm. "Not really." His hands drifted up into my hair, tugging on my scalp, pulling until I gasped. He took his chance to thrust his tongue into my mouth, and I traced it with the tip of my own, sucking on it before pulling back slightly. Cas's fingers dropped to the waistband of my jeans, tugging my beltloops to pull our bodies closer, and I clutched at his shoulder blades, burying my nose in the side of his neck as he fumbled with the button of my jeans, then the zipper. Static energy and anticipation zapped up my spine, as Cas chased my mouth with his, and I didn't realize he'd been guiding me back toward the edge of my bed until my legs collided with the mattress. With a palm on my chest, Cas pushed gently until I fell back, landing on the bed with a slight bounce.

He got to his knees, and the sight had me biting the inside of my lip, hard. I had to keep my head this time, especially if Cas planned to deliver on the promise I read so clear in his eyes. I tangled my fingers in his sandy hair, thick and clean and soft. Cas dipped his thumbs into the crevices of my hip bones, nosing up my stomach and pushing my t-shirt out of the way so he could trace his tongue around my navel. He kissed the skin below as his fingers worked my jeans down past my hips, pulling my boxer briefs down with them.

"W-wait," I stammered. I propped myself up on one elbow, and with my other hand I cupped Cas's cheek. His face was so near my crotch it was like my dick could tell and was trying to bust through my zipper to get to him. "Is this okay?"

Cas laughed. "What?"

"I mean—I dunno. You're new to the whole...guy thing."

"'Guy thing'?" He repeated, brows raised.

"You know what I mean," I said. "The whole, liking guys thing. I'd understand if you—"

Cas pressed a palm to my mouth. "Thor, I have literally been dreaming of getting my mouth on you for weeks. Let me have my fun."

And I mean, really, how could I argue with that?

# 14



Okay, Cas, *moment of truth*. I grabbed the fabric of Thor's jeans and pulled, and to be honest this was a whole thing because his cock made me really work for it. Finally, I had him bare from the waist down, and I ungracefully stood to yank the jeans from his skinny legs, leaving him in his t-shirt and one sock. It was one of those little low socks, stark white against the knobby bones of his ankle. As I returned to my kneeling position, I tried not to make eye contact with his dick yet. I needed to steady myself, so I slid my hands up his thighs, firm and thin, before finally letting myself get a good look at his junk.

Thor watched me, nervous to be on display, his balls hanging over the edge of the mattress and his dick like a goddamn flagpole. For a hot second, I just had to look. From this vantage point it was even bigger—or maybe that was my nerves getting the best of me—rising up from its nest of curly dark hair, bobbing like a lure, hypnotizing me. In my fledgling gay porn adventures, I'd seen a lot of long dicks, but some of them, hand to God, looked like ET's finger. You know, *Elllllii-iooooot.* Kind of horrifying.

Thor's was the opposite. Mesmerizing. Beautiful. I wouldn't have thought a dick could be beautiful, but his was. I wanted to get my lips on him, but I was nervous. Thor and his merciless mouth had worked me into a lather and I wanted to do right by him and the gorgeous cock now twitching eagerly against Thor's belly.

To buy myself a little time, I pressed a kiss to his thigh, and felt it shaking—in fear? In anticipation? I glanced up, and the heavy-lidded gaze peering at me from behind Thor's glasses told me it was the latter, so I wrapped my hand around his shaft and drew it toward me like a lever, marveling at the heat coming off his skin and the weight of it against my palm. The pale rosewood of his crown might be my new favorite color— watching in real-time as a fresh drop of precum beaded at the slit didn't hurt, either. When I gave it a little squeeze, Thor gasped, a sharp aborted breath, and fell back against the bed.

It hit me, then, that no one had ever touched Thor like this. I leaned forward and gave the head of his cock a tentative lick. *Oh, fuck.* At one taste I was immediately addicted, and took as much of his cock into my mouth as I could. I heard a strangled yelp, and Thor's fingers flew immediately to my head, tangling in my hair once more.

Somewhere under my lusty fog, my brain dutifully catalogued each detail of the taste of Thor and the feel of him in my mouth. Tangy, musky. Sweet, salty. Warm, so warm—and a little bitter. When I released him, his dick sprang back to his stomach with a wet slap, and I brushed the underside of his shaft with my tongue, holding him in place with my hands on his hips.

He made the cutest little noises, like he couldn't believe he was actually getting his dick sucked. Each pleasured moan came with an edge of surprise to it. I hollowed my cheeks, pulling him as deep as I could, sucking with everything I had. Sloppy and ungraceful, but eager. I was always one for learning on the job. There was no way in hell I could get his whole dick in my mouth without, you know, dying, so I brought my hands to the party, stroking and teasing the parts of his shaft my lips couldn't quite reach.

Without my hands holding him down, Thor's hips popped up and soon he was thrusting into my mouth with no reliable rhythm. He caught me off guard once and the head of his dick pushed back toward my throat, and I gagged a tiny bit before backing off to tease him with my tongue. I placed one of my palms on his waist, and wiped my mouth on the back of my other hand.

"Sorry," he gasped, his eyes screwed shut tight, not sounding sorry at all.

I kissed his hip bone. "It's okay," I said, thrilled to have him unraveling under my touch.

I decided while I was down here, I should keep exploring. I wanted to taste all of him. So, I wrapped a loose fist around Thor's cock, stroking slowly while I nosed down into his pubes and toward his balls. I wiggled myself into position, lifting his thighs over my shoulders, letting his heels dig into my back. Over the years, I had learned I enjoyed having my balls played with, so I thought maybe Thor would too.

Ever so gently, I used my tongue to scoop one of his balls between my lips, sucking softly before moving to the other. With delicate little tugs, I had Thor absolutely incoherent, and I increased the speed of my hand, jerking him firmly as I used my nose to nudge his sac out of the way. Giving him zero warning, I swiped my tongue over his tiny little hole.

Thor arched his back off the bed with a shocked gasp, so I did it again. Glancing up, I saw that his hands were fisted in the blankets, white-knuckled. I licked him again, and again, and again.

"Oh—*oh*—*oh!*"

He was close. I moved swiftly to take him in my mouth again, and my lips barely made it around the head of his cock before he was firing down my throat, coating the inside of my mouth with his release, hips jerking feebly in the aftermath.

Okay, so.

Plainly, I loved the taste of Thor's cum. That was something I would never have considered even a month ago, but here we were. I swallowed every drop, and he twitched as I released him from my mouth, making sure I missed nothing, cleaning his flushed crown with delicate kitten licks.

Thor's legs were leaden over my shoulders, and he didn't show any signs of moving, his breathing heavy, his arms limp at his sides. I rocked back onto my heels, kissing down Thor's bare leg as I went, until I reached his sock-clad foot. I pressed a final kiss to his ankle before releasing his legs and getting shakily to my feet.

Thor finally regained his sense and sat up. "Oh my God," he said, turning red.

"What?"

"I'm just wearing a t-shirt."

"And a sock," I added.

"What?" He twisted around, looking down at his feet.

I laughed, grabbing his ankle as he squirmed away. "See?"

"Good grief," he said, falling back again and draping his forearm dramatically over his eyes. "This is so embarrassing." With his other hand he grappled for the blanket on the edge of his bed to cover himself.

"What?"

"I don't know, wearing a shirt with my dick hanging out is weird."

"And a sock," I said, laughing. "Don't forget the sock."

"That makes it worse!"

"Nah," I said, I kissed his ankle again. "It's hot."

"*Gods.* Stop."

"I'm serious," I leaned forward, pushing up the fabric of Thor's t-shirt a bit, kissing his hips. "I like it."

We grappled playfully until I finally relented and allowed Thor to wiggle under the covers.

"Okay," I said, "I see how it is. I can suck your dick but I can't look at it."

He covered my mouth with laughing kisses, but I noticed he didn't move to change at all—either to pull off his tee or pull on a pair of boxer briefs. I switched off the light, and slid into the blankets with Thor, reaching into the depths of the silky sheets to palm his bare ass.

He let out a satisfied little huff and snuggled back against my chest. "I'm glad you're here with me," he said.

I smiled, kissing the nape of his neck. "You said."

"Just making sure you knew."

After a while though, Thor got restless, tossing and turning at my side. Eventually, he sat up. "Hey," I whispered. "What is it?"

"You know, my bathroom has a really nice hot tub."

Confused, I said, "Huh?"

"A hot tub," said Thor, peeking at me over his shoulder. "On the balcony."

"I didn't bring any trunks," I said.

Thor stood, pulled off his t-shirt, and winked. The little bastard actually winked. "Me neither."

Oh. "Shit," I muttered, flinging off the covers and scrambling to get out of bed.

Thor laughed, an evil little chuckle he saved for when he knew he had me happily bagged up in some sexy snare. Thor's bathroom was dramatic and beautiful, like his bedroom, with a sliding glass door leading out onto a small balcony with an in-ground hot tub. As he grabbed some clean towels from the linen closet, I took in the décor of the bathroom, which included a giant baroque oil painting of—

"Cernunnos."

"Who?" I turned to Thor, who was watching me with a look of amusement on his face.

"Cernunnos. He was a Celtic god, protector of wild things. It was said under his mediation all the animals of the forest found peace together." He sighed, gesturing at the painting. "Apparently he was always horny on main, too."

I laughed, staring back at the painting. The man featured was indeed nude, one hand wrapped around a massive erect dick. His other hand was held out offering an apple to a doe. Curled by his feet a wolf gazed serenely up at him, and birds flew overhead. It was beautiful in an unsettling and aggressive way. The man was tall and freckled with a pair of enormous horns sticking out from his wild golden hair. In a strange way, he reminded me of Eve in the Garden of Eden, holding the apple and smiling out of the canvas, looking at Thor and me like he knew something we didn't. There was even a snake wrapped around one of the trees in the painting.

I couldn't pull my eyes away, forgetting momentarily why we'd come in here. Thor cleared his throat. "Try not being gay with *that* staring at you every time you shower."

I followed Thor out onto the balcony, where I gasped at the sudden chill. Somehow, I'd forgotten it was November in the mountains. Thor switched on the lights, giving the water a glow like some secret grotto. In the warm, churning water, I reclined back against the edge of the tub, a jet positioned right at a knot in my shoulder blades, and a naked Thor nestled between my legs, resting against my chest. Pretty heavenly, all told.

I lifted Thor's glasses off his face, as they'd fogged up entirely, then tilted his head up for a lazy kiss. The view of the grounds wasn't half bad, either, the crisp night air and the stars on the forest behind the Ambrose family estate. Thor's balcony backed right up onto the rear of the property, and I could see the deep shadows of the tree line.

As I watched, a few of the shadows stirred. At first, it seemed like wind rustling the branches, but as I stared, two sizable shadows detached themselves from the mass of darkness and stepped out onto the grass. A motion sensor light went off, throwing them into sharp relief, and I lurched forward, dumping Thor into the water. He came up, sputtering indignantly and reaching for his glasses where I'd folded them on the edge of the tub.

A wolf and a bear emerged from the trees, and I watched as they shuddered and twitched. It took a moment before I realized I was witnessing something similar to what had happened to Leda, when she'd changed into a swan and back again right in front of me.

Thor cursed softly, watching over my shoulder as I stared in fascination. The bear and the wolf became Thor's brother and father, respectively, and they walked naked over the grounds, not an ounce of shame between them. Each man held something in his hands.

"I forgot," said Thor, sounding huffy. "They always hunt the night before Thanksgiving, just the two of them."

"Oh?"

"And then a big family hunt happens tomorrow night," he continued, each word sounding more bitter than the last.

I turned to look at Thor where he stood in the center of the hot tub, his arms crossed over his chest, and a complicated expression on his face. It was an expression of hurt, and longing, of bitter envy. "Baby..." I said, wondering what I could say.

He hitched up a smile. "It's late," he said brusquely. "Let's dry off and get to bed."

"Thor—"

He grasped my chin and pulled me in for a kiss that tasted of distraction and chlorine. "I still owe you one, if you recall."

Part of me wanted to call him out on his diversionary tactics, but when he wrapped his slim fingers around my dick below the water, I figured there was more than one way to pull him out of the funk his family put him in.

In the morning, we went downstairs, and Thor directed me through the house to the solarium--which was apparently a thing that people had in real life--where the rest of the family already assembled, brunching it up with a sideboard of goodies. Thor opted for a bloody Mary, while I chose coffee. A platter of artisanal pastries, danishes, and croissants looked inviting. I selected a croissant.

Thor's family had enough money to purchase top-tier baked goods, but sometimes fancy people didn't look past the price tag. So, I joined Thor on a little settee in the corner to assess the croissant's merits based on my own exacting specifi-cations.

None of them looked up when we came in. It seemed like I was invisible by association, but to be honest that sort of suited me just fine. I didn't need Thor's family realizing this early that I didn't know which fork to eat with or whatever.

As I assessed the croissant on my little china plate, I felt Thor's eyes on me. "What?"

"Nothing," he said, failing to conceal his grin behind his bloody Mary.

I frowned. "Seriously, what?"

"I just love watching you eat a croissant," he said, going back to picking at his own breakfast.

"I eat them normal."

"You absolutely do *not* eat them normal."

Grumbling, I finished my examination, peeling apart the layers, finding the lamination of the dough to be suitable— and to my delight the fat inside was clearly all butter, not any sort of bullshit that mass-produced pastries contained. I smiled happily as I ate every last crumb.

Thor still watched me. "*What?*"

He shrugged. "You're just cute," he said. "That's all."

Which left me extremely flustered. After a second cup coffee, Thor sighed and asked me under his breath. "We have a set of traditions we always do," he said, with the air of one explaining tradition in question was a virgin sacrifice.

"Oh?"

"You ever play touch football?"

"Yeah, sure," I said. "Why?"

"When my cousins get here, we always have a big game." He grimaced.

"You play?"

Another look of hurt flashed over Thor's face, a direct reaction to my surprise, and it made me ache. But just like last night, he'd arranged his face into something resembling a smile. It was more like a resigned, walk to the gallows sort of smile, but I guess it counted. "Yeah, though I have been trying, unsuccessfully, to get out of it for years. I figured you'd be up to the challenge, but you should know that my family gets real competitive, and the touch game can get kind of...extreme."

"Why does that not surprise me?" I muttered, and Thor's face shone with a genuine smile, albeit a self-deprecating one.

His father, Lysander, entered the room with a palpable storm cloud, commanding everyone's attention before even uttering a word. "Well, this is a disaster," he said.

"What is it?" Thor's mother looked up from her magazine.

"Selvig just called. He had a family emergency and he won't be able to make it."

I looked around, confused as everyone made similar noises of defeat and surprise. "Who's Selvig?"

"Our cook," Thor explained. He turned to his dad. "What are we going to do?"

"Fuck," said Abraxas, ignoring the hiss of admonishment from his mother. "Order Chinese, I guess?"

"This is a disaster," agreed Circe. "Should we call the family and let them know or—"

"Hold on," I interrupted. I looked around the room at the several functioning adults in my presence. "Are you telling me *none* of you know how to cook a turkey?"

They exchanged blank looks, like I'd asked if one of them wanted to take a stab at open heart surgery.

I sighed, standing. "Don't worry, I got this."

"Cas," Thor hissed, tugging my sleeve, "Don't—"

"It's okay," I said, stooping to kiss his forehead. "I can make dinner," I told them.

"Cassian, dear," said Thor's mother. "You don't have to do that. We can just order in."

"It's not Thanksgiving without turkey, Mrs. Ambrose."

"You cook?" Asked Lysander. "Are you any good?"

"I'm alright," I said.

"He's amazing," snapped Thor, and I flushed with pride. He always seemed ready to stand up for me. "But seriously, Cas—"

"It's fine," I said confidently. "Point me toward the kitchen."

"Good man," said Abraxas, clapping me on the shoulder hard enough to make my knees buckle. "Make extra stuffing, yeah?"

———

## THOR

Well, this was an absolute disaster. I had planned to use the intervening hours between brunch and Thanksgiving dinner to brief Cas on the extended family passive-aggressive hellscape he was walking into—and instead, he was catering the whole fiasco.

I was furious at my father, too. Cas may not have realized it, but my family was treating him like staff. They would *never* have agreed to let Rafe Nardini cook dinner if I'd brought him home for Thanksgiving. It was a slap in the face. I'd brought home a potential mate, and they were making him serve us a meal, instead of treating him like an honored guest. I seethed. But Cas didn't know any of this shifter pack politics, and to be honest, I half expected he was just excited to see what my parents' kitchen was like.

In that, at least, they did not disappoint—our kitchen was massive, every appliance state of the art. Usually occupied by Selvig and his employees, I hadn't actually spent all that much time in here. I hadn't spent much time in any kitchen, anywhere.

Another issue emerged. Selvig wasn't simply a chef. He was also a skilled butcher. The turkeys, plural, for tonight's feast had been personally hunted and killed by my father and brother—to which Cas and I bore witness last night. It was a harvest season tradition that the host of the celebration would procure the food, personally. Over time, it had evolved from the entire meal being foraged to a few symbolic set-pieces. For my father, naturally, it had to be the star of the show, the focal point of the meal. So every year, he and Abraxas shifted into their *fauna* and hunted in the acres of land behind the estate until he had a few wild turkeys for Selvig to pluck, dress, and prepare.

I had no idea if Cas knew his way around a freshly killed

bird, but I was about to find out. Trailing behind my father and Cas as they walked into the kitchen, I did my best to bite back a laugh—my dad was pointing out the major landmarks to Cas like he needed the help, and like my dad knew a broiler from his own butt cheek. At any rate, Cas smiled politely, nodding and listening to my father's unnecessary instructions, his eyes sweeping the room and surely making his own mental map.

Cas had dressed casually, but looked devastating in a cream cable knit sweater over a flannel, and jeans that were tight enough to be fashionable, but loose enough that you could tell he thought he was straight when he bought them. At any rate, it made him look rugged and masculine, and truly edible. He asked me to point him in the direction of the Thanksgiving bird.

"...s" I said.

"Huh?"

"It's birds, as in, plural."

"That's no problem. Your parents have enough oven space to pull off a restaurant dinner service."

"Anyway, they're out there."

"Outside?"

"We have sort of a root cellar."

I showed Cas out the rear door from the kitchen and into the earthy, damp basement, pointing. If Cas was flummoxed, he didn't show it. Three wild turkeys, still very much intact, except for the red gashes at their throats, dangled from the ceiling, where they'd spent the previous twelve hours draining of blood into the buckets below.

"Have you ever...butchered before?" It sounded like a weird verb to use in that context.

"I know what I'm doing, Thor, trust me." We went back inside where my father waited.

Cas whipped off his sweater, unbuttoning the top button

of his shirt and rolling his sleeves up. Apparently butchering three wild turkeys was going to be more wet work than he'd originally thought. All I wanted to do was press my lips to the newly exposed triangle of freckled skin where Cas's collarbones met, but life had other plans for me.

"Thor, your cousins will be here soon."

I tried my best to school my expression, but the flinty look in Dad's eyes told me I'd failed. "I was kind of thinking I could stay in here with Cas, in case he needed help."

"It sounds to me like you are trying to avoid playing football with the cousins," he said.

"Dad, never once in my life have I wanted to play football."

He glared at me. I quailed under his gaze, like I always had, buckling immediately, feeling childish and spineless. "Upstairs, and change, now. Cassian will be alright in here, won't you Cas?"

I couldn't look at Cas. I didn't want to see the pitying look on his face as he imagined me fumbling through some sort of approximation of football, while my family mocked my lack of strength, speed, and skill. Touch football my ass—somehow the game always found me with my face in the dirt, let alone the absolute beating sustained by my ego.

Nevertheless, I turned and left the kitchen to go change.

Three excruciating hours later, I limped back into the kitchen. My lip bled freely and I knew soon enough, Cas and I would have matching shiners. Cas was hard at work, wearing the special, focused expression he got when he was cooking, the one I adored. But I hadn't gotten to watch, I thought petulantly. I loved watching him cook.

He must have heard me open the freezer door, in which I now rummaged in search of an ice pack, because I felt the firm weight of his palm on the small of my back. "Hey," said Cas. "Can you tell me which of these wines are okay to cook with? I don't want to use the wrong one and look like an asshole."

I straightened up without turning around. "Anything in the wine cooler under the counter is fair game. The real fancy stuff is in the cellar."

"Of course, it is," he said.

I made to escape but he caught my arm. "Why won't you look at me?"

I turned and had to watch his face morph from surprise to concern to pity, which made everything hurt worse.

"What the hell happened? I thought it was a touch game."

I forced a smile. "Nothing but a little familial rough-housing," I said, I couldn't keep the bitter note from my voice. Cas cupped my face in his hand and leaned down to kiss the swollen skin around my eye, like I'd done to him yesterday. He looked like he wanted to ask some more questions, so I blurted out something about taking a shower and dashed out of the kitchen.

Up in my room, I blasted the shower as hot as it would go, trying to steam clean the shame from my pores. And the mud, too, I guess—there was plenty of that smeared into my skin. When I emerged, squeaky clean, and dressed for dinner, I slid silently down the stairs and back into the kitchen, hoping I could hide in there with Cas until dinner.

The kitchen smelled marvelous, and Cas was up to his elbows in turkey prep, literally. He'd probably have to shower too. I noticed a thin sheen of sweat on the back of his neck, and his scent muddled with the smell of roasting food, blending into something that said, "Home."

I climbed up onto a stool at the kitchen island to watch the muscles in his shoulders move while he chopped vegetables, like I did at the apartment, wishing we were there right now. I sighed, and Cas dropped the knife he was holding. "*Jesus.* Why do you do that?"

"Sorry," I said, but I wasn't. I liked to watch Cas, especially when he didn't know I was looking.

He reached below the table and pulled out a bottle of wine to pour me a glass. A bourjelais, my favorite variety, though I was sure the brand was foreign to him. I sipped and watched as he moved around the kitchen, feeling far more settled than I had since we'd arrived.

Naturally, of course, that was the moment my father chose to come in. Every muscle in my body tensed at his approach, and I tried to look like my swollen lip and black eye didn't faze me in the slightest, like I was the type of guy always getting into scraps who'd just rub some dirt into his bruises and get on with his day.

"How is it going in here, Cassian?"

"Right on schedule, sir," he replied, wiping his brow with a paper towel. "And I'm keeping Thor away from the food, so all in all it's going well."

I stuck my tongue out at Cas, and he grinned. For some reason it didn't bother me when Cas teased me. Something about the timbre of his voice and the twinkle in his eyes told me the ribbing came from a kind place.

"Good, good. I'll let everyone know!"

When he left, Cas exhaled. "So," he said. "What's the deal with the birds?"

"Ugh," I said. "My father hunts for them every year. It's a pride thing."

"He hunts like..."

"Yeah. He shifts into his wolf form, goes into the forest and stalks and kills wild turkeys. It's so we can pretend we hang onto the Old Ways, when in actuality my dad doesn't know the first thing about hunting or foraging for game." I rolled my eyes.

"The old ways?"

"Yeah. It's one of the traditions of our kind—it's a big

feast for the harvest, and it kind of coincides with Thanksgiving so we use Thanksgiving as camouflage. Back in the day, the head of household would hunt and forage the entire meal. But at this point we're all far too civilized for that."

Cas grinned.

"What?"

"Just...starting to get the measure of how your dad operates, that's all."

"Oh, yeah?"

But whatever Cas had sussed out about my dad, he kept it to himself. We passed the rest of the cooking time in peaceful silence. I was grateful for a few quiet moments while Cas did his thing. It helped me feel a bit more grounded, a bit steadier before we had to endure the entire production of a meal my family put on. Cas had to duck upstairs to shower and change, leaving me in charge of his oven timers, though I knew everything would hum along like a well-oiled machine in his absence. Cas didn't leave anything to chance when it came to food.

In truth, I wanted this weekend to be over. My siblings with their mated partners, my cousins with their big impressive *fauna* that had all emerged on time, my parents—it was exhausting to be around them all for this long.

Finally, it was time. We gathered around the massive banquet table in the dining room, Cas's beautiful spread laid out before us, and I couldn't help my surge of pride at my partner who had prepared all of this to feed my family. Everyone sat, and I scooted my chair closer to Cas's so I could rest my palm possessively on his thigh.

My father took his place at the head of the table, and everyone stopped chattering and turned toward him. It was easy, for my father, to command the room. He didn't so much as clear his throat before all eyes were trained upon him. He raised his glass. "Another year, another harvest season. Another beautiful table."

My dad always said the same thing; I could almost recite the speech alongside him. However, I jolted with surprise as he veered off his usual script.

"Everyone," he said. "We have guest of honor this year."

I blanched. One good thing about Cas being in the kitchen all day was he could escape the scrutiny of my entire extended family. However, my dad was about to shine the spotlight directly on his face.

"Our cook called in today, and we would have been eating pizza if it weren't for Cassian here," My dad gestured deferentially toward Cas.

Cas gave a sheepish smile. "Let's not get carried away until you guys try everything."

Everyone laughed, and I relaxed a little. I shouldn't have been so worried—Cas was easy to like. Chances are, by the time we left, Dad would be trying to convince Cas he could do better than me. Dad wasn't done yet, however, and if I thought I could make it through this meal without my family spectacularly humiliating me or my boyfriend—well, you know the definition of insanity.

Dad always made the same kind of grandiose toast. He, of course, knew Cas was human, so I hoped he wouldn't make things too weird this year, but a sinking sensation in the pit of my stomach told me hope wouldn't get me very far.

"Another autumn," Dad began, raising his wine glass. "And how blessed we are by the bounty before us. The many Wild Facets of God have truly bestowed upon us a table full of gifts, and a season of plenty."

"A season of plenty," I intoned, raising my own glass as the rest of the family echoed my father's words. Cas raised his own glass, hastily copying us. We all held our cups aloft as my father continued his speech.

"By the blessings of Cernunnos, Horus, Diana, and the nameless Wild Facets beyond counting, we are granted this beautiful feast," he said. And by the moon that hangs over all of us, my mate and I share it with all of you." He reached for my mother's hand, clasping their fingers together. Cas's eyes widened a bit at the odd prayer but otherwise he concealed his surprise politely.

My father gestured next to my uncle, his eldest brother Ares, seated to his left. Ares stood, pulling a dark, dusty bottle below his chair. He took my aunt's hand and said in formal, ringing tones, "My mate and I bring a gift of mead, to share with our hosts, to celebrate the bounty of the season."

I felt Cas's gaze upon me, and realized I should have coached him for this. Considering he already knew the family secret, everything else had seemed pretty minor. Or maybe I just hadn't wanted to risk telling him anything else that might scare him away. His warm hand came to rest on my knee to give it a squeeze, so I shot him a quick, apologetic smile.

The whole ritual was super extra. Each of my father's siblings and our other guests brought traditional host gifts: mead, meat, bread, salt, "tallow"—which we usually substituted with a boutique soy candle—and "blood"—usually substituted with a dry red wine, honey, and stone. Stone usually came represented by some kind of stylish geode or decorative crystal. Cas leaned over to me and hissed, "Did we bring something?"

The fact that he wanted to participate in my family traditions warmed my heart more than I could say, but of course, it was another instance in which I fell short. Only fully bred shifters and their mated partners participated in this rite. Cas and I were the only ones present who'd be excluded—the shifter equivalent of being relegated to the kids' table. I shook my head, indicating no, and listened to my blowhard family drone on and on.

Finally, things returned to my father at the head of the table. I wondered, not for the first time, why we couldn't take turns saying what we were thankful for, like a normal family. At long last, the blessing was complete and we could drink from our glasses. My arm ached from holding it up for so long.

"I would like to say thank you to the Facets for introducing my son to his first potential mate, Cassian."

All eyes snapped to us, and I found myself praying to all the Wild Facets of God to send a lightning bolt down to vaporize me on the spot. I tried to communicate with my eyes to please, please, shut up, but of course I may as well have begged a statue for all the good it did me. "May they complete their bond, and may their union be blessed, so we can welcome Cassian into our pack and family."

Cas's freckled cheeks were pink, and I didn't trust myself to speak at all.

"And of course, without Cas, we would not have this bounty before us. To Cassian!"

"To Cassian!" everyone echoed, toasting him. Abraxas toasted with particular gusto, his eyes fixated on the giant casserole dish of extra stuffing.

Cas blushed further still and thanked everyone before dropping his eyes to his plate. Under the table, I grabbed his hand, stroking his palm with my thumb. Beneath the embarrassment, I felt another surge of protective pride. Bringing home Cas was clearly the most impressive thing I'd ever done.

It was finally time to eat, and for a while I enjoyed basking in reflected pride as everyone tucked in and complimented Cas's cooking. He was pleased as well, relaxing a bit as the focus shifted off of him and everyone broke down into smaller side conversations.

I should have known better than to think I'd be able to escape this meal with my dignity intact. My father and uncle Ares were always super competitive, dragging the rest of us into their constant posturing. For several years, my uncle had been in the hot seat because his eldest son Ragnar had an embarrassing *fauna.*

Then I came along, with nothing. My uncle was positively giddy to see my father knocked down a peg. The two of them were deeply ensconced in one of their passive-aggressive pissing contests toward the head of the table, so I swung around to where Cas was trying his best to remain invisible to the rest of the family, an impulse I understood too well. Unfortunately, with a room full of predators, he couldn't stay hidden for long.

"So, Cas," said my brother. I snapped my gaze to his, glaring to indicate he should leave Cas alone. "Do you hunt?"

Cas swallowed and cleared his throat, covering his mouth with his napkin. "Pardon?"

"Hunt," Abraxas repeated. "Do you ever hunt?"

"Uh, no," said Cas, his eyes darting to mine. "I've never been."

"That's too bad," chimed in my cousin Magnus. "We go every year on Thanksgiving night. You clearly know your way around preparing game."

Cas frowned, like he couldn't work out if they were making fun of him or not.

"It's a family tradition," said Abraxas with an evil grin. "Big game, fowl, all kinds of...beasts in the woods out back."

"*Abraxas,*" I warned, fingers clenching tightly around my knife and fork.

"Thor never comes. He's far too...civilized." Both Magnus and Abraxas howled with laughter, which was rich coming from a pair of dudes wearing Ferragamo loafers, but whatever. They only stopped cackling when they caught the harsh look on my dad's face at the other end of the table.

Cas looked at me for an explanation, but I suddenly had a lump in my throat. Cas already knew about the family, but it felt like he was finding out all over again—finding out just how much of a loser I really was. Through the family's eyes, surely he'd see he was wasting his time with me. My eyes stayed fixated on my plate, and I pulled my hand back to my lap below the table. I wished I could disappear.

"Cassian," barked my uncle suddenly, making everyone jump.

We all turned toward him.

"What drew you to my nephew?"

Abraxas snickered again and I kicked his shin. Cas frowned and took my other hand boldly where it rested on the table. He shot me a brief smile. "Lots of things."

"It had nothing to do with our family?" The threat hung there, in the air above the table, draped over the crystal chandelier, settling on the expensive linens.

"No," said Cas firmly. "I didn't know anything about Thor's family. I still don't, really."

Oh, damn. Looked like it was my turn in the hot seat. "Thor," my father said, picking up the thread of the conversation. "You plan to bring Cassian along as your potential mate but you haven't prepared him at all for what being part of our family might mean?"

I struggled with myself, trying to find the right words. "We just started dating," I tried. I didn't want Cas to freak out, didn't want my not-so-subtle family to chase him off.

Cas dropped my hand and I realized that was the wrong thing to say. Now he wouldn't meet my gaze.

"He's not one of us," my uncle snapped, addressing my father and ignoring both me and Cas. "No one in our line has had a human mate in living memory."

"He'll never fit in with the rest of the families," chimed in my aunt.

The best-case scenario here was that Cas would leave this dinner table thinking we were part of some kind of mafia.

Which, I guess, wasn't that far from the truth. That's how my dad and his brothers saw themselves: above the laws of men. Untouchable.

"What about their children?" Asked Ares.

"That hardly matters," my father said dismissively, shooting him a look. "They're both males. They wouldn't reproduce biologically anyway."

"Oh my God," I said under my breath. Please, lightning, strike me down. Or, failing that, send a piano to fall on my head.

"My son still carries our line." Dad steepled his fingers and looked across them at me. My insides shriveled. "Science has come a long way. I've been in talks with Leon Templeton. Neither Thor nor Leon's daughter Leda showed any inclination toward proper breeding matches, so we've been hammering out a surrogacy agreement for years. Cassian's humble genetics will hardly matter—"

"That's *enough!*" Someone yelled, slamming their fist on the table. Oh, shit. It was me. "Um..."

I trailed off as everyone stared, my courage bleeding out as quickly as it had come. But I turned to Cas, and he looked so lost that I found some steel.

"Cas is my boyfriend." I put emphasis on the word, hoping to stem all this mate talk that would sound insane to an outsider, and frankly, still seemed pretty insane to me. "And you *cannot* talk about him this way."

My parents looked taken aback. "You have no reason to be so upset," my mother said. "I was just saying to your father this morning that Cassian seems like an exemplary mate. Probably the best you could hope for given..."

"Given *what* exactly?"

"Given, well, your circumstances," she said.

"Besides," said Dad, airily. "Offspring with attractive parents are always more likely to succeed, regardless of blood ties. At the very least, Cassian fits that criterion. Combining Thor's breeding with Leda's will be a perfect genetic match. Good for both families."

"*Stop!*" I yelled. My whole body shook and I realized I'd gotten to my feet. Why did it take so much for anyone in his family to hear me? "This is insane, and *beyond* rude. You can't just plan my whole life, or my relationship without consulting me. Or, Leda's for that matter!"

My father opened his mouth but I steamrollered right over him.

"And—and. Cas is amazing." I chanced a look at him. "He'd be a great match for *anyone.* Anyone would feel lucky for him to choose them. I know I do. And I am *not* going to force him to sit here while you guys go on about him like he's a fucking piece of meat. Come on, Cas."

I held out my hand, and for one heartbreaking moment I feared he wouldn't take it, but he did. I squeezed his fingers and led him from the dining room.

"Thor, I—"

"Stop," I snapped, and Cas flinched. "Sorry, I just don't want to talk about it. Let's go upstairs. We can leave in the morning."

But Cas planted his feet. "No," he said.

"What?"

"I—this is way too much, Thor."

My heart pounded and I felt like a trapped animal. "What do you mean?"

Cas looked pained. He looked uncomfortable, and frankly, he looked hurt, too. "This—" he gestured vaguely at my parents' ridiculous foyer. "They were talking about us having *kids.*" He whispered, like "kids" was an obscene swearword.

"I know, it's just them—"

"When were you planning on explaining the whole 'mate' thing to me?"

"I was going to—"

"Because it sounds a hell of a lot more serious than bringing me for dinner, and that had you all nervous, didn't it? Is it because you knew what I was walking into, here? Some kind of arranged marriage ritual?"

"It's not like that!"

"It isn't? Okay, so, when you didn't want me to come—what, you didn't want me to embarrass you with my, how did your dad say it, 'humble lineage' or whatever the fuck—"

"Cas, *stop*," I said, an edge of desperation creeping into my voice. "You know that's not how I feel."

"Yeah, sure," he said. He took another step away from me. "Listen, Thor—I gotta...I gotta go. I can't be here anymore."

"Please, just wait." The begging tone of my words was unseemly, but I couldn't help it.

Cas shook his head, walking to the staircase. I stood like an idiot, frozen, and the main thing on my mind was a prayer that my family was still ensconced enough in dinner not to have their ears pressed up against the dining room door. My lips pressed together in a line, and the panic rose in my gullet as I stood in the echoing silence. In a matter of minutes, I heard Cas's footfalls and he came down the stairs with a bag over his shoulder.

"Cas, please..." I didn't finish my thought. Please, what, exactly? Even I didn't know.

He shook his head again, and said, "Listen, we'll...we'll talk, okay?"

I nodded, ignoring the lump in my throat. Then, Cas was gone.

# 15



What an asshole. Like, legitimately the world's biggest asshole. That's all I kept thinking, berating myself as I drove away from Thor's house. The knowledge that I was being an asshole, however, couldn't convince me to turn around and drive back, so I kept going.

It had all just hit me, hard. Seeing Leda transform in a controlled environment like her lab, seeing her become a beautiful bird, was very different from seeing a duo of enormous predators emerge from the forest and turn into my boyfriend's dad and brother. At dinner, I sat there, listening to them talking about me like breeding stock, and all at once it hit me that Thor's father could transform into a literal wolf, leap across the table and rip my throat out if I pissed him off too bad. The dude was terrifying enough in his human form. Looking around the table at the rest of Thor's family, it was like I could see the wild animals leering from behind their eyes.

And all I could think was, *Cas, what the fuck are you doing here*? Then, the blessings began and it sounded like old magic, and the more I thought about it the crazier it seemed, until it felt like I couldn't breathe and I had no choice but to bolt.

Maybe Thor could have told me a bit more about what I was walking into, but still. I knew I had fucked up. The look on Thor's face had almost been enough to kill my desire to flee, but then my own sort of animal brain kicked in, and it screamed at me to escape before *I* ended up the centerpiece of their next family meal. I'd packed in such a hurry I was sure I'd left about half my shit in Thor's bedroom. Oh well.

When I finally opened the door to our apartment, exhaustion hit me like a freight train. I dropped my bag on the floor of the living room, looking at the candles on the mantlepiece with an ache in my chest.

Like they had minds of their own, my feet took me down the short corridor to Thor's bedroom (*our bedroom?*), but my tired brain caught up when my hand reached for the doorknob.

I couldn't sleep in there.

I turned my back on the door and retreated to my own room. It had, in actuality, only been about two weeks since I'd slept in there but it felt like forever. The bed was cold and sad looking, but I was bone tired and desperate for sleep so I could stop thinking. Two hours later though, and I'd never felt more awake, like my brain was punishing me. I tossed and turned, and it didn't take a genius to figure out what was keeping me up.

Deep inside, I knew I'd have to make some sort of decision tomorrow, and I knew making it on no sleep was a bad idea. So, I got up, marched to Thor's bedroom, and collapsed on top of the covers.

I'd gotten used to sleeping with…someone tucked snug in my arms. And I felt like a flailing octopus in bed alone. I stuffed one pillow between my knees and hugged the other to my chest, burying my face in it. And if I happened to casually sniff the pillow a few times, well, that was my business.

I was out in minutes.

The following morning, I woke up and laid in bed for a while, but when no epiphany struck me, I got up, got dressed and called Lucy.

"Hey, man, you okay? You don't usually call."

"I know," I said. "I really need to talk."

"Okay." She hesitated a beat. "Aren't you at Thor's parents' this weekend?"

I sighed. "Back early."

"Yikes."

"Yeah."

After a bit of awkward silence, we decided to meet at the coffee shop on campus. Since my phone was almost dead, and I'd forgotten my charger, I sent a quick text once we hung up asking if she could bring me a spare.

Lucy had gotten to the coffee place before me, securing a table and my usual order. When she saw me, I realized I must look as shitty as I felt, because the look that passed over her face was one of intense worry. She immediately stood and pulled me into a hug when I got near the table. Then she held me at arm's length, inspecting me.

"Sit," she ordered. She pointed at the coffee in front of the vacant chair. "Sip.

I did.

"Spill."

I paused. Somehow, when following my knee-jerk reaction to call and confide in her, I hadn't figured out what I would actually *say* to Lucy. I certainly couldn't come right out and say what was really going on—that Thor's magical family had been trying to marry him off for ages but he didn't have any takers so they were okay with him slumming it with a mere mortal like me.

Lucy seemed to sense I was wrestling with something, so she leveled her gaze at me over her cappuccino and said point-blank, "Did you guys break up?"

"No," I said, feeling my stomach drop. "Yes. I don't know."

She frowned. "Sounds complicated."

"It started off great. The rest of his family is almost as good in the kitchen as Thor is." I smiled a little to think about it. "So, their cook quit on Thanksgiving and I offered to make dinner for everyone. They seemed really relieved."

"You spent the whole day working?" She asked me, fondly exasperated.

With a grin, I said, "Yeah. Anyway, they play this big touch football game."

She raised her brows. "And Thor plays?"

"He tried to get out of it," I explained. "His family... they're really rough on him. They're all like these beautiful giants. He doesn't really fit in with them." That was possibly the understatement of the fucking century.

From here, I hesitated, trying to find the right words to get advice from my friend without sounding crazy. "Anyway," I said. "The whole family is...religious." I found myself echoing Thor's own explanation of his family. "They have a lot of traditions and rituals and stuff that he really didn't tell me about beforehand. I was really blindsided."

"Weird how?"

"It's kind of hard to explain."

Lucy's frown deepened, like she knew whatever I held back was pretty critical to the story. "So," she said. "You got blindsided by his family's drama and you—what?"

I chewed my lip. "I left."

"You *left?*"

"Yeah—I just, it was like I was on autopilot. I grabbed my shit and jumped in the car and ran."

"When?"

"What do you mean, when?"

"Like, when did you leave?"

I winced. "In the middle of dinner."

Lucy massaged her temple. "So, Thor's family was being... judgmental or rude or whatever, and you just jumped up and left?"

I looked down at the table and nodded. Obviously, there was more to the story, but yeah, that was the gist.

"Well, that's no good!"

"I know."

"Okay," she said. "Obviously, there's something huge you're not telling me here. And the reason you're not telling me is one of two things."

"Oh?"

"Either you're protecting Thor," she said, hesitating a minute before saying, "or you're afraid of him."

"I think maybe it's both."

"Well," she said, covering my hand with hers. "That tells me you're not done with him."

"No," I said. "At least, not yet."

"Then you know what I'm going to say next, right? You need to talk to him."

"Ugh."

"What's the worst that could happen?"

"I could die."

Lucy laughed. "I'm serious dude. You need to give him a chance to explain his side of things. And I think you probably should apologize for bolting on him like a big coward."

With a groan, I rested my forehead on the table. "AITA?"

"Yeah, Cas. I think you might just be the asshole," said Lucy, but not unkindly. "But I also know you, and I know you aren't always, and I know there's something bigger going on here."

I groaned again.

"Chin up soldier," she told me. "And you can always crash with me if you have to."

Back at the apartment, I mulled over Lucy's advice.

Which was it?

Was I protecting Thor, or was I afraid?

————

## THOR

I couldn't face the thought of returning to the dining room only to confirm that, once again, I had failed. Failed to go a day without humiliating them, failed to be a proper shifter, failed to find a mate—failed, so spectacularly, to seal the deal.

So, I went up to my room, registering that Cas had done a horrendous job of packing, so disturbed by the idea of being stuck with my family––with me––that he'd left half his belongings behind. And, I noted, he'd taken some of mine by mistake. I almost laughed at the thought of Cas trying to fit into my jeans, but I couldn't quite manage it.

Restless, I paced around the room, gathering Cas's forgotten things and folding them neatly to stuff into my backpack. I left out one of his flannels, which I pulled on, warm and familiar as a hug. If he had moved out by the time I got home I was absolutely keeping it.

I sat on the edge of my bed, phone balanced on my knee, praying for it to buzz with a message. It didn't.

I wasn't really sure how long I sat there, but some hours later, as if following orders, I pulled up the train schedule on my phone, booked a ticket, and scheduled an Uber to pick me up. It was the first train out, so it would leave really early. I was hoping if I left early enough, my family would be too hungover to question me about Cas's flight and my own premature departure.

I scrubbed my face with my hands, nudging my glasses up to the crown of my head as I did so. The injustice of all this caught in my throat. For once, I hadn't screwed things up. Sure, I maybe could have prepared Cas a little better, but I'd be willing to bet that ninety-nine-point-nine percent of families didn't discuss surrogacy agreements, breeding, and mating rituals the very first time they met someone.

But, to them, I knew it would still be my fault somehow. If I had made myself appealing as a mating prospect, Cassian wouldn't care about such trivial things as having a bunch of strangers pass judgment on him and plan his whole future.

One all-night anxiety attack and a fugue-state train ride later, I stood on the sidewalk in front of my building. I really, *really* didn't want to go in and face Cas, or face an empty apartment with all his stuff gone. To be honest, I wasn't sure which would hurt more.

As if, for once, the fortunes chose to look kindly on me, my phone blipped. I dropped my bag, scrambling frantically in my pockets to grab it, but it wasn't from Cas. It was Leda.

Leda: *Lab. Now.*

Then the little ellipsis animation appeared and disappeared several times before she added. "Coffee, pls."

I sighed, but in the end, I was grateful for a reason to avoid going home. I swiped into the lab about half an hour later. After setting down the tray from the coffee place, I tucked my bag in the corner and shrugged into a lab coat. Leda beckoned me with an impatient wave and a grunt from where she sat staring at a backlit transparency, much like the one that determined the parentage of the deceased swan primitive.

"What is this?" I asked.

"I compared Rafe's blood to the reptilian John Doe."

"And," I said, dreading the answer. "Is he the father?"

"Not quite," she explained, indicating a few shared markers.

"They are related, though—or could that be a coincidence?"

Leda shook her head. "It would be a staggering coincidence."

"Then, how?"

"I'm not certain—but I've asked him to meet us here."

Soon enough, a quiet knock on the door signaled Rafe's arrival. "Hi, Thor," he said. "Leda."

Rafe looked nervous, and I wondered how much Leda had told him when she'd taken the sample of his blood. "So, guys, what do you need?"

"I need to know if anyone else in your family has been abducted," said Leda bluntly.

"Abducted?" Rafe paled. "What are you talking about?"

Leda's bedside manner might leave something to be desired, but she had cut to the heart of it. I did my best to fill in the gaps, and by the end of the tale, Rafe had staggered over to a stool and now covered his face with his hands. "So," I said, tentatively. "Has anything like what happened to you happened to anyone else in your family?"

"I didn't realize you guys thought I was abducted," he said shakily.

"Leda," I said, "You didn't tell him anything?"

"I didn't want him to freak out," she explained.

Rafe looked ready to liquify.

"Well," I said. "Mission accomplished!"

"So—sorry," said Rafe, interrupting our sniping. "I don't understand—someone else in my family…"

His eyes slid in and out of focus as he screwed up his face, remembering.

"My brother," said Rafe softly. "My older brother—we discussed it at harvest dinner. I mentioned having a missing day after being drugged at a party, and he said something like it happened to him last spring."

"He did?" This had been going on a lot longer than we had originally thought.

"Yeah," said Rafe, looking horrified. "He's kind of a partier though—he played it all off like some big joke."

The three of us stared at the genetic workup from the primitive that was, apparently, Rafe's nephew.

I took the long way home, which was good, because it gave me some time to stew over our discovery, but was bad because as I walked up the street, I saw Cas's Impala parked in its usual spot. My stomach lurched, but I figured it was time to face the music. I couldn't avoid an ugly scene by living the rest of my life pacing back and forth on the sidewalk.

I walked up the stairs, dragging my feet—literally and figuratively—feeling my heart pound harder and harder as I ascended the stairs. It was like I could feel his presence more acutely with every step. By the time I reached the door to our place, I was breathing hard, sweating, my mouth full of saliva, my belly full of a foreign sort of hunger.

When the door swung open, I took a deep, steadying breath. The apartment looked much the same as I had left it, though I wasn't sure what I expected. Closing my eyes, I took another breath and it was like I was underwater, but I could hear Cas calling to me from the surface, like I was looking up at him from the depths. Blurry, muted, but unmistakably there. I couldn't put my finger on what this feeling meant, because Cas was not calling to me; in fact, the apartment was silent as a grave.

The door to our bedroom was cracked and as I approached it, I heard the rumbling snores of Cas's sleepy breathing. Concerned, I checked my phone. It was about eleven in the morning. He must not have slept very well. I pushed the door all the way open, moving silently across the floor as the hardwood gave way to carpet. Looking at the bed, I stalled, swaying where I stood, one foot hovering mid-step like I'd forgotten I needed to put it down to keep walking.

Cas was on his stomach on top of the covers, sinking into my plush white comforter, miles of creamy skin exposed, dusted with countless freckles like little galaxies of brown stars. His back rose and fell rhythmically with his breathing, and he had his face squished into the pillows, sandy hair falling messily across his brow.

I drifted across the room, utterly enchanted. Cas had on only a pair of boxers, and a damp towel draped over the back of the chair near the bed, so clearly, he'd come to bed freshly showered for a morning nap. As I got closer, I pulled deep hits of Cas's scent through my nose, into my sinus, into my lungs. Something odd was happening. I'd, of course, viscerally reacted to Cas's scent before, but nothing like this—like I'd been pulled from a hibernation so long I'd forgotten what being awake felt like.

I sat on the edge of the bed, carding a hand through Cas's cornsilk hair. My fingers caught on a snarl, and he opened his eyes, though they remained heavy-lidded and sleepy.

Instead of a greeting, Cas let out a soft noise, like, "*Mmmmm.*"

I was absolutely gone. The little sound pushed every rational thought from my brain, and before I really realized what I was doing, I'd pushed Cas onto his back, straddling his hips like the very first morning I had kissed him.

He blinked up at me, not seeming surprised, but sort of seeming like...he'd been waiting for me. His pink lips parted, and I braced my hands on either side of his head, leaning down so that our mouths hovered millimeters apart.

"Are you moving out?" I whispered. *Shit.* That's definitely not what I meant to say.

Cas shook his head, dazed. "No."

So, I closed the gap between us and shoved my tongue in his mouth. Cas responded beautifully, like maybe he really had been waiting for me, his big warm palms sliding up my back and gripping my shoulders to hold me close. He sucked on my tongue, moaning around it like my mouth was something fine, something delicious, something to covet. His fingertips dug into my shoulders, and I rocked against him, wishing that I'd taken off my jeans before climbing up here. As if sensing my thoughts, Cas pulled back and panted, "Get naked."

I hesitated. "Don't you...want to talk?"

Cas shook his head, his eyes feverish. "After."

"After?"

In answer, Cas sat up, nearly shoving me off him so he could peel me out of my clothes and I somehow ended up on my back, his tongue trailing down my neck, his hands twisted in mine, pinning me against the bed. He gave my hands a soft squeeze before releasing them, dragging fingertips in a maddening, featherlight caress up my wrists, down my arms and over my collarbones, across my chest to brush against my nipples.

*Cas, wait.* Or, at least, I thought that's what I said. What came out instead was more like a grunt. Or a growl. Cas stopped, peering at me quizzically, because he'd clearly never heard me make a noise like that before. Come to think of it, I'd never heard me make a noise like that before.

"We need to—*ohh.*"

Cas danced his tongue across my nipple, flattening his

tongue to lave over the sensitive bud, then sealing his lips around and sucking hard. He drew away, moving up my chest with open-mouthed kisses, more teeth than lips. "What do we need?"

"We need to talk?" But it came out as a question. It was a clash of the titans: head vs...well, downstairs head.

Cas let his forehead fall to my collarbone. "Okay, fine." He took a deep breath, his whole body shuddering. "I think you need to tell me about this whole mating ritual thing."

I sighed, dragging my fingers up and down the muscles of Cas's back. "So, my brother and sister and their partners, right?"

"Mmm—hmmm." Cas was clearly only half listening, his lips hovering over the pulse point in my neck. Gods, that felt good.

"It's kind of...common for us to pair off young."

"Young?" Cas tensed against me.

"Not gross young," I amended. "It's just that, our kind can identify an ideal partner. It's instinctual. Both of my siblings found their mates right out of high school. They were good matches from other prominent shifter families."

"Like Leda's?"

"Yeah." I cleared my throat. "My dad must have introduced me to dozens of young women when I was in high school, trying to get me to form a mating bond."

"Was he angry when you came out?"

"No," I said truthfully. "It was almost astonishing how quickly he started reaching out to the same families, asking if any of their sons were gay." I poked him in the side. "Or bi."

"That is somehow...really accepting and really gross at the same time."

"Yeah, that's kind of where my dad lives. You heard him at dinner—if I was gay, the actual biology of mating didn't really matter. All that mattered was perpetuating our family line, and making a good match. Anyway, I never had any sort of manifestation of a mating bond."

Cas went silent for a while. It was a lot to process. So, I contented myself seeing how close I really could squish against his body. Very close, as it happened.

"I'm sorry," I whispered. "I should have told them to back off. I shouldn't have let you walk into the lion's den unprepared."

"Pun not intended?"

"Well, actually, my mom..."

"Oh, for fuck's sake."

I laughed.

"I'm so sorry I left." Cas started nuzzling and kissing my neck again, but all at once, he froze. "So, wait."

"Yeah?"

He shoved away from me, sitting up. I rolled off him, awkwardly flopping down onto the mattress. Cas had drawn up, shielding himself, and he had never looked so small to me before that moment.

"What is it?" I prompted.

He rested his chin on his knees, legs curled up tight against his chest. "So, what happens when you find them?"

"Find who?"

"Your real...mate, or whatever?"

I moved so fast it was like I teleported. I kneeled beside Cas and tried to wrap him in my arms, the breadth of his shoulders making it a bit of a challenge. With my forehead pressed against his temple, I whispered in his ear. "It's not going to happen."

"How do you know?" While Cas was very easy to rile up, he didn't often seem meek, didn't often seem truly unsure.

"Call it animal instinct," I hedged, kissing his cheek. I knew if I were honest, this next part would really freak him out.

He laughed a little at my lame joke, uncurling his limbs as he turned to pounce on me. Pinned on my back, I cocked my head to look up into his dimpled smile. Cas lowered his lips, breathing on my neck and said, "How—do—you—know?" He punctuated each word with a kiss to the edge of my jaw.

I groaned, my body igniting under each soft press of his lips. "I could tell the first time we touched," I told him, rolling my hips to press against his hot body. "I felt it again, every time you came home from practice—sweaty," I grabbed his ass, squeezing tight. "Glowing." *Beautiful.* "I felt it when you carried me home from that awful party. Felt it when I kissed you. I knew."

"Knew what?" Cas asked me, and I could feel his heart pounding against my own chest, every inch of us pressed together. He rested his hands on the mattress, bracing himself on either side of my shoulders. His confidence returning, his smile was playful but his eyes smoldered.

This was too soon, way too soon, but I had promised to tell him everything, and there was no way I could stop my mouth running with him all over me like this.

"I knew you were it for me, Cassian Rhodes."

"*Fuck,*" he said on a sharp exhale, and kissed me. Hard. If what I said scared him, he didn't show it. The way he kissed me was fierce; I couldn't breathe. His hands were in my hair, tugging on my scalp.

All the little muscles between my navel and my dick contracted, pulling tight and burning, all while Cas's fingers scorched across my body. I felt something I'd only heard described, felt something I had long since accepted I had been born without.

Something wild, something powerful, was waking up inside me.

I growled into Cassian's lips before pressing my palms to his chest, trying to still him.

"Wait—wait," I said, trying to keep my brain in charge, but I could feel myself slipping, and panic rose in my gut, at war with the desire igniting my skin.

"Why wait?" Cas surrounded me, every inch of his taut, powerful body pressing me into the mattress.

*Oh,* help. I couldn't think, or breathe with him like this. I was so hard my dick ached, and an instinct surged through me to bury it in Cas's body, to stuff him so full his insides had to move around to make room for me. "Cas—*no!*" I squirmed out from under him.

"What?"

"You can't—you don't—"

"*What?*"

My mate was right here, panting with want. Hard and ready, for me. My Alpha side, a part of me I thought did not exist, bloomed in my chest, in my groin. *You could have him,* it said. *He wants you.* I swallowed. I wanted Cas, of course, so badly. *Take him.* The thought had me practically purring. I'd never talked to the wild part of me—largely because I didn't think he existed. I grabbed my own cock, squeezing it— hoping the small offering of pressure would help calm my desire.

Cas took that the wrong way, like I was getting ready. He covered my body with his again, and I melted into the mattress. His teeth on my ear, his cock leaking into the divot of my hip, his gorgeous hot weight thrumming on top of me —it was too much. "*Baby,*" he breathed against my jaw. "*Baby.*"

My kryptonite. I'd never been anyone's baby, but I was his. I marshalled my self-control. Cas was bigger, stronger. But he did not have magic on his side. He wasn't a shifter, and he wasn't the Alpha partner here, either. Something deep inside me snarled. I could take him, if I wanted. But I could also make him listen. My mate, *mine.* I put some steel into my voice. "Cas."

"What?"

"Stop." Something powerful vibrated in my voice, something threatening—something thrilling.

Cas felt it too, and he pulled away. "What's wrong?"

I sighed. "Cassian," I used his full name, to underline the gravity of the situation. "I promised I'd tell you everything."

He brushed his fingers over my cheek. They were firm, warm. Thick. Soft and calloused at the same time. "Tell me."

"This—the mate bond; it's serious."

He cocked his head to the side. "I'm serious about you."

"Cas—stop!"

He looked down at me, pupils blown wide. He looked possessed. He looked drunk. That's what I had heard before. Finding your mate was a heady thing. It could soothe you, like medicine—but it was also like a drug. Addictive and dangerous.

Cas was mainlining the connection blooming between us, but he didn't understand the consequences. And, in truth, neither did I, not really. We weren't the same kind. He legitimately stuck out his bottom lip in a sweet pout. "I thought you said I was yours."

Breathing hard, I tried to explain. "Cassian, what I said, it's true, *but.*"

"What?" His voice was muffled, pure sex as he lowered his lips to my neck again.

"Finding your mate...binding us together..." I shuddered. How did he know how to make my body sing?

Cas bubbled against me, like boiling water. He latched his full pink lips to my neck, sucking hard enough to mark. He might not understand, but on some primal level, his body knew. He ground his dick against mine, making me groan. I had to tell him, I had to— "It's *permanent,*" I said, moaning, writing under his touch. "Once we..." I paused. I wanted this to sound romantic. This was not how this conversation was meant to happen—I couldn't think with Cas's hand stroking my cock.

Cas looked at me, both bold and bashful somehow. "Once we fuck?"

*Oh hell.* I could have come just hearing him say that. "Yes."

He nipped my earlobe, flicking his tongue against it, while tugging and pulling my dick. "Once we fuck," he breathed, "then what?"

"Unnf," I said, eloquently.

"Because," said Cas, pressing every glorious inch of his body against mine, humming with tension and desire. "I wanna fuck."

"Oh my *God.*"

"Right now."

"Please, Cas," I said, though it felt like something tore in my chest as I said it. I bent my arm awkwardly so I could cup his cheek with one hand. "You're not thinking clearly. It's been—it's been an insane few days. There's still a lot you don't know."

Cas slumped, pushing his forehead against mine. He took a deep breath. "Okay," he said.

"Okay?" I barely dared to move, or breathe trying desperately to ramp myself back down.

"Yeah," he said. He kissed my chest shyly before blinking up at me through his lashes. I was relieved to see his hazel eyes had cleared. "Of course, we can wait. You're right. I don't know what came over me."

"It's okay." I wiggled until I was on my side again, and stroked his cheek. "I want to too, obviously."

Cas grabbed my dick again, giving it a squeeze, and I groaned. "Clearly." He grinned. Cas brushed the hair out of my face before trailing his hand down my side, his thumb teasing my hip. "Do you think...um..."

"What?"

He blushed. "Do you think, if we're not gonna have sex, maybe we could have this conversation with some pants on?"

"Oh?"

Cas swiped his fingers down my abdomen, through my pubes. "You're very distracting."

I laughed. "Sorry," I said. "No."

"No?"

With a smile to hide the real vulnerability I felt, I grabbed Cas's hand, kissing his knuckles. "I was really scared you'd be long gone when I got home," I confessed quietly. "So, you're here and that's where I'm keeping you. All of you."

I grabbed his butt.

The rest of the day passed much the same. We stayed in bed, touching, kissing and talking. I told Cas what Leda and I had discovered, and it was like I could watch him visibly packing it away in his mind, to contemplate later. Every time he thought of a question to ask, about shifters, mating bonds, my family, anything—he'd ask it. Sometimes he'd talk through what he'd learned, and I'd answer as best I could and wait patiently for him to recover enough to fool around some more.

Because really, while I knew neither of us was ready to complete our mating bond, there was plenty of stuff for us to share in the meantime.

Some hours later, I found myself draped over Cassian's broad back, kissing the nape of his neck. He was on his belly, chin resting on his folded arms. I rolled my hips in lazy little circles, not really doing anything, just kind of liking the way my dick nestled so nicely in the cleft of his perfect ass.

"Okay, another question," Cas mumbled. He arched his

back, pushing me up a bit. I slid between his thighs, my knees hitting the mattress.

"What is it?" I asked, trailing more kisses down his spine.

"What actually like, *happens?*"

"Happens?"

He cleared his throat suggestively, and pushed his ass up a little more.

"*Oh,*" I said. I smoothed my hands down his sides, holding his hips. Somehow it seemed a little easier to talk when we weren't facing each other. "Well," I said, trying to figure out how to word this. Suffice to say I was glad we'd taken a little time to calm down. "The first time we...*make love—*"

Cas snorted. "Make love?"

I gave his butt cheek a swat. "Hey."

"Sorry."

"Anyway," I huffed. "The first time we—"

"—make love?"

"Will you stop?" Maybe it wasn't easier just because we weren't face to face. My cheeks burned.

Cas laughed.

"Okay, fine," I snapped. "Now you'll never know."

"Alright, alright. I'll be good." He pushed his butt up against me with a soft sigh, possibly by way of apology.

I squeezed his hip bone, digging my knees into the mattress as I leaned down to kiss his neck. Cas moaned, and I thought maybe he was ready for another round. "So, with shifters," I started, trying a different tact, "with mated pairs, there's always an Alpha. The roles don't always shake out until they get together. But they fall into it, like instinct. They fit together."

We rocked against each other in silence for a few minutes, and somewhere in the back of the mind I registered these sheets could probably do with a washing. Cas clenched his ass, tight. The slight squeeze around my shaft as I dragged the head of my leaking cock over his hole had me groaning, my resolve threatening to crack. I almost forgot what we were talking about. "Go on," he prompted, and I was pleased to hear he'd gone a little breathless.

I trailed my tongue down his neck, pressing my teeth to the sharp tendons I found there. With a scrape of my canines I told him, "The Alpha bites their partner." I snapped my teeth in his ear, and he shivered below me. "Right when they come."

"*Fuck*," he whispered. "Why?"

"It's like a claim," I said. "It solidifies the bond between them."

"Woah," Cas breathed. "Does it hurt?"

"Probably, yeah. But I hear it feels good too." I paused. "It's permanent."

"So...what happens if they break up?"

"I don't—I don't really know. I don't think that happens all too often." I kissed his shoulder, again and again and again.

"Okay," said Cas. "So...how do you know who's the Alpha?"

I burst out laughing before I could stop myself.

"What?" Said Cas, annoyed.

Still chuckling, I tangled my fingers in his sandy hair, tugging until his head turned to the side. With his cheek on the pillow, we could both have a full view of ourselves in the mirror above my dresser. "Look at you," I said, half teasing, half reverent.

Cas looked absolutely wrecked, eyes dazed as he stared at our reflection: him on all fours, back arched, ass begging to be spread and bred. His dick bobbed hard between his legs, and I wrapped my hand around the shaft to give it a squeeze. When my thumb brushed the head, he gave a needy little moan and bucked even harder against me. And—I barely recognized myself, flushed and disheveled, something feral in my eyes as I knelt behind Cas, holding his hips, preparing to mount. *Hell.* I needed a cold shower, immediately.

"*Jesus,*" whispered Cas, embarrassed. He turned his face the other way.

I rolled off him, landing flat on my back. "That's why I want you to think about it," I told him. "At least for a little bit. It's a lot."

Cas was quiet for a while. "So," he said, "does that mean we only—"

I pinched his side. "—*make love?*"

He groaned. "Yes. Does that mean we only...do it, one way?"

"One way?" I echoed.

If possible, Cas blushed even further. "Because, there's a lot of stuff I wanna try. With you. Like, all of the stuff. I wanna try all of the stuff. I want you any way you'll have me."

I wrapped him in a tight hug. "We can try anything you like."

# 16



Thor and I didn't put clothes on between him coming home that morning and my alarm going off at five on Monday. I asked him everything and anything I could think of, though a lot of the questions seemed to be coming from my dick instead of my brain. That had to stop. There was a lot more to what I'd been learning about Thor and his family than the sexy part. I made a pact with myself to write down a list of any non-mating-related questions I thought of during the day.

Which meant I had to spend the day *not* thinking about mating.

I didn't know what it was about that word that got me so fucking hot. It was an unusual term, not one I'd ever used outside of a science class, and something about that really turned my crank.

I decided a good long run would help me work off some of this pent-up energy, so I prepared to hit the treadmill, hard. When I got to the gym, I stuffed my earbuds into my ears and picked my favorite machine, far away from the hubbub of the rest of the gym floor. Being here before six certainly had its benefits. I worked myself hard and the run had its desired effect. While I didn't necessarily think too much about the serious questions regarding my future with Thor, at least I wasn't thinking about leaving the gym and diving into bed with him. Okay, well, I thought about that a little. Sue me. But for the most part, I had my head on right to start my day. While it seemed like everything had gone topsy-turvy over the weekend, the rest of the world still continued on as normal, and I found that deeply reassuring.

I was a tiny bit jelly-legged by the time I'd showered and headed out of the locker room. With about an hour before my first class, I figured I'd head to the café and get some studying done over coffee.

With a latte at my elbow, I had settled in to review my notes when someone poked me in the back of the head. Hard.

"Ow," I said, annoyed, pulling my earbud out and searching for my tormentor. It was Lucy, wearing a scowl. "What gives?"

"'What gives,' he says." She threw up her hands, exasperated, before flinging down her book bag and sitting across from me, uninvited. "*Hello?*"

"Uh, hi?"

"Don't take that tone with me," she snapped. "What the hell happened with Thor?"

Oh. "Um..."

"Did Thor come back? Was he pissed you left? Are you okay? Did you break up?"

"Easy, *easy*," I said, raising my palms in supplication, wincing at the barrage of questions.

"Don't you 'easy' me," she said. "I'm serious. I've been worrying all weekend. You seemed so freaked ou—is that a hickey?"

I clapped a hand to the side of my neck. "No?"

"I guess you made up then."

"Yeah," I said. "I mean, kinda."

She gestured, and honestly, I had no idea how to even begin explaining. "Come on, Cas," she said. "I have been really worried about you."

So, I did my best to frame what Thor and I had discussed in a way that wouldn't have Lucy suggesting I have myself committed. "Well," I said, "Thor's family has this weird tradition with like..." how on earth could I phrase this? "Marriage."

"*Marriage?* You guys have only been together for a few weeks! You only just figured out you're bi!"

"I know, I know." If Lucy was already freaked out by *that*, what would she think if she knew the whole truth? Framing the whole "mate" thing as a marriage made it sound a lot more serious, and a lot less like a frantic, sexy game. My stomach twisted uncomfortably. Now that I thought about it, with pants on, in public, it really seemed a whole lot more serious than marriage. Thor's quiet voice, shy and uncertain despite his instinctive sexual confidence rang through my head. *It's permanent.*

"So, what, did he like, propose to you or some shit? Is that why you were so freaked?" She eyed my hickey, and slammed her fist to the table. "Did you say yes?"

"No—I don't know."

"Well, Cas, you gotta know. It's sounding to me like you're even less sure of what's going on than when we talked on Friday. What does Thor have to say about this? Does he want to get married so soon, or is it just his family?"

That sobered me up, too. How much of it came from Thor, and how much of it came from his family pressuring him? "I don't know." I scrubbed my hands over my face. "I don't want to break up, though." I looked at Lucy, so she would know how serious I was. "I am really into this guy."

"Well, good grief, those aren't the only two options, are they?"

*They are if I wanna have sex,* said a voice in the back of my head. I squashed it. "No, I suppose they aren't."

Lucy x-rayed me with her eyes. "There's something you're not telling me, still, isn't there?"

I sighed. "Yeah."

"And you...really can't talk to me about it?"

"No," I was certain of that at least.

She looked troubled. "You're...you're safe, right?"

"What?"

"Thor isn't like—he's not, hurting you?"

I laughed so hard a few people looked around in alarm. "Thor weighs about four ounces," I said, once I had gathered myself, and Lucy grinned too.

"I know, I know. I'm sorry. I had to ask."

"This talk really helped, but please don't worry about me," I told her. Then I frowned. "Don't think badly of Thor, either."

"I don't!"

"You just asked if he was abusing me," I reminded her. My little Thunder God might have me on my knees in the bedroom, but outside of that domain—I couldn't even fathom it.

"Okay, fair. But I don't, I promise. I like Thor a lot—and honestly, I really like the two of you together."

"Yeah?"

"Yeah, man. That's part of why I feel so strongly about this. I like seeing you happy, and you need to talk about stuff or this whole relationship is going to implode."

"Ugh, you're right."

"Duh."

I spent the rest of the day mulling things over, and after classes I made my way back to the apartment. I hadn't lied to

Lucy; her advice had made a lot of sense, and I'd been thinking about all of it. Thor had been right, too. I did really need to be sure about things before we moved our relationship forward. We had just gotten together, and despite the easy rhythm we'd fallen into, this was a very serious step for us to take.

When I walked into the apartment, I found Thor waiting for me.

*Shit.* Just looking at him, with his big eyes and slightly parted lips, I couldn't think. Or move. Or do anything. "Um."

"Listen—" he started, taking a step toward me. I watched the bob of his Adam's apple as he swallowed. He twisted his hands over each other.

"Yeah," I said. "Let's talk. I'll make dinner."

He nodded, perching on his usual seat to watch me cook. I pulled out the cutting board and a knife. I didn't even know what I was making. It would come to me. With my back to Thor, and with something to fill my hands, I thought it might be easier to talk.

"I think you should move back to your bedroom," Thor said quietly.

It tore me up to hear him say it. I dropped the knife, immediately turning to face him. "Are we breaking up?" I blurted, fear bleeding through my voice.

His eyes got huge behind his glasses. "Of course not—unless, do you want that?"

Despite my original plan to maintain some physical distance, I somehow found myself standing between Thor's knees. I took his face in my hands. "No. That's not what I want."

"Oh," he said softly. He slid his glasses up his nose. "Um. Good."

"So—you want me to move back into my room?"

"Well, no, obviously," Thor amended with a sly grin. "But I think you should."

"Why?"

"I think it'll be easier for you to think about...things. If you have some space, and some privacy."

Neither space, nor privacy sounded like something I wanted, but I supposed it was something I needed. It still felt wrong. Deeply wrong. I did my best to shrug off the feeling. "Okay."

I went back to chopping, letting the rhythmic sound of the blade fill the silence between us. Thor didn't say anything for a while, and I wondered what this meant for him. If his kind were used to pairing up and settling down essentially at the onset of puberty, what would it do to him to keep me at arm's length? I brushed it aside. Thor was an adult. He could make his own decisions. And I could make mine.

"I think we should date," I told him.

Thor huffed out a nervous little laugh. "Isn't that what we're doing already?"

"Rolling around in bed together is not dating."

"Oh, so you want me to wine and dine you, is that it?"

I turned to face him, bracing a hand on my hip. "Yeah," I said, bristling. "You have a problem with that? Is courting not a part of your fancy mating process?"

He blushed and gave me a sweet smile. "Alright," he said. "If that's what you want. Prepare to be wooed, Cassian Rhodes."

My heart actually fluttered. God help me, I was so screwed. "Good."

After I finished cooking, we sat together and ate in silence, and it felt like things were settled between us, at least for the time being.

Unfortunately, that let our thoughts drift to other things, namely the discoveries Thor and Leda had made in the lab. "So, someone is out there breeding primitive shifters," I said. "Why?"

"I have no idea," said Thor heavily, pushing his food around on his plate with his fork. He chewed his bottom lip. "Leda and Rafe's missing days are bothering me. Something isn't right about it."

"We already found out it was Benson who drugged you and Rafe," I said. "He admitted it to my face. I could chalk Rafe's incident up to Benson not giving a shit about collateral damage, but Leda? Did he have something against her?"

With a shrug, Thor said. "Maybe he had help, or was helping someone else. I have no idea."

The thought made me furious. Benson drugging someone for the sake of a stupid prank was bad enough—but the idea that he might be working with someone who actively wanted to hurt Thor? I opened my mouth, but Thor held up a hand.

"If someone else was involved, I find it highly unlikely I was the intended target."

"What?"

"Come on, Cas," he said. Thor wore a self-deprecating smile, trying to hide the real hurt behind his words. "If they're after shifters, what on earth could they possibly want with me? Me getting hit was probably just something Benson was happy to accomplish while they went after Rafe."

"None of this makes any sense," I said. Because, while I didn't want to argue that some kind of deranged shifter kidnappers wanted Thor, arguing that they *didn't* want him wasn't great either.

"I know." He sighed. "I think if we can figure out why they're doing this—or even what they're hoping to accomplish—and what's stopping them, we could start piecing some of this together."

"How do we know they're not accomplishing what they want?"

"Because they're leaving the results of their experiments to die off," he said, voice hollow. "If they were going well, they'd be kept, don't you think?"

"Poor things," I said, brushing the back of Thor's hand. He barely reacted, like he was lost in his own thoughts. He'd also barely eaten, which disturbed me. And, offended me a little. "You okay?"

Thor blinked rapidly, like he was coming out of a trance. "Yeah, sorry." He smiled, but it was strained. "Just kind of lost my appetite."

I picked up our plates, scraping Thor's leftover pasta into a Tupperware, knowing he'd be hungry and come back for it later.

With the dinner dishes cleared away, I got the distinct impression that Thor wanted to clear away the thread of the previous conversation as well. He made us a bowl of popcorn and picked a movie, and we spent the rest of the night snuggled up on the couch. I found myself dreading the lateness of the hour, knowing soon we'd be heading off to our separate, lonely beds.

Too soon, it seemed, the movie was ending and Thor was nudging me awake where I'd nodded off against the backrest of the sofa. I really, *really* didn't like the idea of going to bed without him.

True to his promise to woo me, Thor legitimately took my hand and walked me to my bedroom door, like he was escorting me home from a formal date. Standing on the threshold, he brushed his palm over my cheek and stood on tiptoe to offer me a sweet kiss. "Goodnight," he said, and I just about melted with how fucking adorable he was.

I couldn't help the "*Mmm,*" sound that came out of my mouth, and before I really knew what I was doing, my hands snuck out and seized the collar of his shirt, pulling him close to deepen the kiss.

"Cas," he murmured, like a warning, but he stepped in

closer, pushing my back against the wall and I went happily. It was wild how my body seemed to follow his every command. Thor let the kiss continue, heating up before pulling away, leaving me panting and weak-kneed where I leaned against the door jamb.

"Mmm?" I said again, a question this time. This was going to be more challenging than I thought. My hands fell limply to my sides, but Thor caught one. Without breaking eye contact, he pulled my hand up to his lips, brushing a soft kiss to my knuckles. I swallowed. Hell.

"Seriously, Cas," he said, but he was smiling. "*Goodnight.*"

So, for the next several weeks, Thor and I played the dating game. We went out, took long walks, stayed up late talking. I let Thor spoil me and take me to all his favorite fancy restaurants. We kept our clothes on, much to my chagrin. That had been the second ground rule to this little experiment—the first being sleeping apart—and it was proving to be a fucking trial. Still, though, a lot of our nights ended in some hot as fuck make-out sessions on the couch. After the top speed race of the first part of our relationship, I had to admit it was kind of nice to take a breather. Kissing Thor became something I was determined to master. Every time I wrung a new moan or sigh from him, I took my time memorizing how to make it happen again, and again, and again. That part was great.

Sleeping alone sucked. I missed having him tucked beside me every night. He fit so well in my arms that being in bed without him felt wrong.

One of the only good things about being back in my room was that I had a chance to privately explore some of the things Thor and I had discussed. The whole mating ritual still seemed pretty foreign, and I didn't know how I felt about him legitimately biting me, but it was important to Thor, so I decided to see if bottoming was something I'd be into trying.

Somehow, the idea hadn't entered my mind, and I think I

must have had some lingering hang-ups about the whole thing. Based on our respective physicalities and demeanors, and I guess the fact that I'd only ever topped before—did you still call it topping when it was someone with the opposite sex? I made a mental note to look that up, or possibly ask Lucy, because I wanted to make sure I had all the lingo correct. I'd had sex with a few different partners, all women, none of whom had been interested in experimenting with anal. At least, not that they'd expressed to me.

So, I decided to take my ass for a solo flight before I invited anyone else into the cockpit. Oh my *God*, what a horrible metaphor. My first night alone in bed, I spent a while doing some in-depth research. And I meant actual research, not porn research.

The following night, armed with a new bottle of lube, I sprawled out naked in bed because it was definitely time for porn research. I propped my laptop open beside me, and found a video with my favorite gay porn star (the one with the glasses), where he was topping his partner for a change. My skin prickled. It felt weirdly like I was being unfaithful to Thor, jacking off with some other dude's dick on my screen. I hadn't looked at porn since we got together, even when I felt like some self-love, reality proving a million times hotter than any fiction.

Watching the video that I'd jerked off to about a million times when I was first figuring things out, I realized it was doing absolutely nothing for me now. If anything, it had me keyed up and distracted, and one of the major tips I'd found online was to be as relaxed as possible. I slammed my laptop shut. The theatrical moaning cut off abruptly, and now my room was eerily silent. I shivered, before sitting up to coat my hands in lube.

I was *nervous*. Never had I been so nervous to jerk off before. Because like, duh. But this seemed important, weightier somehow, like my body knew how much was riding on this. Which made getting in the mood kind of hard—and made me decidedly *not*.

*Okay, Cas,* I thought. *You can do this.* I decided to go back to square one: thinking about Thor. I did my best to shut off the rest of my brain, thinking only about the sweet weirdo in the next room. His smile, his lips...his lips around my dick. I stroked myself, slow and easy, focusing on Thor.

Well, that worked. Like, embarrassingly quickly. I stroked myself to full hardness, which did not take long with all the sexy images of Thor coursing through my brain. Another tip I'd read was to make yourself as aroused as possible. So, I edged myself for hours, working myself to a frenzy. By the time I was feeling brave enough to move on with my experimenting, I was panting and shaking and dying to come. I swapped hands, brushing my left thumb over the head of my cock as my hips bucked off the bed, chasing the teasing friction of my off hand. With my right hand, I let my fingers slide down, tugging briefly on my balls before drifting behind them to the sensitive patch of skin between my sac and my hole.

A long exhale, then I applied a bit of pressure. The Google gods had informed me it was possible to stimulate one's prostate from the outside, so I figured I could start there, my fingers fluttering across the area, testing to see what might feel—*oh*.

A full-body shiver seized me as I brushed a certain spot. *Holy shit.* Squeezing my dick with my left hand, I kept probing with my questing finger. The angle was a little weird, but I spread my legs, bracing my feet on the mattress, chasing the feeling, spiraling quickly toward orgasm after so much denial. My plan was to slow down again when I got close, and maybe get my finger actually inside, but after being on edge for so long, the differing sensations pushed me off the cliff and I gasped, my cock jerking against my palm as I spurted all over my stomach.

*Woah.* I took that as a good sign.

I kept up with that all week, imagining me and Thor getting sweaty in bed, and every night without fail would find myself naked and gasping for breath, needy as I twisted in the sheets, making myself come again and again and again. When I got brave enough to breach my hole, I found the fullness strange. Not bad strange, necessarily, after the initial burn of the intrusion. Just...an adjustment. Literally.

When I got a bit more used to it, I imagined Thor's slim fingers in place of my own, agile and dexterous, taking me apart, and I came on a strangled moan.

My heart hammered, and I wondered if Thor heard me. The thought was strangely thrilling. Unlike other nights, I kept my finger inside after coming, imagining what would happen if he heard me, if he came in, how that confident, hungry look would flash over his face when he saw the state I was in. I kept probing my prostate even after my dick began to flag, a weak stream of cum still dripping from the head as I increased the pressure. It almost hurt—too sensitive in the aftermath of my orgasm, but I couldn't stop chasing the feeling. I twisted to get a better angle, imagining Thor coming in, pouncing on me, shoving his huge dick— *"Holy shit!"* I blurted. I came again somehow, but I felt it...everywhere. From my scalp to my balls to my toes to my stomach. Another feeble gush of cum dribbled out as my dick twitched, only half-hard as it recovered from my first orgasm.

I kind of felt like I'd licked a battery. In a good way. Quivering, I slid my finger out, heart pounding as I strained to hear if Thor stirred down the hall. My whole body trembled, mini shivers of delight flowing through my veins like electric shocks. I never wanted it to stop, and for a minute there it didn't seem like it was going to.

Holy fucking shit.

Okay.

I was definitely down to get fucked.

———

## THOR

Since we'd begun to sleep apart, Cas seemed unable to keep his hands off himself.

It drove me slowly insane, day by day. There was so much my kind still didn't understand about our nature, about mating bonds, and it seemed now that I'd formally declared Cas my intended, my pull to him had strengthened—despite it being pretty damn strong already.

It was as if all my senses had been tuned in to Cas's frequencies. I laid in bed every night, wide awake and aching, feeling the vibrations in the air from Cas's little gasps and moans, the way his scent saturated the space, and naturally my own imagination conjuring image after image of what he was getting up to between his sheets.

Before I'd met Cas, I had never imagined being the Alpha partner in a relationship. Any sexual fantasies I'd dreamt up usually involved me happily submitting to some huge guy who pinned me down, bent me like a pretzel, and fucked me ten ways to Sunday.

Cas was different. The way he looked at me made me want to take charge, to hold him close, protect him, take care of his needs, his pleasure, all of it. I wanted to lay claim to Cas, and the way he looked at me said he wanted that too.

But for me, it was an instinct I could trust. Cas was human, and he didn't have the crutch of magic to guide him toward choosing me. And he had to be sure.

So, I had to wait.

I had to wait, alone in bed, listening to Cas cheat on me. With himself. Obviously, I knew that wasn't what was happening, but it was hard to be charitable when I couldn't sleep, and Cas seemed to be having the time of his life down the hall. Alone, in the dark, my animal side made its displeasure known, so I lost a lot of sleep trying to calm down the vociferous part of me that wanted to bust Cas's door down.

Then, there was the other thing.

The first time it happened, I almost didn't even notice. But then it happened again.

I came back from class one day, the warm tenor of Cas's voice humming through the door. As I went inside, dropping my keys in the dish, Cas hastily ended the phone call.

"My friend just got here, Dad," he said into his phone. "Gotta go. Love you."

At first, I didn't read anything into it, but Cas calling me just a "friend" more than once drove a little spike of hurt deep in my chest. Finally, one day, my curiosity got the better of me.

"Why do you do that?"

"Hmm?" The pink in Cas's freckled cheeks told me he knew exactly what I was talking about.

"When you talk to your dad, you always call me your friend." I left it at that, not wanting to sound accusatory. Cas never gave me the impression his dad was anything other than loving and accepting, but I didn't really know the guy; there could be something there.

Cas made a face. "I'm sorry. It's shitty. Every time I talk to him I just...I haven't come out to him yet."

"It's something you have to do in your own time," I said. "Do you think he'd be upset?"

"No—he'd love me no matter what," said Cas. He set his phone on the counter and walked toward me. He wrapped his warm hand around my arm, gripping tight to my elbow. "My Dad...he has enough to worry about without me piling it on."

I jerked from his grasp. "Piling *what* on, exactly?"

"Just," he gestured between us, trailing away. He looked desperately uncomfortable. "More issues."

"Oh."

"Thor—"

"No, I get it. It's your call, if you want to tell him." I forced a smile. I knew it wasn't okay to try to dictate when someone else came out, but it was more than that. Cas didn't seem to be implying his dad was intolerant, only that our relationship was some kind of complication that wasn't worth explaining yet. Cas never liked to make waves, and apparently dating me was a huge wave.

I tried not to sulk, I really did. The rational side of me knew Cas had to deal with this in his own way, in his own time, but I couldn't shake the feeling that he was embarrassed of me.

I put it from my mind as best I could, especially because despite my trouble sleeping, everything was going great between us.

A few days before the winter break, I came home to see Cas spring up from the sofa like he'd been waiting for me.

He bounded over, grabbing me by the hand to tug me toward the kitchen island. After boosting me up to sit on the counter, Cas moved to stand between my knees and pulled out his phone.

He made a few taps on the screen then held it to his ear.

"Dad?"

A pause.

"Yeah, I was just—I was wondering if it's okay if I brought someone home for Christmas."

My eyes widened and my breath caught.

"Yes—yeah...his name is Thor. He's...he's my boyfriend."

# 17

CAS

Thor's eyes went wide behind his glasses, and he fisted his hands in the front of my shirt. My heart hammered in my throat as my dad stayed silent on the other end of the call.

I wasn't even sure why I'd put this off for so long, but the longer I waited, the more nervous I was to tell Dad. It was hard to put into words, but I'd lived so long as the kid who never made his life harder that eventually I started automatically shielding him from anything complicated.

The silence stretched on long enough that I crossed from jittery nerves into real fear. Never had my dad said anything to make me consider he was intolerant of LGBTQ folks, but this radio silence was killing me, sending me into a spiral of panic. Based on the look on Thor's face he was right there with me.

Finally, my dad cleared his throat. "His—his name is...*what?*"

Thor groaned; I let out a shaky laugh. "Thor. His name is Thor."

"No shit?"

I grimaced. That was my exact reaction to learning Thor's name the day we met. I ran the knuckles of my off hand up and down Thor's arm in sympathy. "Yeah," I said. "Is it okay? If he stays for Christmas?"

"Of course! Well, I mean, you know what the house is like —but the more the merrier."

"Thanks, Dad," I said, his acceptance meaning more than I could say.

"Well, I say that but you're the one who'll be cooking for everyone, so."

I grinned, grabbing Thor's hand and bringing his knuckles up to kiss them because he still looked terrified. "Okay, great. Thanks again."

"Love you. Can't wait to see you."

"Love you too."

Thor still looked pale after I hung up.

"Was that okay? Sorry, I should have—*umph!*"

He cut me off by grabbing my face and pulling me in for a kiss. "It was perfect. Thank you."

So, Christmas Eve-eve, we pulled into the driveway of my childhood home. Dad and I had lived in an apartment while he was in nursing school, but I had been so little I didn't remember it. He'd only been seventeen at the time. When he met my stepmom, they had saved up to buy this place. It had been a real piece of junk that they rebuilt and turned into a home. I grabbed mine and Thor's bags from the trunk, and as I slammed it closed, I heard the creaky front door swing open, a noise so familiar it squeezed my heart in my chest.

When we got to the front porch, the whole investigative squad was there: Dad; my brother Jesse, who was a sophomore in high school; the twelve-year-old twins Walt and Wanda; and Bart, who was eight.

I hugged my dad and moved down the line to hug the rest

of them. Jesse seemed to have grown a couple inches while I was away this semester. He eyed Thor suspiciously over my shoulder. "That's Thor?"

I groaned and elbowed him. "Yes. Don't be a dick."

"We tried to Google him but—"

"Shut *up*, Bart!" Walt cuffed him on the shoulder.

Bart retaliated, and a scuffle broke out immediately.

D
ad sighed. "Welcome to Casa Chaos, Thor."

Thor stood half a step behind me with his mouth gaping open. "Uh," he said, cheeks pink.

Had this been a huge mistake? I started questioning my sanity, bringing Thor into the mayhem of my home life, but before I could fully descend into anxiety and come up with some faux emergency to get both of us out of here and back to campus, Dad moved past me and pulled Thor into a big, warm hug.

So, I skipped right on past anxiety and right into panic. My dad was a hugger, and I'd forgotten how that might come off to someone like Thor, whose parents greeted him with a curt nod and a stiff handshake. I heard a sharp intake of breath, and Thor blinked at me over my dad's shoulder, rigid in the hug. I flinched, bracing myself.

But then, something happened. Thor returned the hug. It all happened in the span of only a few seconds, but it was huge. Thor looked a bit shaken, his glasses foggy and off-kilter, but he smiled as he ascended the steps to meet the rest of the sibs.

Walt had his hand over Bart's mouth. "We totally didn't Google you."

He laughed. "I'm too boring to be on Google, anyway."

Everyone chuckled except Jesse, whose eyes narrowed.

I cleared my throat. "I'm going to put our stuff up in my room."

"Hold on," said Jesse. He turned to our father. "When Leah stayed over after homecoming, you put her in my room and made me sleep on the couch."

Little shit! Trying to blow up my spot!

Dad looked uncertain, eyes flickering between the two of us. Jesse had really put him in the hot seat. He opened and closed his mouth a few times before saying, "Actually, when Leah stayed over, I reminded you to be a gentleman, and you offered to sleep on the sofa." He gestured between Thor and me. "I don't know which of you, uh, is the gentleman, here."

"Not Cas," muttered Wanda.

"I'll take the couch," said Thor, and Dad shot him a grateful smile. He looked up at me. "I'm much shorter than you. And obviously much more gentlemanly."

"You don't have to—"

"It's fine," he said, putting a hand on my chest.

I caught his fingers and squeezed. "If you insist."

As we went inside, I cringed. I wasn't ashamed of where I grew up, but I couldn't help thinking of Thor's family's house. If this situation had been reversed, I was sure he would have set me up in the world's most lavish guest room—and here I was letting him sleep on the world's lumpiest couch.

It wasn't a bad couch, but it was old as Moses and still smelled like spilled root beer on hot days.

The strange thing was, with every step into my family's cluttered, creaky old farmhouse, Thor grew more relaxed. He was positively floating by the time he set his bag down by the end of the sofa. My Dad handed him a pile of musty throws, saying, "What we lack in spare beds we make up in blankets!"

"Couch looks plenty comfortable," Thor assured him.

We spent the evening at the huge table in the kitchen. I cooked, and the usual chaos reigned as everyone squabbled over the perceived best pieces of chicken, the potato with the crispiest skin, and the corn on the cob with the most butter. Honestly, this is where I belonged: standing in the kitchen, whisk in hand, listening to the people I loved most in the world bicker and laugh.

I startled. Was Thor one of the people I loved most?

I turned to look at him, leaning in to listen as Walt explained to him earnestly that Thor wasn't the coolest Avenger, and my Thor seemed a lot more like Bruce Banner anyway, who was way cooler. Thor slid his glasses up his nose and laughed. As the conversation surged around him, Thor didn't dive in—but he didn't shy away either. He was engrossed, smiling, watching and drinking in my family like they were the most fascinating people in the world.

During a lull in the conversation, he caught my eye and missed his mouth with his fork, stabbing himself. "Ow," he said softly, blushing.

Yes.

I loved him.

The rest of my lovable but meddling family stayed up way too late. I had hoped to get some alone time with Thor, but he was dozing with his head on my shoulder before everyone else had turned in. When I'd shooed them all upstairs, I gently removed Thor's glasses and tucked him in. I brushed a kiss to his temple before shutting off the light. When I got to the stairs, I turned. The pull in my gut was hard to ignore, and I made a mental note to set my alarm so I could sneak down and wake him up the way I wanted.

Upstairs in my old room, I stared at the ancient glow-in-the-dark stickers on the ceiling. I had really hoped to have Thor curled up beside me, that maybe the sleeping arrangements would give me a chance to show him I was ready for everything he offered, ready to dive in, together.

And I missed him.

So much.

I had a hard time falling asleep, so when my phone went off at the ass crack of dawn, I hit snooze—just once. Or at least, I thought I did.

I woke with a start, grabbed my phone and realized it was after ten. Fuck! I pulled on my pajama pants and a hoodie, praying everyone was sleeping in.

No such luck.

Jesse stood in the kitchen burning bacon; the twins and Bart sat on the couch playing video games.

I kissed each of the Super Smash Bros (And Super Smash Sis) on the head. "Merry Christmas Eve, gang. Where's Thor?"

The twins shot each other looks and identical grins, and Bart piped up. "He's a real heavy sleeper."

I realized the three of them were in fact sitting in a row on top of a snoring mound of blankets. A shaggy head of curls poked out one end, and several pale toes out of the other.

"Can he breathe?" I hissed at them.

Wanda shrugged, frantically directing the c-stick on her controller with her thumb.

Walt said, "He wouldn't move. Or wake up."

"This is the only spot all the controllers reach," added Wanda. They all liked to play my old GameCube so much, I didn't have the heart to take it to school.

"Okay, well, in that case, I got next."

I made my way to the kitchen, knowing coffee was the only way to rouse Thor and keep him from getting absorbed in the saggy sofa like a handful of loose change. Jesse stood at the counter mixing pancake batter like it had insulted his mother. I debated giving him a tip on how to avoid over mixing, but decided to keep my mouth shut.

"What, Cas?" He turned around and glared at me.

"What?"

"Whenever you hover, it's because you want to butt in and tell me I'm fucking something up."

"Woah, dude," I said, defensive. "What is up with you?"

"Nothing," he snapped, going back to his breakfast food victims. "And I fucking know how to make pancakes."

"Okay," I said. "I know you do."

I clapped him on the shoulder, making a mental note to ask Dad what the hell was up with him.

Jesse seemed to unclench, and said, "There's coffee."

"Thanks."

I filled a mug and went back to the living room, shooing the sibs off their perch on my boyfriend's back. "You guys want to see something funny?"

They nodded. I crouched by the end of the sofa and held the mug close to the mop of curly dark hair. I blew on the top, wafting the steam toward him, and in point five seconds flat, Thor launched himself off the couch. "I'm up, I'm up. Coffee?" He reached for the mug without having opened his eyes yet. "Why does my back hurt?"

Jesse served us all breakfast with a determined, focused cast to his face. Halfway through our feast, Dad came in through the front door, looking exhausted. I knew he'd taken on some extra shifts at the hospital to be able to spend the whole of Christmas Day with us. Tired, but happy at the sight of us all at the table, he made his way around the kitchen, giving us each a kiss on the brow as he had always done since we were little. He paused awkwardly when he got to Thor, and gave him a one-armed hug instead, but Thor still looked bashful and pleased. My heart soared. It meant more than I could say that my family accepted him so easily.

While I was prepping for dinner, I shooed Thor into the living room to watch Christmas movies with the siblings. Dad sat at the kitchen table, eating a sandwich. I knew he was exhausted, and after working all night, he'd be heading to bed as soon as he finished eating.

I kind of got the vibe that Dad wanted to talk about stuff. He'd been very welcoming of Thor, and accepted my dating a guy without missing a beat, but he was still my dad and I sensed he was waiting for some kind of explanation. Or at least a story. I heard his glass thunk on the table seconds before he asked, "So, how did you and Thor meet?"

My stomach churned, and in that instant, I realized the real reason I hadn't told him about Thor before this. I turned the burner under my stir fry way down and turned to face my dad. "He's...he was my roommate."

Dad looked puzzled. "I didn't think you had a roommate," he said. "I thought your scholarship gave you a single."

I sighed, and took the seat across from him. My guts twisted, and a lump rose in my throat. "I lost my scholarship," I whispered.

"What?"

And then, the whole story was spilling out, somehow. It started with me tanking my paper, and wound all the way through my developing relationship with Thor. My eyes stung as I talked, looking down at my interlocked hands. I couldn't meet my dad's eye.

I heard the scrape of chair legs across the tile, and all at once, Dad pulled me into a hug, squeezing me so tight, resting his chin on top of my head.

"Oh, Cassian," he said. "Why did you feel like you had to keep this from me?"

"I don't know," I said. "I didn't want you to be disappointed in me. I didn't want you to worry."

"Cas, I'm your father," he said. "Despite the fact that it sometimes seems like you're the other half of the parenting duo in this house, that's really not the case."

I sniffled, and said nothing.

"I rely on you far too much," he said, "I know that. And I am so grateful for everything you do for this family." He pulled away, looking into my eyes. "But I don't want you to feel like you can't be a kid."

I scowled.

He laughed. "Okay, so you're not a kid. But you're *my* kid."

"I was just so embarrassed," I confessed. "I couldn't believe I'd fucked up so badly."

Dad cupped my cheeks and kissed my forehead. "We all fuck up sometimes," he said. "And I'm glad you got Thor out of the deal. He seems good for you."

"He is." I cleared my throat, and stood to return to the stove. This had been plenty heart-to-heart for one night. "I um."

"What is it?"

This is something that made me feel like the scum of the earth. I hated myself for it, but I knew I had to be honest. "I was trying to requalify for my scholarship again," I said, "So I can give you guys the money from my summer job this year. But..."

Dad smiled knowingly. "But?"

I hadn't said this out loud, and I hadn't even really admitted it to myself yet. "I want to keep living with Thor, so I'll have to use the money for rent," I said. "I know it's selfish—"

"Cassian, please. For once in your life, please, be selfish."

"Really?"

"Yes, really. We'll be fine."

I looked at him doubtfully.

"Cas, I never intended to rely on you for income. Jesus. We'll be okay."

"Okay," I said. We hugged again tightly, and Dad ruffled my hair before heading upstairs to crash.

Mercifully, the living room emptied at a reasonable hour on Christmas Eve, leaving me and Thor tangled up together on the sofa, the soft twinkling glow of the Christmas tree reflecting in his glasses.

He looked enchanting. I told him that, just to make him blush. Thor gave my chest a half-hearted shove, turning away. I seized his chin to bring his eyes back to my own, hesitating briefly before brushing my lips softly to his. He shivered, closing his eyes with a little hum of pleasure. With a nudge to his hip, I encouraged Thor to climb up into my lap.

He was already hard, rocking eagerly against my crotch. The past few weeks had been an exercise in desperation, our lust relegated to hot and heavy make-out sessions on our couch, dry humping frantically and, when the pressure built too much, shoving our hands down each other's pants, jerking each other to rough completion.

I longed to get naked with him again, and something told me the hour was fast approaching. But not tonight. Not yet.

But, you know. I wasn't made of stone. Planting my feet, I lifted my hips, shoving my pajama bottoms down my thighs. Lowering my bare ass back to the couch cushions, I raised my eyebrows at Thor, who looked down between us like he didn't dare believe what he was seeing. He hastened to squirm out of his own bottoms, but wrapped a blanket around his shoulders, hiding us both from the possibility of spying eyes.

While he held my shoulders, I wrapped a hand around both of our dicks, pressing them together, feeling Thor's heat and getting a weird little thrill at the size comparison. Something about Thor's huge cock dwarfing mine had me boiling over, especially given my solo explorations of the last few weeks. My precum leaked over the head of my dick, thick and fast, and I used my thumb to smear it around. Thor licked his palm and his hand joined mine. We released matching groans, rutting into the slick hole created by our joined hands. He pressed his forehead to mine, and his breath was hot on my face, smelling of cocoa and candy canes. I claimed his mouth, invading with my tongue to taste it all, and he sucked eagerly, swiping the tip of his own tongue against mine. Squeaky, huffing little moans breached the seal made by our lips as we rocked together, trying to stay quiet but encouraging one another.

Thor came first, a muffled sob of pleasure alerting me before the wet heat of his release spattered against my stomach. Before I could react, he slipped down between my legs and took me in his mouth as his knees connected with the floor. The blanket draped over him like a cloak, and I fisted my hands in his thick, silky hair as he worked me with his tongue.

When he took my balls in his mouth, wrapping his long fingers around my shaft, I didn't last much longer, biting down hard on my bottom lip as I came all over myself. Thor lapped the cum from my navel, making me groan, wishing I could peel the clothes off him and cover every inch of his skin with my lips. He climbed back up into my lap, our spent groins radiating heat against each other, a small taste of the complete closeness I hoped we'd be sharing again soon. We kissed slowly, languidly, until I could tell Thor was seconds away from dozing against my lips.

Glancing at the clock above the mantle, I realized with a jolt that it was almost one thirty in the morning. I nudged my nose up Thor's jaw and nipped his ear. "Merry Christmas, baby," I whispered.

He grinned against my cheek. "Merry Christmas."

I drew away to look into his eyes, sleepy and unfocused now, and so endearing. "I..." the words were there, on my tongue. I felt them deep in my bones, and unless I was way off, I read them in Thor's eyes, too. But the moment had to be right. Perfect. I swallowed. "I should get upstairs."

Thor cocked his head, like he sensed what I hadn't said. He kissed my nose. "Goodnight, Cas."

"Goodnight."

———

## THOR

Feeling satisfied, but wishing I still had a warm Cas to snuggle, I punched the sofa cushions around, trying to mold them into a more comfortable shape. I set my glasses on the end table and curled up under the blanket, staying warm and keeping any lingering traces of Cas's smell in my little flannel bubble.

I had just begun to float down into a doze when the stair creaked. Of course, I was hoping it was Cas returning, so I sat up immediately, groping for my glasses. My eager smile faded when I saw Cas's brother Jesse descending the stairs, struggling with two huge garbage bags.

He saw that I was awake and rolled his eyes. "I thought you two were never going to stop humping."

"You *watched* us?" I blurted, mortified. My brain instantly kicked into calculations of escaping the Rhodes household and fleeing into the night, never to be seen or heard from again.

"Gross, dude, no." Jesse crossed the living room and deposited his garbage bags beside the Christmas tree. "I caught one glimpse and that was more than enough."

"Then what're you..."

Jesse sat next to the bags and began emptying them. "I had to wait for the coast to be clear so I could wrap these."

The bags contained gifts, ribbons, wrapping paper, and Christmas stockings. It looked to be hours' worth of work.

Before I could ask, Jesse said, "Dad usually stays up late Christmas eve to wrap everyone's gifts. It's the only chance he has to do it, but he was exhausted, so I shut off his alarm." He glared at me.

"Want some help?"

"No," he snapped. Then he sighed. "Yes."

I moved across the room to sit opposite him, waiting for instruction. He sorted the gifts into small piles for each sibling, and glared at me some more as he fully emptied the bags. "Is everything alright, Jesse?"

"Everything's fine."

"Do—do you not want me here?"

"I don't care." But the look on his face said he did care. About a dozen reasons crossed my mind why this kid could hate my guts without even knowing me. But, before I could hazard a guess as to one of them, he opened his mouth again. "I did Google you."

"Oh?"

"You're rich."

I frowned. "So...you hate me?"

"Kinda."

I chewed on that a moment. "I guess that's fair." Seizing the nearest gift, I began to cut and trim the wrapping paper before folding it crisply at the corners and taping it down.

Jesse was quiet for a while, the only sounds between us the crinkle of paper and the snip of scissors. "Cas always did this stuff."

"Ah."

"'Ah' what?" Jesse narrowed his eyes, his hands frozen as he tied a bow.

"You miss him."

"I do not," said Jesse, incredulous. "He's such an uptight dick."

"Uh-huh."

"Real white knight complex."

"Sure."

"Always bossing us around like *he's* our dad. He's only like four years older than me."

I sighed, leveling my gaze at Jesse, waiting.

He chewed his lip. "I do miss him."

"I know."

"It's really hard without him here."

"He knows. He misses you all, too. But he's gotta do his own thing."

Jesse nodded, looking away. He stuffed a few trinkets angrily into a stocking. "You can't take him away from us."

"What?"

"I've seen the way he looks at you," said Jesse, sounding disgusted, and I couldn't help a small smile. "You're gonna 'Christmas Prince' him."

"What does *that* mean?"

"I don't know, I never watched it! It's some stupid romance movie. You're like the Prince Charming guy and Cas is like the poor Cinderella girl."

I laughed out loud. "Oh, man, please let me be there if you try to call him that."

Jesse scowled at me, and I had to relent.

"Even if I wanted to take him away—which I don't—I couldn't. Cas loves you all more than *anything*."

He scoffed. "He loves you, too."

I blushed. "We'll see."

It was Jesse's turn to laugh. "Uh-huh." A little more silence passed between us and finally Jesse said, "You're okay, I guess."

With a smile, I said, "Thanks. You are too."

Christmas morning with Cas's family was *everything*. I didn't think I'd ever felt so at peace with the whole entire world as I did sitting on the sofa, Cas's arm around my shoulders, watching his siblings open their gifts. I hadn't gotten very much sleep at all. By the time Jesse deemed the gift wrapping complete, it had been almost four, and then around five thirty, Cas's dad thundered down the stairs in a panic because he'd overslept. He'd been equal parts relieved and embarrassed to find the gifts already done, but I'd steered him into the kitchen and fed him some coffee and one of Cas's homemade muffins, and that set him right. He was in high spirits by the time everyone else woke up.

Mostly I observed the Rhodes family experience their Christmas. Seeing Cas in his natural habitat warmed me up inside, even more than the half hot chocolate, half coffee concoction Jesse made me.

This was a family. A real family. And somehow, I must have done something right because I was here, being a part of it.

"Are you alright?" Cas asked me in the car as we drove back to campus a few days later.

I guess I had been fairly silent, staring out the window and recalling a thousand tiny perfect moments from my time at the Rhodes house. Turning to Cas, I smiled. "Yes."

"You're awfully quiet." His hand came to rest on my knee, giving it a gentle squeeze.

I threaded our fingers together. "Just...thinking."

"Thinking what?"

"Your family is..." I searched for the right word.

"Embarrassing?"

"Beautiful."

Cas barked out a startled laugh. "Come on."

I squeezed his hand. "I'm serious."

A flush crept up his neck. "Oh." A pause. "Well, thank you. I think so too."

As we drove, I steeled myself to bring something up that I'd been mulling over for a few days, and I wasn't sure how Cas was going to take it. His family was struggling. They were hardly destitute, but the cracks were there—in little things: the used textbooks, the old appliances. The crack in Cas's father's cell phone, a few generations old. Since we started dating, neither Cas nor I had mentioned that we'd entered into our living arrangements with the assumption it would end after a year.

When we first got together, I had imagined, in the darkest, most shameful corners of my mind, Cas and I running away together, away from the shadow of my father and the rest of my family. I still had all of Cas's rent money, and his security deposit, sitting in a separate bank account. Jesse's anger, his fear, the look on his face had bothered me. *You can't take him away from us.* I never could, and I hadn't lied to Jesse. I would never want to. That family was a part of Cas, and a part of me, now.

"I haven't spent your rent money," I blurted gracelessly.

"What?"

"I still have it all," I said. I looked out the window, not at Cas. "You should have it back, and don't bother paying me for the rest of the year."

"Thor, that's—"

"Please, Cas. I don't want your money and I don't need it."

"I can't—"

"If you don't want it, I'm going to donate it all to charity at the end of the year," I said firmly. I chanced a glance at him. "I'll pick something weird and embarrassing and do it in your name."

Cas was silent.

"Cas—"

"Thor, I really don't know what to say." Well, at least he didn't sound angry. I knew Cas had a lot of pride, and he didn't like showing his vulnerability, but he had to understand I couldn't keep his money in good conscience.

"Just say thank you," I suggested. "Or better yet, don't say anything. Just say you'll buy your dad a new phone."

Cas laughed. "He's had that dumbass broken phone for two years. It was Jesse's."

"So, you'll take the money back?"

"I'll think about it."

Fair enough.

# 18

CAS

Back in our apartment, an electric energy pulsed over every interaction I had with Thor. Bringing him home to meet my family had been huge; I hadn't realized how huge until we'd said goodbye on the front porch. Like seeing my siblings, even Jesse, hug him had unlocked a secret chamber in my heart.

I was ready, ready to grab Thor's hand and jump into the unknown. *Finally*, my libido seemed to shout. Perhaps it was fast to enter into a permanent mating bond like the one Thor described, but every time I saw Thor, the look in his eye said, "home."

The problem was getting Thor to believe that. I'd thought we were on the same wavelength, especially after his offer to refund my rent money, but when we went to bed our first night back in the apartment, Thor did his usual date-night move of walking to my bedroom door, kissing me goodnight, and heading off to his room. Alone.

I was floored. Apparently, he still had some reservations. Okay, fine. It was time for me to pull out the big guns.

"Okay, for real. What is going on with you guys?"

Lucy appeared by my elbow under the pretext of helping me plate up dessert. I fixated on upending the ramekins in front of me. It had been two weeks since we got back from my family's house. Two infuriating weeks with Thor either oblivious to my horny overtures, or playing ridiculously hard to get. "What do you mean?"

Lucy scoffed. "I have never felt even a tingle of desire for a dude," she said in a low voice, "but you two have me so hot I don't know what the fuck is happening."

I grinned. "Nothing's going on," I told her quietly. "I'm trying to throw Thor off his game."

Lucy rolled her eyes. "For fuck's sake, Cas. I'm expecting you to bend him over the dinner table right in front of us."

I had the misfortune of tasting the bourbon caramel sauce at that precise moment, inhaled to laugh, and choked on it. Never mind the fact that it would be Thor doing the bending.

"You okay?" Speaking of, he materialized at my side, rubbing my back as I struggled for breath.

"Wrong tube," I said as I regained control of myself. "Here, will you taste this?"

Thor's eyes went wide as I held the spoon to his mouth. His pink little tongue darted out, pulling the spoon between his lips. With his glasses, Thor's dewy brown eyes seemed giant as he stared me down, hollowing his cheeks to taste the caramel. "*Mmm,*" he said softly as I tugged the spoon back, meeting the slightest resistance as he sucked every drop of sauce from it. His eyes closed, just for a second. "Perfect."

"Yeah?" My voice pitched low and husky.

"Yeah." He blinked rapidly, fluttering those thick lashes. With a blush, I realized my other hand had flown to Thor's waist, thumb teasing the bone of his hip. How had that happened?

We locked eyes for several beats, Lucy looking between us with glee. Thor swallowed, and my eyes followed the movement of his Adam's apple before traveling up to his lips, which he licked, his tongue searching for traces of sweet caramel.

Feeling a bit hot, I released Thor's hip and returned my attention to the dessert on the counter. We had already eaten dinner. For the first time since that fateful meal in September, I had cooked risotto. The gesture had not been lost on Thor, who'd looked up from his plate mid-moan and caught me staring right at him.

It was so on.

I'd invited Lucy and Leda over, and it seemed that the two of them were forming their own bond. Like Thor and me, it seemed that opposites had really attracted in their case. I had to wonder how much Leda had told her, and I still felt a pang of guilt every time I saw Lucy because I felt like I was lying to her. Thor drifted back to the dinner table to chat with Leda, and Lucy elbowed me, clearing her throat. When I glanced toward her, she mimed fanning herself like a proper southern belle. I shoved her.

"Woof," she said, stifling a giggle as she stumbled off a step.

I tried to keep it together while the four of us had dessert, but the energy my Thunder God gave off was like static, searing the air before the arrival of a summer storm. We ate in quiet for a while, until Lucy broke the silence.

"Your apartment always smells so nice," she said politely. "I've been admiring your candles. Leda has some just like that at her place."

"It's sort of a tradition, both her family and mine share," Thor explained. "Each new candle is started with a new beginning in one's life."

"Oh, that's such a sweet idea. What are they?"

He dabbed his lips with a napkin and stood. Beginning at the left-hand side of the mantle, Thor trailed his fingers over the base of each lit candle, the color on his cheeks deepening with each explanation. "I started this one when Cassian moved in," he said. "Cas bought this one when we started the tradition of our weekly dinners."

I loved to watch his shy smile.

"This one when we got together..." he trailed off, confused. *Finally.*

"Well?" Lucy prompted. "What's that last one."

Thor turned back toward me, an unasked question on his lips. Since I'd put the candle up there and lit it, I decided to answer for him.

"It's kind of private," I said, summoning an exaggerated casual demeanor.

Leda choked on a bite of her dessert, and I blushed realizing she would know expressly, specifically, the new beginning marked by that candle. Lucy thumped her on the back. "You okay, babe?"

*Babe!* That was new. I glanced at Thor, momentarily distracted, and he gave me a knowing waggle of his eyebrows. Was it something he could sense happening between them? Or had Leda told him?

Between the four of us, the air was heavy and thick with intention as we poured another round of wine and savored our dessert.

------

THOR

After dinner and dessert—a downright decadent chocolate lava cake with sinful bourbon caramel—Lucy and Leda hung around for a bit, playing cards and having a few drinks. I could barely focus from nerves and anticipation.

After boldly stating tonight would be a 'new beginning' for us, Cas pretended nothing special was scheduled to happen tonight. He was in no rush to get the girls out of the house, though the hand he placed on my shoulder, rubbing little circles with his thumb, seemed to speak volumes of intention.

When Lucy and Leda finally left, I closed and locked the door behind them feeling like I'd had about fourteen double espressos.

My hands shook as I grabbed the sponge to begin the dishes. Hyperaware of Cas's presence across the room, where he reclined on the sofa, I knew I was about fifteen minutes from having no capacity to think about cleaning, and I didn't want all the dishes to sit until tomorrow.

Cas waited patiently until I finished my tidying. I rinsed my trembling hands and crossed to stand before him. His gaze was so sweet. I nudged his foot. "Shall we?"

"Yes."

"Are you sure about this?"

Cas stood, so tall, so strong, and took me in his arms. His big hands braced across my back. "Take me to bed, Thor.

I went weak against him, wondering how on earth I could be the one to lay claim to this man.

Cas led me down the corridor, his thumb brushing over the knuckles of my hand. When we reached my room, our room, I stopped at the doorway.

In theory, it was my bedroom, but I still felt like I had to ask for entry. Once I stepped over the threshold, I'd be my basest self. In some ways, I'd be an animal. I'd be an Alpha. And, I wanted to be that. With every vibrating hormone in my body I wanted to be Cas's Alpha. I wanted to fuck him, claim him, bite him.

But not just that. I wanted to provide for him, care for him, love him. Treat him like royalty until I drew my last breath. But things were different for us, for shifters. The instinct was there for us to trust—a law of nature, like gravity. For Cas, though, it was just an attraction, wasn't it? It was a man, finding another man he liked. He could have anyone he wanted, so why choose me?

He was intelligent, caring, and chivalrous. Beautiful. Tender.

I had to *earn* my right to claim him.

I stepped over the threshold into the bedroom, like a stranger in my own home. Asking. And Cas, God love him, met me there.

He met my gaze and peeled off his clothes until he was perfect and bare. I stared at the broad spread of his chest, the rise and fall of it as he breathed. Naked, Cas moved to the bed. He laid on his back, splayed out on the comforter, his freckled skin pale gold like an offering. "Thor." He said my name like an incantation, and it summoned me to the bed to kneel on the comforter beside him. "I'm yours."

I stripped, hastily, far less graceful in my disrobing than Cas had been. I'd felt so lonely in this bed before him. So, for a while, I just looked, liking to see him there. Cas rolled onto his belly, the toned expanse of his back stretched out before me, perfect ass begging to be spread and claimed. I wanted to tear him apart.

I shook my head, trying to clear it. This wasn't a type of thought I'd had before; it was starting already.

Cas had set this in motion, so I decided to trust him, to trust my instincts. That decision was like a hook in my chest, pulling me forward. I draped over Cas, and he was so, *so* warm. And because I still had no idea what I was doing, I whispered in his ear—half expecting him to deny me. "How can it be me you want?"

Cas arched his spine, pushing his ass against my pelvis and I throbbed against him. This was far from the traditional experience of an Alpha, or so I would have thought. Cas dislodged me from his back and rolled us both, pinning me beneath him. "Thor," he said, determined. "I love you."

The breath whooshed from my body as he kissed all over my face.

"I wanted to tell you. You know, before."

"Gosh," I managed. I craned my neck to kiss him back. "I love you, too."

"Then," Cas said, his voice low and rumbly. "Show me."

Odd, this was something I had studied. I had read about it countless times, feeling envy and loss at the thought that something like this could never be mine. But now, it was. Part of me always wondered if my kind exaggerated these urges to excuse boorish behavior in bed, and perhaps to some degree they did, but a spark of white-hot lust zoomed through me and I shoved Cas onto his back with a strength I had not, until this moment, possessed. Startled, Cas landed with a slight bounce and before he could draw a breath, I was on him, kissing him, biting his full lips.

I thrilled to feel Cas beneath me, struggling to catch his breath; he couldn't keep up with my kisses. I moved my lips down his chiseled jaw, his gorgeous throat, nipping at the spot I would be sinking my teeth into later. He shivered. "*Thor*," he whispered, like he couldn't stop invoking my name. I loved the sound of it in his mouth. "Touch me."

I snuffled against his collarbone, thinking that would be my absolute pleasure. I wrapped my fingers around his dick, relieved to see my hand had stopped shaking. He was hot and hard against my palm. After a few loose strokes, I pulled back, nudging his thighs apart so I could settle between them on the bed.

I could tell I was losing my grip on sanity, my vision going hazy as some horny stranger took control of my mouth. My voice pitched low, to a commanding register, and I said, "Present for me."

Cas's eyes blew wide in surprise. He swallowed nervously, but then he shuddered and something washed over him, softening his features—something primal, something docile and trusting. Blinking lazily, Cas hooked his hands below his own knees, drawing his legs up toward his chest, spreading himself wide.

Gods.

I grabbed the base of my own cock, giving it a firm squeeze and I swear, I almost fainted. For a moment I was paralyzed, not sure what on earth to do with this gorgeous gift splayed out before me. Then, Cas made a high pitched needy little huff, impatient and greedy with his junk exposed, waiting for someone to do something about it.

Waiting for an Alpha to take care of him.

Waiting for me.

"You are..." I cleared my throat. My voice was hoarse and strangled, and I needed to be sure he heard me. "You are so beautiful," I told Cas.

Suddenly bashful, Cas released his legs. "Jesus," he said, turning his face away. "You can't say stuff like that when I have my ass in the air."

"Why not?"

"I don't know," he said, voice muffled behind his hand. "I don't know why I did that either. Yikes."

I slithered up to lay on his chest. "Because I told you to."

"And that worked?" Cas's eyes were clear again as he peeked out between his fingers. The sexy haze draped over us had all but evaporated.

"Apparently." I nuzzled into the little spot below his ear. He seemed nervous and unsure all of a sudden. "We don't have to do this tonight," I told him, though the selfish part of me thought it might kill me if he left my bed.

Cas whined and seized my hand, pressing my palm to his crotch. I wrapped my fingers around his length, felt the slippery spot at the head where he was leaking. "I swear to God," Cas said. "If you don't fuck me right this minute, I might die."

"Well then," I said, putting on a bit of a growl for show. Cas laughed, and finally lowered his hand to look at me again. "You should get back in that other position."

"Oh my *God*," he said, embarrassed.

I nipped his earlobe. "I liked it."

"Ugh, stop."

"No, seriously. I did." I moved away, nudging him to spread his legs again. When he grabbed ahold of his knees, I pushed a soft kiss to the underside of his thigh, trailing my tongue down toward the crease where his leg met his butt cheek. "A lot."

Cas groaned but it seemed like we were getting back to where we needed to be, mood-wise—except now I was the one who was nervous. I didn't have the numbers on it or anything, but I was pretty sure most times there wasn't quite so much negotiation between Alphas and their partners.

"Hey," said Cas, almost a whisper. He reached down to cup my cheek, then pulled me up toward him for a soft kiss. His eyes searched mine. "Where did you go?"

I shook myself. This was crazy. "Nowhere," I said, worrying his bottom lip between my teeth. I pulled back, tugging until he hissed. When I released his lip, I whispered, "I'm right here."

"Good."

Tingles flooded my body, filling my senses, and I felt myself slip back into that Alpha headspace. *Finally.* I relished in it, the bone-deep feeling of rightness that came with not overthinking, for once. Cas on his back with his goods on display was definitely helping. I squeezed his thighs, settling with his calves over my shoulders. "Beautiful," I said again, though that's kind of what had derailed us before, but I couldn't help it. The muscles of his legs, the flushed rosy complexion of his balls drawn up tight, his thick hard cock twitching against his abs...to say nothing of the delicate pink pucker waiting between his cheeks, for me. It was like a secret. No one had ever seen my Cas like this before. *And no one else ever would,* I thought, and the voice in my head was angry. It lit me on fire, the possibility of missing out on this, missing out on him. Someone else being here, where I was. Cas didn't laugh when I growled this time. He shivered.

I needed to get my mouth on him that instant.

I dove right for his ass, nosing along his sac while I laved over his hole, and Cas cursed, crass in the silence of our bedroom. I smiled, flexing my tongue and pressing against the tight ring of muscle, loving the taste of him. Like extra-concentrated Cas. He moaned and fisted his fingers in my hair, shamelessly grinding against my tongue. I'd never done this before, so all I had to go on was my own instinct, my own desire and the pornographic sounds dripping from Cas's mouth as I ate him out.

The newly minted Alpha beast clawing at the inside of my chest spurred me on, until I wasn't certain if I was pleasuring Cas or trying to eat him alive. Perhaps a bit of both.

What I lacked in experience I made up for with enthusiasm; Cas was incoherent and nearly crushing my skull with his powerful thighs. He cradled the back of my head, guiding me to where he wanted my mouth. The rigidity of his muscles told me I could make him come like this.

He whined, a delicious sound, when I drew my mouth away, dragging my tongue over his balls. Cas shifted his hips with a frustrated plea. "Woah," he said softly. He uncurled his spine, propping himself up on his elbows. The tense muscles in his legs relaxed a bit as he stared at me.

"What?"

"Your eyes," he said in a low, syrupy voice. "They're so dark."

I spared a glance for the mirror on the wall, registering that my eyes were glassy and indeed dark, pupils wide and blending with the brown of my iris. Returning my focus to Cas, I tried to gather myself. This was everything I wanted, and I didn't want it to end any time soon. If he came before I could mark him properly, we'd have to wait.

And now that we'd started, I didn't want to wait any longer.

His eyes were dazed, his breath coming in ragged gasps. He was so hard his cock jumped against his belly with the beating of his heart. "Why did you stop?"

I narrowed my eyes. "You were about to go off."

The flush creeping up his chest and neck, bleeding onto his freckled cheeks, told me all I needed to know. "No I wasn't."

The scent of his bashfulness had me dizzy; my dick gave an insistent throb. My dumb hindbrain was taking over and I felt rabid, eager to mount. Not yet, I told myself, lowering my mouth again. I licked a hot stripe from the base of Cas's cock up to taste the slick beading at the silky head, and I decided to linger there, sucking hard on the tip of his dick, tonguing the slit.

It wouldn't be long, I knew. With a weak little noise, Cas let his legs fall over my shoulders again, and he bucked up, trying to shove his cock further into my mouth. We were close enough to making this happen that I felt my blood thrumming in concert with his pulse, and I could tell his body was ready, seeking out the completion only I could give him. I sucked Cas root to tip before drawing off to fumble in my bedside drawer, the tip of my tongue teasing as I groped for the bottle of lube.

My Cas, so strong and solid, but he was falling to pieces with my tongue on him, in him, lapping at the secret parts of him that were just mine. I kissed the inside of his thigh, then scraped my teeth over the sensitive skin there, dusted with downy golden hair. Blinking up at him, I whispered the pad of my lubed-up finger over his entrance, asking.

"God," he breathed, arching his back. "Yes."

I had enough brain cells left to know to be gentle, but when my finger breached the firm, tight ring of muscle and slid into Cas's channel, they fled. I stroked him from the inside while devouring his cock, determined to make this amazing for him.

"Uh, uh, *ohhhh.*"

Cas squirmed all over the bed and it was a challenge to hold him still, strong as he was. The dull pull in my groin grew hotter and harder to ignore, so I doused my hand with more lube and pushed two fingers into Cas, hot and slick and sloppy. He cried out, bucking wildly and tangling his fingers in my hair to keep my lips around his dick, and I was beyond happy to suckle him as I pumped into his ass with my fingers. Soon though, he was pulling harder on my hair, and the tingle against my scalp had me growling around my mouthful.

Cas let out a warning, a strangled, "Baby—!" Coupled with him legitimately yanking my curls to pull my mouth off him. "If you—I can't—I'm gonna—"

I did not need the end of those sentences. Trembling, Cas's calves slid from my shoulders while I hurried to slick myself up. His eyes were wide, staring at my dick like he was a little afraid of it. It was enough to slow me down a little. "What?" I asked, cupping his cheek. I brushed the pad of my thumb over his lip. "You alright?"

"Yeah, just." He gave a nervous little laugh, eyeballing my cock warily. "Go slow, okay?"

I grinned. "As slow as you like," I said, leaning forward to kiss him.

Cas moaned into my mouth and sank his teeth into my bottom lip. "Not too slow, though, yeah?"

I was absolutely beside myself as I pressed the head of my dick against his entrance. Cas's big hands found my waist, guiding me, and when I pushed inside it was kind of like, 'pop!'

"Oh, fuck," I groaned as I slid inside. So tight, so slick and soft, clutching tightly and squeezing. Glancing down I saw I'd barely gotten the head in him but already his ass was choking my dick so tightly I felt like I was going to explode.

Cas grinned, panting. "That's not like you."

"What's not?" I asked, distracted.

"You don't swear much."

I slid in another inch or so. "I do when—*fuck*—when the situation calls for it."

Cas shook like a leaf, but he was still at maximum steel, his cock slapping his belly as I jostled him. "Keep going," he whispered, tugging on my hips.

I pressed further, as slowly as I possibly could, every hair on my body bristled with tension. Hardly daring to breathe, I peeked down between us to where our bodies joined. I was less than halfway. I nudged forward, another tiny thrust to sink in a bit deeper.

"Stop!"

I froze. "Cas—are you alright? Did I hurt—"

"No, you didn't hurt me." He looked up at me, face aglow with warmth and trust. "I really don't think you even could."

I took his hand, kissing his knuckles. "Then what is it?"

"I—I want you to..." he sighed, wilting back against the

pillows, hooking one long leg up and over my hip. "Stop holding back."

"Huh?"

He huffed out a laugh. "I'm not going to break, Thor. You're supposed to like, claim me, right?"

Having this conversation with my dick halfway in his ass was proving next to impossible. My brain did not have enough blood to function. "Yes, I mean, I—what?"

Cas leveled his gaze at me, stretching his arms back to grip the headboard. "You're supposed to be my Alpha."

"Yes?" I still wasn't sure what he was getting at.

"Then show me, Thor," said Cas. "Fuck me. Hard."

Fucking hell. I exhaled, trying to quiet the roaring in my ears. "Alright," I said. I was so nervous to show him this side of myself—a side I didn't really even know yet. A side of myself I didn't trust. "Cas—"

"Baby," he said, laughing again, but it was a desperate sound. "I swear, I'm about to explode. I love you so much. *Please.* Let me have it."

It was the *please* that did it; something broke deep inside me. I wrapped my fingers around Cassian's wrists, holding him down as I snapped my hips. He yelped as I plunged in to the hilt, my pelvis flush against his ass. I drew out and drove into him again, deep and hard, and Cas went wild, thrashing his head, squeezing my waist with his thighs to keep me close.

"Yes—yes! *Ohh.*"

I circled my hips to grind against him, and his body sang to me like a holy instrument. There was no way I was going to last but I simply had to get him there first. Tuning into what his body told me, I shifted my rhythm to short, blunt thrusts, increasing the friction between us, the heat.

I smothered Cas's cries with my mouth, kissing him like I meant to steal the breath from his lungs. I wanted that; I wanted his breath, his sounds, his body, all of him. I wanted to devour him whole. The muffled mews that made it out where our lips met drove me insane, everything in me humming toward climax. *Mine, mine, mine,* I thought, pounding Cas into the mattress with everything I had.

Cas tried to move with me, too big and strong and passionate to be a passive partner, but I wasn't having it. Not this time.

I drew back to bare my teeth, tightening my grip on Cassian's wrists. With a low grow I moved my lips to his ear. "Be still."

Cas trembled below me, but something in my voice had him stop his squirming. His cock jumped and pulsed between us, and I knew he was close. *Now, now, now. Mine.* Erratic, frantic, I increased the pace of my thrusts to a bruising staccato.

I brushed my lips and tongue to the spot on Cassian's neck where it sloped into his shoulder. I could feel his pulse, and a not-so-small part of me thrilled that I could tear out his throat if I wanted. Like his body recognized what I was about to do, like he was born to submit so beautifully, Cas extended his neck, turning up his throat to me and I scraped my teeth over the spot, warning him before I bit down, hard.

"Oh, *fuck!*" Cas yelled, cursing again and again. "Yes, *fuck,* Thor. *Fuck!*" He came so hard I felt his cum splash my collarbone, hot and filthy as I ground my teeth into his neck. The taste of his skin, his sweat, even a little bit of his blood—sent me over the edge and I fired shot after shot deep into Cas, the rhythmic pulsing of his channel clutching my cock like he wanted to pull me in even further.

It seemed to go on, and on, and I couldn't stop humping through my climax. Cas rewarded me with weak, gorgeous sounds, broken moans and little yips. I knew he'd be oversensitive in the aftermath of his own orgasm, but the connection we'd forged was at its peak and I wanted to ride the crest of it forever.

When we finally came down, I laid on Cas's sweaty chest, lazily flicking my tongue over the bite, and each time I connected, he shivered. I couldn't think, or move, but with Cas's arms around me I didn't need to.

All I had was one word, his name, forever on my lips, pressing into his skin. "Cas," I whispered, and my voice sounded drunk. "Cas. Cas. Cas."

# 19



I had pictured my first time with Thor a hundred ways, but in my hottest fantasy I hadn't even come close.

Even when I started coming around to the idea of bottoming, I hadn't expected to love it so much. Thor had no problems at all finding my prostate—which was so fucking good—and then he'd bitten me, which my brain somehow rerouted so I found it pleasurable, as well as painful. I'd come so hard I felt it in my scalp.

The thing was, it was Thor. Of course it was perfect. This after part was pretty perfect too, with the only sound our ragged breathing in the silence of the room. Thor had fully collapsed onto my chest, his softening dick slipping out of me in a gush of lube and cum that, yeah, was gross, but kind of in a hot way? My spent cock gave a feeble attempt at rallying, but Thor's body, surprisingly leaden for such a slight guy, was so warm and soft on top of me that I knew sleep was going to win out. In fact, I listened closer, and yeah, Thor was already making his breathy little snores. He'd seemed larger than life only moments ago, and now he'd shrunk back down, pliant and boneless in my arms. My little Thunder God, finally, back where he belonged.

Round two could wait until morning, or for a few hours at least.

I wrapped my arms around him and squeezed, so happy to be back in this bed with him. Sleeping apart the last few weeks had been awful. It kind of hit me all at once, lying here, how wrong it had felt to sleep apart. The gaunt look on Thor's face, the circles under his eyes, it all started to make sense. He'd shrugged it off, said he hadn't been sleeping well, but that simple statement meant more to me now. I kissed the top of his head, breathing in his scent.

Woah.

With a slight frown in the dark, I took another deep inhale. Either Thor got strangely fragrant during sex, or something had changed how I perceived him. His scent was suddenly so strong, but so comforting, like a hug or a toasty blanket. It made me feel dopey and sleepy. I could hear his heartbeat, too, not just feel it thudding against my own. Freaky. What the hell was in shifter spit? I'd have to ask him about it when he woke up.

The bite on my neck throbbed and ached, but not necessarily in a bad way. The sound of Thor breathing, the warm weight of him on top of me, the heady scent of him, sweat and sex had my eyelids drooping.

I woke up some time later to one of the worst sensations on earth: dried cum matted into body hair. My skin pulled and pinched as I stirred.

"*Unnf,*" I said into the darkness, my throat a bit sore from all the hollering I'd been doing a few hours prior. With a feeble lurch, I groped in the darkness for Thor. The bed was cold beside me and an empty sense of abandonment washed over me, like a withdrawal pang; I couldn't hear his heartbeat. I couldn't smell him. "Thor?"

No answer.

To be perfectly honest, I felt a little hurt. Part of the appeal of this whole Alpha business was having a partner who wanted to take care of you. And here I was, covered in crispy dried jizz, alone in bed after our first night together. I couldn't tell if I was angry or worried. Trying to calm down, I knuckled my eyes. This was crazy, like weird post-sex mood swings. He probably had just gone to the bathroom or something. I moved to the side of the bed, letting my feet hit the floor.

I stretched. *Woah*—ouch. In the moment, telling Thor to really give it to me had seemed beyond hot. And, the way his long dick had filled me so exquisitely, dragging across my prostate on every pass, certainly hadn't inspired me to think rationally. Now though, picturing Thor's dick and like, the maximum possible size of my asshole (not that I'd ever really looked at it, or measured it)—the mathematical logistics alone...ugh. I winced as I put weight on my butt. I was going to be sore AF for a minute. I really needed a hot shower, but maybe during that I'd be up for round two. Plainly I was too sore for us to fuck again yet, but at the very least I felt that I deserved a nice blowjob for my bravery. Where the hell was Thor?

I steadied myself, quieting my pouty thoughts and yes, there––I thought maybe I heard him somewhere in the apartment, but the sound was faint. My senses conflicted, confusing the hell out of me. It was like they were dulled and heightened at the same time in a way I wasn't used to—like I had superhuman hearing and then put in some serious earplugs.

I picked up my jeans from the night before and pulled out my phone. It was only four fifteen a.m., but I knew I wasn't going to be able to fall back asleep without at least washing up first.

Then I heard it.

The noise was soft, coming from behind me. A weird sort of rustling, like wind in a dry grass, but so quiet I almost missed it. My eyes had finally adjusted a bit to the dark and I turned toward the source of the noise. There was something familiar to the rustling sound, but I couldn't place it. Squinting, I noticed for the first time something round nestled into the indent on Thor's pillow.

Like a dumb fucking ape, my first instinct was to poke it. "Ouch!" The thing jumped and like, hissed? And it was spiny. Had Thor left a fucking sea urchin on his pillow?

I flipped my phone around, using the light from the screen to make sense of what the hell I was seeing, because I was way too exhausted and cum drunk to understand this.

Yes, there was something round and spiky on the pillow.

It was definitely alive, and it wasn't a sea urchin.

It was a hedgehog.

*What.*

I jumped out of bed, stumbling over the trail of clothing Thor and I had left on the ground, feeling kind of ridiculous because I was still buck naked. I flipped on the light, like maybe I was imagining things and I expected to see something else when the room was fully illuminated.

I wasn't imagining things.

There was a hedgehog in my bed, where my boyfriend had been sleeping peacefully after some really hot sex. During which, he'd bitten the ever-loving crap out of the side of my neck, as part of his magic family's crazy mating ritual.

His family who could all turn into animals.

I wasn't prone to fits of denial.

"Thor?" I whispered, kneeling on the edge of the bed.

The hedgehog slowly unfurled itself from its roly-poly

position and blinked up at me. Its eyes were black, not brown, small and beady where Thor's were so wide and soulful, but somehow, there was no mistaking them.

"Look at you." I knew how much it weighed on him that he didn't have a *fauna* like the rest of his family. And, given the timing, I felt comfortable taking a little bit of credit that I helped him find this power inside himself. Timidly, I rested my palm upturned on the bed, and Thor snuffed, the spines on his back bristled immediately. Trying very hard not to laugh, I kept my hand still. Eventually, he climbed up onto my hand. He had tiny little paws and wobbly steps, and his nose quivered as he scented the air above the palm of my hand. I held him up closer to my face and scratched the top of his head with one tentative finger. When the spines relaxed, they were kind of nice to touch. "Okay," I said. "Very cool. But I really want a shower. Turn back into you and join me?"

Thor didn't say anything, naturally, but he also didn't shift back into himself.

"Come on," I said.

Still nothing.

Okay, fine. I understood how this was a huge deal for him. In all honesty, I thought if I had eight hours of sleep under my belt it would have been a bigger deal to me too. It was disturbing how little this phased me, but I tucked that away for later examination. For now, I needed a shower. So, I carried Hedgehog Thor into the bathroom and set him in the soap dish.

I cranked the water on hot, stepped under the spray and moaned. Okay, maybe a little bit for show. But I would have thought a naked, wet, me in the shower would have inspired Thor to do the exploration of his new powers later. I glanced at the grumpy pin cushion in the soap dish, who watched me with a nonplussed expression. *Fine.*

I turned my back, and when the steaming water hit the

bite on my neck, I almost lost my footing. The blood rushed to my dick so fast I saw lights pop in my eyes. I was aching hard and overstimulated by the heat of the water on my skin. I dodged out of the spray, knees buckling, and leaned against the cool tile wall to gather myself. Dizzy with need, I turned back to the soap dish to see Thor had balled up again, a uniform ball of short little quills. I couldn't even see his face.

*Fine, jerk, I'll take care of it myself,* I thought uncharitably.

I wrapped a loose fist around my cock but it was way, way too much. Way too sensitive, my own hand like sandpaper against my dick. I turned the shower down to cold and let it sluice over me, but the cold was just as bad—like a million needles stabbing into my pores. Finally twisting the shower dial to a lukewarm, and adjusting the pressure to a weaker setting, I relaxed. The water felt nice, and I was able to calm down, clean up, and I felt like myself again by the time I turned the water off.

Exhaustion crept back in and I carried Thor back to the bedroom to get a few more hours' sleep. I set him on his pillow. "It'd be real nice if I woke up to *you* you," I told him sourly, rolling onto my belly. I was asleep in seconds.

When it was a nice hour of the morning, not an ungodly one, I rolled out of bed, feeling much better. The raw ache deep inside me had retreated to a sweet sort of looseness in my muscles, like after a really good workout, but better. Hedgehog Thor was still balled up on the pillow where I left him. Now that I'd softened up a bit, mentally and physically, I could admit he was pretty damn cute.

I scratched his head again, which he seemed to enjoy, and then scooped him up. "Let's go, Pin Cushion," I said. I tossed on some pajama pants and carried him into the kitchen. If he wasn't going to transform back, I was definitely going to have some fun.

The first thing I did was set him on the rug and nudge him

with my toe. He did the snuffing thing again, spines sticking out every which way like a pufferfish with tiny little stick legs. When he ran, awkward round body wobbling, I took some surreptitious video. I didn't know how much human awareness remained when he was in this form, and I planned to take full advantage and get some cute pics to embarrass him with later. Serves him right.

I filled my camera roll with stupidly cute hedgehog pics. My favorite by far was one where I put Thor in a mug and pretended to take a sip for a selfie. His little face looked so grouchy in the picture that I immediately made it the lock screen background on my phone.

By evening though, I had circled back to worried. Thor sat next to me on the couch while I did some homework, and I glanced at him occasionally, but he showed no signs of turning back into a human. He hadn't eaten or drank anything all day, and I was getting concerned he didn't know how to change back. It seemed a reasonable fear, considering he'd never shifted before last night. "Are you alright?" I asked him.

His only answer was to scoot closer to me on the sofa. I returned to my paper, but soon I felt an insistent tugging on my pant leg. Looking down, I saw that Thor was chomping ferociously on the fabric. I watched in alarm as a bizarre, foamy substance formed around his sharp little needle teeth, spreading a damp spot along the seam of my pajama bottoms.

Thor then used his front paws to smear the foam all over his own head, after which he bent his round, spiny body into a pretzel shape that, frankly defied physics, in order to spit the thick white goo all over his back.

Did...my boyfriend have rabies? Was he having some kind of fit? Panicked, I typed "Hedgehog, rabies," into Google. My mind already hummed with frightening possibilities: did I take him to a doctor? Or a veterinarian? Or like, an exorcist? Oddly, there were no definitive Google results for "magic hedgehog has rabies," or "cursed hedgehog magic seizure."

After reading through a few articles online, my heart rate slowed back to normal. According to most animal sites, rabies in hedgehogs was rare, but it was common for them to do something called "self-anointing." Apparently, if they thought something smelled nice, they would chew on it and smear their spit all over themselves to smell like that thing, so I supposed I should be flattered.

So, sure, he didn't have rabies. The fact remained, however, that I had no idea how to help Thor transform back into a human guy.

By the following morning, I was in a flat-out panic. Not only was Thor still a one-pound ball of fur and quills, but I was pretty sure my fucking mating bite was infected. The bite ached, the skin around it hot to touch and beyond sensitive. Every time I touched it, or my clothes brushed against it, I got instantly hard. The only thing that worked was icing it. Maybe it was so infected I was seeing things, and Thor had gone out of town and I was hallucinating the hedgehog riding around in the pocket of my hoodie.

Shit. I set Thor, if that *was* who it was, on the counter and scrutinized him over the top of my coffee mug. It was definitely him.

I was pretty sure it was him.

I gave him a little saucer of water, and after some more Googling, I made him a scrambled egg, which he ate. Did he need to eat as much as a man? Or only as much as a hedgehog? I truthfully had no idea, and I was so far out of my depth. Thor had classes on Monday, and I obviously couldn't send him like this! Although, the thought of him with a tiny hedgehog-sized backpack conjured up some ridiculously cute mental images.

I picked him up so we could look eye to eye. "What do we do?" I asked him.

No answer.

*Shit. Shit. Shit.* My eyes fell on Thor's phone, which he had left plugged in to charge on the kitchen counter. I didn't know anything about shifters, but Thor knew people who did.

Of course! I scrolled through his contacts and called Leda.

"Thor, good, where have you—"

"Hi, Leda. Um. It's Cas. Thor's um...Cassian. It's Cassian."

"Oh," she said, after a pause. "Hello."

I thought I could hear someone in the background. "Sorry if this is a bad time," I said. "But can you come over?"

"Over...?"

"To Thor's. To our place. We have kind of an emergency."

She paused again. "I'm on my way."

"Thank—" but she had already hung up.

Twenty agonizing minutes later, Leda pressed the buzzer to be let upstairs. To my surprise, and horror, she wasn't alone.

"Hey, man," said Lucy.

I glared at Leda. "I didn't realize you had company."

"We were out. I thought you said it was an emergenc..." Leda blushed. "Oh."

"Oh?"

Leda cleared her throat. "You and Thor."

"Me and Thor...?"

She raised her eyebrows.

"Oh, Jesus," I said, momentarily distracted. "How can you even tell?"

"Is that why you called me?"

"No, actually. Um." Words failed me. I didn't know what to say with Lucy here, so I pointed.

Leda turned and gasped. "Cassian! Is that—"

"Thor, yes."

Lucy said, "Huh."

I blinked at her. "Hold on—"

"Oh," said Lucy. "Should I be more surprised?"

"What the f—"

"To evaluate Lucy as a potential mate, I had to first see how she would react to the honest truth about me. I learned that from you and Thor, actually."

"What? Thor wasn't evaluating me when you—*you*—"

"Yes, and thank goodness he wasn't," said Lucy drily. "You reacted horribly."

"Okay," I snapped. "Fine. I am *also* reacting horribly to *this.*" I pointed at Thor where he sat on the table, watching us.

"It looks like him," said Lucy. "Thor, I mean. Something about the eyes."

"Yes," I said, feeling strangely relieved. "That's what I thought."

Leda adjusted her glasses and approached the table, bending down to examine Thor. "This is fascinating," she murmured.

"Hey wait a minute," I said. I turned to Lucy. I tugged aside the collar of my shirt. "Do you have one of these?"

"No," she said, squinting at my mating bite. She reached out and I dodged away from her.

"Don't even touch me," I said. "I'm experiencing some uh, some side effects."

I watched as Leda picked up Thor and examined him, flipping him right over and prodding his belly. He huffed and tried to shield himself by balling up again.

"Hang on," I said, "You two slept together. Why don't you have a bite?"

"I'm fairly certain Lucy is the Alpha partner," said Leda absently.

Lucy shrugged. "Duh."

Leda set Thor back down on the counter and turned to me. "I always knew his *fauna* gene was merely latent."

"Fabulous," I said. "I called you because he is stuck like that."

Leda shot me a withering stare. "Oh, please, he is not."

"He can't change back."

"How do you know?"

That brought me up short. I supposed I didn't know, for sure, that Thor was stuck. I started to get a little angry. "Well if he's not stuck, he's being kind of an asshole," I said loudly.

Thor snuffed, and the way his spines fell over his tiny forehead made it look like he had grumpy eyebrows.

Leda looked thoughtful. "Everyone experiences their first shift a little differently," she said. "But it's usually something one goes through with one's family."

"Thor's parents!" I couldn't believe I hadn't thought of that before. I grabbed his phone again and opened his contacts app.

With my attention on the phone in my hand, out of the corner of my eye I saw something giant and flesh-colored tumble from the kitchen island to the floor.

"*Don't!*" Thor had crashed to the ground, ass naked, a tangle of skinny limbs. He bounded up, wild-eyed. "Don't call my dad—please!"

Leda, Lucy and I all stared at him, and he stared at us, before looking down at himself and then dodging behind the kitchen island. I grabbed a blanket from the back of the sofa and walked over to him, mutely holding it out. Underneath my overwhelming relief that I wasn't romantically committed to a hedgehog for the rest of my life, I felt the prickles of anger. Thor wrapped the blanket around his waist like a towel.

I set my jaw and glared at him, at a loss for words. I turned to Leda, opened my mouth, but before I could say anything—

"We should go," she said, grabbing Lucy's arm.

"Talk to you later Cas, and uh, Mozel!" Lucy grinned and waved as Leda marched her from the apartment.

When the door swung shut behind them, Thor blinked at me, and I could tell he couldn't see a damn thing as he wasn't wearing his glasses. "Cas," he started, "I know you're mad but…"

I bit back a smile and stomped down the hallway to retrieve his glasses from the bedside table. When he'd slid them in place on his nose, staring sheepishly at me, I found my voice. "How could you do this?"

"What, exactly?"

"Let me freak out for two straight days! I was afraid you were stuck like that!"

"I was—or, I let myself be." Thor frowned. "It's hard to explain."

With a harumph, I sat on the couch. When Thor didn't say anything else, I said, "Well?"

Clutching the blanket around his hips, Thor sat beside me. "I woke up, and I felt—I don't know…" his thick, dark brows knit together. "I felt it happen, and all I wanted was to wake up and show you—"

"But you didn't! I woke up alone! You fucked me, and left me all alone."

"I was still right there," Thor snapped. "It's not like I actually went—"

"Oh, *please*," I said. "That did *not* count."

"Okay, granted." He sighed, leaning forward to cover his face with his hands. "I was fffmmmfphed."

I blinked. "Sorry," I said. "Didn't catch that last bit."

He peeked out at me. "I was *embarrassed*," he said.

The confession startled me out of his indignation for a second. "What?"

"I mean…" Thor trailed away, looking miserable. When he spoke again, his voice was tiny. "You saw."

"Yes, I did."

"And you saw...my brother and my father."

"Yes, Thor, I fucking saw them." I wasn't likely to forget that night.

"Well!" he said, exasperated. "Ugh—I can't—I can't explain while I'm naked."

I raised one brow. "Tough," I said. "You're gonna."

"But—"

"Listen, you could have turned back into you and put some damn pants on any time over the last *two fucking days.*"

"Okay, yeah, that's fair."

I gave him a second to gather himself, gazing sidelong at him on the couch. It made me a bit uncomfortable to realize how much I'd missed him. It had only been two days for crying out loud. Thor adjusted himself, fidgeting like he always did when he was nervous. I was still angry enough that I wasn't going to help him out, so I let him stew for a bit.

Finally, he exhaled. "Like I said—I wanted...when I first felt it happen, I wanted to show you more than anything."

"Then why didn't you?" I looked down, and realized my hand had come to rest on his knee. Apparently, I couldn't not touch him.

Thor shot me a hard look. "Come on," he said. "You *saw.* I've waited so long for this. My whole life, really, to have a *fauna* like the rest of my family and I finally have one, but I'm still..." he blinked rapidly, lashes fluttering over moist eyes. "Tiny. Small." He looked away again. "Weak."

"Hey—"

"No, stop," he said, brushing me off. "You were right. It was selfish. I was hiding. At first, I couldn't figure out how to change back, and then I guess I didn't want to. And then when I did try to change, it was harder. Like I was further away, somehow."

"Then?"

"It seemed harder and harder and then, I felt safe as...."

I couldn't contain my smile. "As a hedgehog?"

He flushed. "Yes. I just wanted to curl up, and keep hiding."

"Well," I said. "That was selfish."

"I know." He paused. "I'm sorry."

"Okay," I said. "We're going to discuss this more, at length, but I have a really pressing question."

Thor cocked his head to the side, confused, and I had to try really hard to not show how much his cute little gestures affected me.

In answer to his look, I yanked my t-shirt collar to expose the wound he'd left on my neck. "Am I dying?"

Thor clucked, looking at the bite. "Don't be so dramatic."

"That's rich, coming from the guy who spent forty-eight hours as a hedgehog because he was a little embarrassed."

"Fair enough," he said, giving me a tiny smile for the first time since he'd changed back. "C'mere. Lean in."

Curious, I extended my neck, leaning toward him. His hot breath on my skin sent chills down my spine. I'd been really angry, a second ago. That mattered a lot less all of a sudden. Thor's soft lips brushed over the bite, and yeah—it had the same effect that any contact had over the past two days, but where the other touches felt like a fearsome itch nothing could scratch, Thor's kiss was like a balm.

"*Woah*," I said. I stretched further, and he peppered my neck with kisses. I frowned. "I'm still mad," I added, like an afterthought.

"I know."

We broke apart. "You can't do this," I said. "*We* can't do this. Pull away, not talk about stuff. We're together."

He touched the mark on my neck with his fingertips. "I know that too."

"Like *really* together. I love you," I said. "This kind of thing—where we don't talk, or run away—has to stop. Now."

"Okay."

"Promise?"

Thor took my hands. "Yes," he said. "I promise. And I'm so sorry."

"And?"

"And, I love you too."

———

THOR

I spent a significant amount of time making things up to Cas. He didn't seem angry anymore, and I was glad. I felt awful for leaving him alone after our first night together. To be honest, it was the last thing I had wanted. I could have stayed in that bed with him forever and died happy.

But I'd changed. I'd shifted!

I had a *fauna.* It was a really lame one, but the fact that I wasn't a total genetic failure was a triumph.

However, every time I looked at Cas, it didn't feel like a triumph. He had loved me, before. He didn't care about my family, or my *fauna,* or previous lack thereof. We'd...we'd been together, and not because of some bizarre fated bond, but because he chose me. And I chose him too. I felt wretched that I'd left him the other night to deal with his mating bite, the afterglow, all of it. It was the worst thing I'd ever done, and I was determined to make it up to him.

Lucky for me, most of what Cas seemed to want in exchange for forgiveness was sexual in nature, and I was more than happy to oblige. We did not get a lot of sleep those first several nights, and I didn't think either of us minded one single bit.

I was happier than I could ever remember being. Having Cas back in my bed, knowing we'd completed our bond had me feeling so secure and settled, it was hard to let anything else get me down. That was, until Rafe knocked on my door one Saturday morning.

I'd known Cassian had experienced a bit of jealousy regarding my past with Rafe, but I thought he'd have gotten over it. However, the look of hostility on his usually kind face took me aback.

"I can't stay long," said Rafe. "I just wanted to bring a few of these by, from my family's private collection."

He set several thick leather-bound volumes on the coffee table. "I looked through my father's catalogue and thought these might be of some use to yours and Leda's investigation."

I flipped through one of the books, lifting the cover gingerly. A more in-depth perusal would definitely require gloves. "These are in pristine condition," I said. "You must thank your father for letting me borrow them."

Rafe flushed. "He doesn't know."

"Ah, well. In that case," I said. "I'll take extra care with them."

Cas stood in the kitchen, openly scowling, and he didn't even offer to make Rafe a sandwich, which was the Cassian Rhodes equivalent of taking off his glove and smacking Rafe in the face with it.

Rafe seemed to sense something, and he squinted at Cas, before turning to me with a knowing look. "Ah," he said. "I'll just, leave these with you and get out of your hair."

"What?"

"I think your mate is feeling a little territorial," he whispered to me.

"What was that?" Cas said loudly.

"Nothing," Rafe and I said.

I don't think Cas believed us, but he let it drop, and as

soon as the door closed behind Rafe, Cas strode across the apartment and we shared a passionate tumble right there on the sofa.

I stayed up the next four nights, engrossed in Rafe's books. They delved a little closer to the mystic arts, which, while fascinating, didn't seem likely to yield any definitive results. However, partway through the third volume, I came across a ritual performed often by a pagan healer, twelfth century.

The name of the village he lived in was familiar, and flicking back through my notes I realized it was the very same village that had run off the original Primitives. Any trace of frustration or sleepiness vanished as I pored over the text. The story was fairly grizzly—the man specialized in cleansing rituals. Comparing this to the history of the primitives, the events lined up to form a grotesque complete picture.

The feral shifters reproduced in the wild, and occasionally one of their primitive offspring would be born with more human traits, so they would sneak into the village under cover of night and leave their children in cradles. I wondered, as I annotated my summary of the story, if changeling myths could be traced back to these instances. The young were *not* human, much like the shifters found by the police were not. This healer would do his best to cleanse the children of the demons he thought were within. He altered them surgically, drained their blood, and performed all manner of cleansing rites. The success rate, as in many medical procedures performed before humans had developed a true understanding of them, was dicey.

It was one of those things—if the child died, the demon had done it. If the child lived, the rite had been successful. I took down all of the details I could, diagramming the rite and listing the ingredients used in the cleansing spells. There were incantations as well—those were harder to discern. The holy man would bleed the child, heavily. The blood would then be stored in a sacred vessel. If the child lived, it was assumed the demon had been contained in the jar, and it was then destroyed in a ritual fire.

"Baby?"

I jumped and looked up to see Cas come down the hallway. He had on plaid flannel pants and his eyes clouded with sleep. "Did I wake you?"

"No," he said. "But I woke up and you weren't there."

I closed the book, stretching. "Sorry, I think I got something here."

"Come to bed," said Cas, his voice a low, throaty purr. "Please?"

And of course, I was powerless to resist. Long after Cas had fallen asleep, though, I laid awake thinking about the rituals, and the thought that someone was recreating something similar turned my stomach. People hadn't gotten less cruel since those chaotic, lawless times. They'd gotten smarter, but that did not translate to greater understanding.

The following day, I brought Cas to see Leda in the lab, where we'd also agreed to meet Rafe.

"You want to do *what*?" Leda looked at me like I was crazy.

"I want to give the police a tip on the case. As much as I can give them."

"Thor, you've got to be out of your damn mind," said Leda. "The police already think you and Cas are suspects in this case, and now you want to give them an excuse to tap your phones?"

"This is beyond us," I said. "It's beyond experimentation and it's definitely illegal. Someone has been kidnapping shifters and creating offspring from their DNA."

"Don't you want to know why?"

"Honestly, I just want it to stop." Cas squeezed my shoulder reassuringly. We had been more in tune than ever over the last few weeks, and I shot him a grateful look for the support.

Leda sighed. "Okay, so what do you think we should do?"

"We need to point him in the right direction," I said. "We can't exactly give them the details without exposing us or our families, but there's got to be something."

Leda was vehemently against tipping our hand at all, and after a lot of debate we decided to sit on it for a while.

Cas and I walked back across campus. "So, we're really going to wait?"

"No," I said firmly. "We don't need Leda's permission to do the right thing. And frankly I think it's pretty suspicious that she doesn't want to."

I explained my plan to Cas. I figured the best bet would be to get the police searching independent research labs in the area. The people doing this had to have resources in order to breed the primitives, and they had to be keeping them somewhere before each experiment had been deemed a failure and turned out.

So, wearing gloves and using generic office paper and a pen I'd taken from the student center, I scrawled a note to Detective Davis.

"CASE NUMBER 10876-GHX-2; illegal genetic testing and cloning. Drugs. Kidnapping." Underneath that, I listed the drugs Leda had found in her own, mine, and Rafe's blood after testing.

"Hopefully this will be enough to get them searching in the right direction."

"Yeah, and hopefully it won't bring them knocking on our door."

Downtown, Cas and I got lunch at a restaurant he'd been wanting to try, and, again wearing gloves, I dropped the letter in a public mailbox.

"Do you think it'll work?" Cas asked me as we drove home.

"I don't know." I sighed. "But without any more samples turning up, I don't know if there's anything else helpful we can determine. Leda's area of study doesn't give her access to forensic equipment or chemicals. It's up to the police, I suppose."

Cas squeezed my knee reassuringly. "Well, you did the right thing. And it's not like we're actually guilty or have anything to do with the bodies. So even if Davis calls us again, what is he going to find?"

I really hoped that was true, but knowing my luck I'd try to do a good deed and end up taking the fall for a bunch of murders.

"Can I talk to you about something unrelated?" Cas asked me.

"Of course."

"And you won't get mad?"

"Uh, oh." I glanced at him and our eyes met briefly before he returned his gaze to the road. "Shoot."

"Why don't you want to tell your family about your *fauna*?"

Ice trickled down my spine. I honestly didn't even really know how to explain it to myself, in so many words. "I will tell them," I said, dodging the question. "I want to deal with it a bit longer on my own, first. I'm waiting for the right moment."

Cas chewed his lip like there was more he wanted to say, but in the end, he let the subject drop as we drove the rest of the way home in silence.

# 20

CAS

It may have taken us a while, but Thor and I finally found something resembling equilibrium following his first shift. Magical drama aside, I couldn't believe how easy it was with him, with us together. And to be honest, the magical drama didn't even come up all that much. He was still embarrassed about the form his *fauna* took, and he was definitely in denial about sharing it with his family, but for now, everything was going so well. I didn't want to push the issue and rock the boat when we were both so deliriously happy in what we'd found together. Why let Thor's family into our little mate bubble?

About a month after Thor's first shift, the weekend after we'd mailed our hint to detective Davis, I found myself in the kitchen, cooking breakfast early on a Saturday. We'd had a lively night, even by our standards, and in all honesty, I was kind of hoping I'd sufficiently worn Thor out so that I could get some work done. Grinning as my brain suffused with images of last night, I flipped the pancakes on the griddle.

I felt a bonk between my shoulder blades and a pair of thin arms slid around my middle. Thor moved as quietly as ever, but since the mating bite, his silent approaches no longer startled me. It was like I could sense him coming before he announced his presence. "Mmmph."

"Morning, Pin Cushion," I said. "There's fresh coffee."

"Bless you," he said. "And we've really got to have a discussion about that nickname."

"Sorry, but that ship has long since sailed." I grinned, in truth, the fact that the pet name annoyed Thor made me even more eager to tease him with it.

I carried on with my cooking, letting Thor fix his own coffee. He hopped up onto the counter, bare legs dangling over the edge. When I looked at him, I got warm all over. His hair was rumpled from sleep, his glasses slightly askew, and he wore one of my flannel button-ups. I smiled. This was one of his favorite things to do, now. He'd worn a few of my things before but now it was like he couldn't get enough, and that was fine by me. I loved seeing him all cozy in my shirts. They were all big on his slim frame, and to be honest that *really* worked for me.

Thor sipped his coffee and watched me cook, and I said, "I have a lot of studying to catch up on today."

From behind his mug, I heard a little snort.

"I'm serious."

Thor nudged my thigh with his foot and set his coffee mug beside him on the counter. "We could do stuff before," he said, blinking innocently from behind his glasses.

That was true in theory, but in practice it definitely wasn't. For someone who had gone the first twenty years of his life with near-zilch as far as sexual contact was concerned, the last few weeks had transformed my little Thunder God into an insatiable, cum-hungry monster. Not that I was complaining, but I did have to leave the bedroom from time to time, and so did Thor.

Thor was totally useless after orgasm. More so after fooling around in the daytime, and even more so after bottoming, which I'd discovered, much to my delight, one lazy Sunday when we'd switched for the first time. He just wanted more. If I fucked Thor in the morning—which, let's be real, I loved to do—I had to be prepared to stay in bed for hours, essentially at his beck and call for when his dick had recovered enough to come again.

That may all sound like griping, but it obviously was not a hardship for me. I was having so much fun, and I was ecstatic to wake up with him in my arms and try new things in bed almost daily. As if we were honoring my secret wish when I'd first come to grips with my feelings for Thor, we had fucked on almost every flat surface in the apartment. There were corners of the place I could barely look at without blushing as I remembered having Thor on his back on the desk in the living room, or him taking me from behind on the rug in front of the fireplace. I'd had rug burns on my knees for days, and each time I felt the sting I couldn't help but remember the burn of his cock stretching me to my limit as Thor put me through my paces. We'd done it against the doorframes, in the shower, on Thor's reading chair. Between my strength and his flexibility, it had been quite a month and the energy between us didn't show any signs of cooling off.

However, the hockey season made serious demands on my time, and I had to maintain my grades as well. Not to mention, you know, going to classes and actually seeing friends from time to time.

Somehow, during my brief introspection, I had subconsciously moved to stand between Thor's bony knees, and he took his chance to lock his ankles together around my waist. How did that happen? My hands dropped to his waist, bunching up the fabric of my shirt against his skin. I frowned, digging my fingers into the bones of his hips. *Oh fuck.* I slid my hands under the bottom hem of the oversized flannel and gasped. Thor was totally bare under my shirt and the idea had me frantic to touch him.

I slid my palms up his thighs, stroking his hips, moving closer so we could kiss, and he made a self-satisfied, greedy noise against my mouth. Little shit.

Thor tangled his fingers in my hair, and just when I was beginning to mentally map the logistics of our position, I pulled away. "Wait."

"Mmmm?"

"Your bare ass is on my counter."

He pulled back, brows raised. "I'm sorry, *your* counter?"

I scoffed. "If you can tell me where the toaster is, we can call it your counter."

"Fair point."

"Still though. This is where I cook. The food. That we *eat.*"

"I know," he said, scooting forward to kiss my neck, correctly assuming that licking the bite he'd left there would crumble my resolve. "You eat my ass, too, though."

My knees buckled. Thor's bravery when it came to talking dirty had increased exponentially over the last few weeks and I fucking loved it. "True," I said. "But our guests don't."

He laughed, embarrassed. His newfound chutzpah only went so far. "Okay, fine," he said, drawing away to cup my cheek. "Take me to bed, and then I'll scrub and sanitize the counter."

I pressed our foreheads together with a helpless groan. I really had to get to the library. My brain did its very best to think quickly given the fact that my body had stopped sending any blood its way. I grinned, an idea for payback taking form. "Okay," I said. "Fine."

Thor looked surprised. We usually played a bit more before I gave in when it came to things like this. With a swift move, I tossed his slim body over my shoulder, where he landed with a startled *oof.* I gave his butt cheek a swat and carried him down the hall.

After kicking the door open, I crossed the room and chucked him on the bed. He landed with a bounce, grinning, but I backed off a step. Thankfully I was still dressed—albeit, a bit disheveled—or I wouldn't have been able to resist. I adjusted my jeans and cleared my throat. "Anyway," I said, and I could see confusion drawing across his face. "I'm just gonna go to the library for a *few* hours, and then I'll be back."

"What?" He sat up, voice strangled.

"Bye!" I turned and dodged the shoe he whipped at me and ran down the hall, scooped up my school bag and dipped out, laughing all the way down the stairs.

---

## THOR

I wasn't really mad of course. And I'd missed him with the shoe on purpose. Smiling and groaning at the same time, I relaxed back onto the pillows. How had I lived without Cas?

The answer was simple: I hadn't, not truly.

I rolled over onto my stomach. It was early so I could grab a quick nap. Cas had worn me out last night, to the point that I'd shot Leda a text message requesting the day off, and if I could make the hours up later in the week. She'd replied with an eggplant emoji and an eye-roll emoji. I think Lucy was having a serious influence over her.

It had been excellent. I had zero experience in general, and Cas had zero experience with men, so we liked to try new things and compare notes. I didn't know if it was my Alpha side, or my twenty-year-old guy side, or my Cassian-Rhodes-is-Fine-as-*hell* side, or a combo therein, but I could not get enough of him. My mate. The thought was warm and comforting, like slipping into a steaming bath and soaking away all my tension.

Since Cas had escaped my horny clutches, I hoped he made the most of his time at the library and came back ready for other activities. As for me, I'd nap for an hour and then make the most of my own solitary time. I hoped to work on my novel for the first time in weeks. Sending the tips off to the police had been like a weight off my shoulders.

Smiling contently at the breakfast waiting for me in the warmer for when I woke up, I drifted off to sleep.

A crash and a muffled curse woke me, and disoriented, I sat up. The shades were pulled tight, and without my glasses, I couldn't see a damn thing. I groped for my glasses, but my phone was in the kitchen.

I heard another bang and frowned. Cas was making a great deal of noise, like he'd come home drunk or something. Still groggy, I rolled to the edge of the bed and stretched. *Bang.* What on earth was he doing out there?

I walked down the hallway, yawning. As I rounded the corner into the living room, I said, "Cas, what is—"

I stopped dead. The front door of our apartment was swung open, the latch visibly busted. Books and papers, my notes—my research, littered the floor and every possible surface. Too late, I realized the scent of the person in the room with me was foreign. I felt, rather than heard, them moving behind me.

It was not Cas.

His voice was muffled, but he said, "You weren't supposed to be home."

A massive forearm clamped around my windpipe before I could even react. My hands went to fight against the grip, instinct screaming at me to free my airway, but it was useless. He was much, *much* stronger. My feet left the floor and I had a split second to be embarrassed that my dick was hanging out before real terror coursed through me. Before I remembered that I could shift, my assailant pressed a piece of wet, dirty fabric over my nose and mouth.

"Just as well," the guy said, "I can't make heads or tails out of these notes."

I registered a sickly, burning, chemical smell, but it was kind of sweet.

When I woke yet again, I was in a pitch-black room. I couldn't see my damn hand in front of my face, even if I'd had on my glasses. What *had* happened to my glasses? I felt around, but came up empty. A chill seeped up from the floor into my bare legs. I still wore nothing but Cas's flannel, so I clutched it tightly against me like a life jacket.

I was still groggy, and dizzy, and my throat burned. I did what every dumbass in every dumb movie did in this situation. I called out. "Hello?"

No answer. Now that my eyes were adjusting a bit to the dark, I could see I was in a very small room with an earthen floor and no windows. I felt around the walls and found they were made of stone, suggesting an unfinished basement. The room in which I was being held was about the size of a closet. And like a closet, it had a thick wooden door. "*Hello?*"

Again, no one answered, so I increased the ferocity of my pounding, the volume of my yelling, because that was certainly easier than dealing with the reality of my situation.

Soon enough my hands and throat started to hurt, so I slumped to the ground with my back to the door. I tugged my flannel so I had something to sit on. The indignity of sitting bare assed on a dirty basement floor, was, quite frankly, too much on top of everything else. So, I scrunched down, drew my legs up to my chest, and turned over everything that had happened in the last...while, to see if I could figure out what the hell was going on.

Facts. Facts were good. There weren't many, but I clung to them as tightly as I clung to the neckline of Cas's shirt. First, this wasn't a random abduction. Whoever this was, he knew me, and (fact two) he was after my notes. Maybe if I explained my shorthand, he would let me go. Then, there was fact three. He clearly didn't know that I could shift. Only Cas, Leda and Lucy knew, since I hadn't even told my family yet. I hadn't managed to pull off a shift during my capture, so there was a chance he still didn't know. I assumed he wouldn't have left me this unsupervised if he knew—not that I could turn into anything big or strong enough to bust the door down. However, I was in a basement with an earthen floor. I had yet to test the limits of my burrowing capabilities.

Did hedgehogs even burrow?

Well, I was fucking gonna.

I felt the bottom of the door, trying to suss out the gap between it and the floor. Hedgehog me was pretty tiny, but it still seemed like too tight of a gap. Last thing I needed was to get stuck, Winnie the Pooh style, under the door in some creep's basement. So, despite my fight or flight response being heavily weighted toward flight, I convinced myself to stay put. I had to seize my moment. So, I waited.

Sure enough, the door creaked open eventually and a huge dark figure stood framed in the entrance. "You done yelling?" He pitched his voice low and weird, like he was putting on an accent to disguise it.

I didn't answer. I was aware I was about as menacing as a kitten, especially squinting at him, near-blind without my glasses. So, I figured staying silent was my only bargaining chip in this power exchange.

He grabbed me by the arm, tugging me forward, and I stumbled, stubbing my toe and of course I had to open my mouth. "I can't see," I snapped. "If you want me to read you anything I'm going to need my glasses."

My host did not deign to answer me, which I supposed wasn't a huge surprise. He frog-marched me up the stairs, out of the basement, into a much brighter room. After shoving me into a chair, he slapped something into my hand. My glasses! I jammed them on my face so fast I nearly poked my eye out. After a quick scan of my surroundings, I saw that I was in a shockingly normal dining room. From what I'd experienced of this gentleman's hospitality thus far, I had been expecting something more like Frankenstein's lab.

I recognized my notebooks immediately, piled high on the table before me. He placed a stack of blank lined paper at my elbow. "You copy," he grunted, still doing that weird Christian Bale Batman thing with his voice. "In full longhand."

"Why don't you tell me what you're looking for?"

He laughed. Okay, that was disconcerting. The hair on my neck prickled. Now that I had my glasses, I could see that he had a bandana around his face, big sunglasses, and a baseball cap. He'd also doused himself in enough cologne to choke me, disguising his scent. Under that thought, I could still tell he was human, not shifter.

I flicked my gaze to each of the windows in the room and he laughed again. "Don't even think about it." He crouched beside me, and I squeezed my knees closed, my face burning hot with shame. I felt something cold around my ankle, and peeked down to see him fastening a handcuff around me, and the other end to the leg of the table, which was bolted to the floor. Terrific.

Not to put too fine a point on it, but this was fucking insane. Here I was, chained to some guy's table, setting about copying massive amounts of research notes, like I was doing a PhD dissertation from the set of *Misery*. I could try shifting, but I wasn't super confident in my abilities and he was standing right there at my shoulder.

So, I copied. I wrote, and wrote, and wrote. I wrote until my hand cramped and my eyes blurred, even with my glasses. But the guy didn't move. Eventually, he called a halt, and marched me back to the basement. I hated myself for my meekness, but apparently it made him trust I'd be too much of a coward to attempt any kind of escape: I wasn't locked in the closet again, merely locked in the cellar. However, he did take back my glasses, leaving me to feel around in the blurry dark for a toilet on my own. I suppose I should have been grateful that I even found one down here.

I gulped water from the tap, not knowing when I'd get another chance, and after that I felt every inch of my prison. It was sealed up tight like a fortress and my stomach dropped as I realized I was definitely not the first person to be kept here. I thought of Leda, and Rafe, afraid and alone. But they had no memories of this place—how? Had they been unconscious the whole time?

After realizing I was just the latest in a series of prisoners, I fled immediately to the closet where I'd originally been held, slammed the door, and cried like a baby.

I did my best to muffle the noise against my knees, hiding as much as I could within the safety of Cas's well-worn shirt, because this really had been humiliating enough without my budget Kathy Bates hearing me sniveling like an idiot. Considering this was the worst thing that had ever happened to me, by a significant margin, I tried not to be too hard on myself.

When I finally cried myself out, as silently as possible, all the fear and adrenaline left me in a whoosh. I was exhausted. I curled up, shivering on the cold floor, burying my nose in the sleeve of my shirt and trying to smell a little of Cas.

# 21



I managed to get a lot done at the library, especially considering I was still mentally in bed with Thor. In fact, I had gotten enough of a jump on my work that I could spend the rest of the day, night, and tomorrow catering to his voracious appetites.

I had my phone on airplane mode, which I often did when I was studying. I had expected a flood of texts, and possibly a spicy pic or two when I switched it back on. Nothing. That was weird. I felt a quiver of unease. He hadn't been truly angry, had he?

I shot off a quick message to let him know I was heading home before gathering my things. I had my eyes on my phone screen as I left the library, and as such collided with someone coming the other way down the hall.

"Oh, sorry—" But when I looked up and saw Benson. I broke off, scowling.

Benson looked nervous, like he was afraid I was going to

haul off and punch him again. I'll admit, it was tempting. "Cas, come on. Are you still mad?"

"Still mad that you tried to date rape my boyfriend? Uh, yeah. I'm still mad."

Benson hushed me and stepped closer. "Look, man. I didn't set out to hurt Thor," he said.

"Oh please," I said, turning to leave. I didn't need to stand here and listen to his bullshit excuses.

But Benson grabbed my sleeve. I faced him again, and something dangerous must have read on my face because he released my arm and took a step back. "Someone paid me."

"What?"

"Someone offered me money, and threatened to blackmail me if I didn't do it."

He was obviously lying. "Why would someone do that? Who was it?"

"I don't know." He lowered his voice. "Someone had footage of us... in Kendrick's office. They emailed it to me, threatening to send a copy to the Dean if I didn't do what they said."

"You're full of shit," I said.

"Cas, I'm not, I promise."

"You are such a jackass. Only you would try to cover up one shitty crime by doing another one. Why didn't you call the police?"

"I couldn't lose my spot on the team, man. Besides— nothing even happened to Thor."

"You're fucking unbelievable," I said.

"You can't tell anyone about this!"

"Like hell I can't," I said. "Fuck off, Benson."

My head spun as I left Benson calling after me. I practically ran home. Clearly Benson had a connection to whoever was kidnapping shifters and breeding the primitives. I had to get home, confer with Thor, and maybe even call Detective Davis. This could be a huge lead.

When I got to our building, I saw that someone had jammed something in the front door to keep it propped open, probably just someone expecting a package or something, but I felt a prickle over my skin, a weird sort of awareness that I couldn't place. The feeling of unease increased with every stair I climbed, such that I took the last several two at a time.

I about barfed up the bagel I'd eaten at the library when I got to the door of the apartment, or rather, what was left of it. It swung sadly, the wood by the strike plate splintered. "Thor? Thor!" My voice pitched high, sounding young and scared as I burst through the broken door, panic mounting. I couldn't smell him, I realized. I couldn't feel his heartbeat. He wasn't here. Looking around the room, I forced myself to take in the scene. The TV was still here, Thor's stereo and the game systems. Not one of Thor's expensive liquor bottles had been disturbed. Nothing seemed to have been taken, but the place had been thoroughly ransacked. Notebooks, papers, books lay strewn all over the floor, an image that twisted in my guts, reminding me cruelly of the night we'd hooked up on this very floor, surrounded by these very books.

Something high-pitched, like the buzzing of a mosquito, whined inside my head. I checked every room, under the beds, in the closets, yelling for him. He wasn't here. *He wasn't here.*

An hour later I sat on the couch, flanked by Lucy and Leda. Lucy had her arm around my shoulders. The apartment was full of police officers, jotting things in notebooks, asking me an endless list of only slightly differentiated questions.

All I could think was the last thing I'd done was refuse to touch him.

"Mr. Rhodes?" I looked up, startled. One of the officers stood in front of me.

Lucy nudged me gently. "Sorry," I said. "What was that?"

"Detective Davis here would like to ask you a few questions."

Davis was there with his hard-faced partner, who re-introduced himself as Sargent Stark. They requested to speak to me in private, but my throat constricted and I couldn't even answer. "We're staying right here," Lucy snapped, giving me a little squeeze.

Detective Davis looked very grave as he asked me to tell the story. "Start from the beginning," he said, pen poised over his notebook.

As I recounted the story, such that it was, he took copious notes, but Stark interrupted me.

"Mr. Rhodes," he said sharply. "When exactly did you move in?"

I frowned. "Early September," I said. "Why?"

"And did you know Thor Ambrose prior to moving in?"

What the hell did this have to do with it? "No," I said. "I found his ad at the student center."

"And were you aware of his family's net worth before you answered the ad?"

"Of course not—"

"What does this have to do with anything?" Lucy asked the guy aggressively, cutting across my answer.

"The questions are standard, Miss," said Davis. He shot his partner a look, but it was ignored.

"When did the two of you become romantically involved?

I flushed. "Just before Thanksgiving."

He jotted down a note. "And where were you this afternoon?"

"*What?*"

"Answer the question, Mr. Rhodes."

"I—I was on campus."

"Can anyone corroborate that?"

"Now, hold on," said Leda, placing a firm hand on my shoulder. "What exactly are you implying?"

"We have to ask these questions?"

"Why would he abduct his own boyfriend and then *call you* about it?"

I was on my feet, and I didn't remember getting up. "I swiped into the library with my student ID." I said, barely keeping my voice under control. "I checked out a study room with the librarian."

Stark leveled his gaze at me, nodded, and made yet another note. Detective Davis looked conflicted. "Thank you, Mr. Rhodes. We'll be in touch."

"That's it?"

It was apparently, because then they were gone, leaving the apartment cold and empty. I sank back down onto the couch, covering my face in shaking hands. Feeling a flurry of movement at my side, I looked up to see Leda gliding gracefully around the kitchen, looking for cookies and setting the kettle on to heat for tea. "You should come and stay with me tonight," said Lucy.

I shook my head. "I have to stay here. In case he comes home." I cleared my throat, trying to swallow around the lump. I checked my phone, praying for a call or a text. But Thor's phone was here. His wallet, his keys, everything. I set his phone beside mine on the coffee table and stared at them both. I'd have to make sure to keep them both fully charged.

Lucy handed me a steaming mug and my throat tightened even further. It was the same mug I'd put Hedgehog Thor in to take the picture of the two of us. My eyes burned and I rubbed them angrily with the heels of my hands.

The police had mentioned getting in touch with Thor's family, so I'd given them the contact information for his parents. I wondered if they would call me when they heard. Should I call them? I hadn't considered what the proper protocol might be in this situation. I hadn't considered much of anything. My brain was a worthless pile of scared mush. I couldn't think clearly. With a vague desire to have something to do, I stood and wandered around the living room, picking up the books and torn pages that Thor's abductor had left behind. Many of the books were gone, and a lot of Thor's notebooks. I stacked the remainder neatly on his desk. He hadn't gotten a lot of joy out of those books, but he'd had a reverence for them, always taking care to treat them well. Of course, we'd given in to the building attraction between us and snapped, coming together like a car crash. My brain filled with images of Thor laid out for me as I made him come for the first time...

A tear escaped. I couldn't remember the last time I'd really cried, but at the moment I felt like something gaping and dark and angry had opened up in my chest. Something raw and painful, and with every second passing, every breath, it hurt worse. Like the wound of the Fisher King, it would never heal. All at once I couldn't breathe. What if something horrible happened to him? What if...? I couldn't even think the words.

My vision blurred, and somewhere in the fog I registered a few soft hands pulling me back toward the sofa. The whole afternoon had been moving in curious time jumps, and the next time my brain turned back on, I was curled on the couch, my head in Lucy's lap, my feet in Leda's. Lucy stayed the night, sitting with me on the couch until almost four a.m., staring at my phone, waiting for it to ring. Leda left, heading to the lab around nine, filled with fresh determination to find something else to help with the case. Lucy must have gone to crash in my old bedroom at some point because another funny sort of time-skip later, I was alone in the living room. I wasn't sure if I'd fallen asleep or just zoned out—but I scrambled up to check the phones. No missed calls.

When I finally did fall asleep, it was with my phone tucked up near my chin so it would wake me if it rang.

———

THOR

It took me two more full days of solid copying to finish transcribing my notes, by which point my fingers felt like they were about to fall off. Part of me thought I could make some omissions, or factual "errors" but in truth, I didn't have the energy for subterfuge, and I had no idea what he was after. I was given water, but no food, so when I finished the final page and he sent me downstairs again, my jelly legs stumbled and I hit the floor of the basement.

I bit my tongue to keep from crying out, not that it would do me any good. The door slammed shut, plunging me into darkness again. I kept hoping he would forget to reclaim my glasses after a session of transcribing, but I had been unlucky thus far.

I curled up in the closet, trying to detect a remaining hint of Cas's scent on my soiled flannel. There wasn't much left beneath the stench of my own fear sweat. The asshole had still not given me any pants, so with every movement, every time a piece of my bare skin touched the floor, I felt a sickly swoop of shame in my gut. Never had I felt so vulnerable, so exposed.

Yesterday, when he sent me back down here, I had mapped my prison as well as I could. The basement consisted of at least three rooms, but I found one metal door, barred shut, and who knew what lay beyond it. I had the distinct impression I didn't want to find out.

Now, panic clawed my throat. I huddled in my corner, knees drawn up tight under my chin. I had finished the notes, so now what?

I had serious doubts that he would just let me go. This was different than the others—though I had to assume it was the same perpetrator. Leda and Rafe had only suffered one missing day, and judging by the fact that their memories were blank, he'd kept them in a haze of drugs the entire time. Unless he had something unheard of that could literally erase my memories of the last few days, I'd remember. I might not be able to identify him, but I could give the police *something*. This man wasn't an idiot. He must know he couldn't let me go.

The one bullet remaining in my chamber was that I could shift. However, I had only done it once, and I'd been half asleep. I cursed myself for not practicing more. I hadn't found a single spot where I could breach the defenses of this damn basement. There wasn't a single crack in the walls or floors that I could find, not even one small enough for a hedgehog to slip through. I'd have to wait until I was topside, if he ever brought me up there again. I had entertained the idea of practicing now, to see if I even *could* shift on command, but a tiny voice in the back of my head suggested there might be some kind of security system down here, and that would give me away even if I was successful

So, I waited, and worried, and finally fell into an uneasy sleep.

A smell woke me up, a simple one, but heavenly. Beside my head on the floor was a plate. And when I felt my way toward it, I discovered it held toast and jam. My survival instinct warned me that there might be something more to this offering than breakfast, but I was simply too hungry to care.

I finished the three slices of toast and then stood to stretch my legs. Heavy footfalls on the stairs had me breaking out in cold sweat. For all the good it did me, I scrabbled back away from my breakfast plate to cower in the corner, hating myself as I went for being such a coward.

Sure enough, after a few moments, the door to the little closet swung open. Without a word, my captor grabbed me by the upper arm and yanked me to my feet. He dragged me, stumbling, across the uneven floor, and though I couldn't see, I was familiar enough with my basement prison to know he was pulling me away from the staircase, and toward the locked and barred metal door.

Abandoning any pretext of bravery, I struggled, yanking against the iron grip around my arm, planting my heels on the floor. Of course, I had no idea what was behind that door, but every instinct I possessed told me it wasn't likely to be something pleasant. I think the strength of my struggles surprised him, because after two days with no food and no escape attempts, he probably expected me weak and pliant. But adrenaline surged through me, and I pulled and kicked and fought with a hysterical desperation that allowed me the briefest freedom as I yanked my arm from his grasp.

He cursed, and I fled, clambering ungracefully up the steps to the basement door. Of course, it was locked, but I yanked on the handle, screaming and hollering myself hoarse, hoping there was someone who'd hear me. No one came, not even a curious mailman, and soon enough he caught up to me and pressed a damp rag to my face. I held my breath as long as I could, but I couldn't do that indefinitely, and once again I found myself sucked under.

When I came to, my head ached, and I was on my back, strapped down and completely naked. Not that I'd been fully dressed before, but the fig leaf of false modesty—not to mention the sliver of comfort—provided by Cas's shirt had meant more to me than I realized. I struggled impotently against the thick leather straps, my face burning with humiliation at how weak and exposed I was. Powerless. I couldn't budge an inch, but I couldn't stop fidgeting, wanting nothing more than to cover myself.

Movement behind me, and I about broke my own neck craning my head to the noise. "*Shh,*" came a soft voice, a hand on my head. I twisted from the touch, but he laughed. He put on my glasses, tucking them in place almost tenderly, bringing bile up my throat. I blinked in the harsh light of the medical lamp shining from above. It illuminated my bare body and I squirmed, the shame itching like insects on my skin.

Now that I had my glasses on, I squinted and adjusted the light so I could look around. Looks like I finally found myself in some sort of Frankenstein lab, like I'd expected when he first brought me here. Be careful what you wish for, I suppose.

"I need something else from you, before I release you," the man behind me said, and I flinched. "I intended to gather it before Thanksgiving, but that plan was bungled. When I learned your findings would be of more use than your DNA, I set my sights on that. Never did I imagine I'd get access to both."

Had I been free, I would have jumped, but as such I merely jerked against the restraints. He released a soft chuckle and my mind raced. *He was going to release me? Or was that merely a euphemism?* My guts clenched and churned, my meager breakfast of toast like a hot ball of lead in my stomach.

I didn't trust myself to answer, but he walked into my field of vision and grabbed something from the counter. It was a small plastic jar with a screw-on lid, like the kind doctors used for urine samples.

I stared at him in disbelief. "You want my pee?" I blurted.

He let out a full belly laugh, loud but strangely muffled behind the bandana that hid his face. "Close, but not quite."

What. The. Fuck.

I had to be misunderstanding him, right? Right?

"With your...unique condition, I must admit I'm quite eager to study your samples."

I couldn't help the disgusted noise that slipped out of my mouth. He drew a key from a ring at his belt and busied himself with the straps at my wrists, freeing my hands. Paralyzed, I couldn't decide if I wanted to cover myself or try to fight, so in my infinite wisdom I opted for a very feeble attempt at both. I covered my cock and balls with my left hand and took a swipe at him with my right. Of course, the rest of me remained completely immobilized, so it was easy enough for him to dodge my pathetic strikes.

"So, I take it you're right-handed." He snagged my left wrist, drawing it away from my crotch and strapping it down to the table, securing the padded cuff once again with the padlock. "You can do this yourself, or I have a machine that'll do it for you. I'll give you five minutes to decide."

He left the sample cup within reach of my hand, adjusted a few cranks on the table to bend my prone body into a seated position instead, and left the room—but not before removing my glasses and turning off the light.

# 22



I took a few days off from classes, or at least, Lucy contacted my advisor on my behalf and gave her the gist of what was going on. Apparently, having your boyfriend vanish into thin air qualified one for a short leave of absence, though I noted with a bite of annoyance, on the form where it said "relationship," they had written, "roommate."

The problem, though, was all this time I had to sit around all day, staring at both Thor's and my phones. The detectives came by once again, and like before, Sargent Stark badgered me and implied more than once I must have Thor locked in a trunk somewhere. His partner, Davis, was much kinder, and the second time he came alone.

"How are you holding up?" He asked gently when I let him into the apartment. He looked like he was in his mid to late thirties, but more worn down than I'd imagine someone at his age should look, reminding me a lot of my dad.

I shrugged. Glancing down at my shirt, I saw I hadn't changed out of my pajamas today. With a start, I realized I couldn't remember the last time I'd put clean clothes on. I tried to give myself a surreptitious sniff, but I couldn't be fucked really to go put on deodorant or change.

Davis closed the door quietly behind him and followed me into the kitchen. I gestured vaguely at the kitchen island, indicating he could take a seat. "Coffee?" I asked him.

"Please."

I nodded, my back to Davis as I got the coffee going. While I got some mugs from the cabinet, I listened to him fidget.

"My CO doesn't know I'm here."

"CO?"

"Commanding officer." Davis cleared his throat. "Stark thinks this is a cut and dry missing person's case."

"Yeah," I said, hands shaking. "He fucking thinks I did it."

"I don't think you did it."

I turned back toward him. "You don't?"

"No, Mr. Rhodes, I don't. But I do think you know something."

We stared at each other for a beat. I placed a mug in front of Davis, then turned to fridge to grab milk, buying myself some time. When I straightened up, I said, "If I knew anything that would help get Thor back, I would tell you."

"I believe that," said Davis. "But the case is larger than just the disappearance of Mr. Ambrose. Tell me, what do you know about your boyfriend's family?"

My guts clenched, swooping nervously. Was he asking what I thought he was asking? "Not much," which on some level, was true. "I've only met them once."

"The Thanksgiving you spent at their home?"

"Yes." This guy was sharp. I'd have to be very careful what I said, because while I certainly hadn't harmed Thor, I could still accidentally expose his entire family.

"And how did you find them?"

"What do you mean?"

"Were they...welcoming? Did they have any traditions you found peculiar?"

"Some," I said. I had a suspicion he was dancing around the matter at hand, and I decided my best bet was to be as honest as I possibly could without giving them all away, especially because he at least believed I had nothing to do with this. "But they were alright, I suppose."

He stirred milk into his coffee. "And..." he hesitated. "Does Thor—how does he fit in with them?"

I weighed my possible answers, and decided to go all-in and trust Davis. He was looking for Thor. That's all that mattered. "He didn't, historically," I said, staring him in the eye. "But very recently he started uncovering a new...side of himself."

"Is that so?"

"Yes."

"Very well. Now, I wonder if you could tell me a bit more about what was missing, after the break-in."

"Nothing valuable," I said. "Like I told the officers, our TV, Thor's laptop, stereo, nothing like that was touched."

"What was touched?"

I pointed to Thor's desk. "His books. And his notes. Research."

"Research?"

"Yes, He—" I hesitated, and then threw caution to the wind. "He was doing a project." I stared pointedly at Detective Davis. "For his family. About them."

Davis looked alarmed. "Do you know what exactly was missing."

"No," I said with a pang. "Thor writes everything in a weird sort of shorthand. His notebooks would be a disaster to anyone else." *Even me.*

Davis scribbled furiously in his own notebook before

snapping it shut. "Thank you, Mr. Rhodes, this has been very helpful."

"It has?"

"I'll be in touch," he said, and then he hesitated for a moment before he wrote on the back of his business card. "If you think of anything else, this is my personal number."

Davis thanked me for the coffee, and left.

I was alone again, and I hated it. I tried to summon up a smidge of surprise that Detective Davis had all but admitted he knew about Thor's family and their powers, but I honestly didn't care. I didn't care about anything except waiting for the phone to ring, and Googling missing person's statistics, as if I could find one source that could give me a shred of hope. It had been five days since Thor disappeared.

I collapsed on the couch. I felt a pull in my gut and tried to remember the last time I'd eaten. I certainly hadn't cooked in days, but I didn't have much of an appetite. I massaged my stomach. Now that I thought about it, it didn't really feel like hunger.

It was more like a tug, like someone had lodged a fishhook in my abdomen. With a frown, I sat up. The tugging lessened when I moved, but then began again. Harsher. Stronger.

My throat ran dry and my pulse quickened. I stood, and the tug subsided again, for a moment, before returning. Insistent. Drawing me on. To the door. Down the stairs. I followed the tug in my belly until I reached the lobby. The sensation vanished so quickly it was like it had never been there. Perhaps I was truly losing it.

The lobby was empty. I stared blankly until a flurry of movement caught my eye. Something small and brown dashed past the front door. A rat, was my first thought. Then I froze.

I felt a heartbeat that was not my own. But, to be honest, it may as well have been mine. I needed to feel it just as badly; it pumped life into my body as if it were. I ran to the door and flung it open, frantic. Tiny, brown, covered in spines. Filthy. With those fucking eyes blinking up at me.

"Hey, Pin Cushion," I said, and my voice cracked.

I crouched and Thor ran immediately into the palm of my hand. He balled up, hiding his little face, and I could feel him shaking. I had done some research about hedgehogs and knew they didn't like the cold, and it was very brisk outside the door. I shut it, cradling the spiny ball to my chest. It took a surprising amount of self-control not to squeeze him.

Part of me didn't even believe it, and I didn't think I'd really be able to relax until it was my Thor that I was seeing, but this was good too. So good. I ran back up the stairs, holding him close to my heart.

I set Thor on the counter and just looked at him. Poking his spines like I had to be sure he was real. It took almost an hour for him to un-ball and totter around on his little paws. I ached to see his human face, to touch him, to pull him into my arms, but he was here, and that was all that mattered.

His quills were covered in dirt, the soft tan fur of his belly stained from travel so close to the ground. First, I made him a scrambled egg, which he wolfed down at a shocking pace for one with such a tiny body, and then I knew he wouldn't want to be dirty. So, I picked him up and carried him to the bath-room, filling the sink with warm, soapy water. I set him down in the water and let him paddle around a bit before fetching a spare toothbrush from the linen closet.

Cooing gently, I dipped the soft bristles of the toothbrush into the water and used it to scrub Thor's quills. He seemed to like that. I felt a pang that he didn't turn back into himself, but recalled his words a month ago when he'd said he felt safer as a hedgehog, where he could curl up and hide.

Thor perhaps needed that, but I needed *him*. I coursed with guilt, feeling selfish, as I had no idea what he had been through the past several days.

A prickle of something I couldn't name washed over me. He had no idea what *I'd* been through. While my instincts told me Thor hadn't run off, I couldn't help remembering what happened after the first time he shifted. How he'd been exploring his own power and left me to fend for myself.

But we had talked. At length. He'd promised me that would never happen again.

Looking at him splashing about, occasionally peering up at me with fathomless black eyes, I knew I trusted him. He would come back to me when he was ready.

I dried him off with a fluffy hand towel, and by the time he was blinking and swaying on his paws. I hadn't been sleeping all that well, either, so I figured an early night wouldn't kill us. I fired off a quick text to Lucy, to let her know Thor was home and unhurt and I'd call her in the morning.

I rested on my back, sleeping in our bed for the first time since he'd been taken because I couldn't face sleeping there without him. Gently, I put Thor on his pillow and he sank into the soft down, huffing and puffing with his spines erect.

I brushed a fingertip over his head and whispered, "I'm so glad you're home, Pin Cushion."

With another little huff, Thor ambled over to nestle against the crook of my neck. The scrape of his quills was the most welcome sensation I'd felt in a long time; the prickle soothed me more than the softest touch.

And with Thor there, I slept.

I woke to something tickling my face. I sneezed. Then, I froze. Thick, dark hair obscured my vision. A warm, solid weight covered my body. Bare skin pressed tight against me, draped over me, falling limp between my thighs. I didn't think I'd ever been more torn in my life: I wanted to grab him by the shoulders, shake him awake, see his smile and hear his laugh, but I also wanted to stay tranquil with him in my arms, endlessly comfortable, for as long as we could.

I settled for a half measure, and squeezed his body like I'd wanted to yesterday. His human form could withstand my hugs.

He let out a huff, not unlike the one made by his hedgehog self. I didn't want to speak, or startle him, so I squeezed again and breathed him in. Thor. He was home. He was safe.

His lips brushed against my chest, and the simple gesture had my eyes prickling. *Fuck.* I sucked in a breath, trying to hold myself together.

"Cas?" Thor's eyes found mine, unfocused without his glasses.

"I'm here," I whispered, and it was a trial to get the words out around the lump in my throat. "I'm here, baby."

He nuzzled into my chest, pressing close. I realized for the first time he was naked. It made sense, considering how he'd gotten home, and usually the merest suggestion of a bare Thor had me hard and wanting, but now all I wanted was to press him against me, let him crawl inside my own skin and hide there. And I didn't even know what had happened yet.

I turned my face into the pillow. *I will not cry.*

But he spoke again, his voice tiny, lips pushed against my trembling skin. "Cas?"

It was like I felt my name rather than heard it. "Yeah?"

"Just..." he sighed. His exhale released a pulse over us both, and the lean muscle of his tight body melted against me. "Checking."

Several hours of sleep later, bundled up in my clothes, and looking more tiny and frail than he had even in his hedgehog form, Thor told me what happened. He had on my sweatpants, one of my hockey jerseys, and my hoodie, drowning in fabric, clutching it close to him like armor. I fidgeted as he talked, watching Thor adjust to his backup glasses. The wire frames suited his narrow face, but they didn't look like *him* the way his old glasses did.

He curled up, limbs knotted tightly, in his customary reading chair. I sat on the sofa, my hands twitching, because all I wanted was to pull him into my lap, squish him close and absorb his pain onto my own skin, but if there was one thing I had learned from Thor, it was that he would come to me in his own time.

In the wake of his tale, Thor came back to me, bit by bit, piece by piece. Some nights, I would fall asleep with him in my arms and wake up with a hedgehog curled up on my chest, and some nights the opposite. But we were getting there.

It was strange, at first, Thor very much wanted to be naked together, but he did not want to be touched. I didn't know what to make of that, so I let him curl against me and held him, but I didn't move things further than that. I let him direct my hands, position my body like a doll's, and I figured that was him coming back to himself: my bossy little Thunder God, telling me what he needed in his own way.

After telling me what happened, I convinced Thor to call Detective Davis, who to his credit had listened carefully and asked pointed questions about Thor's research. I had gripped Thor's hand for comfort when he had to again discuss what happened in that basement. Thor took care to remember his route home, and was able to describe the outside of the house. He detailed his escape, and the biological samples he'd found and destroyed. Davis thanked him, and left us alone again, promising to call if there were any updates on the case.

After repeating his story to Detective Davis, Thor was furtive, avoiding my gaze. I wanted to explain to him that there was nothing he had to hide from me, but I felt saying the words aloud would only make him feel worse.

We went back to class; I went back to cooking. Thor smiled a bit more each day. The school made him talk to someone, which was good. I had no idea what all they discussed, but I supposed that was the point of therapy.

One Sunday morning, two weeks after Thor had returned to me, I woke up to a soft, wet heat around my dick.

My hands flew to Thor's head, tugging on his hair to pull him off me, to bring his face up closer to mine. "Hey," I whispered.

"Good morning," he said, and I swore I saw the gleam of mischief in his big brown eyes that had been sorely lacking recently. His lips were plump and pink and slick with spit.

"What are you doing?"

He cocked a thick eyebrow and grinned. "Sucking your dick," he said, matter of factly, and we both laughed. I pulled him closer to me, and we lazed in bed kissing for a while instead.

After that, I almost would have thought things were back to normal. We'd mess around, and perhaps I was a bit more gentle with him than I would have been, but otherwise the same as before—except for one thing.

Thor would not let anything touch his dick.

I almost didn't notice. He'd just taken to bottoming, which, when Thor did it, was bottoming only in name. He would climb on top of me and ride hard, clawing the skin of my chest, grabbing my wrists to hold me down or direct my hands. I'd eat him out, finger him, fuck him. He'd suck me off, and with our usual physical whirlwind it took me a few bouts to realize he was keeping his dick out of the equation.

Then, one day, I was on my back, grasping Thor's waist as he rode my cock, rolling his spine just so, and he looked— perfect. I was so happy to look up at him, so happy he was back here with me, safe. Every time we fucked it was a gift. It had been before too, of course, but it felt heavier now. It embarrassed me a little but now when we got close like this, I'd get a bit emotional. Never in my life had I cried during sex, but suddenly it took everything I had not to every time I was inside him. Sometimes I'd catch myself off guard, too focused on not bawling my eyes out to realize how close I was to coming.

My hips jerked off the bed, my whole body bowing as I came explosively. "Oh *shit*—sorry—"

Even as I apologized, I held Thor tight, still bucking into him, his ass flush against my lap. He moaned as I ground against him, trying to offer what friction I could even as I came down. In one heartbeat I rolled us, kissing his neck, nuzzling the sweaty skin of his shoulder. I slid my tongue down his throat, savoring the perfect dip where his collarbones met before moving down to tease his pink little nipples, hard and sweet to roll between my lips.

I nosed through the soft fluff below his navel, preparing to suck him down and swallow him whole, but he froze, and then zoomed out from under me faster than I would have thought possible. He sat on the edge of the bed, his back to me, and said, "I'm fine."

His harsh voice startled me, because he obviously was *not* fine. "Hey—"

"Sorry," he said, his voice immediately softer. He peeked over his shoulder at me, a little half-smile on his face. "Just, don't worry about me."

I squirmed onto my knees beside him, kissing his temple, of course worried. "Alright."

And just like that, he was gone, and I heard the shower running down the hall.

———

THOR

I turned the shower on as cold as it would go, stepping under the spray, though by the time I'd gotten to the bathroom I was already half-soft, deflating more by the second. Being back home with Cas, I felt safe again, for the most part. Being so close to my bonded mate smoothed the rough edges down, his very presence like a warm bath and a bite of chocolate.

I felt guilty though, like I didn't deserve his comfort. I felt gross and soiled, no matter how hard I scrubbed my skin in the shower, sometimes multiple times a day. Cas was so gentle, and so pure that I felt as though too much contact with me would contaminate him somehow.

It was also odd to *need*. Odd was putting it lightly. It rankled, irritating like a splinter. Needing Cas so badly reminded me that I was weak, that I had been so afraid. A few times, I imagined what would have happened if the man who'd taken me had tried to abduct Cas instead. First off, he probably wouldn't have gotten two hundred pounds of furious Cas out of the building without a few broken ribs. Second, Cas would never have submitted so easily. He would have refused to copy the notes, torn pages from the books and destroyed the research to keep it out of his hands. He would never have allowed himself to be strapped down and humiliated—

*Don't think about that.*

The fact was, I was used to dealing with things on my own. *Poorly,* said a snide voice in my head. The school insisted I visit a counselor, which also rankled. The guy was an idiot. So, after the first session I bagged out of the rest, and spent the hour twice a week sitting in a tree on campus. It was freezing and the bark dug into my butt, but it was isolated and private. I felt guilty lying to Cas about where I was, but it was only sort of a lie. I was working through what happened just—my way.

The biggest shock by far had been Cas explaining about Detective Davis. I had given an official statement to the police, but Davis had come by the apartment a few days later to ask a few more questions, off the books.

Davis was the serious sort, troubled by what we discussed, but he was kind enough. The way he asked questions was cathartic, like a doctor stitching up a wound: it hurt when it had to and he didn't yield, but he meant no malice and only tried to help. Part of me wondered if I should warn my parents that a detective was sniffing around us. However, I was angry with them. Cas had called them when I was missing, and the police had talked to them as well. I couldn't face talking to them when I first got back, so Cas had called them again.

They hadn't called me yet.

I left those thoughts behind and finished my shower. I hadn't meant to snap at Cas, especially after sex. I grabbed a towel and padded back to our room to see Cas sitting cross-legged on the blanket, wearing nothing but an intense expression. Before I could open my mouth, he snapped. "Get over here. We need to talk. Now."

Because I was powerless to deny him, I dropped my towel and climbed onto the mattress.

Cas simply stared at me, waiting, damn him. He knew me too well. I fidgeted with the edge of the blanket. A lump rose in my throat, and with it the sensation of a kettle about to boil and blow its lid.

Cas reached out to place a hand on my shoulder, and I cringed from his touch. He drew his hands away. "I'm sorry."

That galvanized me. "Stop," I bit off. The word burst out of my mouth before I could recall it, snappish and irritated.

Cas balked. "Excuse me?"

Of course, I was screwing this up. I covered my face with my hands. "That's not what I meant—or, it was. I don't know."

"C'mere," said Cas, heaving an exasperated sigh. When I looked out from behind my hands, Cas was leaning back against the pillows, his arms open. He was so open, always. Waiting for me. I curled up with my head on his chest, my ear over his heart, listening to it beat. Once we'd settled against each other, the bond between us flowing like light and warmth in a feedback loop, Cas inhaled and said, "Okay. Let's try this again."

"I just meant—stop apologizing," I said, my voice calmer because we were touching. I didn't think that was a mate bond thing. That was just Cas. "I feel like I should be apologizing."

Cas laughed. It was a sad, shaky, nervous laugh, utterly devoid of real humor. "I'm sorry," said Cas hastily. "That was awful of me. I just—Thor, I don't know how you could blame yourself for this."

"I know you don't," I said, the snap returning to my voice.

Cas traced the outline of my jaw with his fingertip. "Then tell me. Help me understand."

This was something I too had been struggling with. Perhaps if I'd given the dumb school therapist half a chance, he could have helped me figure it out. But that was me. Why figure out something calmly with help when you can struggle with it alone until it eats you alive?

"When I was—" I didn't want to say the words, and Cas rubbed a little circle on my neck with his thumb, so I knew he understood. "I tried so hard not to think of you."

I felt him tense, and hastened to explain.

"I mean—I couldn't." I clutched at his arms as they surrounded me. "I didn't want any part of you associated with —with that."

By way of answer, Cas gave me a little squeeze. I could almost feel the lump in his throat as if it were rising in mine.

"So, I shut you away. But now, now that I'm home, it's like the opposite."

I felt Cas frown, his cheekbone brushing against the crown of my head. "What do you mean?"

My voice was so quiet I could barely hear myself, but I knew Cas could. "I didn't want any of *that* associated with *you*."

"So that's why you don't want me to suck you off?"

Cas was so blunt sometimes, but it was needed. I laughed, and Cas chuckled too, and the tension eased a bit. "Yes," I said. "Every time something comes close to touching me, it's like I'm back in that basement."

"I understand."

"I'm just not—I'm not ready to be touched like that again, yet."

Cas nodded against me, running his fingers up and down my spine. He squeezed me tight, and his voice was quiet and serious when he said, "I just missed you so much."

The confession made me ache, but I still wasn't ready. "I missed you too."

Of course, Cas understood. He felt some type of way about the whole thing, obviously, but had I really expected less of him? For some reason, though, I felt like it would be easier if he raged. Easier if he was furious at me for giving in. This was almost like...he just accepted I was too weak to fight.

"You wouldn't have," I mumbled.

"I wouldn't have...what, exactly?"

"Let him." I left it at that, my face burning.

In a blink, Cas had shoved me from him, and I flopped on the bed, startled. "Are you serious?"

"I don't know," I said, my voice sulky and sullen.

Cas grabbed my chin, and I flinched, but he did not apologize this time. His eyes were fierce, his fingers firm as iron. "Thor," he said, his voice barely controlled. "If it had been me, you bet your ass I would have done *anything* he asked me to."

I didn't answer, just blinked at him as his eyes bored into mine.

"I would have done anything if it meant surviving," Cas said. "If it meant coming back to you."

"Promise?" I hated the way my voice came out tremulous and weak.

Without releasing my chin, Cas pulled me in for a quick, hard kiss. "With all my fucking heart."

I got a call from Davis the following day. He asked if Cas and I were free to meet, and I could tell by the tone that the news wasn't good, but I agreed that he could come over to discuss the case.

As I hung up, Cas wrapped himself around me. "What did he say?"

"Nothing good," I said with a heavy sigh. I closed my hand into a fist, pressing it to my forehead. "He's on his way over."

Cas opened the door for Davis about twenty minutes later. "Detective," he said.

"Guys," said Davis with a nod.

I poured the three of us a drink and we sat in the living room, Cas and I on the sofa and Davis in my reading chair. Cas slid one arm around me, gripping my opposite hip and grounding me. Davis looked at us with his tired, kind eyes and heaved a breath. Before he could speak, I said, "You didn't find anything."

Davis sighed. "You're right. We followed your tip and found the house where I believe you were held, but the location had been entirely scrubbed. We weren't able to get any usable evidence."

I closed my eyes, leaning forward to brace my elbows on my knees. "Naturally."

Cas rubbed my back. "But you still believe that's where Thor was held?"

"I do," said Davis. He ran a hand through his hair. "I think we need to agree to be honest with each other for this investigation to continue."

I sat up, glancing at Cas. I raised an eyebrow, and he nodded. "I think that's for the best," he said.

We all stared at each other in silence for a bit, and Detective Davis said carefully, "I received an anonymous tip regarding the case of the triple homicide. The one with the disfigured bodies, including the one you gentlemen found."

"Yes. We sent it to you."

"I thought as much. What I'm about to say might sound a little insane, but I think there might be something...paranormal at play here."

"Well, I am shocked," said Cas loudly.

I couldn't help it. I burst out laughing. This whole thing was surreal. "Me too," I said. "Shocked."

Davis gave a small smile and said, "Alright. Fair enough. I need you guys to start at the beginning, and tell me everything you know."

# 23



After our big talk, clearing the air with Davis, things approached normal. Thor's shoulders came down from around his ears; I adjusted to the look of his thin, wire-framed glasses, and I still didn't touch his dick. Much. Sometimes I woke up with it squished against my leg, but I felt like that was hardly my fault.

Given Thor still had aversions to being touched there, but no other aversions to us having sex, it became my personal mission to master the art of making Thor come untouched. This was great fun. It took me a while to get the hang of it, but we got there. Using a determined combination of my dick, fingers, and tongue—obviously not all at the same time—I became an expert on Thor's prostate. I felt bad for the down-stairs neighbors because Thor was really loud when he got going, when I pegged him just right to make him come apart for me.

And yeah, maybe I spoiled him outside the bedroom, too, cooking a world tour of his favorite foods and leaping to my feet any time he needed something that wasn't within arm's reach. He seemed to like that, crinkling his nose with a good-natured eye roll each time.

There were other lingering reminders that weren't going away any time soon. Coping with trauma, I learned, was not a linear process. I couldn't say I handled everything perfectly, but I did my best. There was one ugly incident where Thor woke up screaming, convinced someone was climbing in our bedroom window. He startled me from a dead sleep, and I flung myself out of bed, bellowing at a non-existent intruder, and smashed my toe so hard on the door jamb I saw stars. I swore loud enough to wake the dead. Two a.m. with a nearly broken toe, my heart about to explode out of my chest, I admittedly was not at my best. I'd turned around and snapped at Thor, who spent the next thirty-six hours as a hedgehog, sleeping in one of my shoes instead of in bed with me.

It took a lot of coaxing and scrambled eggs to get him to forgive me and transform back into a human.

But, for the most part, we did okay. I was over the moon that he had returned unharmed—physically at least. I never took for granted an opportunity to be close with him.

One point of contention between us involved Thor's family. I didn't like to push him where they were concerned, but I still thought he should tell them he'd come into his power, had a *fauna*. I hoped they'd be proud of him, but I was also livid they hadn't come by to check on him. Even *my* dad had been calling regularly to make sure we were both doing okay.

One morning, however, there was a knock on our apart-ment door. It was Sunday, and Thor was curled up on his chair catching up on some reading for class. I was in the kitchen, fixing some leftover fried chicken to make chicken and waffles. All of this comfort food meant a lot of extra time on the treadmill for me, but I didn't mind. Thor, of course, could stand to put on a few pounds.

Another lingering effect of his kidnapping was that Thor wore my clothes more often than he wore his own. They swam on him, making him look even skinnier, but I'd always liked him in my stuff and if it comforted him, even a little, it was fine by me. Thor uncurled his limbs to answer the door, and his sister Circe stood there in all her glory. She was wearing a crisp forest green pantsuit, looking starkly formal and put together, compared to Thor and myself, still in our pajamas.

"Circe?"

"Are you sick?" She asked immediately, taking in his baggy sweats and giant t-shirt.

I clenched my fists and chewed my tongue. If he was sick, it wasn't like any of them could be fucked to find out, or even check on him.

"No, just..." he cast around for a suitable excuse. "Lazy Sunday."

I fumed. Like he needed an excuse to be comfy in his own home on a weekend. Thor had been painstakingly putting himself back together over the last several weeks, and now of course his family was here to do their best to undo all of that.

Circe shook herself, looking embarrassed, almost like she hadn't meant to ask that. "Sorry," she said. "I didn't mean that —I just. Anyway."

Clearly Thor had learned his exquisite communication skills from his family. "You here for lunch, Circe?" I asked her from the kitchen.

"No, thank you, Cassian." She turned to her brother. "Thor, I have your invitation for the Nardini's party."

Thor mumbled something under his breath.

"What?"

He cleared his throat. "Nothing. I hadn't realized it was coming up. What's the theme this year?"

"Formal masquerade." Circe rolled her eyes. "It should be fun, though. And you have a plus-one this year."

Thor caught my eye and grimaced, but his sister saw it. She pinched his side. "Come on," she said, and her tone softened. "I miss you. And you should see the family. Plus—" she gave me a once over. "You've *got* to show off Cas."

"Sounds like fun to me," I offered, and Thor wrinkled his nose.

This was how I found myself standing in my own bedroom for a change, trying on a way-too-expensive suit that Thor insisted on buying for me. It was from the kind of shop where like, I didn't even see him pay for it, and the salespeople knew him when he walked in the door. It fit so well, not like the leftover funeral suit I borrowed from my dad to wear to my high school prom. I could tell it cost a fuck load because Thor hadn't even let me know the price. I tried to insist on paying, but he shot me a ball-shriveling look so I let the subject drop. Plus, I took it as a good sign that he was back to wanting to take care of me.

I was self-conscious, having never worn anything so fine, but looking in the mirror, I had to admit I looked good. The jacket, pants, and vest were black, crisp, and tailored perfectly. Thor had picked me out a mask, a simple one like the ones superheroes wore, plain black. The only spot of color in my outfit was on my tie, which was patterned with ornate scarlet skulls.

"You ready?" Thor called from the living room.

I could tell from his voice he was nervous, so I quit primping and left my room. Thor stood in the living room and I almost had a fucking stroke. He looked *incredible*. He hadn't let me see the suit he'd picked out for himself, and if he was going for the biggest possible impact, he was sure as fuck successful.

It had been a while since I'd seen Thor in anything other

than pajamas (or naked), and even before, I'd never seen him dressed this formal. He cleaned up good. Real good. The suit was navy blue, with a black brocade pattern, tight and tailored, and it fit his slim body like a dream. It highlighted the angles of him, the buttoned-down strength and confidence, that had drawn me to him. Instead of a traditional masquerade mask, Thor had pinned a sheer strip of silk chiffon from ear to ear, navy blue and dark, covering the bottom half of his face like a veil. It fluttered when he breathed, and there were delicate silver chains draped across the surface.

Thor shifted from foot to foot as I stared at him before wrinkling his nose and turning away. "It's too much, isn't it? I look ridiculous...I—"

I seized his hand, spun him back to face me. "You look," I said, leaning in to kiss his temple. "So beautiful."

"You don't think I should change?"

"Unless you're changing into nothing so I can fuck you this instant, don't you dare change."

I could tell by the crinkles around his eyes that he was smiling behind the fabric. "The car will be here any second, so I don't think we have time for that."

I grumbled a bit, but allowed him to take my hand. "Where are your glasses?"

He pulled a face. "I went with contacts. Is it weird?"

I shook my head. In all honesty, I was struck dumb. Thor's doe eyes blinked at me from above the mysterious curtain of fabric, lashes fluttering as he waited for me to respond. "Not weird," I said. "You know I love your glasses. But this whole...I mean, the look..." I licked my lips. "It works."

With a sly smile, he said. "Good."

We waited for the car sent by Thor's family, hand in hand on the sidewalk. One of the side effects, or knowing Thor, the intent, of the veil was that I found myself staring, hypnotized, because it was *almost* sheer enough for me to see his lips. And I wanted to see them. Fuck. How on earth was I going to make it through this party?

The car arrived, not a limo, but a town car with a privacy screen. So, honestly, part of me was tempted to see if Thor wanted to fool around, but I could tell he was way too nervous. We popped a bottle of champagne, like in the movies, and were a bit giggly by the time we arrived. I kept laughing because Thor had to move his veil every time he wanted to take a sip.

I suppose I worried, too. I didn't know how to behave. Like, was Thor having to pretend we were just bros? Or was the shifter community really fine and dandy with the gay thing? But, when the car pulled up, Thor got out, took my hand and escorted me up the front walk. He rested his head on my shoulder, linking our arms and pulling me along. It was clearly a romantic gesture, and I would have dipped him and kissed him hot and sloppy like that famous photo from V-J Day, but he was wearing the damn veil and I didn't want to slobber all over it.

Except, I did.

I did want to slobber all over it. I wanted Thor, wearing nothing but the veil, splayed out naked on our bed. I took a deep breath, trying to will my body to calm down, and for my brain to stop coming up with all those unhelpful images.

We ascended the front stairs into the huge foyer, all eyes upon us. Rather, all eyes were on Thor. That's how it felt, but maybe it was just me. I almost tripped over the last step because I couldn't look away. I had to say something, something logical and small talk-y. "So, what is this, like a hotel?"

Thor groaned. "No," he said. "It's the Nardinis' house."

"No shit?"

He giggled. It was a nervous one, but it was a laugh that was honest, and caught off guard. When we first met, even when I thought we might be just friends, just roommates, I had loved that startled little laugh. I hadn't heard it in some time. The unguarded giggle made me feel a prickle of hope that while Thor might be changed, perhaps things between us didn't always have to be shadowed by what had happened to him.

I squeezed his hip.

That fucking suit was going to be the death of me.

Hell. I had a brief moment of short-circuiting, trying to decide if Thor was prettiest in the suit, in my huge clothes, or entirely bare. Then I was back to thinking about Thor entirely bare and I needed to get a grip before I made a scene.

Just inside the door, where there was an honest-to-goodness coat check girl, we found Thor's dad. Despite his elaborate mask, there was no mistaking him, an absolute giant among the other partygoers. Thor, who had seemed so stunning and confident mere seconds ago, wilted as Lysander descended upon him.

"Thor!" he said in his booming voice. "There you are. While you're here I wanted you to keep an eye out for Dr. Kendrick—he should be around somewhere. It's a perfect chance to do some networking."

Unbelievable. Thor was still recovering from his ordeal, and not only had his dad not bothered to check on him at all, but he wanted Thor to use the party as a work function, instead of what he sorely needed it to be—a chance to cut loose.

"Fantastic," said Thor heavily. "Cas, drink?"

But he was gone, lost in the crowd before I could even reply. Lysander wasn't quite done with me yet, and pointed out some other notable guests, offering to hook me up with his business associates for internships, and any other kind of connections I might need. "You're part of the pack now, Cas!" he said, despite having derided my "humble" breeding not too long ago. This whole party was the crème de la crème of shifter society, a yearly shindig where they could all schmooze and preen and brag and marry off their children.

To be honest, the whole thing gave me the heebie-jeebies, like I was some kind of mob wife now that I was mated to Thor.

"You certainly clean up well, Cassian."

I turned to find two staggeringly beautiful masked women arm in arm standing behind me.

"Leda!" Thor's dad swooped in, kissing her on both cheeks. She wore a knee-length vintage looking black dress, black pumps, and a mask that looked like Phantom of the Opera, but black and sparkly.

"Hey, man," said Lucy, from behind an intricate white lace mask. She had on a white jumpsuit with a plunging neckline that highlighted her sculpted arms and shoulders, her hair side swept into an elegant low knot at the base of her neck.

It hadn't even occurred to me that the girls would be here; I'd been so distracted by Thor in his suit. "This is Thor's father, Lysander Ambrose," said Leda as he shook Lucy's hand.

Lysander soon moved away to greet some other new arrivals, and Lucy said, "That's his dad? Oh man, poor Thor."

"I know, I know." Speaking of, where had he gotten to? "I'll catch you guys later," I said.

I wound my way through the crowd, and found Thor at the bar. I hurried over and placed my hand on the small of his back. "Hey," I whispered.

He turned, a martini in one hand. His other hand fell to my waist, and the heat of his palm seemed to sear my skin through the layers of my suit. "What's up?" He asked.

"Leda and Lucy are here," I said.

"Huh," said Thor, tugging his veil aside to sip from his drink. "I knew Leda was coming, but she must be pretty serious about Lucy if she brought her."

I mulled over that for a minute, but became distracted by the rigidity of Thor's stance and the tension in his brows. "Are you alright?"

He shrugged. "I don't know," he said. "I always feel like an outsider at these things. And now, technically, I fit in—I have a *fauna*, I have you, but I still feel like the kid with his nose pressed against the glass."

I cupped his face in my palm, my thumb sliding over the soft, dark fabric of his veil, and then up to brush his cheek, peeking out over the top. "We can just leave," I told him. If the party wasn't fun for him, I had no qualms bailing.

Thor mock gasped. "And waste these amazing outfits?"

I leaned in. "I have absolutely no intention of wasting them," I said in his ear, my voice husky.

Thor took a shaky half step back, looking flustered. "Tempting," he said. "But no. Dad wants us to go back to the house after this, and we're having a family brunch in the morning." A defiant gleam sparked to life in his eye. "I'm going to tell them."

"Oh yeah?"

He nodded, his eyes sweeping over the party, where everyone danced, talked, drank, and relaxed, mingling without a care in the world. Thor stood beside me, his shoulders moving up toward his ears. Fuck this.

I snaked an arm around his waist. "Let's dance."

---

THOR

The pressure of Cas's hand on the small of my back steered me toward the dance floor before I could really protest. The lights were low, and everyone around us sparkled. I supposed, though, that could have been from the champagne and the martini I'd guzzled.

Cas took my hand and pulled me close so we could sway together.

"You have any idea how to do this?" Cas asked me.

"Nope. But I like our way."

Cas squeezed my hand, and I glanced around at the big ballroom. These were, for the most part, people I'd known in one capacity or another since I was born, but with them I never felt at ease. Having Cas here helped, but I still felt like I couldn't relax. Something had the hairs sticking up on the back of my neck. Twisting my head each way, I kept expecting to find someone staring at me.

"Hey." Cas's voice was soft, just for me.

"Yeah?"

"How can I help you relax?"

I pondered for a minute, and Cas rested his cheek on the top of my head. "Tell me something."

"Like what?"

"Anything."

We danced in silence for a while, honestly barely moving, while Cas thought. "Well," he said. "I love you. Very much."

"I knew that."

Cas gave my side a little pinch. "You said it could be anything."

"I lied," I said, grinning now. I peered up at him, so striking in the plain black mask. "Tell me a *new* thing."

"Okay," said Cas, and he spun me a little faster so I stumbled into his chest, laughing. "Well, how about this: did you know how much I missed you?"

"I did."

He leaned in close, his lips almost touching the shell of my ear. "Did you know how much I'm missing your cock?"

I froze and almost fell over. "Wh-what?"

Cas nudged me to get us moving again. We danced in silence together for a minute, and I kept tripping over my feet, wondering if I'd misheard him. After a moment, he gave my ear a sharp nip. "You look so gorgeous tonight," he told me, letting his lips touch my skin this time. "Did you know that?

I flushed with pleasure. "I didn't," I lied; of course Cas had told me already.

"I've been remiss, then."

"Clearly."

"I can't decide if I want to take you home and peel that fucking suit off you, or get on my knees for you right here."

"Jesus, Cas," I said, turning my face to hide against his chest. I heard the quickening of his pulse, and my body went tingly all over. I couldn't look at him. I *couldn't*.

"It's true," he said.

"Oh." Chancing a quick glance up at him, I saw he was smiling down at me, eyes dark and sparkling behind his mask.

"I love when you're flustered," he said. "It's usually me who's all tied in knots."

"You're just teasing me."

"Well, not *just*." Cas slid his hands down to grab my butt and press me close. I gasped; he was hard as hell in his tight slacks. "There someplace we can sneak off to?"

We absolutely should not even be entertaining this idea, but the thought of hiding somewhere in this awful pretentious house full of shifter aristocracy and fucking my mate sent a thrill up my spine. With a start, I realized I'd seen it as a foregone conclusion that I was ready to take Cas again, ready to be touched that way again. The notion sent a fission of lust coursing through me. "Let's go."

We skirted through the crowd on the dance floor, slipped to the edge of the room and dipped out through the rear door. I didn't think anyone saw us go, and Cas tugged on my hand, giving it a squeeze. "Where?"

I had to pause to remember. It had been years since I'd seen any other room in this place, but I knew the library was on the second floor. Sure enough, the first set of double doors I tried lead us into Rafe's father's private library. It was dark, the only light coming from the lights on the lawn outside. I shivered, nervous and jumpy. Were we really about to do this?

Cas strolled through the stacks, and I could tell he was giving me some space to decide. He passed one shelf of books. "You have a preference?" He asked, trailing his hand down the spines of some of books.

"Huh?" I asked, loosening my tie.

Cas pulled a book out, pretending to leaf through the pages. "Is there any part of the Dewey Decimal System that gets you hot?"

I laughed, and it echoed weirdly in the empty silence of the library. To one side of the room, a wooden desk stood before a wide array of floor-to-ceiling windows. They looked out over the grounds, with its fountain surrounded by statues and topiaries. It was beautiful, in a stiff uptight way. I could see the moon, shining down over the water in the fountain like beaten silver.

Leaning back on the desk, I turned back to Cas. "Here."

"Yeah?"

"Yeah," I said. "Right here. I like this desk."

Cas laughed and closed the distance between the two of us, bracketing my waist with his arms to brace his hands on the desk. He pushed his forehead against mine, and I could feel the heat of his breath through the fabric of the veil.

I moved my hands to peel it from my face but Cas grabbed my wrist. "Leave it on," he said, nosing up against my jaw. "It's so hot."

I was already in danger of bursting the zipper of my slacks.

Cas kissed down my neck, working fast to further loosen my tie and unbutton my shirt and vest. His palms on my waist were hot and firm as he held me against the edge of the desk. The sharp wood dug into my tailbone. Cas finally undid my last button and pulled open my shirt before getting to his knees. I wanted to bust at the sight of him, sandy hair mussed, devilish eyes glinting behind his mask, lips plump and pink. I reached down to take his chin in my hand, dragging my thumb over his bottom lip.

From his position on his knees, Cas blinked up at me. "Hey," he said softly. "If you're not ready for this, we don't have to do anything. I got a bit carried away."

I raised my eyebrows, unable to hold back a laugh. "Oh, did you?"

"Fair," he said "At first I was just trying to distract you from all the stress of the party. I didn't think you'd take me up on it."

"Kind of late to backpedal now, Cas," I said, gesturing at my state of rumpled, partial undress.

"So," said Cas, "You're sure you want this?"

"Cassian," I said, seizing his hand and pressing it to my crotch, wanting him to feel how I strained against the zipper. "I'm sick of letting what happened keep me from having you exactly how I want you."

"Yeah?"

"*Yes.*"

"Okay," he said, "Thank God." And grabbed the waistband of my slacks and yanked.

When Cas pulled down my boxer briefs and bared my junk to the draft of the library I gasped, and when he took the head of my dick between his lips, I moaned. Cas must have been serious when he said he'd missed my cock, because he sucked me like he was a starving man and this was the first meal he'd had in days. First, he hollowed his cheeks and took me deep enough to make himself gag, and then backed off to tease with his tongue, using his hand to pump my shaft and running the tip of his tongue under my foreskin. The fear of discovery heightened every sensation; never mind the fact that I hadn't had Cas's mouth on my dick in weeks.

Cas looked up at me, lips stretched around my shaft, wearing his mask, and it was by far the hottest thing I'd ever seen. Feeling filthy, I traced my finger along Cas's cheek, feeling myself in his mouth and I nearly lost it.

Cas pulled back, tonguing the slit at the head of my dick before saying, "That all you got?"

With a low rumble in my chest, I tangled my fingers in Cas's hair, holding his head while I fucked his mouth, snapping my hips and letting my balls slap his chin. His mouth was perfect and wet and slick, so hungry as he remained pliant on his knees, open and willing and all mine. Something in my chest constricted, something primal and possessive that had been hibernating for a while. I pushed Cas's forehead until he released my cock with a wet plop. He panted, looking up at me, a thin string of spit connecting his lips to my dick. Good *gods.* "Up," I said.

Cas rocked onto his heels, wiping the back of his hand over his mouth, and stood. I moved aside, and with a firm hand between his shoulder blades I guided him to bend forward over the desk. He went willingly, and I briefly knelt to reach around him and undo his belt. "Pocket," grunted Cas, and before I pulled down his pants, I felt in his pocket at found a small packet of lube. I grinned, and gave his ass cheek a little bite. "You were very confident in your ability to get lucky," I said.

Cas peeked over his shoulder, giving a coy shrug. "Hey, a man can dream."

"You dream about my dick?"

"Every day," said Cas, without missing a beat. I grinned, rolling my eyes, but the beast waking inside me preened.

I stood, my dick still wet with Cas's slobber, and I pressed it against his bare ass and nosed the back of his neck.

"Oh, baby," said Cas, pushing eagerly against me. "I've been missing this."

"Yeah?" I said, moving my hand to Cas's face, stroking his cheek before shoving two fingers into his mouth. "Suck," I commanded, and he did. My knees buckled as Cas worked his tongue over my fingers. He was hungry and needy and driving me wild.

I slid one spit-slick finger into Cas, and then the other, fingering him roughly, making sure to tease his gland and get him moaning for cock. When I pulled away, he whined, and I watched in satisfaction as he reached down to take himself in hand. With no idea what possessed me, I drew back and gave Cas an open palm smack on one perfect ass cheek. He yelped, turning back to look at me once more. "Fuck, Thor," he choked out.

I balked. "Too much?"

Cas bucked back against me, so hard I almost toppled over, balance impaired with my pants down around my ankles. "Not enough," he gasped.

So, I palmed his cheeks, rough, and spread him wide. I released them, bracing one hand on his tailbone as I slicked up my dick with Cas's lube. "Ready?"

"Yes," he said, "God yes."

I lined up, took a deep breath, and pushed inside. Cas groaned, and I couldn't tell if it was pleasure or pain. It had been quite a while since I'd had him like this. "You alright?" I asked.

"Yes, just. *Fuck*. It's been a minute."

I faltered, turning unsure again in the span of one shaky breath. "I'm sorry."

Cas shot his hand back, stretching his arm at a strange angle to grab my thigh. "Don't you dare be sorry," he said, breathless. "Fuck me. Hard. I need you."

And of course, I could not deny him. His breathy plea fired through me like I could hear it in my blood cells. I drew back, watching Cas's rim cling to me as I dragged out, leaving just the tip inside, before slamming back in.

"Fuck!" Cas yelped. We were lucky the band in the ballroom was loud, because that shout had been enough to wake the dead.

I opened my mouth to stammer another apology, but Cas didn't need it, apparently—he braced his hands on the desk and rammed himself backward, impaling himself on my dick. Well, fine. So, I gritted my teeth, gripped Cas by his hips, and rawed him. Sweat broke on my forehead as we moved together. I hadn't realized how much I'd been aching for this, how much I needed it, needed Cas. From the sound of it, he'd needed it too. He clenched around me, the velvet heat of his channel stroking my dick like it had been made with me in mind. We fit together like puzzle pieces—feral, rabid, horny puzzle pieces.

I hammered into Cas, pressing our sweaty thighs together, breathing so hard I was afraid of inhaling my mask and choking on it. Cas said something, his voice muffled with his cheek against the surface of the desk. "What?" I gritted out.

"Gotta come," Cas said, panting. "Please, please baby."

"No," I growled, startling myself. "Not yet." With a hand between Cas's shoulders, I slowed my stuttering hips, reaching my free hand up to yank the mask from my face so I could breathe. So I could kiss Cas.

So I could bite him.

From the corner of my eye, I saw Cas's hand creeping over the edge of the desk. Plainly, he was too desperate to come to be trusted with use of his hands. "*No,*" I said again, and the quiet thunder of my Alpha voice sent a fissure through the body pressed below me, punctuated by a delicious squeeze around my cock. I grabbed his wrists, stretching him out before me over the rich wooden surface. Cas gripped the opposite edge obediently, white-knuckled, pinned in place by my command, my hands, my cock shoved deep inside him. I stilled entirely and Cas squirmed, trying desperately to get some friction so he could get off, and I didn't have it in me to torture either of us much longer.

We had been too many weeks without this.

I released one of his wrists in favor of fisting my fingers in his hair, tugging his head to the side to expose the scar I'd left when I'd marked him as mine. Frantic to claim Cas again, I lowered my lips to his neck, kissing the mark before sinking my teeth into the spot. Cas came with a yell, spurting all over the front of the mahogany desk, and I fucked him through it, my forehead pressed against the nape of his neck until I erupted, painting Cas's insides, emptying myself into him until we slowed, still joined, and rocked slowly together against the desk. It seemed we couldn't stop the motions of our bodies, gentle swaying like we stood on the deck of a ship, tossed by rolling waves.

I clung to Cas, lingering far longer than was wise. We'd been lucky no one had intruded on our moment, another amorous pair—or worse, my family—could have easily wandered in. But I needed a bit more. I was sure Cas was not comfortable, bent in half and squashed against the unforgiving wood of the desk's edge, my dick still in him, but I couldn't let him go yet.

When we'd cleaned up and dressed, grinning slyly as we stuffed our dicks away, and adjusted our suits best we could, Cas pulled me in for a tight hug. When he drew away, his eyes glistened behind his mask. Before I could comment, he cradled my face with one warm palm, kissed me soft and sweet, and drew away so he could pin my veil back in place. "I missed you so much, Pin Cushion."

"I missed you, too."

# 24

CAS

Looking at Thor, how flush his face was, coupled with the scent of sex clinging to us both, I thought perhaps we could do with some fresh air. While I was getting absolutely skewered just moments ago, I couldn't help but notice how pretty the grounds were.

"Wanna take a walk?" I asked him. "Cool off a bit?"

"Yeah," he said. "That'd be nice."

I held out my hand for him to take, and when he grabbed it, I smiled. His hand was small and warm. I had no idea how this beguiling, demure man could transform into such an aggressive sex demon. Truly, it felt as though that side of Thor belonged only to me.

"What?" he said, uncertain.

"What, what?"

"You're staring."

I flushed. "It's nothing."

He gave me a suspicious little squint, but otherwise let it go. At the door of the library, I pulled him back toward me so

I could whisper in his ear. "Also," I said. "When you slapped my ass? So hot."

Thor's cheeks pinked above his veil, eyes going wide. "Oh, gosh. I can't believe I did that. I didn't hurt you, did I?"

I laughed. "With your cute little spank? No. Your dick on the other hand..."

Thor squawked and shushed me, flapping his hands as we sidled back into the corridor.

I seized his fingers, bringing them up to my lips for a kiss. "I love you."

"I love you, too. Now, let's get outside before everyone in this party gets a good look at us. Or worse, a good hard sniff."

*Oh, shit.* I hadn't even thought of that.

The cool night air hit my face and I sighed. It was shaping up to be a really good night. I still had a bit of a champagne buzz, the stars were out, Thor held my hand, and there was a nice little walking path around the expansive grounds that surrounded this monstrosity of a house. Dotting the landscape were stone benches, little alcoves between sculpted hedges that had me thinking Thor and I could spend the rest of the night out here, maybe fooling around again in one of these little hidey holes. Then I stepped down a little too hard on the path, sending a jolt that went straight up to my sore ass. I winced. Maybe not.

Our sex in the library had been filthy and urgent, and so, so fucking good. Alpha Thor was hot as hell, but it was way more than that. We'd been messing around and having sex regularly since he'd worked through most of what had happened to him, but it wasn't like that. I loved anything we did, but when Thor accessed that part of himself, it let me find a different side of me, too. When he took me like that, I was full—in more ways than one. I was complete. The span of heartbeats when his pleasure peaked and we were as close as two people could possibly ever be, I think that's when I most understood the whole 'mate' thing.

I brushed his knuckles with my thumb as we walked. The fresh air cooled our faces, and I hoped, dispersed the scent of sweat and sex that floated around us both like a cloud of perfume. We amused ourselves by making up stupid stories about the statues, making our way slowly from the back acreage to the side yard, following the brick pathway.

As we stopped to admire a particularly lewd statue, someone bumped into me. "Woah," I said, staggering.

The guy waved a distracted hand at me. "Ah, sorry—no, not you. Just bumped into someone..." I realized he was talking into a cellphone as he walked. He passed by Thor and me, gesticulating with his free hand as he carried on his conversation.

It took me a second to realize Thor had released my hand and stopped moving. His entire body was rigid, trembling, his eyes wide and terrified over the top of his veil.

"Thor?"

He didn't answer, his eyes getting a glazed sort of look.

I frowned and stepped closer to him. "You okay, Pin Cushion?"

When he still didn't react, I placed a gentle palm under his elbow, and he swayed on his feet, his entire body going from stiff to limp as he staggered and almost fell against me. He grabbed for the lapels on my jacket, fingers clutching tight and feverish. "*It's him.*"

"Him who?"

Thor moved his hand to my upper arm, gripping hard enough to bruise. I could feel him shaking as he pressed closed to my side.

"Oh," I said stupidly, as realization dawned. Instinctively, I flung out an arm in front of Thor, stepping forward to place my body in front of his as we stared at the guy's retreating back. I hadn't gotten a good look at him. "Do you know him?"

Thor nodded. In the dim light of the courtyard, I squinted into his face. At first, I thought his pupils had blown wide in fear, but now his entire eyeballs seemed black.

"Holy—what's happening to your face?" Before my eyes, the pale skin of his face erupted with a covering of soft pinkish hair, a small patch darkening over the bridge of his nose.

"I don't know," said Thor, panic in his voice. He raised his free hand to touch his own cheek. "What the f—*ow!*"

He hunched over, and through the beautiful brocade fabric of his suit, the points of innumerable quills had begun to protrude. "Are you shifting?" I asked him, looking around frantically, making sure we were alone.

"I was trying not to," Thor said, his voice hysterical. "I was panicking and I felt it started but I didn't—not here—"

I tore off my mask and his before grabbing his face in my hands. "Hey, stop," I said, keeping my voice level and calm. "You're okay. It's just you and me here. You're okay."

He held my gaze, and after several labored breaths, his eyes returned to normal, and the fur and spines shrank back into his skin.

"There," I said gently. "Now, tell me—who was that?"

"Dr. Kendrick," he said. "Leda's boss."

"Hold on—Professor Kendrick? From school?"

"Yeah, I—wait, how do you know him?"

"That's the teacher's office I..." all of a sudden, my conversation with Benson outside the library came screaming back to me. I had forgotten all about it in the wake of Thor's disappearance. "Benson."

"Pardon?"

"Benson told me someone was blackmailing him when he drugged you—that he had footage of us trashing the office, that it hadn't been just me. It must have been him!"

Thor staggered over to a bench and collapsed onto it, covering his face with his hands. "This doesn't make any sense," he said.

"Why not?"

"Dr. Kendrick isn't human."

"Huh?"

"The man who..." he trailed away, but I knew what he meant. "He was human."

I frowned, thinking hard. "Is there any way for someone to...sort of, pass? As a shifter? Like technically before you had a *fauna,* you were still a shifter."

Something clicked into place at my words, because Thor shot straight up from his seat. "We have to go. Now. Right now."

He took off across the lawn and I hurried to catch up with him. "What is it?"

"My father said—he told me Kendrick was working on a gene therapy for shifters. Something that could give a person a *fauna* who was born without one. Like me—or, like I thought I was. I didn't think that much of it because I thought Dr. Kendrick was already a shifter."

"So, you think he's been trying to give himself a *fauna*? But why?"

"I have no idea—but we need to—"

We rounded the corner of the building in time to see Kendrick helping someone into his car. It was Leda, and Thor's parents were getting into the back seat. "What the hell is Leda doing with him?"

"She has to know," said Thor. "That's why she didn't tell him about our findings—he already knew! They were his aborted primitives. That's why she didn't want us to tell Detective Davis what we knew." The betrayal on his face was like a knife to my throat. He shoved his hand in his pocket and grabbed his phone. He tried dialing his parents, and Leda herself, but went straight to voicemail. He drew back his fist like he was about to throw his phone across the lawn but I seized his wrist. "Fuck," he swore. "We have to follow them."

"How?" I said. "They're already pulling away."

We watched as the car pulled out from the Nardini's driveway and disappeared into the darkness.

"Okay," I said. "We have to go find Lucy, and tell her what's going on. Maybe she knows something without realizing it."

Thor nodded absently, still squinting into the night, like he could discern the car's destination by watching its taillights. I led Thor back inside, and almost immediately ran into Lucy. "Hey guys," she said casually. "Have either of you seen Leda?"

We exchanged a look, and I filled Lucy in. She peeled the mask off her face, leaving it on the bar, expression dire. She shook her head. "She wouldn't do that."

"Luce, we just *saw* her."

"There has to be some other kind of explanation!"

"Well, we're not likely to find out if we can't go after them—"

"What's going on?"

A tall guy in an iridescent green suit and a lacquer mask covered in leaves appeared beside us. It was Rafe. "We figured out who's behind all this shit," I said. "Do you have an address for Dr. Kendrick somewhere?"

Rafe paled behind his mask. "His home, yeah, he RSVP'd to the party."

"He wouldn't have brought them to his house," said Thor, annoyed. "He has to have a lab facility somewhere."

A buzzing sound cut the air between us. Thor pulled his phone from his pocket. "It's a text from Leda," he said. His brow furrowed. "It just says Castor, in all caps."

"What the fuck does that mean?"

"Castor...he was Leda's son in ancient Greek mythology..."

"Her computer!" Said Lucy.

We looked at her.

"It's a custom rig. She calls it her baby. It's in her bag in her car."

Down in the garage below the Nardini estate, we found Leda's car, but of course it was locked. "What do we do?" Thor asked.

I shucked out of my jacket and tossed it to Thor, before picking up a heavy wrench from a tool chest by the wall. "Sorry, Leda," I muttered, and swung the wrench with all my strength to smash the passenger window. Lucy swore, Thor jumped a mile, and Rafe brought his arms up to shield his face. The alarm blared, but I ignored it, searching until I found Leda's computer bag.

"Security's going to come down any minute," said Rafe. "We can find an address on the way. I'll drive."

"No, it's too dangerous," said Thor.

Rafe crossed his arms over his chest. "None of you can drive."

"Why not?"

"Well, you've all been drinking—and none of you has a car here."

Shit. The guy had a point. "Fine, let's go."

We jogged across the garage where Rafe parked his Lexus and piled in. I rode shotgun, Thor and Lucy got in the back, opening Leda's computer and trying to get into it.

"It's asking for a password—try Castor."

"It worked!"

As Rafe drove aimlessly, waiting for Lucy and Thor to give him a destination, I pulled up Detective Davis's contact information in my phone, my thumb poised over the call button.

"Got it!"

I pressed down. "Detective Dav—"

"I got an address."

"Mr. Rhodes?"

"I have a name and I have an address. You ready?"

I heard some scuffling in the background and Davis said, "Go."

I relayed the information. "We saw him get in his car with Thor's parents and his assistant, Leda Templeton."

"Alright. I'll get some backup and check it out. Do you think this guy is armed?"

"Yes," I said, though I had no idea. "Definitely dangerous. He's kidnapped at least four people."

"Okay," said Davis, sounding out of breath. "I'm heading to the precinct as we speak. Go home, wait by the phone. I'll call you."

Yeah, right. "Of course."

"Cassian," said Davis, like he didn't believe me. "You can't go in there. The police will handle it. Wait at home."

"Yes," I said blandly, already hanging up. Wait at home my butt cheek. I typed the address into Rafe's navigation system. "Let's go."

———

## THOR

In the back seat of Rafe's SUV, I pored over Leda's computer. According to the GPS, we were about an hour from Kendrick's lab.

"She's got a lot of stuff in here," I said. "A lot she never shared with me—enough to put Kendrick away."

"I told you," said Lucy. "She wouldn't hurt you, dude. Not on purpose. He must have something on her."

Given Kendrick's approach with Benson, it would not surprise me.

The air in the car was tense, and as he drove, we gave Rafe and Lucy all the details they were missing.

"I don't get why he wants a *fauna* so badly," said Cas. "Clearly he's been fooling all of you guys well enough without it."

"That's another thing I don't understand," said Rafe. "There's a scent difference between humans and shifters. How has he gotten along all this time without anyone finding out?"

"Synthetic pheromones," I said. I had just pulled up the document on Leda's computer. She had apparently run tests on the primitives' skin, finding foreign traces of something synthetic. When she identified it as a synthetic pheromone, she'd surreptitiously tested Kendrick's clothing. "Our families were too enamored by Kendrick and his research to investigate much further."

When we finally got close to Kendrick's lab, a small facility set deep in the woods, we pulled up Google maps to consider the best approach.

"It's the middle of the night—I can't imagine he has much staff here," I said.

"Still, who knows what kind of crazy mad scientist shit he has going on in there?"

Cas chewed his lip. "Should we wait for Davis?"

I shook my head. "No way. He definitely brought my parents here for some reason, and I can't imagine it's a good one."

Cas put a hand on my shoulder. "I know you're worried about your family and Leda. But it might not make the most sense to run in their half-cocked."

"We don't have time to waste. Who knows how long it'll take Davis to get here with backup?"

"Thor, it's not like your parents rushed off to rescue you when you were missing."

I felt like Cassian had slapped me. "Yes," I said coldly. "Thank you for reminding me."

The silence was thick and awkward.

"I'm not waiting," I said. "I have to go in—"

"Thor, you're going to get yourself killed!"

There it was. Cas was the only person I'd ever met who didn't think of me as helpless, as worthless. Or so I'd thought. He must have sensed he said something unforgivable, because he immediately tried to backtrack but I held up my hand. "Thank you, for your concern," I said in a flat, deadened voice. "But I'm going in. You're welcome to stay here and inform Davis where I've gone."

I took off through the woods on foot before he could stop me. I had Leda's map of the area, sent from her computer to my phone. I'd made it a few yards into the trees when I heard the sound of sticks snapping behind me.

"Don't you dare try to go in there without me," said Cas. He grabbed my hand. "I got your back, Pin Cushion. Always."

Choked up a bit, I nodded. "Thank you."

We made our way through the trees, following the map. When the trees started to thin, my phone suddenly lost its signal. "Damn," I said. "I lost service."

"Doesn't matter," said Cas. He pointed. "We're here." Ahead of us, the trees gave way to green grass, and in the distance was a small, stark grey building, more closely resembling a bomb shelter than a scientific lab.

Looking at my phone, with the little x where the bars usually sat in the top right-hand corner of the screen, I said, "This isn't a coincidence."

Cas pulled out his phone, finding the same result. "I'm sure you're right. Doesn't change anything though."

"Nope, it does not."

"Do you have a plan?"

Kind of. There was a chance Kendrick still didn't know

about my *fauna*. My caution during my escape from his house, and the fact that Davis had not uncovered any traces of surveillance equipment when he searched the place, had me thinking that possibly I still had that ace up my sleeve. We had the element of surprise on our hands, because he also didn't know we had the location of his lab.

Unless this was a trap.

But then, like Cas said, it didn't change anything.

"I think I should shift. I can hide in your pocket, and we can sneak in. Then, if you get caught, I can make a break for it."

"Okay," said Cas, but he looked doubtful. "You're the best secret weapon we've got, so I say let's do it."

I stripped out of my suit, folding it neatly and tucking it in the hollow at the base of a tree. With no idea what sort of security Kendrick might have, I had to make sure we didn't leave many traces. I pulled out my contacts, and handed Cas my glasses, which had been in my jacket's interior pocket.

Cas looked at me appreciatively.

"Now is not the time," I said, bracing my hands on my hips.

"Right, right," he said, flushing. "Okay, let's do this."

When I'd shifted and gotten my bearings, the darkness alive to my nocturnal vision, Cas scooped me up and tucked me in the interior pocket of his suit jacket. "I'm gonna leave your phone here," said Cas loudly, though he knew I couldn't answer him. "Kind of suspicious if I get searched and have two."

Good thinking. I rode in the warmth and comfort of Cas's pocket, trying my best not to prick him with my spines. From my spot, I couldn't see anything but the inside of the pocket. Cas described everything out loud in a low voice, but I hoped he would stop doing that once he got inside.

"There's a chain-link fence surrounding some kind of

grassy enclosure," he muttered. "I think we're at the rear of the facility."

"I'm going to have to climb the fence, but I don't want to squish you."

It was all very disorienting, and when Cas landed on the other side of the fence, I felt like I'd been thrown in a sack and tossed over a cliff.

"You okay, Pin—"

A blinding light shone even through the layers of fabric of Cas's jacket.

"Shit," said Cas. "Two security guards, I think they have—"

I heard the unmistakable sound of electricity zapping before Cas cried out in pain and went down. Luckily, when he fell, he didn't squash me like an insect. I remained still in his pocket, hoping that whoever tased Cas didn't search him before bringing him inside.

With my ears straining, I waited until motion stopped, and I heard a door click. I poked my nose out of the pocket, and wriggled until I could see where I'd been brought. It seemed as though they'd removed Cas's jacket and brought him somewhere else. I was in some kind of security office. I shifted as quickly as I could, grabbed my glasses from Cas's pocket, and checked the monitors. I saw two men hauling an unconscious body into a room with some kind of holding cell. The monitors were black and white, and I couldn't fully distinguish faces, but the unconscious body was obviously Cas, and there was one other person in the holding cell. Looking at the monitors, I saw innocuous lab space, clean and empty. Kendrick must have sent most of his staff home—but where was he? There had to be some rooms not covered by security footage.

The guards left Cas in the holding cell and left the room. I watched their progress on the monitors, assuming they'd be coming back here. I hid in a broom closet, and hoped to God the two weren't in the mood to do some late-night cleaning. I grabbed a bottle of some disinfectant spray, thinking I could spray at least one of them in the face if they opened the door.

The voices were muffled when they returned to the office and from what I could gather, they were the last two people onsite, besides Kendrick, and they were clocking out, per Kendrick's request. That told me they were paid well enough to look the other way regarding some things, but Kendrick didn't trust them as witnesses to whatever he was planning for tonight.

I wasn't sure whether that was encouraging or horrifying.

Waiting for them to gather their things and leave, I glanced around the closet, and found a pair of huge coveralls hanging on a peg. I pulled them on, cuffing the sleeves and legs, but there were no shoes to be had. Oh well. At least I wouldn't be attempting this rescue mission ass-naked. Once the door clicked again, I watched the security monitors to make sure the guards had left the building. Despite the fact that Kendrick's security personnel were hardly my allies, the fact that I was now totally alone in this building hit me and I froze. Cas was incapacitated, my parents were Lord knows where, and Kendrick had all the cards.

I took a deep breath, counting to ten and trying to calm myself down.

I pushed my way out of the security office, knowing when I left the monitors behind, I'd be flying blind, and Kendrick could find me at any second. The hallways were clearly marked, and I eventually found my way to the room called "Specimen Containment B," which was the room I'd seen with the holding cell.

I swiped a security key card, and used it to get into the room. Cas jumped up, looking a little worse for the wear. "There you are!"

"Hey," I said, approaching the holding cell. "Are you alright?"

"Yeah, I'm fine," he said, though he looked far from it. "Your mom was in here—she had some kind of implant in her neck. A computer chip or some shit I don't know. She said it kept her from shifting. Kendrick just came in. He doesn't know you're here."

"What about my dad and Leda?"

"I haven't seen them. He just took your mom, told her they had some 'catching up to do' and something he wanted to show her in the surgical theatre."

I wracked my brains, but I was certain none of the security monitors showed a surgical theatre. "Okay," I said. "I'll find them, and then come back and get you."

"Wait, what? No! You have to let me out so I can help you!"

I leaned in for a quick kiss through the chain link. "Sorry, Cas. It's way too dangerous."

"You have *got* to be kidding me."

"I'll come back once I've got the others," I promised. I felt guilty but I couldn't allow my mate into such a dangerous situation. There was no way to keep Cas from being by my side unless he was locked up, safe for now.

"Thor Ambrose I'm going to kick your—"

I closed the door before I could hear what else he had to say, and moved quietly down the hall toward the elevator. The sub-level basement required me to swipe the security card for access, and I hoped it wouldn't send any kind of alert to Kendrick, but unfortunately there wasn't much I could do about it if it did.

My stomach leapt up into my throat and it struck me how colossally stupid this was. Barefoot, unarmed, and ready to take on an unhinged scientist.

The elevator emptied into a poorly lit basement hallway,

and the hairs on the back of my neck stood up as I moved forward as silently as possible. Another supply closet stood to my left, and I ducked inside, hoping to find some kind of, anything, I could use as a weapon. No such luck, but I did see access to the vents.

Without any better options, and because my life had clearly devolved from any semblance of normalcy, I climbed up a shelving unit and got to work prying open the vent. It was a tight fit, and with my weight, the vent creaked ominously. I climbed back down, and stripped naked for the second time tonight. As an afterthought, I rummaged around the shelves for a few rubber bands and knotted them around my wrist.

*Gods help me, if someone catches me climbing bare-assed into a vent, let them kill me,* I thought. I took the rubber bands and looped them around the ends of my glasses, creating a sort of makeshift harness before shifting. I was able to slip the rubber band over my head and drag my glasses along beside me. It wasn't as silent as I'd have liked, but I imagined my human self crawling through the vents on my hands and knees would have made much more noise. At each intersection, it took me a few moments to orient myself, knowing the vents probably didn't run exactly parallel to the corridors.

Eventually, I heard the whirr and beep of surgical equipment, and I followed the noise to the entrance to the vent system, looking down on a *very* grizzly tableau.

Down below, what looked like a dentist chair and some sort of veterinary operating table had been positioned side-by-side in the sterile white space full of equipment. I could make out the one-way glass that must indicate the viewing chamber on the other side of the surgical area. If what Cas said was correct, my mother was on the other side of that glass.

A door directly below my vantage point opened. I couldn't see the door but I heard it creak. Someone in a lab coat wheeled in a gurney with a mass covered in a sheet. My heightened senses recognized the synthetic pheromone scent of Dr. Kendrick as I stared at the back of his head. He wheeled the gurney to the empty veterinary table and unveiled the thing upon it.

I recognized my father's *fauna* immediately. I was as familiar with it as I was with his human form. However, I'd never seen him so cowed. He wore a muzzle, and stirred feebly as if he had been sedated. Kendrick transferred him to the surgical table, and connected some straps around his paws and his middle, and one around his neck.

Kendrick beckoned to someone, and I watched Leda approach, scrubbed up like she was ready to perform a surgery. The information on her computer proved to me that she was here under duress, but I still couldn't ignore the bite of anger seeing her assist Kendrick.

I watched in confusion as the two of them began pulling a series of odd items from a chest—a strip of cloth, a candle, a piece of charcoal. A small brazier. The items looked especially strange around the high-tech surgical setup. Leda prepared the surgical instruments while Kendrick used the charcoal to draw a series of symbols on the floor. He then removed his lab coat, under which he was bare-chested, and he drew a matching sigil on the skin of his chest.

That's when I recognized it—the sigil had been depicted in the book I'd read, the one with a ritual for exorcising the demon from a shifter-born infant. It seemed that had been the piece of my research that Kendrick had really been after when he forced me to copy my notes over for him. Based on the setup, it seemed like he was trying to legitimately excise my father's *fauna* and use his own body as the sacred vessel to contain it.

My head spun, but I couldn't look away from the bizarre blend of science and occult taking place before me. I noticed

Kendrick's entire torso was littered with half-healed surgical scars—as if this was merely his latest in a series of attempts to give himself a *fauna*.

He fitted my father in his wolf form with an IV and a set of tubing that went from the inside of his paw, through some sort of device, and then back to a spot under his ribs where he'd inserted some kind of torquer.

When he flipped on the machine, I watched my father's blood flow from one end of the tubing, through the machine, and then back into his body. Another tube, originating from the machine, flowed up an IV stand, which Kendrick inserted into a vein in his own arm, like he was giving himself some sort of blood transfusion from my father's *fauna*. Beside the surgical table, sat another table with an array of trays on it, each filled with some sort of liquid. Kendrick then pulled out his scalpel and got to work.

My stomach turned as I watched him filet the skin from my father, who came to partway through and began to howl and snarl, horrible animal screams that I'd never heard him make. I wished to go deaf, wished to never hear my father make sounds like that again. I squeezed my eyes shut. *He's killing him,* I thought. *He's skinning my father alive right in front of me.* The howling stopped eventually, though the echoes of it vibrated through my skull, and I didn't think I'd forget them any time soon.

I opened my eyes in time to see Kendrick peeling several large sections of wolfskin from my father's body, laying them reverently on silver trays arrayed on the symbols drawn on the floor. Leaving my father to bleed, he made his way over and sat himself in the dentist chair.

Apparently, it was Leda's turn. I couldn't make out what he was saying, but he clearly was giving her some sort of instructions. She picked up a syringe, injecting him with something just above his nipple.

It must have been local anesthesia, because Leda next picked up a scalpel and started slicing the skin off his pec. I kept praying her hand would slip and she'd sever something essential, but her hand was as steady as I'd always seen it. Despite the numbing agent, Kendrick's muscled chest corded with exertion. He was clearly in a lot of pain.

Leda worked free a patch of skin above his heart roughly the size of a cocktail napkin, peeling it from Kendrick's body. She crouched beside a piece of wolfskin on the floor, swapping them. Then, as if this whole thing hadn't been horrifying enough, she sewed the furry patch of skin directly to Kendrick like some kind of taxidermy patchwork quilt.

The smell of burning sage filled the room, and Leda waved a smudge stick over Kendrick's body. She then repeated the process six more times, painstakingly replacing specific patches on Kendrick's body with pieces of my father, all while the machines pumped his blood into Kendrick's body. Finally, it appeared to be done—Leda covered Kendrick's body with a linen sheet, and then burnt the pieces of human skin over the brazier, chanting all the while. I caught snippets of Latin, Hebrew and Gaelic, but I couldn't understand the words.

Perhaps the ritual would kill him. Kendrick bled freely despite the stitches, and the chamber stank of blood. I truly hoped my mother wasn't watching this. I didn't know how either of them could survive this mutilation, and my father was losing a lot of blood that was being sent directly to Kendrick. This was fucking sick. He'd plainly lost his mind— there was no way this would work, would it?

Kendrick was hooked to a heart monitor, and the pattern of beeps was erratic at best—he was as weakened as he'd ever be. Now was my chance. I slid out of the rubber bands I'd been using to tow my glasses and shifted. Fumbling briefly in the dark, I found my glasses and jammed them on my face, but while I was trying to decide how best to get down there, the vent gave a creak, and then there was only the scream of straining metal before the bottom fell out of my world.

I fell naked to the floor, the wind shoved from my lungs as I landed hard on my back. Something definitely snapped in my left arm, and I couldn't even scream in pain. Which was probably a good thing, considering I'd done just about everything I could to blow the element of surprise.

Still wheezing, struggling to catch my breath, I rolled onto all fours, and looked up at Kendrick, who slumped unconscious in the chair. My father hadn't stirred either.

"Thor!" Leda said, running to my side to help me up. I grabbed Kendrick's discarded lab coat and pulled it on. That may not have been a strict priority, but being vulnerable and naked was very distracting, and I needed every ounce of focus I possessed. I held my injured arm close to my body, thankful it was my left one so I could still button the coat over myself.

"So you got my text," said Leda.

"Yeah—fat lot of good it did me. We're too late. Why did you help him?"

"He threatened my family," said Leda. "When he found out about my relationship with Lucy, he threatened her, too. We have to—"

But I ignored her. The stupid lab coat was huge on me, like an Ebenezer Scrooge nightshirt. I hobbled across the surgical theatre to the door beside the two-way mirror. It was locked on my side, and when I opened it, my mother came careening out. She hugged me, and all I could do was grunt in pain as my injured arm was squashed against my rib cage.

"Dad," I wheezed. "Get Dad."

She nodded tearfully and ran over to him, just as I heard the monitor connected to Kendrick flatline. *Oh, thank the gods.*

"Thor," said Leda, grabbing my shoulder. "This place is full of hostages—specimens."

"Can you find them?" I asked her. "Detective Davis is on the way with backup—if you can get them out of here before the police arrive—"

"I'm on it." She turned and strode from the lab.

"Cas is in Specimen Containment B," I hollered after her.

I could finally inhale a decent breath, so I followed after my mother, gritting my teeth at the pain in my arm. As Kendrick flatlined, Dad's body convulsed on the gurney, and he shifted back into his human form, bleeding, struggling, and screaming. The screams turned from feral howls to human shrieks about partway through, and as the last bit of grey fur retreated into his body, he passed out cold.

My mom and I worked together to undo the restraints around him, painfully tight now that he was in his much larger, human form. "He's alive," my mother said, tears falling freely down her face. "He's definitely alive." She had shaking fingers on his pulse point, but I was sure it was their mate bond that told her Dad still had life in him.

Behind me, a resounding bang shook the relative quiet of the room, and I spun to see what fresh hell had landed on us. A tall man in a rumpled black suit and a gas mask burst through the door, brandishing a long, sinister-looking blade.

"*Pin Cushion!*"

I had to blink about a million times to comprehend what I was seeing. No way Leda could have gotten to him that fast, so Cas must have found his own way out of holding. But where did he get the knife? And the gas mask? "Cas?"

He pulled the mask off, revealing the freckled face I loved, and I was so shocked and relieved that I missed the sound of the heart monitor beeping back to life behind me.

# 25



I'd found my way to Thor, but that's where the good news ended. Because surrounding him was a fucking horror movie.

The gas mask I had nabbed from a hook on the wall was a precaution—I'd seen enough movies to know that evil scientist lairs were usually not what they seemed.

The scene I took in hardly made sense to me, but I had time to register a huge, broad man lurch from a medical exam table and come behind Thor. Before I could cry out in warning, a massive forearm clamped under his chin, sprouting thick grey hair as Thor was hauled off his feet.

"*Ack*," he said, trying to claw the hand away, thrashing in the giant's grip.

I surged forward, brandishing my knife—that I'd found when I'd stumbled across the employee commissary—thinking it was as good a weapon as I was likely to find. Now though, the eight-inch blade seemed a piddly thing faced with the half-man, half-wolf, all monster thing doing its best to strangle the breath from Thor right before my very eyes.

The monster, now unrecognizable from the distinguished man we'd seen at the masquerade ball, could only be Dr. Kendrick. He'd been tall then, but now he towered, his face contorted and twisted, showing lupine features: fangs, and hair, lopsided on his face as the rest visibly struggled to retain its humanity. It was like he was trapped in a state of shifting between man and wolf, and the result was horrifying.

I suddenly had some doubts about the plan to charge in without waiting for Davis or any other police backup.

"Don't move," he said, raising one clawed hand to point at me, his voice growly and threatening. "Or I'll tear out his throat."

Thor locked eyes with me, still struggling for breath. Paralyzed, I didn't know what to do. I was strong, and fast, but the two-inch-long iron-grey spikes now protruding from the end of Kendrick's fingers gave me pause. There was no way I could reach them before he made good on his threat.

"It's not worth it," Kendrick told me. "He'll leave you."

This was about the last thing I'd expected him to say. "No, he won't."

"You think that little love bite will stop him? He'll fuck you, make you pretty promises, but the animal inside won't be satisfied with a human. Isn't that right, Freya?"

For the first time, I caught a glimpse of Thor's mother, crouched over another upturned medical exam table with the unconscious form of Thor's dad. She looked up at Kendrick, clearly lost. "What?"

"Can you feel him, from me now? It was never the man you loved. It was the beast."

"What the fuck are you talking about?" I asked, looking between Thor's mom and the crazy guy about half a second away from fileting my boyfriend's throat. "What is he talking about?"

I watched as recognition dawned on Freya Ambrose's face. "Ken?"

"I can't believe how long it took you to recognize me," he said, his attention now fixed on Thor's mother.

"You've...you've changed quite a bit since I knew you," she said carefully, standing. "What are you doing? What is all this?"

"Once your father introduced you to *him*, it was like you never saw me at all," said Kendrick. "You couldn't help it, though, could you, Freya? It was in your nature."

"No, Ken, I didn't—" Thor's mother's eyes flew to his father, still unconscious on the floor. I wasn't even certain if he still breathed.

"I have his beast, now," said Kendrick. "His *fauna.*"

"That doesn't change who she loves," I said, trying to get the guy's attention back on me.

"It was the only real difference between us," said Kendrick, like he was trying to make a logical case for love. "We worked together so closely at school, inseparable, and then when she met *him* it was like a switch flipped in her, and I didn't exist any longer."

"We were never together," said Thor's mother. "You were my closest friend, Ken. It broke my heart when you left school, I never knew—"

"Never knew I'd discovered your furry little secret? Well, I did. And I knew without one of my own, I'd never be what you needed. It was easier than you'd think, faking my way in with a shiny new identity. You're all the same. As long as I was rich and confident, none of you even suspected I didn't belong in your little club. And now, I do belong."

I watched this whole melodrama unfold, still worried

about Thor losing oxygen. Kendrick wasn't done with me yet, though.

"I can help you," Kendrick said to me. "I can give you a beast, too."

"No thanks," I said, holding up the knife defensively. "No offense man, but the budget Scooby-Doo wolfman look is *not* an improvement."

I caught Thor's eye again, and he shot me a meaningful look, his eyes darted to his mother. Either this mating bond was serious and I could read his thoughts—or I was about to do something spectacularly stupid. Honestly, maybe both. I lunged to the side and grabbed Thor's mom, hoping she'd understand I would never truly hurt her. I held my knife to her neck, looking quickly to find the chip Kendrick had implanted in her skin.

"You let him go," I said, "Or I'll take her out."

I caught Thor's minuscule nod, knowing then I'd understood his plan perfectly, and I watched as behind his glasses his pupils went wide and black, just like they had at the masked ball. Kendrick frowned—like he knew I wouldn't actually ever kill someone, but he hesitated, just for a second. It was enough. All at once, Thor rammed his head back with all his strength, and Kendrick let out a real, animal yowl of pain. Thor had partially shifted again, the quills on his back erupting as he forced them backward. I dug the point of my blade into Freya's skin below the chip, hoping I wasn't about to kill my boyfriend's mom, and yanked out. She let out a shriek, but I shoved her forward. "*Go!*" I said.

Freya lunged toward Kendrick, her satin evening gown shredding like tissue paper as she shifted. By the time she collided with Kendrick, her *fauna,* a huge fucking lioness, had emerged, and was clearly not happy with Kendrick's treatment of her mate, or her cub.

Kendrick dropped Thor, but several of his quills remained

stuck in Kendrick's face and chest, and Thor cried out in pain as they yanked out of his skin and he hit the ground. But he rolled to the side, and I flew at Kendrick, brandishing my chef's knife.

I dug the knife into the meat of his shoulder, and he yowled again, and I felt his claws rake my side, doing a pretty good job of shredding my suit and opening my chest up, and face to face I could see one of his mad eyes still had an extra-long hedgehog quill stuck in it, and a few others stuck in his face that fell around our feet like pine needles as we grappled for the knife. Freya raked her claws over Kendrick's back, and fastened her immense jaws around his neck. Before she could clamp down, Kendrick freed one hand and clawed at her face. Instinctually, she dropped back with a hiss to protect her eyes.

I went for the knife again but it was really fucking stuck in his shoulder, and since that was my only weapon, I didn't want to let go of it. However, Kendrick had ten really good weapons at the end of his fingers, and he buried them into the flesh below my rib cage, and I felt the warm gush of blood down my side. "*Cas!*" came a voice. "Let go!"

I obeyed Thor on instinct, hitting the ground like a bag of rocks, and I watched as Thor seized a now empty syringe from the surgical table, stab it viciously into Kendrick's neck, and hammer down the plunger with his thumb, sending however many CCs of air directly into his bloodstream. It didn't take long, his body still trying to decide if it was man or wolf, for the embolism to take hold. Kendrick gasped for breath, his eyes rolling, and he collapsed on the ground.

Looking around myself, I saw that I'd fallen in a large puddle of blood. "Huh," I said.

"Cas!"

That was a voice I liked, a lot. I stood to move toward it. Lightheaded, I tried to hang on to the knife, but I felt it slipping from my grasp, and I floated like a feather, until the floor hit me. "*Ow,*" I said stupidly. I tried to move, lying in a puddle of uncomfortable wet, but my limbs weren't listening.

A big weight fell on my legs, and I caught a glimpse of Kendrick's fucked up face, stuck full of holes from Thor's quills. A soft hand fluttered around my head like a moth.

"Cassian?"

I stared, fixated, as drops of blood oozed ruby-bright from all the holes in Kendrick's face. I finally worked the knife loose, the handle slick in my hand, maybe my blood, maybe his. Thor had kicked some serious ass, I thought dumbly, despite being totally unarmed. All he had was his cute little spines.

"Aha," I said, and my voice sounded far away—like I had headphones on but I was yelling. "The quill *is* mightier than the sword."

Thor's pretty face swam in front of me, my vision going a little misty. Then I heard the last words the love of my life would say to me before I passed out cold.

"You're an idiot."

———

THOR

They wouldn't let me ride in the ambulance with Cas, and I think I might have accidentally landed a hysterical punch to Detective Davis's jaw when they wheeled Cas out on the gurney, trying to take him away from me. He still gave me a ride to the hospital though.

My mother and father rode in another ambulance.

Getting to the hospital was a blur, but I should have known something was off when the police didn't take a statement from me. I was preoccupied, anyway. Cas had lost so much blood. I'd called his dad, who'd arrived a few hours after

I did, while Cas was in surgery, getting sewn up and pumped full of emergency transfusions.

I'd paid for a hotel room near the hospital for Cas's dad and all his siblings, who'd insisted on coming, but Cas was still in a coma when they went there for the night. I stayed at Cas's bedside, holding his hand, and trying not to register how pale his skin was. His pulse was so feeble I was afraid if I dozed off it would fade to nothing. The doctor said it wouldn't be problematic if Cas took a day or two to come out of his coma, but my heart was in my throat the entire time. The bond between us demanded I be there. I knew it was irrational, but I felt like I had to will his lungs to expand, and his heart to pump blood to replace the blood he'd lost. At some point, I realized a cast had appeared on my left wrist.

I must have drifted off at some point, leaning forward with my head rested on my folded arms, clutching one of Cas's hands.

"Thor?" A soft voice whispered in my ear and I startled awake.

"Huh? Who—Cas—?" I flailed, blinking in the overbright light. Cas was where he'd been for thirty hours, still asleep.

Behind me, his father, Adam, and brother Jesse had come in. I sprang up, ignoring the crick in my neck and the pinch in my lower back. "I'm sorry, I only dozed off for a second, have the doctors been in?"

"It's alright," said Adam, squeezing my shoulder. "I was trying to wake you so you could go home. We can sit with Cas."

Jesse stood beside him, the concerned expression on his face bringing his resemblance to both Cas and their father into sharp relief. He held two coffee cups in his hands and handed one to me.

Looking down at the cup, I was horrified to feel a lump

rising in my throat—quick and hard and painful, like an animal trying to claw its way out.

I burst into tears.

Adam Rhodes took the coffee from my hands in the nick of time, because I flung myself at Jesse, exploding all over the poor kid. He stood, rigid and understandably terrified as I unloaded unabashed sobs onto his shoulder.

"Uh," he said awkwardly, patting my back.

I drew back, gulping, making a damn spectacle of myself. "Oh my god," I said. "Oh shit. I'm so sorry—I just—"

But before I could finish Jesse pulled me back into another hug. It was definitely a sort of bro hug, but I could feel him struggling to keep his own composure as we clung to one another. It only made me cry harder, and I felt like a total idiot. Cas's father rubbed my back, making soothing sounds, and every attempt of theirs to calm me down only made me lose it even more.

In a moment where I gasped for breath, I heard something stir behind me.

"*Baby?*" I whipped around to see Cas blinking blearily at me. "What's wrong? Are you okay?"

"Hell," I said, hiccoughing and wiping my eyes. My glasses were all fogged up from the hug attack I had perpetrated on Jesse, and when I leaned over to Cas he raised his hands to take them off my face. As if he wasn't lying here after almost bleeding to death, Cas polished my glasses on the front of his hospital gown and put them back on my face.

"What is it, Pin Cushion? What's wrong?" He still seemed foggy, his words slurring together, but I was so glad he was awake.

I cupped his face. "Nothing, now."

He drifted off to sleep again shortly thereafter, leaving me with his family, feeling embarrassed as hell. "It's okay," said

Jesse. "I cried in the car on the way here, so I was all wrung out."

I laughed, shaky and overtired, staggering back to my chair next to Cas's bed. "Thor," said Adam gently. "Please, go home and get some rest."

His fatherly concern was about to overwhelm me all over again when someone cleared their throat. Detective Davis sidled into the room. "Excuse me," he said. "I'm so sorry for intruding. Do you think I could speak to Mr. Ambrose for a moment?"

"Of course," said Adam, ushering Jesse from the room. "We'll just be down the hall, Thor."

"Thank you," I told them earnestly. "Both of you."

When the door clicked softly behind them, I turned my attention to Davis. "May I sit?" he asked.

I nodded. My nerves were still shot, but my grip on Cassian's hand grounded me. Davis occupied the other empty visitor's chair, a manilla folder balanced on his thighs. He leaned forward, pulling the bedside table between us, and laid the folder on it. "What is this?" I asked him, a strange sort of dread coiling inside me.

"My case report." He slid the folder toward me. "It's the only copy."

I looked up at him, uncomprehending. "I'm sorry?"

"My commanding officer wants this whole business buried, quickly and quietly. Your family, Mr. Rhodes, and Ms. Templeton remain the only witnesses, and considering the original Jane and John Does were never human, Sergeant Stark insists Kendrick's crimes were victimless."

Fury must have crossed my face, because Davis laid a hand on the folder. I looked at Cas, lying in a hospital bed. *Victimless?* "Kendrick had staff," I said. "People who took his money and turned the other way while he carried out these horrors. Leda said there were more specimens at the—"

"Miss Templeton euthanized the remaining non-human test subjects and destroyed Kendrick's research. Officially, we have nothing."

"*What?*"

"Thor," he said, using my given name for the first time. "This is not where I stand on the issue. At all. I would pursue this case to its fullest extent, but I wanted to leave the choice to you."

I stared at Davis. "Why?"

"Because pursuing it could bring serious scrutiny down on your family and everyone you know." The implication in his words was delicate, but effective.

I toyed with the edge of the folder. "What does Stark plan on releasing about the case?"

"Just that Kendrick was a deranged man, a sex criminal who used access to medical supplies to aid in his crimes. He died at the scene, so he's not likely to mount an alternative explanation."

What Davis said was true enough, of course, but it didn't feel right, somehow. "Wouldn't there still be investigations into the kidnappings? The sex crimes?"

Davis placed his hand on my forearm and squeezed. "I have spoken to everyone else involved, and none of them wish to press charges."

The absolute *injustice* of this was likely to choke me where I sat. Cassian must have sensed my distress, because he stirred, his eyes fluttering in sleep. I gripped his hand, feeling the warmth of his palm to steady myself.

Davis looked at me, his warm eyes full of conviction. "Say the word, Thor, and I will pursue this with everything I've got. You deserve justice."

I let the thought play out. Without anyone else in my family as a witness, and given the paranormal nature of the crimes, I couldn't imagine a scenario in which Detective

Davis's career survived this investigation. I didn't even know if anyone would ever believe him. Besides, he was right about one thing. Kendrick was gone, his research—my research—destroyed. It was done. "No," I said. With my free hand, I pushed the folder back toward him, unopened. I stood, brushing the fringe from Cas's forehead. "Thank you, Detective Davis. But I think I'd like to put this behind me."

He nodded, stood, and stuck out his hand. "Of course," he said. "I'll give you some privacy. If Mr. Rhodes feels differently—you have my number."

I shook his hand, and he was gone.

I gathered Cas's hand in both of mine, wondering if I'd done the right thing.

# 26



I could not wait to get out of this fucking hospital. Everyone who came in, peering down at me like I was inches from death, grated on my last nerve. The food was disgusting, too. I had a suspicion that Thor's influence had something to do with the fact that I remained here an extra day after waking up from my teensy, *mild* coma, considering the doctor looked positively terrified of him when he came in to insist I remain for one more day of "observation."

My father and siblings had to return home, but I'd be visiting them for a few days after I was discharged from the hospital. It was late, and Thor had not been home in four days. Lucy had brought him a few changes of clothes, and he'd been sleeping upright in a visitor's chair. It made me fucking uncomfortable just to look at him trying to sleep all pretzeled up.

"Will you please go home," I snapped, annoyed. I tossed the spoon onto my dinner tray after finishing up my pudding, the only tolerable thing to eat in this place. "You're making me crazy."

"Sorry," said Thor. "No. I'm not letting you out of my sight or you might do something stupid again."

"'Again?'" I echoed.

"Charging into a mad scientist lair with nothing but a kitchen knife definitely counts as stupid."

"It was a good plan," I said, crossing my arms. "I stand by it."

"Uh-huh."

"Well, if you're going to stay, can you at least come here and sleep on the bed with me?"

Thor shot me a withering stare, but I wasn't about to back down this time.

"Why not?"

"I could open up your stitches!"

"Let me put it this way," I said firmly, and I sat up in bed, trying my best not to grimace. "Get your ass in here, or I'm going to get up and check myself out."

The hall was dark, the ward quiet, but Thor still peered out into the hallway before shutting the door and drawing the curtain. I knew I was fine; I wasn't even hooked up to an IV any longer. Thor climbed onto the bed as if it and I were made of glass, likely to shatter at any moment. The hospital bed was narrow, nothing like Thor's magnificent Cal king back at our apartment, but even the slight weight of his presence on the thin mattress loosened something in my chest, and I let out a long sigh.

"Will you just get in here?" I asked him, remembering the morning all those months ago when he'd essentially sassed me into bed with him. I rolled onto my side, encouraging Thor to be the big spoon, which was kind of funny considering when our bodies lined up his face pressed between my shoulders. Twin exhales, one from each of us, and I felt the tension seeping from his body, too. He'd needed this, as much as I had.

His hand fell to my hip, the light whisper of his touch through the thin cotton of my hospital gown left me aching for more. It seemed as though he was nervous to lay even the full weight of his palm against my skin, but I needed it, needed the feel of him as close as he could be. I seized his fingers and brought them to my lips, kissing his knuckles before pressing his shaking hand to my heart so he could feel it beating.

At that, Thor curled against my back, slotting his hips behind my ass, and finally relaxing his arm over my side to hold me. His breath puffed nervously over the nape of my neck, warm little gusts. It seemed each exhale danced over the scar from the bite he'd left on my neck, sending electric pulses down my spine. I shivered in his arms.

When Thor had placed that bite there, it had been a promise. A promise of love, sure, but in some ways, more importantly, a promise that I could always trust him to take care of me. That I could trust him with the most fragile, vulnerable side of myself—a side of myself I had never let anyone else see. The weight of that promise felt heavy on my chest, as I laid here at, arguably, my most vulnerable. Recovering from wounds, draped in the crepe thin fabric of the hospital gown. Exposed. Wounded. Afraid.

Suddenly desperate, suddenly terrified—it was like I needed Thor to make good on that promise again. I needed to let myself fall just so I could know that he would catch me. Holding my breath, I gave a tentative wiggle, pressing my bare back against Thor, feeling the rough scrape of his jeans against my thighs and the skin of my ass.

I felt more than I heard him inhale, a sharp little gasp, and his fingers tightened around mine where I held his palm to my chest. Stilling, I waited for his breathing to even out again, for the span of a few heartbeats. I pressed back again, lingering this time, clenching my thighs and feeling as much of him as I could. Thor released my hand, his fingers straying down my front, igniting me even with the barrier of the johnny.

"Cassian..." my name was a plea, a warning, but it was also a siren call. My full name in Thor's mouth did things to me.

My cock stirred, and I felt his thickening against the skin of my ass, but with his hand once again resting on my waist, he pushed himself away. Mere inches of space, but the cold draft suddenly skating over my back raised goosebumps, and a whine that came from deep in my throat. "Please," I whispered.

Thor groaned, pressing his forehead against the nape of my neck. "This is *not* why I agreed to get in this bed."

"And yet, here we are." I fought to keep my voice steady, my tone light. I was afraid if I revealed how badly I wanted this he would fear for my sanity. "Please," I said again, reaching back to grab for his thigh, to press us close together. "I am *fine*," I said, but my voice broke. I hoped Thor chalked it up to me trying to remain quiet, but I could tell he wasn't fooled.

"What is it?" He asked, and I felt him moving around, shifting to prop himself on one elbow.

I dropped my shoulder back, looking up into his face. I chewed my lip, unsure why it was so difficult to get the words out.

Thor touched my cheek, smoothed his fingertips over my brow. "We're both safe, now."

"I know," I said. "I...this is hard for me."

Thor brushed our lips together, feathering more kisses to the corner of my mouth, up my jaw, letting his breath tickle the shell of my ear. "Just tell me what you need, Cas, and I'll do it for you."

"I just need—I need you." I whispered it, like a secret, and a lump rose in my throat. My voice grew a bit louder, but the words still came in shaky fits and starts. "I can't describe it—

it's like an itch, like something burning on my skin. Please, Thor—just..."

"Just what?"

"Take care of me. Please."

Thor drew away, blinking at me in surprise. The moonlight spilling in through the blinds on the window cast eerie silver shadows on his face. No doubt he'd never heard me this needy before; I'd never allowed myself to be. He hesitated only a fraction of a heartbeat before kissing me like he meant to consume.

His lips were soft and insistent as he kissed me, demanding. He bit my lower lip, gently, and pulled back before releasing, then tracing the tip of his tongue over the seam of my mouth. "Of course," he said. "I'll always take care of you."

He nudged my shoulder, encouraging me to move back to my side. His lips latched to my neck, maddeningly close to the scar that somehow remained so sensitive, all these months later. He traced the edge of the bite with his tongue, somehow just as erotic as his fingers inching their way down the vee of my hip. "Please," I said, and this neediness threatening to overwhelm me had me squirming, so I struggled to regain some measure of control over these proceedings. "Just fuck me, Thor, Jesus Christ."

He huffed in my ear, his hand sliding around to cup the meat of my ass cheek, digging his fingertips into my flesh. "I never pegged you for such a bossy bottom," he said, nipping the corner of my jawbone.

With a growl of frustration, I rammed my ass back against his groin and said, "You're not pegging me at all, right now."

Thor laughed a low, throaty chuckle that told me he understood the game we were playing now. His hand had always seemed small to me, certainly much smaller than mine, but when he spread his palm on my abdomen, pressing firmly, the thrumming power I felt in his slim fingers had my toes curling. "Oh baby," he said softly. "I'll give you everything you need."

Thor had never called me baby before. In fact, he'd never called me anything other than Cassian, or Cas. It was thrilling. Part of me resisted the pet name even as the—much larger—part of me preened, knowing I was his and no one else's, and that there was no one else I trusted with this fragile, delicate, submissive side of myself. The side that begged to be led, held, and cherished.

His hot hand smoothed down my side, stroking the skin of my thighs, and I felt him wriggling behind me and knew he was sliding his jeans off—at least partway. With his gentle hand guiding me, Thor pressed my thigh up toward my chest, directing me to hook my own arm around it, and there was something so *filthy* about lying here in an open-backed hospital gown, a garment, really, tailor-made for me to be fucked in.

Thor pulled the thin blanket up over us both, and seized a container of Vaseline from the side table, left by the nurses on one of their visits. When his dexterous fingers found my hole I arched against him, keeping a hold of my leg, spreading myself the best I could to let him work me open, ready me to take his cock. He took his time, and this was something I did not expect. In theory, we should be screwing as quickly and silently as possible, but it was like Thor knew I needed time, knew I needed gentle attention and extra care. I imagined him not even caring if someone walked in on us, as long as he was doing the job thoroughly.

When he withdrew his fingers, I whined, clenching around nothing, chasing the feeling of fullness with an impatient huff.

"Shh," he soothed, guiding the fat head of his cock to slide over my hole, teasing as he rutted gently against my ass, squashing my cheeks together as he pumped his cock between them. "Trust me."

And of course, I did. But that didn't mean I was going to be patient. I clenched, pushing shamelessly against him, knowing my desperation, my hunger, all of it was safe in Thor's careful hands. When he finally pushed past the tight rim of my hole, we both sighed in exquisite relief. With a steady, slow thrust, Thor pushed in until we were entirely flush together, my ass settled against his groin, and part of me would have been happy to stay like that all night.

Then, tiny little thrusts of Thor's hips as he rocked into me, and he wrapped a lubed-up fist around my cock, sweeping his thumb over the swollen head. I leaked into his palm, as he focused all the attention of those devilish fingers on the sensitive ridge below the head of my dick. His movements were slow, agonizing. My dick throbbed in his hand as I reached an impatient hand back to cup Thor's ass and bring him closer to grind against me. I wanted him to let loose and fuck me like he meant it, but also, I really didn't want to explain to the doctor how I'd reopened my wound.

Thor's hand left my cock, returning first to my hip, then down to my balls, fluttering everywhere he could reach below the scratchy cotton of the johnny. He plastered himself to my back, kissing the slope of my shoulder, allowing the movement of my hips to synch with his own as he pulled all the way out and glided back in. He took me apart from inside as he stirred up my guts with that monster dick of his, pressing my hip forward to change up the angle of his thrusts. I released my leg, draping it over his side, offering myself up as wide as I could while still maintaining some sort of plausible deniability on this tiny, rickety bed.

"Oh *fuck,*" Thor cursed softly. He stilled his hips and I felt his hand rummaging around beneath us.

"What?" I hissed, kind of annoyed, bearing down hard on

his meat and wriggling because we'd had a really good rhythm going.

He let out a breathless little laugh. "I thought I pressed the nurse call button."

I had to stifle my own laugh behind my arm, panting as Thor got moving again, letting his teeth scrape along my shoulder blade.

The laugh let some of the tension out of the room, lightening the mood and reminding us that things were alright, really. We'd made it through some serious crazy shit and now all we had to worry about was bringing each other pleasure.

And my little Thunder God was up to the task, for sure. He positioned my body below his confident hands, rolling his spine, pumping his hips with a fluid sort of grace that illuminated every part of me from the inside out.

"Please, tell me you're close," he rasped in my ear, panting against the side of my neck like a wild animal.

But I knew I didn't need to answer him, my body sang under his touch and he knew it better than he knew his own. Pumping his hips quick, with blunt, shallow thrusts he made sure the head of his cock dragged over my prostate on every pass, each wave of pleasure cresting closer and closer until there was no space between them and I came apart in his arms. Thor cupped his palm around my dick just in time, catching the thick, eager spurts as he buried his nose into the side of my neck, inhaling the smell of me and holding me tight against him with fingers like iron, certain to leave little bruises on my hips.

Thor's thick cock pulsed, and his moan vibrated down my spine where he muffled it with a mouthful of my neck. I felt him, marking me inside as he already had outside. I clenched my tired muscles around him, trying to extend his pleasure, trying to keep him deep inside for as long as I could hold out.

Thor often liked to linger inside after—and sometimes, he

would pull out only to trace my tired rim with his fingers, as he did now, smearing his release around my hole in a way that should have been disgusting but honestly made me wish for the stamina to go another round with him straight away. It was filthy and primal, possessive, and I fucking loved it. The tips of his fingers were so gentle as he pushed his cum back inside, like he wanted part of him to remain deep in my core. I hummed, satisfaction slipping over every inch of my skin in a cloud of sex and Thor's uneven breaths.

When he pulled away, I let out an indignant sort of squawk. "Where the hell do you think you're going?" I asked, annoyed that he had shortened our quiet afterglow by allowing the cold draft of sterile air to sting and smart over my abused hole, now feeling *quite* exposed as I laid on my belly in a cum-drunk stupor.

"We have to clean up," he said, and his voice was low and thick, and the way he looked at me, wrecked on the bed, it seemed like it was the last thing he wanted to do. Luckily, hospitals came equipped with many convenient amenities, and shortly thereafter we were both shiny clean and sanitized, Thor's pants back in place as he held me close to his chest. With each shared breath the voice inside telling me to be strong, telling me not to *need*, drew further and further away.

Thor tucked his nose up under my ear, nuzzling in there and breathing deep. "I love you," he said.

I squeezed his hand. "I love you, too."

———

## THOR

Cas was home visiting his family, and I was an absolute wreck. I spent most of my time pacing around the apartment. It was like my fight or flight response had not had a chance to calm down since before Kendrick's lab—despite the frantic, desperate intimacy we had shared in the hospital, I didn't imagine that I'd be able to settle until I had my mate by my side, safe and secure in our home.

I had planned a sort of surprise for Cas—though I oscillated frequently between thinking it barely counted as a surprise, and thinking it was way too much, and we'd been through a lot and perhaps nothing else really had to change just yet. He was due to come back tomorrow, and I had an entire day to kill before then, determined not to harass him while he spent some solo time with his father and siblings.

So, I girded myself to do the thing I had been dreading since I'd found out from an orderly that my family had checked out of the hospital.

I went to go see my parents.

After taking the train and an Uber to their house, I started to feel nervous. It was a different sort of nerves than the low-grade trepidation I normally felt arriving at their house.

In all honesty, I had no idea what to expect when I rang the bell—and it certainly wasn't my mother answering the door, looking like she had not slept in days. I stared, trying to recall the last time I'd seen her without a full face of makeup, every hair perfectly in place on her head, and I realized there wasn't one. Even when she stayed home sick with a cold, she used a little bit of bronzer.

"Thor," she said, sounding distracted and as tired as she looked.

"Hey, Mom," I said, and though it wasn't customary, I pulled her into a hug. She sure looked like she needed it. She clung to me as we stood awkwardly in the foyer, and when she drew away, her eyes were more than a little misty. Afraid of the answer, I asked, "How's Dad?"

Something spasmed across her face, and she buried her face in her hands. She didn't answer, but drew me deeper into the house, which was eerie and quiet, like my mother and perhaps a few restless ghosts were the only ones in residence. Despite the fact that my siblings had moved out and it was always just the two of them here now, the house never really seemed so vast and empty to me as it did that afternoon. Mom served us tea herself, which was odd enough.

"Where's Selvig?" I asked her, considering she still did not answer my question about my father.

She pursed her lips, and held her teacup in rigid fingers, her knuckles white as she struggled to keep the cup from clattering against the saucer in her trembling hands. "Your father sent him away."

"And--"

"And Circe, and Abraxas. He doesn't want to see anyone." She paused. "He tried to send me away, too."

"What?" My father, without my mother, simply did not make sense. Despite their many faults, their loyalty to one another had never faltered, and a world where they weren't a united front didn't compute.

"He—he doesn't want to see anyone," she repeated, looking down into her teacup like she was trying to divine her future from its dregs.

"But—you're his wife," I said. "His mate."

She shrugged, and I could see the strain draped around her like a jacket.

"What's his problem?"

With a miserable look on her face, she said, "He's still ill."

"Ill?"

"His—he can't—his *fauna* is gone. Dr. Milmore just left." She chewed a hangnail, something I had literally never seen my mother do. "She said the procedure would have killed a lesser man. It's a wonder your father even survived—but he's still..." She drifted off, looking distracted and lost again.

I had figured as much, based on Kendrick's ramblings. I

had not known that my parents had anticipated the condition to be temporary. My parents' primary medical doctor was a shifter, and she lived several hours away. They obviously couldn't see her for emergencies, but they brought her in on anything that had to do with our unique genetics.

I, of course, had seen her innumerable times as an adolescent.

"I don't know what to do, Thor," my mother said, her voice soft and helpless. "I feel like he's drifting away from me and I can't do anything to stop it."

Looking at my mother, helpless and afraid, guilt on her features because I knew that on some level she blamed herself for Kendrick stealing my father's power, I felt a white hot ball of fury growing in my belly.

"Where is he?" I asked her.

"Upstairs—but," she began, but I didn't wait.

I took the stairs two at a time, and marched down the hall to the master bedroom. When I opened it, I found it to be empty. Confused, I wandered back toward the staircase, wondering where he would have holed up. For some reason, my feet drew me down the carpeted hallway to the door of my old room. I didn't know why I thought I'd find him in there, but find him I did.

And, I could understand why my mother was afraid. My father looked like half a corpse. He sat in my old chair by the window, staring out over the sweeping grounds behind our house. Even the look of his defeated form didn't still my anger.

"What the hell are you doing?"

He didn't startle at my outburst, just continued gazing out the window and said, "Go away."

"No," I said.

He sighed, and my eyes darted around the room, lighting on an untouched breakfast tray, and my old bed that didn't appear to have been slept in. "You've gotten awfully defiant, lately," said my father mildly, as if I wasn't trying to intervene on his mental breakdown.

"Well, you've gotten even more bullheaded lately," I snapped. Then, I repeated my question. "What are you doing, Dad?"

At last, he turned to face me, and it struck me how sunken his flinty eyes had become in such a short time, how gaunt his cheeks. "I have nothing to say, Thor."

"Not even to mom?"

"Your mother..." he swallowed, and to my horror I realized my father was near tears. "I don't want her to see me like this."

"I understand that," I said, still angry. "I wouldn't want her to see you taking this goddamn pity party either. You're stronger than this, Dad, or at least, I thought you were."

"Not any longer," he said. "I'm not anything, now."

Now, meaning—without a *fauna*. It stung. After all these fucking years, it shouldn't have. Now that I had a *fauna*, it shouldn't have stung. After all that I'd been through—his distaste should not have been able to hurt me any longer. But it did. I stuffed the hurt down, deep inside, suffocating it. "You're a lot of things, Dad, but a coward wasn't ever one of them."

He didn't rise to the bait, but said, "Everything about me worth being, he stole."

"No," I said. "Just because your *fauna* is gone—you're still you, Dad. Didn't you listen to Mom at that lab? She doesn't care about your power, at all. She loves *you*. She still does. She needs you. She's terrified she's losing you, and it's selfish that you won't just admit that you need her, too."

"I'm very tired, Thor. Please, just go."

I clenched my jaw. "Fine," I spat. At the bedroom door, I paused. "I was never nothing, Dad. I was never broken. Not before, and not now. And neither are you."

The following morning, I listened eagerly for Cas,

wanting to meet him at the door. When I heard him on the other side of it fumbling for his keys, I opened it wide, leaning against the door frame to block his path. "Welcome back," I said.

He squinted at me, suspicious, adjusting the strap of his duffel bag. "Hey, you."

I stepped aside, allowing him into the apartment. His eyes swept immediately over the mantle, where two new, unlit, candles were waiting patiently in our lineup. Cas didn't comment, and he seemed to understand there was something afoot.

Scrutinizing the rest of the living room, his eyes found nothing else out of the ordinary, so with one final quizzical look at me, where I leaned against the counter, feigning nonchalance, he moved down the hallway toward the door that had once been to his. He pushed it open with his hip, and gasped, turning back toward me.

"It's empty!" he said, hurt crossing his face. "I don't—"

"I decided having a roommate isn't for me," I said casually. "Didn't really like sharing my space with a casual acquaintance."

"Oh?"

"Yeah. And I just changed my major, so I need a dedicated place to work."

"That's cool," said Cas, grinning, playing along now. "What's your new major?"

I grinned back. "Creative Writing and Literature."

"Congratulations, man. This is a great place though, shame you don't need a roommate. The kitchen is beautiful."

"Well," I said, grabbing Cas by the lapels of his jacket. "I found my boyfriend and I needed more privacy."

"Oh yeah?" His eyes darkened, as he allowed me to tug him down the hallway toward our bedroom.

"Definitely. We get pretty loud," I said, leaning in to suck on the side of Cas's neck. I left a searing kiss on the side of his jaw. "And he's *real* possessive of that stove."

Cas laughed, tackling me onto the mattress. "Possessive of more than the stove, I think."

I practically purred as Cas ran his tongue over my collarbone, dropping his bag carelessly on the carpet. "Wait—wait," I said. "I actually have some more news."

"You are *full* of surprises," Cas said, punctuating the statement with a thrust of his hips against mine where he had me pinned to the mattress.

"I bought the building," I said.

"You—what?"

"Yup. The money I'd been saving to move—I used it for a down payment."

"Why?"

I shrugged. "I thought it was more important to stick down roots here. The money from the renters on the other floors will more than keep us solvent if..."

"If what?"

"If you wanted to take some time to decide what you want to do. You could cook, work, send money home to your dad and the kids. Go to culinary school."

"Culinary school?" Cas choked on the words, like he'd never heard of them before.

"Or fuck, I dunno, you could start a YouTube cooking channel. Write a cookbook. Whatever you want, Cas."

"Why?"

I laughed. "What do you mean why?"

"Why would you do this?"

"Because I love you," I said. "And I think it's time for both of us to stop planning our lives around what others expect of us. I know your family situation is different than mine, and that's why I want to help."

"Thor, I—"

"Please, Cassian, for once, let someone take care of you."

"You amaze me, Pin Cushion, you know that?"

"Yeah," I said, and I really, truly believed him. "I do."

The End.

I hope you all loved reading Thor & Cassian's love story, and if you did, taking a few seconds to drop a rating on Amazon would make my day!

**If you want more Thor & Cas, sign up for my mailing list to get a free sweet and spicy bonus short!**

**Visit emmalinestrange.com/subscribe**

Cheers,
Em

PS: Curious how Detective Davis copes with his new knowledge of the Paranormal? Read on for a sneak peek of *Dress the Neck Becomingly,* the next book in the *Sanguis Et Fauna* world.

# DRESS THE NECK
# BECOMINGLY
## PROLOGUE

SINCLAIR

If I squinted just right at the pavement, I could almost still see the bloodstain. Never mind the fact that the night I'd produced the stain and tonight were separated by a dozen decades; never mind the fact that the alley had been repaved with asphalt in place of uneven cobbles.

It didn't matter, because I could never forget that stain— its color, its shape.

How could I ever forget the night I died?

I had followed the history of the building beside the alley since that night, from afar. I watched, and waited, for the property to go up for sale. Fifty years ago, I'd snapped up the deed, but I had never found the courage to return here, to this building, this alley, this city. Until tonight.

Something told me it was time.

If I closed my eyes, I could hear the shouts, feel my ribs breaking. I could smell the smoke, feel the heat of the fire on my skin as I bled on the stones, listening to my livelihood burn. That entire night rushed through me in an instant where I stood, swaying on the sidewalk.

However, I hadn't come all this way to be undone by the sense memory of cruel men long dead, of the slap of fists, by the shuttered windows or the puddles on the street that filled with rain just the same shape as they had a century ago. I was tired, and I missed my home.

I'd been running for over a hundred years.

Living as a shadow left me feeling wrung out and drained. This building had been my home, had been the last place I'd been happy. I barely remembered what that felt like, but I thought perhaps it was time to reclaim that feeling.

I'd run from what had happened to me, run from what I'd done. I'd never known the one who'd made me, and I'd never wanted to know. He hadn't wanted to know me, either. As I lay dying in the alleyway, watching the reflection of flames in the dirty puddles, he'd whispered in my ear, "Do you want to be saved?" I hadn't, but he'd turned me anyway, and left me to transform in the gutter.

I'd fumbled through a hundred years on my own, happy to hide from the memory of the night I'd died. But of late, I'd been struck by some sort of pull, like the opposite of wanderlust. A deep, unshakeable restlessness, a need to fill the empty place inside where most people kept the knowledge of who they were.

I had no reason to believe the one who'd made me would still be here, in this city that like the rest of the world had changed so much since that night, but it seemed as good a place to start as any.

When I approached the door, I smiled to see it was still the very same as when I'd left it. The key and its lock were as old as I was, and the satisfying *clunk* of the mechanism sounded like coming home.

I wondered when anyone last set foot in here. The dust

settled on everything was thick and soft and pillowy, well acquainted with the creak of the floor, old friends with the spiders in the corners. When I'd purchased the building fifty years ago, it had been a dress shop, and ghosts of that life remained in the stacks of faded hat boxes and waifish dress forms, huddled together behind the till counter. I didn't mind them. Ghosts held no malice for me.

I stood in the center of my dusty little kingdom, feeling at peace for the first time in a hundred years.

It was good to be back.

# CHAPTER ONE
## PRACTICAL ETTIQUETTE FOR SINGLE GENTLEMEN

ROYCE

What had I been thinking?

Perched on the stool at the corner of the bar, I took a gulp from my beer. I'd ordered my same old usual. Several, actually. I may as well have been wearing a sandwich board that read, "I don't belong here."

It had taken me six weeks of denial, two weeks of drunken pining, and five days of psyching myself up to get here. I didn't know what miracle I'd hoped to achieve by dragging my ass to a trendy, queer nightclub downtown instead of the pub down the street from my apartment.

No matter where I sat, I was still the same old boring Royce Davis I'd always been.

The same old boring Royce Davis who'd been dumped on his ass nine weeks ago by his boyfriend of three years.

"I need more, Royce."

"More what?" I'd asked, floored, when I'd come home from an eighteen-hour shift to Derek and his suitcase. I'd just wrapped up an investigation that had left me...changed. It had shattered the very foundations I'd thought the world was built on. All I'd wanted was to come home, to my normal apartment, my normal life. Instead, I'd had the normal fucking rug pulled out from under me.

Derek had shaken his head sadly. "Just...more."

Whatever the fuck that meant.

But I guess I knew on some level, because here I was with some bullshit point to prove. I could be spontaneous. I could be exciting. I could try new things. I could be...*more.* I would have laughed if it wasn't so damn pathetic.

I'd put on my hippest outfit, such that it was, and dragged myself out of the house in an Uber. Now I sat here like a bump on the proverbial log, and all I wanted to do was go back to my place and crawl into bed. I drained my beer glass and set it on the bar.

"What are you drinking?"

I looked away from the bar and almost choked on my tongue. The most beautiful guy on the fucking planet had approached my lonely seat, any sound of his footsteps camouflaged by the pounding beat of the club music. I looked around, trying to find someone else he might be speaking to because it sure as hell couldn't be me, but there was no one. Not even the bartender had approached my little storm cloud in like, half an hour. But this guy was here, standing far too close, and he was moving in closer. My knees widened to make room for him like I'd been given a command. He gave me a soft, shy little smile, one pointy canine poking out over his plump bottom lip as he fluttered his lashes, eyes fixed on me like I was the most fascinating man in the room.

He was probably drunk.

Or high.

Jesus, he looked young. Way too young for me, and possibly too young to be in this club, which was twenty-one and over. "How old are you?" I blurted.

He laughed, his nose scrunching up, the dusting of freckles on his cheeks drawing my eye as the strobing lights splashed across them. Leaning in, he let his lips brush my ear as he whispered, "Old enough."

When he pulled away, he fixed me with an oddly intense stare. His eyes shone a hypnotizing grey-green out of his smooth, pale face.

"That's not going to cut it for me," I said.

He tilted his head to the side, fiddling with the collar of my shirt and said, "And why is that?"

"I'm a cop."

Without missing a beat, he let his lips brush my ear again, his breath ghosting over my cheek as he whispered, "In that case, what will it take to convince you to cuff me?"

I huffed out a nervous laugh. "Why don't you show me your ID?" Good *Lord,* what was I thinking? This had to be a new personal low and definitely not a sexy play to run on a prospective hookup. I had truly hit rock bottom: ID'ing some hot twink to figure out how gross it would be if I clumsily flirted with him.

"What shall I call you?" He asked, fishing in the pocket of his sinfully tight jeans. The way he spoke was weird, like he was performing in a play or something.

"Da—Royce," I said. "My name is Royce."

"Royce," he said, like he was tasting it. I found myself instantly warm at the sound of my name in his perfect mouth. "It suits you."

"Thanks," I said, taking a peek at the ID he slipped into my hand. A sensation like vertigo punched through me, and I almost slipped sideways off the stool. He leaned in, steadying me with surprising strength. I caught a whiff of his skin—like, fresh mint, woodsmoke, and snow. Confused, I straightened up, and saw him putting his ID back in his pocket, like time had skipped. When had I handed it back to him?

"Now that you have ascertained that I am of age, may I legally buy you a drink?"

I frowned. Maybe I was tipsier than I thought. I opened my mouth, but his intense stare pulled me in, distracting me. "I was about to head home, actually," I found myself saying.

He draped his arms around my neck and brushed his nose against mine. "Even better."

"You're way too young for me," I said feebly, even as desire sputtered to life in my gut. Was I really about to do this?

He batted his thick lashes at me and said, "I don't think I am."

"Is that so?"

He sucked my earlobe into his mouth, then nibbled it before whispering, "I'm an old soul."

I threw way too much cash on the bar, focused more on the smooth pair of lips on my neck, the tongue flicking over my pulse point, and the beautiful body in my arms. We stumbled out the door of the club, and he continued sucking on my neck while I ordered us an Uber.

Buzzed on beer and drunk on my own daring, I slid my hands down to cup his ass, pulling him closer while we waited for our ride. When I turned to capture his mouth, he placed a finger to my lips. "Not yet," he said.

"Why?"

With an evil grin, he said, "I want all of you, all at once. In private."

*Fuck me.*

Soon we were in the back of some poor lady's SUV and I could not have been fucked about automobile safety as he climbed up to straddle my lap, grinding against me and teasing my neck with his lips and tongue.

We stumbled through my front door, pawing at each other's clothing, sending fabric flying as we banged into walls and furniture. I was pretty sure I heard a lamp break, but I wouldn't have been able to stop had the apartment been on fire—and when his fleet fingers found their way to the fly of my jeans, I was fucking gone. His kisses were hard, aggressive, lots of teeth and I offered the same, sucking and biting marks into his slender neck.

Tangled up and somewhat naked, we made it to my bedroom, and with a firm hand on my chest he guided me to sit on the edge of the mattress. With practiced grace, he peeled off his skin-tight boxer briefs, kneeling between my thighs to work my feet free of my jeans, which had tangled around my ankles. Lust smoldered in those grey-green eyes, an impish smile lighting his face as he moved to straddle me on the edge of the bed.

"How do you like it?" I asked, leaning in to whisper in his ear the way he'd done to me at the club. I ran my palms down his back, his skin smooth and petal-soft.

His breath caught in his throat as he answered. "Rough."

Music to my fucking ears. I rolled us, twisting to get us further up the bed with his perfect, lithe body pinned beneath me. I thanked my lucky stars I had some lube, but as I groped in my bedside table, I realized I didn't have a single condom. Derek and I had always used them—but it had been quite a while since we even attempted sex, even before we broke up.

My confidence faltered. Maybe that's what Derek had meant when he said he longed for more. More skill between the sheets, more adventure. More fireworks. He'd never said, but maybe I was an absolute zero in the sack. "Hey." A soft voice brought me back to the present, back to the criminally beautiful, naked guy in my bed *now.* "Are you alright, darling?"

I released an embarrassed laugh around the lump in my throat. *Oh Christ, Davis. Get more pathetic. Seduce some kid for an anonymous hookup and then sob all over him.* I had no idea why the soft endearment had thrown me so much, but looking into his arresting eyes, I faltered. It was an odd thing for such a young guy to say. Maybe he was, as he said, an old soul. I kissed his nose. "Yeah," I said gruffly, then seized his jaw to deliver a rough, sloppy kiss to his mouth, which he returned eagerly. "I just uh," I stammered. "I don't have any protection."

His gaze burned in the half-light of my bedroom. "If you say you're negative, I trust you. Risk it?"

"Risk it," I confirmed, sounding so unlike myself that I almost stopped. Almost. Thinking about Derek had me reeling, wanting to do something reckless, something stupid, something possibly dangerous. Looking down at the beauty pinned against my pillow, I thought, *what a way to go.*

I raised up on my knees between his splayed thighs, taking in the tight lines of his body. The adorable freckles on his cheeks spread down over the pale expanse of his chest, and I leaned over to kiss a few of them. He tangled his fingers in my hair, giving the strands a soft tug, like he wanted to remind me he'd asked for a rough fuck, not a tender love-fest.

I growled against his navel, the soft skin of his belly cool and light under my lips. Drawing back, I nudged his hip. "Over," I said, feigning confidence with my gruff tone. He grinned, rolling over onto his hands and knees obediently, and I saw the freckles adorned his perfect ass, too. Hell. I gave one round cheek a gentle swat, and he smiled wickedly over his shoulder before perching with his back arched, his hands on my headboard, knees spread.

I kneaded his sweet, freckled ass with both hands before spreading him wide to get a look at his hole. The puckered skin around his opening was a delicate ballet pink, and I couldn't wait to see what it looked like stretched around my dick. I slicked up my fingers, then gave my cock a few strokes, warming the lube in my hand before massaging his rim with my thumb. I teased until he whined and I pushed my fingers inside, stroking the slick, silky skin of his channel until he begged for more. Pulling my fingers out as slow as I possibly could, I pressed a kiss to his shoulder. "Ready?"

He let out a whispered curse, then softly, "Yes."

I lined up the head of my dick with his sweet little hole and pushed in, slow at first until I was seated inside him and he felt so fucking good, felt like exactly what I needed. I gasped as he squeezed around me, arching his back further. We groaned in unison as we adjusted to each other, and after a few thunderous heartbeats I began to move.

I caressed every inch of his body bent over in front of me, finding the freckles on his shoulders with my lips. As my tongue danced over his flesh, I found a faded scar at the nape of his neck. He shuddered when I kissed it, so I swept his hair aside and lavished attention on the area. Each little shiver had him clench deliciously around my dick.

He'd asked for it rough and I planned to give it to him, but it had been a minute, and I didn't want to humiliate myself by going off too soon, so I started with long, powerful thrusts that had him sighing and moaning on each stroke, pushing his greedy ass back toward me. Soon we fell into a wordless synchronicity, moving together like we'd been making each other come for years.

He didn't have to say out loud that he wanted it harder, because I could read the hunger in his body. With my hands on his tiny waist, I drove into him with brutal, blunt thrusts, making sure to angle my dick just right to nail his prostate. I stroked in and out, ramming him harder and faster against the headboard, and if his yelps and moans were anything to go by, he was thrilled to take what I was dishing out. He bucked back against me, surprising strength in his little body like a briefcase bomb, giving as good as he got.

I was close already, but something told me we'd be fucking more than once tonight, so I really let him have it, wrapping a slippery fist around his dick, pumping him till he came into my hand with a pretty moan. With an arm around his torso, I yanked him upright, slamming his back against my chest, gulping for air as he collapsed in my arms. I came hard as I held his body close, filling him with pulse after pulse, groaning with each twitch of my release.

I ran my hands over every inch of his chest, his skin still cool and dry to touch, while I sweated like a pig. The shame of it curdled the post-nut euphoria and I pulled away, feeling weird and soiled after slobbering and sweating all over the pure-looking angel in my arms. He turned toward me with a small, needy sound as I drew back, his eyes dazed, the very picture of debauched innocence.

"Where are you going?" He fell on his back, stretching.

"Just..." I gestured at my sweaty body and his cum-covered belly. "Going to get something to clean us up."

In a blink, he'd moved to kneel before me, wrapping slim arms around my thick waist to pull me down on top of him, startling me once again with his strength. "I think not," he said, raking his nails across my back.

I shivered. "But..."

"You have a beautiful mouth, Royce," he said, sliding his fingers up into my hair. Pushing gently, he guided my head down his chest. "Why not put it to use?"

Jesus Christ. Okay, so maybe there was a demon hiding behind that angelic smile—perhaps he wasn't the wide-eyed innocent he appeared to be. And to be frank, the idea of getting my mouth on his body had my guilty thoughts melting away like snow in spring. There'd be plenty of time for self-loathing later.

———

## SINCLAIR

Leaving my den earlier that evening, I had not the faintest idea what I craved more: a feed or a fuck.

Sometimes, it was difficult to be sure. I'd been back in Douglas Crest for several months now, and while I made every effort to keep to myself, to remain small and invisible, my kind ran in a fairly closed community. I was not the only predator in this city. Never before had I stayed long in a city when I learned I wasn't the only one. Besides, most vampires never stayed in one place for long—I'd figure out who they were, see if I could learn from them, and they'd move on eventually. This this was different. I was finally home, and I had things to learn. When I was first turned, I had no room for curiosity, my mind consumed only with survival, not unraveling the mysteries of self. Now though...I'd lived long enough to have to start to wonder.

When I entered the club tonight, I spent some time dancing, twirling and grinding on the floor to the pounding music with the other writhing, needy bodies, letting the scent of sweat ignite my prey drive until it thrummed below my skin. I searched the sea of revelers with a detached sort of want, still unsure which way my instincts would ultimately lead me.

Laying eyes on the bedraggled, weary-looking man at the end of the bar, I was still unsure, but I knew immediately it was him I wanted. Until I got close enough to smell his blood, I didn't know if I was about to give him the night of his life or put him out of his misery. Judging by the forlorn look upon his sweet, honest face, either would have been alright by him. He was thick and sturdy, with creamy skin that flushed beautifully, and tired hazel eyes. His face was scruffy, his hair thick and brown and curly, and his shoulders slumped. He carried himself like an old man, though he couldn't have been older than forty. The sight of him had me yearning to lift the burdens from his shoulders and smooth the tension from his brow.

*Royce,* he'd said his name was. A lovely name, truly, a king's name. I hadn't told him my name, yet. But I knew the moment I'd scented his neck that he would learn it soon enough. A hunter's instincts were rarely wrong.

Tonight would not be enough for me to drink my fill of Royce.

After he'd dutifully lapped the seed from my belly, and—to my utter delight—made a meal from the mess he'd made in and around my ass, I was hard again and beyond ready for another romp. Royce took me deep into the silky, wet warmth of his mouth and I was surely a goner. My instincts had steered me well indeed: Royce had a generous and talented mouth and as he swallowed around the head of my cock I released, spilling down his throat as I arched my back off his bed in pure ecstasy.

He sucked my cock until it wilted between his lips before kissing his way back up my chest. God, his lips, his tongue, his entire mouth. Humans usually required something of a refractory period between bouts, and Royce was no different. But he was energetic and amorous, and our bodies came together again and again like they'd been designed expressly for each other's pleasure. After riding his thick cock and then letting him fuck me aggressively into the mattress again, I had made up my mind.

Royce was mine.

It had been simmering in the back of my brain since the club, brewing as he gallantly verified I was old enough to bed, and boiling over now as he bent me in half and fucked me to blissful delirium. After several hours of energetic lovemaking, my darling Royce seemed utterly spent, his human stamina at its end. Or so he thought—he had never spent the night with someone like me before, so naturally he did not know the heights to which he could be pushed.

I draped over his broad chest, soaking up the warmth of his soft, sturdy body like a snake digesting a meal upon a sunbaked stone. By design, I had lined up our groins so I would know immediately when he was ready again, but his cock-drunk, sleepy face told me he didn't foresee fucking me again tonight.

Pity, because I was surely not done pleasing him yet. I kissed him, softly at first, the corner of his mouth, then nipping his lip until I felt him smile. I blinked at him, waiting expectantly. "I would very much like to make you climax again," I told him.

He slid a warm hand through my hair, stroking my scalp with a tenderness I'd come not to expect from casual lovers. "I don't know if that's possible."

"Afraid of falling in love with me?" I teased, pressing kisses to his chest.

"Afraid my heart will give out," he said with a laugh.

I peeked up at him through my tousled fringe. "Risk it?"

He sighed, closing his eyes, a surrender. I grinned against his clavicle and teased my way down his body, loving the smell of him—he smelled of blood and sweat and life.

I adored sucking cock. There was something about a throbbing erection—it had everything I loved, everything I thrived upon: sex, and blood. Sustenance and pleasure. The urge to feed from Royce was a strong one, but I would not. Not tonight. Not yet.

It took quite a bit of coaxing before he hardened again under my ministrations, allowing me to draw one more orgasm from his wrung body, the taste of his seed exquisite upon my tongue, perhaps even better than his blood would have been.

It had taken quite a while to get him there a fourth time, but of course I did not tire as humans did. I relished in the patience I could take with lovemaking, and clearly Royce appreciated my efforts, seizing my arms and pulling me toward him for grateful kisses and sweet murmurs. Unfortunately, with night waning, it was time for me to leave.

Royce seemed close to slumber, providing me the perfect opportunity to slip out into the night and return to my den before the rising of the sun. I disentangled from Royce's embrace, loath as I was to do so. He opened one eye. "Hey," he said.

"Go to sleep," I said softly, standing by the edge of the bed. "I should go."

He extricated one hand from the tangled nest of blankets and raised it to brush his calloused fingertips over the skin of my ribs, trailing down toward my hip. "Stay."

The intimacy of this gesture had me utterly arrested, and I was powerless to deny his command. I could stay for a little while; there were still several hours before the dawn. When I knelt on the mattress, Royce drew me immediately into his arms, into his warmth, holding me close to his chest so I could feel his heart beating, feel the hollow echo of it in my own, silent chest. I sighed. This was something to which I could easily grow accustomed. I snuggled in, the sound of his pulse, the scent of sex lulling me into a state of purest relaxation.

I could tell by his breathing that Royce was already drifting, but before his heart slowed completely, he pulled me closer. One strong hand cradled the back of my head, the other coming to rest upon my ass, holding me secure like my body was something precious.

It had been quite some time since I had been held like that.

My kind had no cause to slumber, but occasionally our minds would slow, and drift, allowing us to enter a restful state. It only occurred if we were truly at peace, secure and safe. It was a rare thing, so imagine my surprise when I was startled by a fiery stripe of searing pain across my back. I hissed, alert at once with my fangs distending and dripping venom.

Disentangling myself from my sweet, slumbering Royce, I leapt from the mattress. I realized in distress that I'd been so comfortable in his embrace that I'd lost track of time.

It was dawn. The pain lancing across my bare back came from the infernal rays of sunshine slithering through the slats in Royce's sheer window dressing.

If I hoped to make it home to my den without hideous, blistering burns, I would have to transform.

Dammit all to hell. I would have to forgo my attire and effects from the night before, leave it all behind here, which would be very confusing for Royce. There was nothing for it, I supposed. With not even time to leave a note, I called upon the powers of the night and slipped into my bat form, fluttering to the sill. Bats were creatures of the night, of course, but the sun didn't burn me the way it did when I walked upon two legs. Here, I paused, taking a final look at my new lover sprawled bare on his back, his lovely body rendered boneless and sated by my hand. The thought stirred a possessive flare in my heart as I took in the beautiful array of purple bruises my lips had left like a collar around Royce's neck. I probably shouldn't have marked him so aggressively, but I hadn't been able to help myself. Besides, when he woke, he'd have something to commemorate our first evening together—a calling card, if you will. I'd nipped and sucked my marks on the tender flesh of his throat, down his chest, and a few other places in my passion, leaving little flesh memories of my lips and teeth on his body like a field of violets.

The sight was tempting, to be sure. I longed to crawl back into bed and wake him with my mouth around his morning hardness, but I had to return to my den lest I be exposed even further to the traitorous rays of the sun. Royce was not ready for the whole truth of me yet, of that I was certain. With one last look at the marvel of his skin against the blankets, so rumpled by our loving, I flew out the window.

---

For updates and other titles by Emmaline Strange, as well as book recommendations, free shorts, and more, subscribe to STRANGE BEDFELLOWS at emmalinestrange.com/subscribe

# ALSO BY EMMALINE STRANGE

**High Fantasy Romance**

*Crown of Aster*

**Paranormal Romance**

The *Et Fauna* Shifter Universe:

*Mighty Quill*

*A Walrus & A Gentleman*

*Dress the Neck Becomingly*

# ABOUT THE AUTHOR

Emmaline Strange is the author of *Mighty Quill*, *Crown of Aster*, *A Walrus & A Gentleman*, and *Dress the Neck Becomingly*. She loves to write and read about smooching. She lives in Boston with her husband, dog, and cat, all of whom she loves to smooch. When not smooching, she can usually be found doting on her plants, baking, or watching far too much television. Ms. Strange is a lover of all things nerdy, from *Dungeons & Dragons*, to *Lord of the Rings*, to the MCU.

She enjoys iced coffee, long walks on the beach, complaining about her feet after long walks on the beach, and long sits on the couch to recover from long walks on the beach.

For updates on upcoming projects, come say hello on social media, where she's always talking about writin', readin', and... well, not so much 'rithmetic.

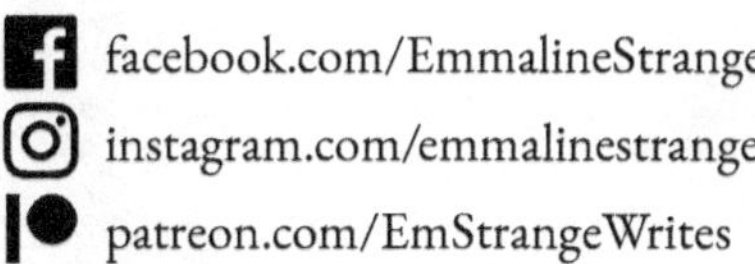